**"KNEEL TO ALFAR,
AND SWEAR HIM THY LOYALTY,
OR A TRAITOR'S DEATH
SHALT THOU DIE!"**

The thin tissue of Rod's self-control tore, and rage erupted. "Who the hell do you think you are, to tell me what to swear! You idiot, you dog's-meat gull! He's ground your ego into powder, and there's nothing left of the real you! You don't exist anymore!"

"Nay—*I* exist, but *thou* shalt not!" The warlock yanked a quarterstaff from the peasant next to him and smashed a two-handed blow down at Rod.

Rod ducked inside the swing, coming up with his dagger in his hand, but a dozen hands seized him and yanked him back, the sky reeled above him, framed by peasant faces with burning eyes. He saw a club swing down at him—then pain exploded through Rod's forehead, and night came early.

THE
Christopher Stasheff
WARLOCK
ENRAGED

ACE SCIENCE FICTION BOOKS
NEW YORK

This book is an Ace Science Fiction original edition,
and has never been previously published.

THE WARLOCK ENRAGED

An Ace Science Fiction Book/published by arrangement with
the author

PRINTING HISTORY
Ace Science Fiction edition / December 1985
Second printing / March 1986
Third printing / July 1986

ISBN: 0-441-87334-0

Ace Science Fiction Books are published by The Berkley Publishing Group,
200 Madison Avenue, New York, New York 10016.
PRINTED IN THE UNITED STATES OF AMERICA

1

For some time now, I've been getting worried about the steadily increasing number of hopeful historians on this Isle of Gramarye. There weren't any when I came here—none that I was aware of, anyway. Then Brother Chillde started keeping his chronicles, and, first thing I knew, there were five more just like him. Not that this is all bad, of course— Gramarye'll be much better off if it has an accurate record of its history. What bothers me is that each one of these young Thucydideses is conveniently forgetting all the events that make his own side look bad, and definitely overdoing it more than a bit, about the happenings that make his side look good. I'm mostly thinking of the Church here, of course, but not exclusively—for example, I know of one young warlock who's taken to keeping a diary, and a country lord's younger son who's piling up an impressive number of journals. So, in an effort to set the record straight, I'm going to set down my version of what happened. Not that it'll be any more objective, of course; it'll at least be biased in a diff–

"'Tis *my* place, Delia!"

"Nay, Geoffrey, thou knowest 'tis not! This end of the shelf is mine, for the keeping of my dolls!"

"'Tis not! I've kept my castle there these several weeks!"

Rod threw down his quill in exasperation. After three weeks of trying, he'd finally managed to get started on his history of Gramarye—and the kids had to choose this moment to break into a quarrel! He glared down at the page...

And saw the huge blot the quill had made.

Exasperation boiled up into anger, and he surged out of his chair. "Delia! Geoff! Of all the idiotic things to be arguing about! Gwen, can't you..."

"Nay, I cannot!" cried a harried voice from the kitchen. "Else thou'lt have naught but char for thy.... Oh!" Something struck with a jangling clatter, and Rod's wife fairly shrieked in frustration. "Magnus! How oft must I forbid thee the kitchen whiles I do cook!"

"Children!" Rod shouted, stamping into the playroom. "Why'd I ever *have* 'em?"

"Di'nit, Papa." Three-year-old Gregory peeked over the top of an armchair. "Mama did."

"Yeah, sure, and I was just an innocent bystander. Geoffrey! Cordelia! *Stop* it!"

He waded into a litter of half-formed clay sculptures, toys, and pieces of bark twisted together with twigs and bits of straw that served some fathomless and probably heathen purpose known only to those below the age of thirteen. "What a mess!" It was like that every day, of course. "Do you realize this room was absolutely spotless when you woke up this morning?"

The children looked up, startled, and Cordelia objected, "But that was four hours ago, Papa."

"Yeah, and you must've really worked hard to make a mess like this in so short a time as that!" Rod stepped down hard—into a puddle of ocher paint. His foot skidded out from under him; he hung suspended for a split second, arms thrashing like the wings of a dodo trying to fly; then his back slammed down to the floor, paralyzing his diaphragm. For an instant of panic, he fought for breath, while Cordelia and Geoffrey huddled back against the wall in fright.

Then Rod's breath hissed in and bounced back out in a howl of rage. "You little *pigs!* Can't you even clean up after yourselves!"

The children shrank back, wide-eyed.

Rod struggled to his feet, red-faced. "Throwing garbage

on the floor, fighting over a stupid piece of shelf space—
and to top it off, you had the gall to *talk back!*"

"We didn't . . . We . . ."

"You just did it *again!*" Rod levelled an accusing forefinger. "Whatever you do, don't contradict me! If I say you
did it, you *did* it! And don't you *dare* try to say you didn't!"

He towered over them, a mountain of wrath. "Naughty,
stupid, asinine brats!"

The children hugged each other, eyes huge and frightened.

Rod's hand swept up for a backhanded slap.

With a crack like a pistol shot, big brother Magnus appeared in front of Cordelia and Geoffrey, arms outspread to
cover them. "Papa! They didn't mean to! They . . ."

"Don't try to tell me what they were doing!" Rod shouted.

The eleven-year-old flinched, but stood up resolutely
against his father's rage—and that made it worse.

"How *dare* you defy me! You insolent little . . ."

"Rod!" Gwen darted into the room, wiping her hands on
her apron. "What dost thou?"

Rod whirled, forefinger stabbing at her. "Don't you even
try to speak in their defense! If you'd just make your children
toe the line, this wouldn't happen! But, oh no, you've got
to let them do whatever they want, and just scold them, and
that's only when their behavior's *really* atrocious!"

Gwen's head snapped back, stung. "Assuredly, thou'rt
scarce mindful of what thou sayest! 'Tis ever *thou* who dost
plead leniency, when I do wish to punish . . ."

"Sure, *when!*" Rod glared, striding toward her. "But for
the thousand and one things they do that deserve spanking,
and you let them off with a scold? Use your head, woman—
if you can!" His gaze swept her from head to toe, and his
lip lifted in a sneer.

Gwen's eyes flared anger. "'Ware, husband! Even to
thine anger, there doth be a boundary!"

"Boundaries! Limits! That's all you ever *talk* about!" Rod
shouted. "'Do this! Do that! You *can't* do this! You *can't*
do that!' Marriage is just one big set of *limits!* Will you
ever . . ."

"Peace!" Magnus darted between them, holding out a
palm toward each. "I prithee!" His face was white; he was

trembling. "Mother! Father! I beg thee!"

Rod snarled, swinging his hand up again.

Magnus stiffened; his jaw set.

Rod swung, with his full weight behind it . . .

. . . And shot through the air, slamming back against the wall.

He rolled to his feet and stood up slowly, face drained of color, rigid and trembling. "I told you never to use your 'witch powers' on me," he grated, "and I told you why!" He straightened to his full height, feeling the rage swell within him.

Geoffrey and Cordelia scurried to hide behind Gwen's skirts. She gathered Magnus to her, but he kept his face toward his father, terror in his eyes, trembling, but determined to protect.

Rod stared at them, all united against him, ready to pick him up with their magic and hurl him into his grave. His eyes narrowed, pinning them with his glare; then his eyes lost focus as he reached down inside himself—deep down, reaching across an abyss—to the psi powers that had lain so long dormant, but which had been awakened by the projective telepathy of Lord Kern, in another universe, one in which magic worked. His powers weren't as readily accessible as his family's; he couldn't work magic just by willing it, as easily as thinking, but once he'd drawn them up, his were at least as great as theirs. He called those powers up now, feeling their strength build within him.

"Mother," came Magnus's voice, across a huge void, "we must . . ."

"Nay!" Gwen said fiercely. "He is thy father, whom thou dost love—when this fit's not on him."

What did that mean! The powers paused in their building . . .

A smaller figure entered his blurred field of vision, to the side and a little in front of the family group, gazing up at him, head tilted to the side—three-year-old Gregory. "Daddy is'n' there," he stated.

That hit Rod like a bucketful of cold water; the complete, calm, sanity of the child's tone—so open, so reasonable— and the totally alien quality of the words. His eyes focused in a stare at his youngest son, and fear hollowed his vitals—fear, and a different anger under it; anger at the futurians who had kidnapped him and the rest of his family away from this child while Gregory was still a baby. The desertion, Rod feared, had totally warped the boy's personality, making him quiet, indrawn, brooding, and sometimes, even weird. His gaze welded to Gregory's face, his fear for Gregory burying his anger at the rest of the family; it ebbed, and was gone.

"Who's not there?" he whispered.

"Lord Kern," Gregory answered, "that Daddy like thee, in that Faerie Gramarye thou'st talk of."

Rod stared at him.

Then he stepped closer to the boy. Magnus took a step toward Gregory, too, but Rod waved him away impatiently. He dropped to one knee, staring into the three-year-old's eyes. "No . . . no, Lord Kern isn't anywhere—except, maybe, in his own universe, that Faerie Gramarye. But why should you think he was?"

Gregory cocked his head to the other side. "But didst thou not, but now, reach out to touch his mind with thine own, to draw upon his powers?"

Rod just gazed at the boy, his face blank.

"Gregory!" Gwen cried in anguish, and she took a step toward him, then drew back for Rod still knelt staring at the child, his face blank.

Then he looked up at Gwen, with an irritated frown. "What am I—a bear? Or a wolf?" He raked the children with his glare. "Some kind of wild animal?"

They stared back at him, eyes huge, huddled together.

His face emptied again. "You think I am. You really think I am, don't you?"

They stared back, wordlessly, eyes locked on him.

He held still, rigid.

Then he swung up to his feet, turning on his heel, and strode to the door.

Cordelia darted after him, but Gwen reached out and caught her arm.

Rod paced out into the bleakness of a day veiled by clouds. A chill wind struck at him, but he didn't notice.

• • •

Rod finally came to a halt at the top of a hill, a mile from home. He stood, staring down at the broad plain below, not really seeing it. Finally, he sank down to sit on the dry grass. His thoughts had slowed in their turmoil as he walked; now, gradually, they sank away, leaving a blank in his mind. Into that, a niggling doubt crept. Softly, he asked, "What happened, Fess?"

The robot-horse answered, though he was a mile away in the stable. Rod heard him through the earphone embedded in his mastoid process, behind his ear. "You lost your temper, Rod."

Rod's mouth twitched with impatience. The robot's horse body might be a distance away in the stable, but the old family retainer could see into him as well as if they were only a foot apart. "Yes, I do realize that much." The microphone embedded in his maxillary, just above the teeth, picked up his words and transmitted them to Fess. "But it was more than simple anger, wasn't it?"

"It was rage," Fess agreed. "Full, thorough, open wrath, without any restraints or inhibitions."

After a moment, Rod asked, "What would have happened if my family hadn't been able to defend themselves so well?"

Fess was silent. Then he said, slowly, "I would hope that your inborn gentleness and sense of honor would have protected them adequately, Rod."

"Yes," Rod muttered. "I would hope so, too."

And he sat, alone in his guilt and self-contempt, in silence. Even the wind passed him by.

Quite some while later, cloth rustled beside him. He gave no sign of having heard, but his body tensed. He waited, but only silence filled the spaces of the minutes.

Finally, Rod spoke. "I did it again."

"Thou didst," Gwen answered gently. Her voice didn't blame—but it didn't console, either.

Something stirred within Rod. It might have risen as anger, but that was burned out of him, now. "Been doing that a lot lately, haven't I?"

Gwen was silent a moment. Then she said, "A score of times, mayhap, in the last twelvemonth."

Rod nodded, "And a dozen times last year, and half-a-dozen the year before—and two of those were at the Abbott, when he tried his schism."

"And a third with the monster which rose from the fens . . ."

Rod shrugged irritably. "Don't make excuses for me. It still comes down to my losing my temper with you and the kids, more than with anyone else—and for the last three months, I've been blowing up about every two weeks, haven't I?"

Gwen hesitated. Then she answered, "None so badly as this, my lord."

"No, it never has been quite as bad as this, has it? But every time, it gets a little worse."

Her answer was very low. "Thou hast offered hurt to us aforetime. . . ."

"Yes, but I've never actually tried it have I?" Rod shuddered at the memory and buried his head in his hands. "First, I just threw things. Then I started throwing them without using my hands. Today, I would've thrown Magnus—if Gregory hadn't interrupted in time." He looked up at her, scowling. "Where in Heaven's name did you get that boy, anyway?"

That brought a hint of smile. "I did think we had, mayhap, borne him back from Tir Chlis, my lord."

"Ah, yes!" Rod stared out over the plain again. "Tir Chlis, that wonderful, magical land of faeries and sorcerers, and—Lord Kern."

"Even so," Gwen said softly.

"My other self," Rod said bitterly, "my analog in an alternate universe—with magical powers unparalleled, and a temper to match."

"Thou wert alike in many ways," Gwen agreed, "but temper was not among them."

"No, and witch powers weren't either—but I learned how to 'borrow' his wizardry, and it unlocked my own powers, powers that I'd been hiding from myself."

"When thou didst let his rage fill thee," Gwen reminded gently.

"Which seems to have also unlocked my own capacity for wrath; it wiped out the inhibitions I'd built up against it."

"Still—there were other inhibitions that thou didst learn

to lay aside, also." Gwen touched his hand, hesitantly.

Rod didn't respond. "Was it worth it? Okay, so I had been psionically invisible; nobody could read my mind. Wasn't that better than this rage?"

"I could almost say the sharing of our minds was worth the price of thy bouts of fury," Gwen said slowly, "save that . . ."

Rod waited.

"Thy thoughts grow dim again, my lord."

Rod only sat, head bowed.

Then he looked up. "I'm beginning to hide myself away from you again?"

"Hast thou not felt it?"

He stared into her eyes; then he nodded. "Is that any surprise? When I can't trust myself not to explode into wrath? When I'm beginning to feel as though I'm some sort of subhuman beast? Sheer shame, woman!"

"Thou art worthy of me, my lord." Her voice was soft, but firm, and so was her hand. "Thou art worthy of me, and of thy children. I' truth, we are fortunate to have thee." Her voice shook. "Oh, we are blessed!"

"Thanks." He gave her hand a pat. "It's good to hear. . . . Now convince me."

"Nay," she murmured, "that I cannot do, an thou'lt not credit what I say."

"Or even what you do." Rod bowed his head, and his hand tightened on hers. "Be patient, dear. Be patient."

And they sat alone in the wind, not looking at each other, two people very much in love but very much separated, clinging to a thin strand that still held them joined, poised over the drop that fell away to fallow lands below.

Magnus turned away from the window with a huge sigh of relief. "They come—and their hands are clasped."

"Let me see, let me see!" The other three children shot to the window, heads jammed together, noses on the pane.

"They do not regard one another," Cordelia said dubiously.

"Yet their hands are clasped," Magnus reminded.

"And," Cordelia added, troubled, "their thoughts are dark."

"Yet their hands are clapsed. And if their thoughts are dark, they are also calm."

"And not all apart," Gregory added.

"Not *all*—not quite," Cordelia agreed, but with the full, frank skepticism of an eight-year-old.

"Come away, children," a deep voice bade them, "and do not leap upon them when they enter, for I misdoubt me an they'd have much patience now with thy clasping and thy pulling."

The children turned away from the window, to a foot and a half of elf, broad-shouldered, brown-skinned, and pug-nosed, in a forester's tunic and hose, wearing a pointed cap with a rolled brim and a feather. "Geoffrey," he warned.

The six-year-old pulled himself away from the window with a look of disgust. "I did but gaze upon them, Robin."

"Indeed—and I know that thou'rt anxious. Yet I bethink me that thy parents have need of some bit more of room than thou'rt wont to accord them."

Cordelia flounced down onto a three-legged stool. "But Papa was so angered, Puck!"

"As thou hast told me." The elf's mouth tightened at the corners. "Yet thou dost know withal, that he doth love thee."

"I do not doubt it. . . ." But Cordelia frowned.

Puck sighed and dropped down cross-legged beside her. "Thou couldst scarce do otherwise, if he did truly become as enraged as thou didst tell." He turned his head, taking in all four children with one gaze. "Gentles, do not reprehend; if you pardon, he will mend."

They didn't look convinced.

"Else the Puck a liar call!" the elf cried stoutly.

The door opened, and the children leaped to their feet. They started to back away, but Puck murmured, "Softly," and they held their ground—warily.

But their father didn't look like an ogre as he came in the door—just a tall, dark, lean, saturnine man with a rough-hewn face, no longer young; and he seemed dim next to the red-haired beauty beside him, who fairly glowed, making the question of youth irrelevant. Still, if the children had ever stopped to think about it, they would have remarked how well their parents looked together.

They did not, of course; they saw only that their father's

face had mellowed to its usual careworn warmth, and leaped
to hug him in relief. "Papa!" Magnus cried, and "Daddy!"
Geoffrey piped; Cordelia only clung to his arm and sobbed,
while Gregory hugged the other arm, and looked up gravely.
"Daddy, thou hast come back again."

Rod looked into the sober gaze of his youngest, and
somehow suspected that the child wasn't just talking about
his coming through the door.

"Oh, Papa," Cordelia sniffled, "I do like thee so much
better when thou'rt Papa, than when thou'rt Lord Kern!"

Rod felt a chill along his spine, but he clasped her shoulder and pressed her against his hip. "I don't blame you,
dear. I'm sure his children feel the same way." He looked
up over the children's heads, at Puck. "Thanks, Robin."

"Now, there's a fair word!" Puck grinned. "Yet I misdoubt me an thou wilt have more such; for there's one who
doth attend thee." He jerked his head toward the kitchen.

"A messenger?" Rod looked up, frowning. "Waiting *in*-
side the house? . . . Toby!"

A dapper gentleman in his mid-twenties came into the
room, running a finger over a neatly trimmed mustache.
Hose clung to well-turned calves, and his doublet was re-
splendent with embroidery. "Hail, Lord Warlock!"

Gwen's face blossomed with a smile, and even Rod had
to fight a grin, faking a groan. "Hail, harbinger! What's the
disaster?"

"Nay, for once, the King doth summon thee whiles it's
yet a minor matter."

"Minor." The single word was loaded with skepticism.
Rod turned to Gwen. "Why does that worry me more than
his saying, 'Emergency?'"

"'Tis naught but experience," Gwen assured him. "Shall
I 'company thee?"

"I'd appreciate it," Rod sighed. "If it's a 'minor' matter,
that means social amenities first—and you know how
Catharine and I don't get along."

"Indeed I do." Gwen looked quite pleased with herself.
Catharine the Queen may have spread her net for Rod, but
it was Gwen who had caught him.

Not that Catharine had done badly, of course. King Tuan
Loguire had spent his youth as Gramarye's most eligible

bachelor—and it must be admitted that Rod had been a very unknown quantity.

Still was, in some ways. Why else would Gwendylon, most powerful witch in circulation, continue to be interested in him?

Rod looked up at Puck. "Would you mind, Merry Wanderer?"

The elf sighed and spread his arms. "What is time to an immortal? Nay, go about the King's business!"

"Thanks, sprite." Rod turned back to Gwen. "Your broom, or mine?"

Gwen bent over the hanging cradle swathed in yards of cloth-of-gold, and her face softened into a tender smile. "Oh, he is dear!"

Queen Catharine beamed down at the baby. She was a slender blonde with large blue eyes and a very small chin. "I thank thee for thy praise . . . I *am* proud."

"As thou shouldst be." Gwen straightened, looking up at her husband with a misty gaze.

Rod looked around, hoping she was gazing at someone else. On second thought, maybe not. . . .

Catharine raised a finger to her lips and moved slightly toward the door. Rod and Gwen followed, leaving the child to its nanny, two chambermaids, and two guards.

Another two stood on either side of the outer doorway, under the eagle eye of the proud father. One reached out to close the door softly behind them. Rod looked up at King Tuan, and nodded. "No worries about the succession now."

"Aye." Gwen beamed. "Two princes are a great blessing."

"Well I can think of a few kings who would've argued with that." Rod smiled, amused. "Still, I must admit they're outnumbered by the kings who've been glad of the support of their younger brothers."

"As I trust our Alain shall be." Tuan turned away. "Come, let us pass into the solar." He paced down the hall and into another chamber with a wall of clerestory windows. Rod followed, with the two ladies chattering behind him. He reminded himself that he and Gwen were being signally honored; none of the royal couple's other subjects had ever been invited into their majesties' private apartments.

On the other hand, if Gwen had been the kind to brag, *they* might not have been invited in, either.

And, of course, there was old Duke Loguire. But that was different; he came under the alias of "Grandpa." And Brom O'Brien; but the Lord Privy Councillor would, of course, have access to the privy chambers.

On the other hand, Rod tried not to be too conscious of the honor. After all, he had known Tuan when the young King was an outlaw; exiled for courting Catharine; and hiding out in the worst part of town, as King of the Beggars— and unwitting party to the forming of a civil war. "As long as they grow up friends," he reminded Tuan, "or as much as two brothers can."

"Aye—and if their friendship doth endure." A shadow crossed Tuan's face, and Rod guessed he was remembering his own elder brother, Anselm, who had rebelled against their father, and against Queen Catharine.

"Then must we take great care to ensure their friendship." Catharine hooked her arm through Tuan's. "Yet I misdoubt me, my lord, an our guests did come to speak of children only."

"I'm sure it's a more pleasant subject than whatever he had in mind," Rod said quickly.

"And 'twould have been cause enow, I do assure thee," Gwen added.

Catharine answered with a silvery laugh. "For thou and I, mayhap—but I misdoubt me an 'twould interest our husbands overlong."

"Do not judge us so harshly," Tuan protested. "Yet I must own that there are matters of policy to be discussed." He sighed, and turned away to a desk that stood beneath the broad windows, with a map beside it on a floor stand. "Come, Lord Warlock—let us take up less pleasant matters."

Rod came over, rather reassured; Tuan certainly didn't seem to feel any urgency.

The young King tapped the map, on the Duchy of Romanov. "Here lies our mutual interest of the hour."

"Well, as long as it's only an hour. What's our bear of a Duke up to?"

"'Tis not His Grace," Tuan said slowly.

Rod perked up; this was becoming more interesting. "Something original would be welcome. Frankly, I've been getting a bit bored with the petty rebellions of your twelve great lords."

"Art thou so? I assure thee," Tuan said grimly, "I have never found them tedious."

"What is it, then? One of his petty barons gathering arms and men?"

"I would it were; of that, I've some experience. This, though, is a matter of another sort; for the rumors speak of foul magics."

"Rumors?" Rod looked up from the map. "Not reports from agents?"

"I have some spies in the North," Tuan acknowledged, "yet they only speak of these same rumors, not of events which they themselves have witnessed."

Rod frowned. "Haven't any of them tried to track the rumor to its source?"

Tuan shrugged. "None of those who've sent word. Yet I've several who have sent me no reports, and mine emissaries cannot find them."

"Not a good sign." Rod's frown darkened. "They might have ridden off to check, and been taken."

"Or worse," Tuan agreed, "for the rumors speak of a malignant magus, a dark and brooding power, who doth send his minions everywhere throughout the North Country."

"Worrisome, but not a problem—as long as all they do is spy. I take it they don't."

"Not if rumor speaks truly. These minions, look you, are sorcerers in their own right; and with the power they own, added to that which they gather from their sorcerer-lord, they defeat the local knights ere they can even come to battle. Then the sorcerers enthrall the knights, with their wives and children, too, and take up lordship over all the serfs and peasants of that district."

"Not too good a deal for the knights and their families," Rod mused, "but probably not much of a difference, to the serfs and peasants. After all, they're used to taking orders—what difference does it make who's giving them?"

"Great difference, if the first master was gentle, and the

second was harsh," Tuan retorted. His face was grim. "And reports speak of actions more than harsh, from these new masters. These sorcerers are evil."

"And, of course, the peasants can't do much, against magic." Rod frowned. "Not much chance of fighting back."

Tuan shuddered. "Perish the thought! For peasants must never resist orders, but only obey them, as is their divinely appointed role."

What made Rod's blood run cold was that Tuan didn't say it grimly or primly, or pompously, or with the pious air of self-justification. No, he said it very matter-of-factly, as though it were as much a part of the world as rocks and trees and running water, and no one could even think of debating it. How could you argue about the existence of a rock? Especially if it had fallen on your toe...

That was where the real danger lay, of course—not in the opinions people held, but in the concepts they knew to be true—especially when they weren't.

Rod shook off the mood. "So the chief sorcerer has been knocking off the local lordlings and taking over their holdings. How far has his power spread?"

"Rumor speaks of several baronets who have fallen 'neath his sway," Tuan said, brooding, "and even Duke Romanov, himself."

"Romanov?" Rod stared, appalled. "One of *the* twelve great lords? How could *he* fall, without word of it reaching us?"

"I could accomplish it—and I am no wizard." Tuan shrugged. "'Tis simplicity—close a ring of iron around his castle under cover of night, then hurl an army 'gainst his barbican, and siege machines against his towers. Invest the castle, and trust to thy ring of knights and men-at-arms to see that not a soul wins free to bear off word."

Rod shuddered at Tuan's *sangfroid*. "But he had a couple of esp– uh, witches, guesting in his tower!"

"More than 'guesting,' as I hear it," Tuan answered, with a grim smile. "They were thoroughly loyal to Milord Duke, for he had saved them from the stake and embers. They've been of great service tending to the ill and injured and, I doubt not, gathering information for him."

Rod frowned. "They must have been very discreet about

it. We make it a practice, in the Royal Coven, not to pry into the minds of anyone except your enemies."

"Or those who might become so," Tuan amended. "Who's to say his witches did more? Nay, once Catharine showed them the way of it, and thou and thy good wife did aid her in forming that band into a battle-weapon, all the lords did learn, and followed suit."

"And Romanov's witches couldn't give him enough advance warning?" Rod pursed his lips. "This sorcerer *is* effective. But speaking of mental eavesdropping, that's a way to check on the rumors. Did you ask any of the Royal Witchforce to try and read Romanov's mind?"

"I did. They could not find him."

"So." Rod pursed his lips. "What minds *did* they hear, to the North?"

Tuan shrugged. "Only what should be. The plowman followed his oxen, the milkmaid coaxed her swain—naught was there to bring alarm, save that the warlock who listened, could not find the minds of any knights or barons."

"How about vile thoughts, from evil sorcerers?"

Tuan turned his head slowly from side to side.

"So." Rod's gaze strayed back to the map. "On the face of it, nothing's wrong; it's just that the Duke of Romanov seems to have taken a vacation to parts unknown, with all his aristocratic retainers."

"Thou dost see why I do suspect."

Rod nodded. "Sounds fishy to me, too . . . not that I can't understand why the noble Duke would want to take off for a while, though. I've been feeling a bit too much stress lately, myself. . . . Gwen?" He turned, to find Gwen standing near. "Been listening?"

"I have." She smiled. "And I do think thou dost make a great coil of naught."

"Well, I wouldn't exactly say we're making a lot of fuss." Rod locked gazes with Tuan. "Where's the weeping and wailing? The yelling and hair-tearing?"

"'Tis even as thou sayest," Tuan turned to Gwen. "I do not see great danger here, Lady Gwendylon—only the abuse of witch-power, over those who have it not."

"And witches ganging up on normals," Rod added. "But that can all be cured by even more witches—from the good guys. After all, we have a vested interest in the public's opinion of witches, dear."

"In truth," Gwen said firmly, "and we cannot have the folk afeard that witches will seek to govern by force of magic."

"Of course not," Rod mumured, "especially when every right-thinking individual knows it has to be done by force of arms."

Tuan frowned. "How didst thou speak?"

"Uh, nothing." Rod turned to Gwen. "How about it, dear? A family vacation, wandering toward the North?" When Gwen hesitated, he added, "I don't really think there's any danger—at least, none that you and I can't handle between us."

"Nay, surely not," Gwen agreed, but her brow was still furrowed.

"What, then? The kids? I really don't think they'll mind."

"Oh, certes they will not! Yet hast thou considered the trials of shepherding our four upon the road?"

"Sure." Rod frowned. "We did it in Tir Chlis."

"I know," Gwen sighed. "Well, an thou sayest 'tis for the best, my husband, we shall essay it."

2

Rod turned the key in the lock, pulled it out, set it in Gwen's palm, and wrapped her hand around it. "Your office, O Lady of the House." He studied her face for a second and added gently, "Don't worry, dear. It'll still be here when you get back."

"I know," she sighed, "yet 'tis never easy to leave it."

"I know." Rod glanced back at the house. "I'll get halfway down the road, and start wondering if I really *did* put out the fire on the hearth."

"And thou dost, but call it out, and an elf shall bear word to me," Brom O'Berin rumbled beside them. "Mere minutes after thou hast uttered it, an elf shall spring out of the ingelnook to douse thy hearth—if it doth need."

"I thank thee, Brom," Gwen said softly.

The dwarf scowled, becoming more gruff. "Nay, have no fear for thine house. Elves shall guard it day and night. Ill shall fare the man who doth seek to enter."

Rod shuddered. "I pity the footpad Puck catches! So come on, dear—there's nothing to worry about. Here, anyway. Time for the road." He grasped her waist, and helped her leap to Fess's saddle.

"May we not fly, Papa?" Cordelia pouted. Her hands were clasped behind her back, and a broomstick stuck out from behind her shoulder.

Rod smiled, and glanced at Gwen. She nodded, almost imperceptibly. He turned back to Cordelia. "As long as you stay near your mother and me—yes."

Cordelia gave a shout of joy and leaped onto her broom. Her brothers echoed her, drifting up into the air.

"Move out, Old Iron," Rod murmured, and the great black robot-horse ambled out toward the road. Rod fell into step beside him, and turned back to wave to Brom.

"A holiday!" Geoffrey cried, swooping in front of him. "'Tis ages since we had one!"

"Yeah—about a year." But Rod grinned; he seemed to feel a weight lifting off his shoulders. He caught Gwen's hand and looked up at her. "Confess it, dear—don't you feel a little more free?"

She smiled down at him, brightening. "I do, my lord— though I've brought my lock and bars along."

"And I, my ball and chain." Rod grinned. "Keep an eye on the links, will you? . . . Magnus! When I said, 'Stay near,' that meant altitude, too! Come down here right now!"

The tinkers strolled into the village, gay and carefree, smudged and dirty. Their clothes were patched, and the pots and pans hanging from their horse's pack made a horrible clattering.

"This is rather demeaning, Rod," Fess murmured. "Additionally, as I have noted, no *real* tinker family could afford a horse."

"Especially not one fit for a knight. I know," Rod answered. "I'll just tell them the last stop was a castle, and the lord of the demesne paid us in kind."

"Rod, I think you lack an accurate concept of the financial worth of a war-horse in medieval culture."

"Hey—they had a *lot* of pots." Rod grinned down at his own primitive publicity agents. "Okay, kids, that's enough. I think they know we're here."

The four little Gallowglasses slowed their madcap dancing, and gave their pots and pans one last clanging whack with their wooden spoons. "You spoil *all* the fun, Papa," Cordelia pouted as she handed him the cookware.

"No, just most of it. Magnus? Geoff? Turn in your weapons, boys. Gregory, you, too—ah, a customer!"

"Canst mend this firkin, fellow?" The housewife was plump, rosy-cheeked, and anxious.

Rod took the little pot and whistled at the sight of the long, jagged crack in the cast iron. "How'd you manage *that* kind of break?"

"My youngest dropped it," the goodwife said impatiently. "Canst mend it?"

"Yeah," Rod said slowly, "but it'll cost you a ha'penny."

The woman's face blossomed in a smile. "I have one, and 'twill be well worth it. Bless thee, fellow!"

Which sounded a little odd, since "fellow" was a term of semicontempt; but Rod blithely took out a hammer and some charcoal, laid a small fire, and got busy faking. Magnus and Gregory crouched on either side of him, obstensibly watching.

"This is the manner of the crafting of it, Gregory," big brother Magnus said softly. "Let thy mind bear watch on mine. The metal's made of grains so small thou canst not see them..."

"Molecules," Rod supplied.

"Aye. And now I'll make those molecules move so fast they'll meld one to another. Yet I must spring them into motion so quickly that their heat will not have time to spread through the rest of the metal to Papa's hands, the whiles he doth press the broken edges together—for we'd not wish to burn him."

"Definitely not," Rod muttered.

Gregory watched intently.

So did Rod. He still couldn't quite believe it, as he saw the metal spring into cherry-redness all along the crack, brighten quickly through orange and yellow to near whiteness. Metal flowed.

"Now quickly, cool it!" Magnus hissed, drops of sweat standing out on his brow, "Ere the heat can run to Papa's hands!"

The glow faded faster than it had come, for Gregory frowned at it, too; this part was simple enough for a three-year-old.

Simple! When only witches were supposed to be telekinetic, not warlocks—and even the best of them could only move objects, not molecules.

But there the pot stood, round and whole! Rod sighed, and started tapping it lightly with the hammer, far from where the crack had been—just for appearances. "Thanks, Magnus. You're a great help."

"Willingly, Papa." The eldest wiped his brow.

"Papa," Gregory piped up, "Thou dost know that elves do 'company us..."

"Yeah." Rod grinned. "Nice to know you're not alone."

"Truth. Yet I've thought to have them ask for word from their fellows in the North...."

"Oh?" Rod tried not to show it, but he was impressed. Three years old, and he'd thought of something Tuan and Rod had both overlooked. "What did they say?"

"The goodwives no longer call warnings to the Wee Folk ere they empty garbage out upon the ground," Gregory's eyes were large in his little face. "They no longer leave their bowls of milk for the elves, by their doors. Each house now hath cold iron nailed up over its door, whether it be an horseshoe or some other form, and hearths go unswept at eventide."

Rod felt a chill and glanced at a nearby tree, but its leaves were still. "Well, I guess no housewife there is going to find sixpence in her shoe. What are the elves doing about it?"

"Naught. There is some spell lies o'er the plowed land there, that pushes against all elfin magic. They have turned away in anger, and flitted to the forests."

Rod struck the pot a few more times, in silence.

"Is this coil in the North so light as thou hast told us, Papa?" Gregory finally asked.

Rod reflected that, for a three-year-old, the kid had one hell of a good vocabulary. He put down his hammer and faced the child squarely. "There's no *real* evidence, yet, that it's anything major."

"But the signs..." Magnus murmured.

"Are not evidence," Rod answered. "Not firm evidence—but I'm braced. That's why we're travelling in disguise—so we can pick up any rumors, without letting people know we're the High Warlock and Company."

"Thou dost not wish our presence known, for fear the evil folk will hide till we've gone by?" Magnus asked.

"No, because I don't want to walk into an ambush. Not that I expect to, mind—I just don't want to take any chances." He gave the pot a last tap and held it up to admire. "You boys did a good job."

"We shall ever do our best, for thee," Magnus responded. "Papa . . . if thou dost gain this firm evidence that thou speakest of . . . What then?"

Rod shrugged. "Depends. If it's nothing major, we'll fix whatever's wrong, and go on to the northern seacoast for a couple of weeks of swimming and fishing. You've never tried swimming in the ocean, boys. Let me tell you, it's very different from the little lake near our house."

"I shall hope to discover it," Gregory piped. "Papa . . . what if the evidence is of great wrongness?"

"Then you three boys will turn right around, and take your mother and your sister right home," Rod said promptly.

"And thou . . . ?"

"I'm the High Warlock, aren't I?" Rod grinned at them. "They gave me the title. I've got to live up to it."

Gregory and Magnus looked at each other, and locked gazes.

"I prithee, my lord, calm your heart," Gwen eyed him anxiously as she laid the campfire. "'Twas not the forester's fault that we may not hunt."

"Yeah—but the way he dragged Magnus in, as though he were some kind of criminal!" Rod folded a hand around his trembling fist. "He should only know how close he came to disaster! Good thing Magnus remembered his disguise."

"'Twas not the child's self-rule that troubled me." Gwen shuddered. "My lord, if thou couldst have but seen thine own face. . . ."

"I know, I know," Rod snapped, turning away. "So it's not surprising he reached toward his knife. But so help me, if he had touched it . . ."

"He would have died," Gwen said simply, "and men-at-arms would have caught us on the morrow."

"Oh, no, they wouldn't," Rod said grimly. "They wouldn't've dared touch the High Warlock!"

"Aye—and all the land would have known we ride north." She sighed. "I rejoice thou didst throttle thy temper."

"No, I didn't, and you know it! If you hadn't butted in and taken over, raining thanks and praise on the forester, as though you were a waterfall..."

Gwen shrugged. "'Twas naught but his due. A less kind man would have beaten the child, and haled him off to his knight's gaol."

Rod stared, appalled.

Gwen nodded. "Oh, aye, my lord. And the law allows it. Nay, more; for this good warden who did find our son, might be censured if his lord did know of his forbearance."

Rod shuddered. "I'm glad I let him go, then. But, my lord! It's not as though the boy'd been trying to bring down a deer! All he was after was a rabbit!"

"Even so, the Forest Laws would say 'twas theft," Gwen reminded him. "Every hare and goose—nay, each mouse and sparrow—doth belong unto the manor's lord; and to hunt them is to steal!"

"But how do these people *live?*" Rod cupped an empty hand. "We didn't do badly today, for tinkers—we made a penny and a half! But we had to spend the penny for a chicken, and the half for bread! What would we live on, if nobody broke a pot?"

"The law..." Gwen sighed.

"Well, it won't, for long." Rod curled the hand into a fist. "I'm going to have a few words with Tuan, when we get back to Runnymede!"

"Do," Gwen said softly, "and thou'lt have proved the worth of this journey, even an we find naught wrong i' the North."

"I'm afraid that's not very apt to happen." Mollified, Rod watched her stare at the kindling. It burst into flame, and he sighed, "I'd better see how the kids are coming along with their foraging." He stiffened at a sudden thought, staring at her. "We *are* allowed to gather berries, aren't we?"

Rod sat bolt upright with a hissing-in of breath, staring about him, wide-eyed.

The night breathed all around him, hushed. Far away, crickets and frogs wove counterpoint that darted harmony with the myriad of stars. The land lay deep in peace.

Rod sagged against the prop of his arm, relieved by

reality. Adrenalin ebbed, and his hammering heart began to slow. He couldn't even remember the nightmare—only that, vaguely, the face was Lord Kern's.

This had to stop. Somehow, he had to break this spell. Somebody moaned; not surprising, the way he felt.

Then he stiffened, all his attention concentrated on his ears. Whoever had moaned, it hadn't been him.

Then, who...?

The sound came again, louder and closer. It wasn't a moan, really—more of a grinding sound. Not moving, Rod murmured, "Fess?"

"Here, Rod." Being a robot, Fess never slept. In fact, he scarcely ever powered down.

"Hear anything out of the ordinary?"

"Yes, Rod. The sound is that of rock moving against rock. When the frequency of its repetitions is accelerated, there is a discernible Doppler shift..."

"Coming, or going?"

"Coming—and rather rapidly, I should..."

Trees at the edge of the meadow trembled, and a huge, dark form came into sight. The silhouette was crudely human.

Rod was on his feet and darting over to Fess. He yanked a light out of the pack, aimed it at the dark form, and pressed the tab. "Gwen!"

Gwen raised her head just as the beam struck the huge figure.

If it was female, it was a caricature. If it had breasts, it also had shoulders like a fullback's and arms like a gorilla's. It did have long fingernails, though—and they glinted dangerously in the actinic glare. Its face was blue. It flinched at the sudden stab of light, lips drawing back in a snarl—revealing fangs.

"Black Annis!" Gwen gasped in horror.

The monster froze for a moment, startled by the beam—and Rod snapped, "Magnus! Cordelia! Wake the babies and get into the air!"

The elder children snapped out of sleep as though they'd been jabbed, galvanized by Gwen's mental alarm. Geoffrey rolled up, sitting, knuckling his eyes and muttering. *"Not* a baby! Six!" But Gregory just shot straight into the air.

Then the monster roared, charging, and caught up
Geoffrey with one roundhouse swipe. He squalled, but in
anger, not fright, and wrestled his dagger out of its sheath.
But Rod thundered rage, and the monster rose into the air,
then slammed down onto its back. Geoffrey jabbed the huge
hand with his dagger, and Black Annis howled, dropping
him. He shot into the air, while Rod stalked toward the
horror. Red haze blurred his vision, obscuring all but Black
Annis struggling to its feet in the center of his field of view.
The familiar roaring thundered in his ears, and power thrilled
through every vein. One thought filled him, only one—to
see the creature torn to bits.

Behind him, though, Gwen retreated, keeping her face
toward the monster, pulling Magnus and Cordelia by their
hands, along with her.

The monster floundered to its feet and turned toward
Rod, its face contorted with hate, claws lifting to pounce;
but Rod's arm was raising, forefinger stiffened to focus his
powers.

Gwen's eyes narrowed, and her children squeezed their
eyes shut.

Black Annis exploded into a hundred wriggling fragments.

Rod roared in rage, cheated of his revenge; but Gwen
cried to her two youngest, "Rise and follow!"

For the wriggling fragments kept writhing and, as they
fell to earth, ran leaping away, long-eared and puff-tailed,
fleeing back toward the wood.

Rod clamped his jaw and ran after them.

But Gwen was beside him, pacing him on her broomstick, gripping his arm and calling to him through the blood-
haze. Distantly through the roaring, he heard her: "My lord,
it was not real! 'Twas a phantom, made of witch-moss!"

That stung through; for 'witch-moss' was a fungus pe-
culiar to this planet, telepathically sensitive. If a projective
esper thought hard at a lump of it, it would turn into whatever
he or she was thinking about.

Which meant there had to be a projective esper around.

Gwen was tugging at his arm, falling behind. "Softly,
mine husband! Fall back, and wait! If this monster was
made o' purpose, 'tis toward the purposer that these conies

we've made from it do flee! Yet if that villain doth take sight of thee, he'll flee ere we can seize him!"

"I'll blast him into oxides," Rod muttered, but sense began to poke through his battle-madness.

"A pile of dust cannot tell us what we wish to know!" Gwen cried, and, finally, Rod began to slow. The master who had made this monster, was nothing; what mattered was the one who'd pulled *his* strings. *That* was the ogre who'd threatened Rod's children. "Black Annis eats babies," he muttered, and the rage began to build again.

"Black Annis is an old wives' tale!" Gwen's voice whipped, and stung through to him. "In Tir Chlis she did truly live, mayhap, but not in Gramarye! Here, she's only crafted out of witch-moss! Here, 'tis a sorcerer who doth scorn babes!"

Rod halted, trembling, and nodded. "And it's the scorcerer we've got to catch—yes! But to find him, we have to question the minion that sent the monster against us!" His lips pulled back against his teeth. "That questioning, I think I'll enjoy!"

Gwen shuddered, and implored, "Hold thyself in check, I prithee! Knowledge is our goal, not joy in cruelty."

"Just tell me where he is. Who's spotting? . . . Oh. The kids." He stilled, listening mentally for his children's call—and muttering, "Fess, to me. When we need to ride, we'll need full speed."

The great black horse drummed up beside him, just as Cordelia's cry came, "Here!"

Rod leaped astride Fess, and they tore off through the night. The robot's radar probed the darkened landscape, and Fess hurdled fallen trunks and streams as though he rode a close-clipped steeplechase course. Gwen swooped above the trees; but Fess broke from cover as she began her downward strike.

Her target was a high-walled wagon with a roof. A woman stood in its open door, silhouetted by candlelight. She darted a glance at Gwen, then whirled, to stare first toward the north, and Cordelia, then toward the east, and Gregory, then toward Geoffrey, then Magnus. She darted back inside, slamming the door; but she reappeared at the driver's seat, catching up the reins. Her horses lifted their heads and turned out into the meadow, pulling the caravan about...

And she stared, appalled, at the horde of rabbits who filled the meadow—and the great black horse who thundered up behind them.

Then both her arms snapped out straight, fingers pointing—The rabbits leaped together, melded, coalesced, metamorphosed—and a lion, wolf, and bear whirled about, to turn on Rod.

He howled in rage and glee as the blood-haze enfolded him again, obscuring all but the monsters. They were release; they were justification for lashing out with his power. He would blast them; then his path would be clear, to smear the woman over the meadow grass.

The wolf was gaunt, with eyes of fire, impossibly huge. The bear, shambling upright, had a human face; and the lion's mane was flame, its teeth and claws were steel.

Rod hauled on the reins and Fess dug in his hooves, throwing his weight back, plowing up the meadow in his halt, as Rod rose in the stirrups, stiffened arm spearing out.

The wolf exploded.

Rod's head pivoted deliberately.

The lion's mane expanded, flame sweeping out to envelop its body. But the beast didn't seem to notice; it bounded on toward Rod, roaring.

Rod's eyebrows drew down, his brow furrowing.

The lion's head whipped around in a full turn and whirled spinning away. Fess sidestepped, and the body hurtled on by, to collapse in a writhing heap.

Rod pivoted toward the bear, his sword hissing out of its sheath; then the beast was on him. A great paw slammed against the side of Rod's head. For a moment, he was loose in space, the blackness shot with tiny sparks; then the earth slammed into his back, and his insides knotted, driving the breath out of him. But the blood-haze still filled his sight; he saw Fess rearing up to slam forehooves into the bear's shoulder. It stumbled, but came on, manlike face contorted in a snarl.

Rod clenched his jaw, waiting for breath, and glared at his sword-blade. Flame shot down its tip, billowing outward as though it were a blowtorch with a three-foot blast.

The bear halted, and backed away, snarling.

Rod's diaphragm unkinked, and he drew a labored breath, then thrust himself to his feet, staggering toward the bear.

It threw itself on him with a roar.

He swung aside, squinting against pain, glaring at it. It flared like magnesium; but it had barely begun its death-howl when its fires flickered, guttered, and went out. Where it had stood, only ashes sifted to the ground.

Rod stood alone in the darkness, swaying, as the haze that filled him darkened, faded, and retreated back within him. He began to realize that a breeze was blowing...

Fire.

He'd left a burning corpse. The breeze could spread that flame over all the meadow, and into the woods.

He swung toward the remains of the lion—and saw Gregory floating near it, ten feet away, staring at the charred hulk. Even as Rod watched, bits of it were breaking loose, and moving off through the meadow grass. He turned toward the bear, and saw Geoffrey turning it into a herd of toy horses, which galloped toward the wood.

"We cannot leave such large masses of witch-moss whole," Gwen's voice said softly behind him, "or the first old aunt, telling of a frightful tale, will bring it up unwittingly, in some horrible guise."

"No." The last of the anger ebbed, and remorse rushed in to fill its place. Rod spoke roughly to counter it. "Of course you couldn't. What happened to the witch?"

"She fled," Gwen said simply.

Rod nodded. "You couldn't follow her."

"We could not leave thee here, to fight unaided." Cordelia clung to her mother, watching her father out of huge eyes.

"No." Rod turned to watch his two youngest dismember the remains of what had been horrors. "On the other hand, if I hadn't stayed to fight them, you could've just taken them apart, and still had time to follow her."

Gwen didn't answer.

"Where's Magnus?" Rod sighed.

"He did follow the witch," Cordelia answered.

Air blew outward with a bang, and Magnus stood beside them. Rod usually found his sons' appearances and disappearances unnerving, but somehow, now, it seemed remote, inconsequential. "She got away?"

Magnus bowed his head. "She fled into the forest, and I could no longer see her from the air."

Rod nodded. "And it would've been foolish for you to try to follow low enough for her to get at you. Of course, if I'd been following on Fess, it would've been another matter."

Nobody answered.

He sighed. "How about her thoughts?"

"They ceased."

Gwen stared down at Magnus. "Ceased?" She looked up, eyes losing focus for a few seconds; then her gaze cleared, and she nodded affirmation. "'Tis even as he saith. But how ... ?"

"Why not?" Rod shrugged. "I was telephathically invisible for years, remember? Sooner or later, somebody was bound to learn how to do that whenever they wanted."

"My lord," Gwen said softly, "I think there is more danger in these Northern witches, than we had thought."

Rod nodded. "And, at a guess, they're better mind readers than we gave them credit for—'cause they certainly knew we were coming."

Gwen was silent, digesting that.

Rod shrugged, irritably. "Oh, sure, it's possible this one sorceress has a hatred for tinkers, especially when they come in families—but, somehow, I doubt that. Conjuring up a Black Annis for the average wanderer is a bit elaborate, No, they've spotted us."

He straightened his shoulders and clapped his hands. "All right, so much for our night's adventure! Everybody back to bed."

The children looked up, appalled.

"Don't worry, Mommy'll give you a sleep spell." Gwen's lullabies were effective projective telepathy; when she sang, "Sleep, my child," they really did.

"My lord," Gwen said softly, "if they do know of our presence ..."

"We'd better post sentries. Yes." Rod sat down cross-legged. "I'll take first watch. I haven't been sleeping well lately, anyway."

•   •   •

When the night noises prevailed again, and the only child-sound was deep and even breathing, Rod said softly, "They're being very good about it—but the fact is, I blew it."

"But it is distinctly improbable that you could have caught the projective, in any event," Fess's voice answered him. "Banished her, certainly—possibly even destroyed her, though that certainly would have been quite dangerous. But attempting to immobilize an esper, without killing her, would be ten times more dangerous."

Rod frowned. "Come to think of it, why didn't she just hop the next broomstick?" He had a sudden, vivid vision of Gwen in an aerial dogfight, and shuddered.

"Why leave her caravan, if she did not have to?" Fess countered.

Rod winced. "*That* hurts—that my rage hamstringed things so much that she didn't even have to strain to get away!"

"Still, that is only a blow to your pride," Fess reminded him. "The object was accomplished; the danger was banished."

"Only temporarily," Rod growled, "and the next time, it might banish *us*, if I let my rage block off my brain again."

"That is possible," Fess admitted. "And the danger must be considered greater, now that there is reason to believe the enemy knows your identities and direction."

"And can guess our purpose," Rod finished. "Yes, we can be sure they'll attack again, and as soon as possible. . . . Fess?"

"Yes, Rod?"

"Think it's time yet to send Gwen and the kids home?"

The robot was silent for a moment; then he answered, "Analysis of available data does not indicate a degree of danger with which your family, as a unit, cannot cope."

"Thank Heaven," Rod sighed. "I don't think they'd be very easy to send home, just now."

"Your children *have* become intrigued."

"Children, my eye! It's Gwen I'm worried about—her dander's up!"

Fess was silent.

Rod frowned at the lack of response; then his mouth tightened. "All right, what am I missing?"

The robot hesitated, then answered, "I don't think they trust you out alone, Rod."

3

"We're getting pretty close to the Romanov border now, aren't we?"

"Aye, my lord. 'Tis mayhap a day's journey further." Gwen was holding up bravely, but she did seem tired.

Rod frowned. "Look—they know we're coming; there's no point in keeping our disguise. Why're we still walking?"

"To save fright, Papa," Gregory looked down at his father, from his seat on Fess's pack. "If the good peasant folk see us flying north, they would surely take alarm."

Rod stared at his youngest for a moment, then turned to Gwen. "How old did you say he was? Three, going on *what?*"

But Gwen frowned suddenly, and held up a hand. "Hist!"

Rod frowned back. "The same to you."

"Nay, nay, my lord! 'Tis danger! Good folk come, but flee toward us in full terror!"

Rod's face went neutral. "What's chasing them?"

Gwen shook her head. "I cannot tell. 'Tis human, for I sense the presence—yet there's a blank where minds should be."

Rod noted the plural. "All right, let's prepare for the worst." He put two fingers to his mouth, and blasted out a shrill whistle.

Like tandem firecrackers, Magnus and Geoffrey popped out of nowhere, and Cordelia swooped down to hover behind them. "Why didst thou not but think for us, Papa?" Magnus inquired.

"Because we're up against an enemy that can hear thoughts farther than whistles. All right, kids, we've got to set up an ambush. I want each of you high up in a tree, doing your best imitation of a section of bark. Your mother and I'll take the ground. When the enemy shows up, hit 'em with everything you've got."

"What enemy, Papa?"

"Listen for yourself. Mama says it's human, but nothing more."

All four children went glassy-eyed for a moment, then came out of their trances with one simultaneous shudder. "'Tis horrible," Cordelia whispered. "'Tis there, but—'tis not!"

"You'll know it when you see it," Rod said grimly, "and just in case you don't, I'll think 'Havoc!' as loudly as I can. Now, scoot!"

They disappeared with three pops and a whoosh. Looking up, Rod spotted three treetops suddenly swaying against the wind, and saw Cordelia soar into a fourth. "Which side of the road do you want, dear?"

Gwen shrugged. "Both sides are alike to me, my lord."

"What do you think you are, a candidate? Okay, you disappear to the east, and I'll fade into the left. I keep trying, anyway."

Gwen nodded, and squeezed his hand quickly before she sped off the road. Leaves closed behind her. Rod stayed a moment, staring north and wondering; then he turned to the underbrush, muttering, "Head north about ten yards, Fess."

The robot sprang into a gallop, and almost immediately turned off the road onto Rod's side.

The leaves closed behind him, and Rod turned to face the roadway, peering through foliage. He knelt, and let his body settle, breathing in a careful rhythm, watching the dust settle.

Then, around the curve of the roadway, they came—a dozen dusty peasants with small backpacks and haunted faces. They kept glancing back over their shoulders. The tallest of them suddenly called out, jerked to a halt. The others hurried back to him, calling over their shoulders to their wives, "Go! Flee!" But the women hesitated, glancing longingly at the road south, then back at their husbands. The men turned their backs and faced north, toward the enemy, each holding a quarterstaff at guard position, slant-wise across his body. The women stared at them, horrified.

Then, with a wail, one young wife turned, hugging her baby, and hurried away southward. The others stared after her; then, one by one, they began to shoo their children away down the road.

Then the men-at-arms strode into sight.

Rod tensed, thinking, "Ready!" with all his force.

They wore brown leggings with dark green coats down to midthigh, and steel helmets. Each carried a pike, and a saffron badge gleamed on every breast. It was definitely a uniform, and one Rod had never seen before.

The soldiers saw the peasants, gave a shout, and charged, pikes dropping down level.

Rod thought the word with all his might, as he muttered it to Fess: "Havoc!"

He couldn't have timed it better. Fess leaped out of the underbrush and reared, with a whinnying scream, just as the last soldiers passed him. They whirled about, alarmed, as did most of their mates—and Rod leaped up on the roadway between peasants and soldiers, sword flickering out to stab through a shoulder, then leaping back out to dart at another footman even as the first screamed, staggering backward. Two soldiers in the middle of the band shot into the air with howls of terror, and slammed back down onto their mates, as a shower of rocks struck steel helmets hard enough to stagger soldiers, and send them reeling to the ground.

Rod threw himself into a full lunge, skewering a third soldier's thigh, as he shouted to the peasants, "Now! Here's your chance! Fall on 'em, and beat the hell out of 'em!"

Then a pike-butt crashed into his chin and he spun backward, vision darkening and shot through with sparks; but a roar filled his ears and, as his sight cleared, he saw the peasant men slamming into the soldiers, staves rising and falling with a rhythm of mayhem.

Rod gasped, and staggered back toward them; there was no need for killing!

Then another thought nudged through: they needed prisoners, for information.

He blundered in among the peasants, took one quick glance at the remains of the melee, and gasped, "Stop! There's no need . . . They don't deserve . . ."

"Thou hast not seen what they've done," the peasant next to him growled.

"No, but I intend to find out! Look! They're all down, and some of 'em may be dead already! Stand back, and leave them to me!"

A rough hand grasped his shoulder and spun him around. "I' truth? And who art thou to command, thou who hast not lost blood to these wolves?"

Rod's eyes narrowed. He straightened slowly, and knocked the man's hand away with a sudden chop. It was ridiculous, and really shouldn't have made any difference to anybody— but it would work; it'd get their cooperation. "I am the High Warlock, Rod Gallowglass, and it is due to my magic and my family's, that you men stand here victorious, instead of sprawling as buzzard's meat!"

He didn't have to add the threat; the man's eyes widened, and he dropped to one knee. "Your pardon, Lord! I . . . I had not meant . . ."

"No, of course you didn't. How could you tell, when I'm dressed as a tinker?" Rod looked around to find all the peasants kneeling. "All right, that's enough! Are you men or pawns, that you must kneel? Rise, and bind these animals for me!"

"On the instant, milord!" The peasants leaped to their feet, and turned to begin lashing up the soldiers with their own belts and garters. Rod caught the belligerent one by the shoulder. "How are you called?"

Apprehension washed his face, and he tugged at his forelock. "Grathum, an it please thee, milord."

Rod shrugged. "Whether or not it pleases you, is a bit more important. Grathum, go after the women, and tell them the good news, will you?"

The man stared, realization sinking in. "At once, your lordship!" And he sped away.

Rod surveyed the knot-tying party and, satisfied everything was well under way with the minimum of vengeful brutality, glanced up at the trees and thought, *Wonderful, children! I'm a very proud daddy!*

The branches waved slightly in answer. Rod could have bent his mind to it, and read their thoughts in return; but it still involved major effort for him, and he couldn't spare the concentration just now. But he turned toward the underbrush, and thought, *Thanks, dear. It was nice to see you throwing somebody else's weight around for a change.*

"As long as 'tis not thine, my lord? Thou art most surely welcome!"

Rod looked up, startled—that was her voice, not her mind. Gwen came marching up, with the women and children behind her. Grathum hurried on ahead, face one big apology. "'Ere I could come unto them, milord, thy wife had brought word, and begun their progress back."

She had obviously run the message on her broomstick; the wives were herding their children silently, with covert glances at her, and the children were staring wide-eyed.

Rod turned back to Grathum. "Any more of these apes likely to be following you?"

The peasant shook his head. "Nay, milord—none that we know of. There were more bands—but they chased after others who fled. Only these followed the high road, when we who escaped to it so far as this, were so few."

"'Others who fled?'" Rod frowned, setting his fists on his hips. "Let's try it from the beginning. What happened, Grathum? Start back before you knew anything was wrong."

"Before . . . ?" The peasant stared at him. "'Tis some months agone, milord!"

"We've got time." Rod nodded toward the north. "Just in case you're worried, I've got sentries out."

Grathum darted quick looks about him, then back at Rod, fearfully. Rod found it unpleasant, but right now, it was useful. "Several months back," he prompted, "before you knew anything was wrong."

"Aye, milord," Grathum said, with a grimace. He heaved a sigh, and began. "Well, then! 'Twas April, and we were

shackling our oxen to the plows for the planting, and a
fellow hailed me from the roadway. I misliked his look—
he was a scrawny wight, with a sly look about him—but
I'd no reason to say him nay, so I pulled in my ox and
strode up to the hedge, to have words with him.

"'Whose land is this?' he did ask me; and I answered,
'Why, o' course, 'tis the Duke of Romanov's; but my master,
Sir Ewing, holds it enfeoffed from him.'

"'Nay,' quoth this wight, ''tis not his now, but the Lord
Sorcerer Alfar's—and I hold it enfeoffed from him.'

"Well! At this I became angered. 'Nay, assuredly thou
dost not,' I cried. 'An thou dost speak such treason, no man
would blame me!' And I drew back my fist, to smite him."

Rod's mouth tightened. That sort of fit in with his overall
impression of Grathum's personality. "And what'd he do
about it?"

"Why! He was gone ere I could strike—disappeared!
And appeared again ten feet away, on my side of the fence!
Ah, I assure thee, then fear did seize my bowels—but I
ran for him anyway, with a roar of anger. Yet up he drifted
into the air, hauling a thick wand out from his cloak, and
struck down at me with it. I made to catch it, but ever did
he seem to know where I would grasp next, and ever was
his stick elsewhere; and thus did he batter me about the
head and shoulders, till I fell down in a swoon. When I
came to my senses, he stood over me, crowing, 'Rejoice
that I spared thee, and used only a wooden rod—nor tossed
a ball of fire at thee, nor conjured a hedgehog into thy
belly!' . . . Could he do such, milord?"

"I doubt it highly," Rod said, with a dry smile. "Go on
with your story."

Grathum shrugged. "There's little more to tell of that
broil. 'Be mindful,' quoth he, 'that thou dost serve me now,
not that sluggard Sir Ewing.' The hot blood rushed to my
face, to hear my lord so addressed; but he saw it, and struck
me with the wand again. I did ward the blow, but he was
behind me on the instant, and struck me from the other
side—and I could not ward myself, for that the arm that
should have done it, was beneath me. 'Be mindful,' quoth
he again, 'and fear not Sir Ewing's retribution; ere the har-
vest comes, he'll not be by to trouble thee further.' Then

he grinned like to a broad saw, and vanished in a crack of thunder."

Rod noted that all this junior wizard seemed to have done, was teleport and levitate—but he had used them to give him an advantage in a fight!

"This worm of a warlock was fully lacking in honor," Gwen ground out, at his elbow.

"Totally unethical," Rod agreed, "and, therefore, totally self-defeating, in the end. If witches and warlocks went around behaving like *that,* the mobs would be out after them in an instant—and how long could they last then?"

"Forever," Grathum said promptly, "or so this Lord Sorcerer and his sorcery-knights do believe. They fear no force, milord, whether it come from peasants or knights."

The fright in his tone caught at Rod. He frowned. "You sound as though you're talking from experience. What happened?" Then he lifted his head as he realized what someone like Grathum might have done. "You *did* report this little incident to Sir Ewing, didn't you?"

"I did." Grathum bit his lip. "And I wish that I had not—though it would have made little difference, for each and every other plowman on Sir Ewing's estates told him likewise."

"The same warlock in each case?"

"Aye; his name, he said, was Melkanth. And there was no report of him, from any other manor; yet each had been so visited by a different warlock or witch. Naetheless, 'twas our Sir Ewing who did rise up in anger and, with his dozen men-at-arms, rode forth to seek out this Melkanth."

Rod clamped his jaw. "I take it Sir Ewing found him."

Grathum spread his hands. "We cannot think otherwise; for he did not come back. Yet his men-at-arms did; but they wore this livery thou seest on those who pursued us." He jerked his thumb back over his shoulder at the heap of bound soldiers. "Aye, they came back, these men that we'd known since childhood; they came back, and told us that Sir Ewing was no more, and that we served His Honor Warlock Melkanth now."

Rod stared, and Gwen caught at his arm. That jarred Rod back into contact with reality; he cleared his throat, and asked, "Anything odd about 'em? The way they looked?"

"Aye." Grathum tapped next to his eye. "'Twas here, milord—in their gazes. Though I could not say to thee what 'twas that was odd."

"But it was wrong, whatever it was." Rod nodded. "What'd the soldiers do? Stay around to make sure you kept plowing?"

"Nay; they but told us we labored for Melkanth now, and bade us speak not of this that had happed, not to any knight nor lord; yet they did not say we could not speak to other peasant folk."

"So the rumor ran?"

"Aye. It ran from peasant to peasant, till it had come closer by several manors to our lord, Count Novgor."

Rod kept the frown. "I take it he's vassal to Duke Romanov."

"Aye, milord. The Count called up his levies—but scarce more than a dozen knights answered his call; for the others had all marched forth to battle the warlocks who challenged them."

"Oh, really! I take it rumor hadn't run fast enough."

Grathum shrugged. "I think that it had, milord; but such news only angered our good knights, and each marched out to meet the warlock who claimed his land, thinking his force surely equal to the task."

"But it wasn't." Rod's lips were thin. "Because they went out one knight at a time; but I'll bet each one of them ran into this Lord Sorcerer and all his minions, together."

Grathum's face darkened. "Could it be so?"

Rod tossed his head impatiently. "You peasants have got to stop believing everything you're told, Grathum, and start trying to find out a few facts on your own!...Oh, don't look at me like that, I'm as sane as you are! What happened to Count Novgor and his understrength army?"

Grathum shook his head. "We know not, milord—for fear overtook us, and we saw that, if the sorcerer won, we would be enslaved to fell magic, and our wives and bairns with us. Nay, then we common folk packed what we could carry and sin' that we would not have the chance to fight, fled instead, through the pasture lanes to the roadway, and down the roadway to the High Road."

"So you don't know who won?"

"Nay; but early the next morning, when we'd begun to march again, word ran through our numbers—for it was hundreds of people on the road by then, milord; we folk of Sir Ewing's were not alone in seeing our only chance to stay free—and word ran from the folk at the rear of the troupe, to us near the van, that green-coated soldiers pursued. We quickened our pace, but word came, anon, that a band of peasants had been caught up by soldiers, and taken away in chains. At that word, many folk split away, village by village, down side roads toward hiding. But when we came to high ground, we looked back, and saw squadrons of soldiers breaking off from the main host, to march down the side roads; so we turned our faces to the South, and hurried with Death speeding our heels—for word reached those of us in the van, that the soldiers had begun slaying those who fought their capture. Then did we take to a byway ourselves; but we hid, with our hands o'er our children's mouths, till the soldiers had trooped by, and were gone from sight; then back we darted onto the High Road, and down toward the South again. Through the night we came, bearing the wee ones on litters, hoping that the soldiers would sleep the whiles we marched; and thus we came into this morning, where thou hast found us."

Rod looked up at the sky. "Let's see, today . . . yesterday . . . This would be the third day since the battle."

"Aye, milord."

"And you, just this little band of you, are the only ones who made it far enough south to cross the border?"

Grathum spread his hands. "The only ones on the High Road, milord. If there be others, we know not of them . . . and had it not been for thee and thy family, we would not be here, either." He shuddered. "Our poor Count Novgor! We can only pray that he lives."

Air cracked outward, and Gregory floated at Rod's eye level, moored to his shoulder by a chubby hand.

The peasants stared, and shrank back, muttering in horror.

"Peace." Rod held up a hand. "This child helped save you from the sorcerer's soldiers." He turned to Gregory, nettled. "What is it, son? This wasn't exactly a good time."

"Papa," the boy said, eyes huge, "I have listened, and . . ."

Rod shrugged. "Wasn't exactly a private conversation. What about it?"

"If this Count Novgor had won, these soldiers in the sorcerer's livery would not have been marching after these peasant folk."

The folk in question gasped, and one woman cried, "But the bairn can scarcely be weaned!"

Rod turned to them, unable to resist a proud smirk. "You should see him think up excuses not to eat his vegetables. I'm afraid he's got a point, though; I wouldn't have any great hopes for Count Novgor's victory."

The peasants sagged visibly.

"But it should be possible to get a definite answer." Rod strode forward.

The peasants leaped aside.

Rod stepped up to the bound soldiers. He noticed that one or two were struggling against their ties. "They're beginning to come to. I think they might know who won." He reached out to yank a soldier onto his feet, then turned to the peasants. "Anybody recognize him?"

The peasants stared and, one after another, shook their heads. Then, suddenly, one woman's finger darted out, to point at the soldier on top of the third pile. "But yonder is Gavin Arlinson, who followed good Sir Ewing into battle! How comes he to fight in the service of his lord's foe?"

"Or any of them, for that matter? Still, he'll do nicely as a representative sample." Rod gave the soldier he was holding, a slight push; the man teetered, then fell back down onto his comrades. Rod caught him at the last second, of course, and lowered him the final inch; then he waded through the bound men, to pull Gavin Arlinson onto his feet. He slapped the man's face gently, until the eyelids fluttered; then he called, "Magnus, the brandy—it's in Fess's pack."

His eldest elbowed his way through to his father, holding up a flask. Rod took it, noting that nobody seemed to wonder where Magnus had come from. He pressed the flask to Arlinson's lips and tilted, then yanked it back out quickly. The soldier coughed, spraying the immediate area, choked, then swallowed. He squinted up at Rod, frowning.

Just the look of the eyes made Rod shiver. Admittedly,

the glassiness of that stare could be due to the head knock he'd received; but the unwavering, unblinking coldness was another matter.

Rod pulled his nerve back up and demanded, "What happened to Sir Ewing?"

"He died," the soldier answered, his tone flat. "He died, as must any who come up against the might of the Lord Sorcerer Alfar."

Rod heard indignant gasps and muttering behind him, but he didn't turn to look. "Tell us the manner of it."

"'Tis easily said," the soldier answered, with full contempt. "He and his men marched forth to seek the warlock Melkanth. They took the old track through the forest, and in a meadow, they met him. But not Melkanth alone—his brother warlocks and sister witches, all four together, with their venerable Lord, the Sorcerer Alfar. Then did the warlocks and witches cause divers monsters to spring out upon Sir Ewing and his men, while the witches cast fireballs. A warlock appeared hard by Sir Ewing, in midair, to stab through his visor and hale him off his mount. Then would his soldiers have fled, but the Lord Sorcerer cried out a summoning, and all eyes turned toward him. With one glance, he held them all. Then did he explain to them who he was, and why he had come."

"I'll bite." Rod gave him a sour smile. "Who is he?"

"A man born with Talent, and therefore noble by birth," the soldier answered tightly, "who hath come to free us all from the chains in which the twelve Lords, and their lackeys, do hold us bound."

"What chains are these?" Rod demanded. "Why do you need freeing?"

The soldier's mouth twisted with contempt. "The 'why' of it matters not; only the fact of enslavement's of import."

"That, I can agree with—but not quite the way you meant it." Rod turned to his wife. "I call it hypnosis—instant style. What's your diagnosis?"

"The same, my lord," she said slowly. "'Tis like to the Evil Eye with which we dealt, these ten years gone."

Rod winced. "Please! Don't remind me how long it's been." He submitted to a brief but intense wave of nostalgia, suddenly feeling again the days when he and Gwen had only had to worry about one baby warlock. And, of course, a thousand or so marauding beastmen....

He shook off the mood. "Can you do anything about it?"

"Why...assuredly, my lord." Gwen stepped up to him, looking directly into his eyes. "But dost thou not wish to attempt it thyself?"

Rod shook his head, jaw clamped tight. "No, thanks. I managed to make it through this skirmish without rousing my temper—how, I'm not sure; but I'd just as soon not tempt fate. See what you can do with him, will you?"

"Gladly," she answered, and turned to stare into the soldier's eyes.

After a minute, his lips writhed back from his teeth. Rod glanced quickly at the thongs that held his wrists, then down to his lashed ankles. His muscles strained against the leather, and it cut into his flesh, but there was no sign it might break. He looked back up at the soldier's face. It had paled, and beads of sweat stood out on his forehead.

Suddenly, he stiffened, his eyes bulging, and his whole body shuddered so violently that it seemed it would fall apart. Then he went limp, darting panicked glances about him, panting as though he'd run a mile. "How...Who..."

Gwen pressed her hands over her eyes and turned away.

Rod looked from her to the soldier and back. Then he grabbed Grathum and shoved the soldier into his arms. "Here! Hold him up!" He leaped after his wife, and caught her in his arms. "It's over, dear. It's not there anymore."

"Nay...I am well, husband," she muttered into his doublet. "Yet that was...distasteful."

"What? The feel of his mind?"

She nodded, mute.

"What was it?" Rod pressed. "The sense of wrongness? The twisting of the mind that had hypnotized him?"

"Nay—'twas the lack of it."

"Lack?"

"Aye." Gwen looked up into his eyes, a furrow between her eyebrows. "There was no trace of any other mind within his, my lord. Even with the beastmen's Evil Eye, there was ever the sense of some other presence behind it—but here, there was naught."

Rod frowned, puzzled. "You mean he was hypnotized

and brainwashed, but whoever did it was so skillful, he didn't even leave a trace?"

Gwen was still; then she shrugged. "What else could it be?"

"But why take the trouble?" Rod mused. "I mean, any witch who knows more than the basics, would recognize that spell in a moment."

Gwen shook her head, and pushed away from him. "'Tis a mystery. Leave it for the nonce; there are others who must be wakened. Cordelia! Geoffrey, Magnus, Gregory! Hearken to my thoughts; learn what I do!" And she went to kneel by the bound soldiers. Her children gathered about her.

Rod watched her for a moment, then turned back to Arlinson, shaking his head. He looked up into the man's eyes, and found them haunted.

The soldier looked away.

"Don't blame yourself," Rod said softly. "You were under a spell; your mind wasn't your own."

The soldier looked up at him, hungrily.

"It's nothing but the truth." Rod gazed deeply into the man's eyes, as though staring could convince him by itself. "Tell me—how much do you remember?"

Arlinson shuddered. "All of it, milord—Count Novgor's death, the first spell laid on us, the march to the castle, the deepening of the spell..."

Rod waited, but the soldier only hung his head, shuddering. "Go on," Rod pressed. "What happened after the deepening of the spell?"

Arlinson's head snapped up, eyes wide. "What more was there!"

Rod stared at him a moment, then said slowly, "Nothing. Nothing that you could have done anything about, soldier. Nothing to trouble your heart." He watched the fear begin to fade from the man's eyes, then said, "Let's back it up a bit. They—the warlocks, I mean—marched you all to the castle, right?"

Arlinson nodded. "Baron Strogol's castle it had been, milord." He shuddered. "Eh, but none would have known it, once they'd passed the gate-house. 'Twas grown dank and sour. The rushes in the hall had not been changed in a month at the least, mayhap not since the fall, and each window and arrow slit was shuttered, barring the daylight."

Rod stored it all away, and asked, "What of the Count?"

Arlinson only shook his head slowly, eyes never leaving Rod's.

Rod leaned back on one hip, fingering his dagger. "How did they deepen the spell?"

Arlinson looked away, shivering.

"I know it's painful to remember," Rod said softly, "but we can't fight this sorcerer if we don't know anything about him. Try, won't you?"

Arlinson's gaze snapped back to Rod's. "Dost thou think thou canst fight him, then?"

Rod shrugged impatiently. "Of course we can—but I'd like to have a chance of winning, too. Tell me how they deepened the spell."

The soldier only stared at him for a time. Then, slowly, he nodded. "'Twas done in this manner: They housed us in the dungeon, seest thou, and took us out from our cage, one alone each time. When my turn came, they brought me into a room that was so dark, I could not tell thee the size of it. A lighted candle stood on a table, next to the chair they sat me in, and they bade me stare at the flame." His mouth twisted. "What else was there?"

Rod nodded. "So you sat and stared at the flame. Anything else?"

"Aye; some unseen musicians played a sort of music I never had heard aforetime. 'Twas a sort of a drone, seest thou, like unto that of a bagpipe—yet had more the sound of a viol. And another unseen beat on a tambour . . ."

"Tap it out," Rod said softly.

The soldier stared, surprised. Then he began to slap his thigh, never taking his eyes from Rod's.

Rod recognized the rhythmn; it was that of a heartbeat. "What else?"

"Then one who sat across from me—but 'twas so dark, I could tell his presence only by the sound of his voice— one across from me began to speak of weariness, and sleep. Mine eyelids began to grow heavy; I remember that they drooped, and I fought against drowsiness, yet I gave into it, finally, and slept—until now." He glanced down at his body, seeming to see his clothing for the first time. "What is this livery?"

"We'll tell you after you've taken it off," Rod said shortly. He slapped the man on the shoulder. "Be brave, soldier. You'll need your greatest courage when you find out what's been happening while you were, uh . . . while you 'slept.'" He turned to Grathum. "Release him—he's on our side again." And he turned back to Gwen, just in time to see the children, as a team, wake the last soldier, while Gwen supervised closely. "Gently, Magnus, gently—his mind sleeps. And Geoffrey, move slowly—nay, pull back! Retreat! If thou dost wake him too quickly, thou'lt risk driving him back into the depths of his own mind, in shock of his waking so far from his bed."

The soldier in question blinked painfully, then levered himself up on one elbow. He looked down and stared at his bound wrists. Then he looked up, wildly—but even as he began to struggle up, his eyes lost their wildness. In a few seconds, he sank back onto one elbow, breathing deeply.

"Well done, my daughter," Gwen murmured approvingly. "Thou didst soothe him most aptly."

Rod watched the man growing calmer. Finally, he looked about him, wide-eyed. His gaze anchored on Gwen, then took in the children—then, slowly, tilted up toward Rod.

"All are awake now, husband, and ready." Gwen's voice was low. "Tell them thy condition, and thy name."

"I am named Rod Gallowglass, and I am the High Warlock of this Isle of Gramarye." Rod tried to match Gwen's pitch and tone. "Beside me is my lady, Gwendylon, and my children. They have just broken an evil and vile spell that held you in thrall." He waited, glancing from face to face, letting them take it in and adjust to it. When he thought they'd managed, he went on. "You have been 'asleep' for three days, and during that time, you have fought as soldiers in the army of the Lord Sorcerer, Alfar."

They stared at him, appalled. Then they all began to fire questions, one after another, barking demands, almost howling in disbelief.

They were building toward hysteria. It had to be stopped. Rod held up his hands, and bellowed, *"Silence!"*

The soldiers fell silent, as military discipline dug its hooks into their synapses. But they were primed, and ready to explode, so Rod spoke quickly. "What you did during those days was not truly your doing—it was the 'Lord' Sorcerer's and his minions. They used your bodies—and parts of your minds." He saw the look that washed over the soldiers' faces, and agreed, "Yes. It was foul. But remember that what you did was *their* crime, not yours; there is no fault of yours in it, and you cannot rightly be blamed for it." He saw their foreboding. Well, good—at least they'd be braced, when Grathum and his peasants told them what had been happening. He glanced from face to face again, holding each set of eyes for a moment, then breathed, "But you can seek justice."

Every eye locked onto him.

"You have pursued these goodfolk, here . . ." Rod jerked his head toward the peasants. ". . . southward. You have passed the border of Romanov, and are come into Earl Tudor's land. Wend your way on to the South, now, with the folk you did chase—only now, be their protectors."

He saw resolve firm the soldiers' faces.

Rod nodded with satisfaction. Southward you go, all in one body, to King Tuan at Runnymede. Kneel to him there, and say the High Warlock bade you come. Then tell him your tale, from beginning to end, even as Gavin Arlinson has told it to me. He will hear you, and shelter you—and, if you wish it, I doubt not he will take you into his army, so that, when he marches North against this tyrant sorcerer, you may help in tearing him down."

Rod glanced from face to face again. He hadn't said anything about guilt or expiation, but he could see remorse turn into fanaticism in their expressions. He turned to Grathum. "We can trust them. Strike off their bonds."

Grathum eyed him uncertainly, but moved to obey.

Rod felt a tug at his belt, and looked down.

"Papa," said Gregory, "will the guards allow them to speak to the King?"

"I'll have to see if I can get you a job as my memory." Rod turned away to fumble in Fess's pack, mumbling, "We did bring a stylus and some paper, didn't we?"

"We did," the robot's voice answered, "but it is at the bottom, under the hardtack."

"Well, of course! I wasn't expecting a booming correspondence on this jaunt." Rod dug deep, came up with writing materials, and wrote out a rather informal note, asking that the bearer be allowed to speak with Their Majesties. He folded it, tucked the stylus away, and turned to Cordelia. "Seal, please."

The witchlet stared at it, brow puckering in furious concentration. Then she beamed, and nodded.

"All done?" Rod tested it; the paper was sealed all around the edges; molecules from each half of the sheet had wandered in among the other half's. Rod grinned. "Thanks, cabbage." He turned to Grathum, handing him the letter. "Present this to the sentry. Not being able to read, he'll call the captain of the guard, who'll call for Sir Maris, who'll probably allow only two of you to come before Their Majesties—and even then, only when you're surrounded by ten of the Queen's Own Bodyguard. Don't let them bother you—they'll just be decoration." He pursed his lips. "Though I wouldn't make any sudden moves, when you're in the throne room . . ."

Grathum bobbed his head, wide-eyed. "E'en as thou dost say, milord." Then he frowned. "But . . . milord . . ."

"Go ahead." Rod waved an expansive gesture.

Grathum still hesitated, then blurted, "Why dost thou call thy lass a 'cabbage?'"

"'Cause she's got a head on her shoulders," Rod explained. "Off with you, now."

4

The family watched the little company march off southward. When they had disappeared into the woodland, Rod turned back to his family. "Thank you, children. I was very proud of you."

They blossomed under his praise. Cordelia caught his hand and returned, "And *I* was proud of *thee*, Papa, that thou didst not lose thy temper!"

Rod fought to keep his smile and said only, "Yes. Well, every little improvement counts, doesn't it?"

He turned to sit on a convenient rock. "We could use a little rest, after all that excitement."

"And food!" Geoffrey plopped himself down on the grass in front of Rod. "May I hunt, Papa?"

"No," Rod said slowly, "there *are* those laws against poaching, and this tinker disguise still seems to be useful."

"But it doth not deceive the sorcerer and his coven," Magnus said, folding himself down beside Geoffrey.

"True, but it does seem to make the folk we encounter more willing to talk. Grathum said things to the tinker, that he was careful to hold back from the Lord High Warlock."

"Indeed," Gwen confirmed. "He was so overawed that his true feelings did not even come into his mind, when he knew thou wert noble."

"Which I still don't believe," Rod noted, "but he did. That's what's important. So we remain a tinker family, on the surface."

"Then, no hunting?" Geoffrey pouted.

"Yes," Rod nodded. "No."

"But we're *hungry!*" Cordelia complained.

"There is an answer to that." Gwen opened a bundle and spread it out. "Biscuits, cheese, apples—and good spring water, which Magnus may fetch."

Magnus heaved a martyred sigh and went to fetch the bucket.

"I know," Rod commiserated. "It's not easy, being the eldest."

Magnus set the bucket down in the center of the family ring and scowled at it. With a sudden slosh, it filled with water.

Rod gazed at it, then lifted his eyes to his eldest. "I take it you remembered the last brook we crossed?"

Magnus nodded, folding himself down cross-legged. "Though milk would be better."

"You may *not* teleport it out," Rod said sternly. "How do you think the poor cow would feel? Besides, it'd take too long to cool, after Mama pasteurized it."

"She could heat it in the cow," Cordelia offered.

"Haven't we done that poor beast enough meanness already?"

"Rabbit would be better," Geoffrey groused.

Gwen shook her head. "There is not time to roast it. We must yet march northward a whiles this day, children."

Geoffrey sighed, and laid a slice of cheese on a biscuit.

"Will we cross into Romanov this night, Papa?" Magnus asked.

"Not if I can help it. That's one border crossing I want to make in daylight."

"There are surprises enough, under the sun," Gwen agreed. "We need not those of the moon, also."

Cordelia shrugged. "We know the range of witch-powers. What new thing could they smite us withal?"

"An we knew of it," Gwen advised her, "'twould not be surprise."

"Besides," Rod said thoughtfully, "I don't like what your Mama said, about that depth-hypnosis not having any feel of the mind that did it."

The children all stared up at him. Magnus voiced for them. "What dost thou think it may be, Papa?"

But Rod shook his head. "There are too many factors we don't know about."

"We do know that the Tyrant Sorcerer is aged," Gregory piped up.

The others stared at him. "What makes thee say so?" Cordelia demanded.

"I heard the soldier speak thus, when he told Papa of the battle with Count Novgor."

"Such as it was." Rod searched his memory, and realized Gregory was right. But it was such a slight reference! And "venerable" didn't necessarily mean "old." He glanced at Gwen, and found her eyes on him. He turned back to Gregory. "Very good, son. What else do we know?"

"That he has gathered other witches and warlocks about him!" Cordelia said quickly.

"That they are younger than he," Magnus added, "for Grathum did not mention age when he spoke of the warlock Melkanth."

"He did not say Melkanth was young, though," Gregory objected, "and neither he nor the soldier said aught of the other sorcery folk."

Magnus clamped his jaw, and reddened. "Other than that there were more than a few of them—and enough to defeat a dozen armed men!"

"Well, he did use the plural," Rod temporized, "and Grathum and Arlinson both probably would've mentioned it, if they'd been old."

Magnus glanced up at his father gratefully.

"Still . . ." Rod glanced at Gregory, whose face was darkening into obstinacy. ". . . that *is* something we've guessed, not something we *know*. We've got to be ready to change that opinion in a hurry."

Gregory's expression lightened.

"We know there is a crafter of witch-moss among them," Gwen said slowly, "and I would presume 'tis the one we met with two nights agone."

"Probably," Rod agreed, "and at least one of their witches is good enough at telekinesis, to come up with fireballs."

"That doth take skill," noted Gwen, who could light both a match and a barn a mile off.

"And a projective who can manage a quick hypnotic trance that's good enough to hold a dozen demoralized soldiers," Rod mused. "Presumably, that's the tyrant himself."

"Thou dost guess, Papa," Gregory reminded.

Rod grinned. "Good boy! You caught it."

"And one among them can plan the use of all these powers, in such wise as to easily defeat an armed force," Geoffrey said suddenly.

Rod nodded. "Good point—and easy to miss. What was their strategy?"

"To gobble up first the peasants, then the knights," Geoffrey's eyes glowed. "They began with the small and built them into strength, then used them to catch something larger. They should therefore attack Duke Romanov and, after him, some others of the Great Lords—Hapsburg and Tudor, most likely, sin' that they are nearest neighbors. Then they might chance attack on the King and Queen, sin' that they'll have the Royal Lands encircled—or, if they doubt their own strength, they might swallow up Bourbon, DiMedici, and Gloucester ere they do essay King Tuan."

The family was silent, staring at the six-year-old. Rod reflected that this was the child who hadn't wanted to learn how to read, until Rod had told him the letters were marching. "That's very good," he said softly, "very good—especially since there wasn't much information to go on. And I did say strategy, when I really meant tactics."

"Oh! The winning of that one battle?" Geoffrey shrugged. "They sent witch-moss monsters against the armed band, to busy them and afright them. Then, the whiles the monsters held their attention, the other warlocks and witches rained blows on them from all sides. 'Twas simple—but 'twas enow; it did suffice."

"Hm." Rod looked directly into the boy's eyes. "So you don't think much of their tactician?"

"Eh, I did not say that, Papa! Indeed, he did just as he should have—used only as much force as was needed, and when and where it was needed. I doubt not, had Count

Novgor proved stronger than he'd guessed, he'd have had magical reserves to call upon." Geoffrey shook his head. "Nay, I could not fault him. His battle plan in this skirmish may have been, as thou hast said, simple—but he may also be quite able to lay out excellent plans for elaborate battles." He shrugged. "There is no telling, as yet."

Rod nodded slowly. "Sounds right. Any idea on the number of subordinate warlocks and witches?"

"Four, at the least—one to craft witch-moss, and direct her constructs; one to fly above, and drop rocks; two, at least, who did appear and disappear, jumping from place to place within the melee, wreaking havoc and confusion. There may be a fifth, who threw fireballs; and also a sixth, who did cast the trance spell."

"Hypnosis," Rod corrected.

"Hip-no-siss." Geoffrey nodded, with intense concentration. "As thou sayest. And, of course, there was the Tyrant-Sorcerer, this Alfar; it may have been he who cast the trance spell, which would make his lesser warlocks and witches only the five."

Rod nodded. "So. We can be sure there're Alfar, and four subordinates—but there may be more." He checked his memories of Gavin Arlinson's account, but while he was checking, Gregory confirmed, "'Tis even as Geoffrey doth say. Word for word, he hath counted them."

Geoffrey cast him a look of annoyance. "Who did ask thee, babe?"

Gregory's face darkened.

"Children!" Gwen chided. "Canst thou not allow one another each his due share of notice?"

Cordelia sat up a little straighter, and looked virtuous.

Rod leaned back on his hands, staring up at the sky. "Well! I didn't know we knew all that much! I expected you children to help out on the odd jobs—but I didn't expect *this!*" He looked down at his brood, gloating. "But—if they've got all that going for them—why did they worry about some escaping peasants? Why did they send their brand-new army to chase them down?"

"Why, 'tis simply said!" Geoffrey looked up, startled. "'Twas done so that they might not bear word to Duke Hapsburg, or Earl Tudor—or e'en Their Majesties!"

They were quiet again, all staring at him.

Geoffrey looked from face to face. "But—'tis plain! Is't not?"

"Yes, now that you've told us," Rod answered. "But what bothers me, is—*why* doesn't Alfar want anyone to know what he's doing?"

"Why, 'tis even plainer! He means to conquer the Duke, and doth not wish any other Lord to send him aid!"

His brothers and sister watched him, silent.

Rod nodded, slowly. "Yes. That's what I was afraid you were going to say."

Count Drulane and his lady rose, and all their folk rose with them. At the farthest end from their dais, the family of tinkers rose, too—though Gwen had to prod Geoffrey into putting down his trencher long enough to remember his manners.

"A good night to you all, then," the Count intoned. "May your dreams be pleasant—and may you wake in the morning."

The habitual phrase fell rather somberly on their ears, considering the tenor of the table conversation. The Count may have realized it; certainly, his departure through the door behind the dais, with his lady, was a bit brusque.

Gwen leaned over to Rod and murmured, "Is such fear born only of silence?"

Rod shrugged. "You heard what they said. The peasants are used to meeting Romanov peasants at the markets, and suddenly, they're not there. And the Count and Countess are used to the occasional social call—but there haven't been any for two weeks, and the last one before that brought rumors of the Romanov peasants being upset about evil witches."

"*I* would fear," said Magnus, "if such visits stopped so suddenly."

"Especially if you had relatives up there," Rod agreed, "which most of them seem to. I mean, who else are the knights' daughters going to meet and marry?" He clasped Magnus's shoulder. "Come on, son. Let's help them clean up."

"Geoffrey, *now!*" Gwen said firmly and the six-year-old

wolfed the last of his huge slice of bread as he stepped back from the table. Then he reached out and caught his wooden cup just as Rod and Magnus lifted the board off its trestles and turned it sideways, to dump the scraps onto the rushes.

"'Tis not very cleanly, Papa," Cordelia reminded.

"I know, dear—but when you're a guest, you do what your hosts do. And make no mistake—the Count and Countess are being very kind, to let a family of poor tinkers spend the night in their castle."

"Especially sin' that their own smith doth mend their pots," Magnus added, as he turned to carry the board over to the wall. Rod followed, and they waited their turn to drop their board onto the growing stack.

"It must be that the witches have done it," the serf in front of them was saying to his mate. "When last I saw Horth—mind thou, he that is among Sir Orlan's hostlers?—he did say an evil warlock had come among the peasants, demanding that they pay him each a penny ere Midsummer."

"And Midsummer hath come, and gone." The other peasant shook his head. "What greater mischief ha' such warlocks brewed, ere now?"

As they dropped their board, Magnus looked up at Rod. "Such words strike greater fear into my breast than doth the silence itself, Papa."

"Yes," Rod agreed, "because it threatens us, personally. That's the real danger, son—and not just to us." He clasped Magnus around the shoulder as they went back. "The peasant reaction. Your mother and I, and Queen Catharine, with Tuan's help, were beginning to build up the idea that espers could be good guys—but one power-grabber can undo all that, and send the peasants out on witch-hunts again." He broke off, grinning at the sight of Cordelia and Geoffrey, struggling toward him with one of the trestles between them. "Hold it, you two! You're just not big enough to handle one of those things, yet—with just your hands, anyway!"

Cordelia dropped her end and glared up at him, fists on her hips. "I'm a *big* lass, Papa!"

"Not yet, you're not—and you won't be, for at least five more years." Under his breath, Rod added, *God willing*. "But you're a real sweetheart, to try and help. Mama needs you, though, to help clean a spot for our blankets."

Cordelia shuddered, and Geoffrey pointed out, "It'd be more pleasant outside, Papa."

"We're after gossip, not comfort." Rod turned him around and patted him on his way. "Go help Mama; she needs someone to talk a cat into staying near us all night."

Geoffrey balked.

"Cats *fight* rats," Rod reminded.

Geoffrey's eyes gleamed, and he scurried back toward Gwen.

Rod picked up his end of the trestle. "Okay, up!"

Magnus hoisted his end, and turned toward the wall. "E'en an witches could conquer all of Gramarye, Papa, they could not hold it—against such peasant fear and hate." He shrugged. "We number too few."

"Watch the personal references." Rod glanced quickly about, but none of the peasants were close enough to have heard. "Good thing none of them wants to be seen near a tinker. . . . No, son, an evil esper, such as this Alfar, *could* hold power—but only by a very harsh, cruel, absolute rule."

Magnus scowled. "'Tis as bad as witch-hunts."

"Worse, for my purposes—because it'd stifle any chance of democracy on this planet. And I want Gramarye's telepaths to be the communications system for an interstellar democracy, some day." Rod straightened, eyes widening. "So *that's* it!"

Magnus looked up, startled. "What, Papa?"

"Where the futurians come in—you know, the villains who kidnapped us all to Tir Chlis?"

Magnus's face darkened. "I mind me of them—and of the peril they placed us in. But what sign of them is there in this coil, Papa? I see naught but an aged wizard, who hath at long last struck out in bitterness and sense of being wronged."

"That's what they want you to see. Okay, son, up onto the stack—heave!" They swung the sawhorse up onto the top of the stack, and turned away to go get the other one. "But if there's the likelihood of a repressive government showing up, there's a high probability of totalitarians from the future, being behind it."

Behind his ear, a methodical voice intoned, "Generalizing from inadequate data . . ."

"But surely that is not enough sign of their presence," Magnus protested, "only the harshness of Alfar's rule!"

"You've been talking to Fess again," Rod accused. "But keep your eyes open, and you'll see more signs of their hand behind Alfar. Myself, I've been wondering about what your mother said—that there's no trace of a mind, behind that 'instant' hypnosis spell Alfar used on these soldiers."

Magnus stared in consternation. "But . . . Papa . . . how could that . . ."

"Up with the trestle," Rod reminded, and they bent to pick it up, and started toward the wall again. "Think, son— what doesn't? Think, that is. What can do things, but doesn't think?"

Magnus was silent as they hoisted the trestle to the top of the stack. As they turned away, he guessed, "A machine?"

"You *have* been talking to Fess, haven't you?" There was a brief, nasty buzz behind his ear. "I'd call that a good guess."

"But only a guess," Magnus reminded him.

"Of course." They strolled up to Gwen where she knelt, just finishing spreading their blankets out over the rushes. "Managed to banish the vermin, dear?"

"Indeed." She glanced at him. "Cordelia and I did think to gather fresh rushes the whiles we were on our way here, so we'll sleep sweetly enow."

Something about the phrase caught Rod's attention. He stared down at the blanket, then lifted his gaze slowly to look deeply into Gwen's eyes.

She tilted her chin up and turned to her sons. "And bear thy manners in mind, for we sleep in company, here."

The children stared at her, then frowned at one another in puzzlement, then turned back to her. "Why wouldst thou think we might not?" Magnus asked. Geoffrey piped in, "We're *good* boys, Mama!"

"Aye," Gwen answered, turning to Rod, "and so must thou *all* be."

In the middle of the night a low groan began, swelling in volume and bouncing back and forth between the stone walls, until it filled the whole hall.

Rod shot bolt upright, panic clamoring up inside him

jarring his brain. Rage answered, and struggled against it.

A bluish white light filled the hall, showing all the servants shocked upright, staring in fear and horror. Cordelia screamed, burying her face in Rod's midsection, and Gregory burrowed into Gwen's skirts.

Magnus and Geoffrey glared truculently upward, even as they backed away against the wall.

Above them all, the great hall was filled with a throng of pale, glowing spectres in antique gowns and ancient armor, all blue-white, and translucent.

And facing the Gallowglass family.

The male closest to them lifted an arm with the weight of centuries, and his voice rolled out, thundering, "Thou! 'Tis thou who dost disturb our rest, thou and thy get! Name thyself, and step forth from thy craven guise!"

Gwen laid a restraining hand on Rod's arm, but the rage was building, and he shrugged her off, incensed that she should dare to remonstrate with him. He glared up at the ghost, throwing his shoulders back and issuing his words one by one. "I am Rodney Lord Gallowglass, High Warlock of Gramarye! And who are you, who dares so address me?"

"I am Arendel, first Count of Drulane!" the ghost bellowed. "'Tis in my hall thou dost stand! Wherefore hast thou come, and why hast thou disturbed my rest—mine, and all of my line's! Speak, sirrah! Now!"

The rage surged higher. "Speak with respect to thy betters, feeble ghost! Or from this place I shall banish thee, to leave thy wraith wailing in the void between worlds!"

The ghost stared a moment, with the empty darkness of its eyes. Then its face creased, and broke open, and laughter spilled out—harsh, mocking laughter, that all the ghosts echoed, ringing from one to another, clamoring and sounding like brazen gongs, until all the Great Hall rang with it, while spectral fingers pointed at Rod.

And the rage built to fill him, striving to master him; but he held himself rigid against it and, in a last attempt to avoid it, cried, "Fess! To me, now! In the great hall!"

"Why, then, mannikin, work thy will!" the ghost sneered. "Hale me down, and grind me under! Work thy wonders! Show us this power thou canst employ, against ghosts!"

Steel hooves rang on stone, and the great black horse

charged into the hall, rearing to a halt bare inches from a peasant couple, who scrambled away in panic.

Arendel turned his wrathful gaze on Fess, staring in outraged anger. "What beast is this thou dost summon! Hast thou no shred of courtesy within thee, that thou wouldst bring thine horse into a lord's hall?"

"Fess," Rod bellowed in agony, "What are they?"

"Rrr . . . Rrrodd . . . th-they awwrr . . ." Suddenly, Fess's whole body heaved in one great convulsion, neck whiplashing; then his head plummeted down ·to swing between his fetlocks. He stood spraddle-legged, each knee locked stiff.

"Seizure," Rod snapped. "They're real!"

Arendel stared in disbelief for a moment; then he threw back his head, and his laughter rocked the hall. "Elf-shot! He summons his great aid, his model of all that is powerful and perfect—and 'tis elf-shot!" And his merriment rolled forth, to batter against Rod's ears.

Then Rod's own natural fury broke loose, his indignation that anyone should mock disability, make a joke of the truest companion he had known from earliest memory—and that fury poured into the building rage to boil it over the dam of Rod's willed control. The red haze enveloped him, and the icy, insane clarity stilled his thoughts, ringing one clear idea: *Ghosts could be exorcised.* Rod bent his brows, eyes narrowing, and a thunderclap exploded through the hall, crashing outward from a short, balding man wearing spectacles and a green chasuble over a white robe. He blinked about him, stupefied. "I was . . . What . . . How . . ."

"Welcome, Father," Rod breathed, in a voice of dry ice.

The priest blinked, seeking Rod out with watery eyes. "But I was even now saying Matins, in the monastery chapel! How came I here?"

"Through my magic," Rod grated, "in response to the ill manners of this churlish dead lord! Exorcise him, Father—for his soul's barred from Heaven whiles he lingers here!"

The ghost roared with rage, and his fellows all echoed him, with screechings and roarings that made the priest wince and cry, "'Tis a foretaste of Hell!"

"Banish them," Rod cried, "ere they linger to damn themselves!"

The priest's face firmed with resolve. "'Tis even as thou sayest." And he held up one palm toward the ghosts while he fumbled in a pocket with the other, beginning a sonorous Latin prayer.

Lord Arendel shrieked, and disappeared.

With a wave of wailing despair, the other ghosts faded.

In the sudden, soft darkness, Magnus cried, "There! Against the eastern wall! Nay, stop her, seize her! Mother, a light, I prithee!"

Sudden light slashed the darkness—a warm, yellow glow from a great ball of fire that hung just below the ceiling, and Magnus and Geoffrey were diving toward a woman in a blue, hooded cloak, who hauled out a broomstick and leaped onto it, soaring up through the air to leave them in a wake of mocking laughter. Magnus shouted in anger, and banked to follow her, but she arrowed straight toward the window, which was opened wide to the summer's night. She trilled laughter, crying, "Fools! Dost not know the witches are everywhere? Thou canst not escape Alfar's power, nor hope to end it! Hail the Lord Sorcerer as thy master, ere he doth conquer thee—for Alfar shall rule!"

With a firecracker-pop, Gregory appeared, directly in front of her, thrusting a stick toward her face. It burst into flame at its tip. The witch shrieked and veered to the side, plummeting toward the open door, but Cordelia swirled in on her broomstick to cross the witch's path, hurling a bucketful of water. The fluid stretched out into a long, slender arrow, and splattered into the witch's face. She howled with rage and swirled up and around the great hall while she dashed the water from her eyes with one swipe of her hand. Magnus and Geoffrey shot after her, closing in from either side. At the last second, the witch clutched at a great whorl of an amulet that hung on her breast, cried, "Hail, Alfar," and disappeared in a clap of thunder.

The hall was silent and still.

Then a low moan began, and spread around the outside of the chamber. It rolled, building toward a wail.

Magnus hung in the center of the hall, beneath the great fireball, his eyes like steel. Slowly, his mouth stretched wide.

Gwen's voice cut like a knife blade. "Nay, Magnus! Such

words are forbidden thee, for no gentleman may use them!"

For an instant, shocked stillness fell again. Then one woman began to giggle incredulously. Another gave a little laugh, but another laughed with her, then another, and another, and the horror in the hall turned into full-throated laughter—with an hysterical edge to it, perhaps, but laughter nonetheless.

Then the Count of Drulane stood on the dais with his quaking wife behind him, gazing out about his hall silently.

One by one, his servants and thralls saw him, and fell silent.

When the whole hall was quiet, the Count turned to a waiting servant. "Light fires, that we may thank this lady for her good services, and be done with her flaming light."

The servant turned to the task, and others leaped to join him.

The Count turned to the priest and said gravely, "I must thank thee, reverend Father, for thy good offices."

The priest bowed. "My office it was, and there was small need to thank me."

"Naetheless, I do. Still, Father, I own to some concern, for these were the spirits of mine ancestors. Are their souls destroyed, then?"

"Nay, milord." The priest smiled. "I' troth, I misdoubt me an a soul can be annihilated. Yet even an 'twere, 'twould not be now; for I saw no need for exorcism. Nay, I merely did bless this hall, and pray for the souls of all who have dwelt here, that they might find rest—which they did."

"And I had feared thou wouldst attempt to blast them with power of thine own," Gwen said softly to her husband. "How is't thou didst think of the clergy?"

But the rage had ebbed, and Rod was filled with guilt and remorse. He shrugged impatiently. "Just an odd fact."

"It was, i' truth, for thou hast never been greatly pious. Where didst thou learn it?"

The question poked through Rod's miasma; he frowned. Where *had* he learned that ghosts could be banished by clergy? "Common knowledge, isn't it?" He glowered at her. "Just came to me, out of the blue."

"Nay," said little Gregory, reaching up to catch his hand. "'Tis not from the *blue* . . ."

"Who asked *you?*"

Gregory flinched away, and self-disgust drowned Rod's irritation. He reached out to catch the child around the shoulders and jam him against a hip. "Oh, I'm sorry, son! You didn't deserve that!"

The priest was still reassuring the Count. "They have fled back to their graves, milord—and, I hope, to their well-earned afterlives."

"For some, that will be a blessing," the Count said noncomittally.

Rod looked up from the shame filled ashes of his wrath. "Shall I send you home now, Father?"

The priest looked up, appalled, and the Count said quickly, "Or, an thou dost wish it, Father, we can offer thee hospitality and, when thou art rested, guardsmen and a horse, to escort thee south, to thy monastery."

"I thank thee, milord," the priest said, not managing to hide his relief.

The Count inclined his head. Then, slowly, he turned to Rod; and he spoke softly, but his words cut like fire. "'Twas ungentlemanly of thee, Lord Warlock, to come, unannounced and disguised, into mine household."

Rod met his gaze, despite the shame that permeated him. He'd lost his head in fear and panic, and aimed at the wrong enemy—and now, to top it off, the Count was right.

How dare he be!

It worked; he summoned up enough indignation to raise his chin. "Deeply do I regret the need for such deception, milord Count—but need there was."

"What?" The Count frowned. "Need to wake mine ancestors from their sleep?"

Rod answered frown for frown. "Be mindful, milord— that raising was no work of ours. 'Twas the doing of a vile wi– uh, sorceress."

"Aye." The Count seemed embarrassed. "'Tis even so, milord; I had forgot."

"But the witch would not ha' been here," Geoffrey whispered, "had we not been."

"Shut up, kid," Rod muttered.

"I prithee, judge not all us witches by her," Gwen pleaded. "There be only a few such wicked ones. And, as thou hast seen, ever will they flee the might of the Royal Coven."

The peasants didn't seem all that much reassured.

"Make no mistake," Rod advised. "The Tyrant Sorcerer, Alfar, does send his agents out to prepare his conquests—and, as you've seen, he has come this far to the South already." He turned back to Count Drulane. "That is why we have come in disguise—to learn all we can of Alfar's doings."

The Count gazed at him for several seconds, then nodded slowly. "Aye, I am captain enough to understand the need of that."

"I thank you for your understanding," Rod gave him a slight bow. "But we must not trouble your keep further this night. The witch has fled, and we have learned all that we can." *Especially now that our cover's blown.* "We will thank you for your hospitality, and take our leave."

The count returned the bow, not quite managing to hide his relief.

Rod smiled, turned, and marched toward the door.

Magnus blinked, then jumped to follow his father, shoulders squared and chin high.

The other children looked about them, startled, then hurried after Magnus, with Gwen shooing them along.

The peasants pressed back, making way for them.

Rod stopped by Fess and reached under the saddle for the reset switch. He threw it, and the robot's head came up slowly. Rod caught the reins and led the black horse away with them.

They came out into the open air, and Geoffrey heaved a sigh of relief.

"Clean!" Cordelia gasped.

Rod was silent for two paces; then he nodded. "Yes. You did want to sleep outdoors, didn't you?"

"Crickets be more musical than snores," Magnus assured him.

"And if I must needs sleep with animals, I had liefer they be large enough to see clearly." Gwen brushed at her skirts. "Faugh!"

"No argument there," Rod assured her. "Come on; we'll just go a quarter-mile or so past the gate, and bed down for the rest of the night."

They passed through the gatehouse, across the draw-bridge, and out into the night.

After a few paces, Rod let a sigh explode out. "Now! Next time you disagree with me, Gregory, *please* wait until we're alone! Because you never know, I might be right."

"Yes, Papa," the little boy said, in a little voice.

Rod frowned. "I don't mean to be hard, son—but there's a very good chance that, if that witch hadn't been there to harry us, there might've been another one of Alfar's crew, to try to spy out the territory *and* spread rumors that'd worry the folk. I mean, all that worried dinner-table talk was *probably* genuine—but it is strangely convenient for Alfar, isn't it?"

Gregory was silent.

To cover his guilt feelings, Rod turned to Fess, muttering, "Recovered, Circuit Rider?"

"Nearly," answered the robot's voice. "I had never encountered convincing evidence of the existence of a medium, before this night."

"Well, maybe you still haven't," Rod mused.

"Who hath not what?" Magnus looked up with a frown. "Oh! Thou didst speak with Fess." He nodded, satisfied; the children had long ago learned that they could not hear Fess's thoughts, unless he wanted them to.

"Mayhap he still hath not what?" Cordelia asked.

"Seen a medium," Rod explained, "a person who can talk to ghosts, or make them appear."

"Oh." Cordelia nodded. "Thou speakest aright, Papa. He hath not."

"Oh, really? Those ghosts looked genuine, to me."

"They were not," Magnus assured him. "They had no greater thought than a mirror."

Rod frowned. "Odd simile."

"Yet 'tis apt," Gwen affirmed. "They had no true thoughts of their own; they mimicked what was there laid down for them."

"Laid down?" Rod still frowned. "By whom?"

"By the witch," Magnus explained. "She did call up the memories laid in the stones, and throw them out to us."

Rod stared. After a few seconds, he said, "What?"

"Some witches there be, milord," Gwen explained, "who

can lay a hand on a ring, and gain the full sense of the person who wore it, even to the pattern of his or her thoughts."

Rod gazed off into space. "Yeah . . . I think I've heard of that. They call it 'psychometery,' don't they?"

Gwen shrugged. "I know not, my lord; such are the words of thy folk, not ours."

" 'Tis all one," Cordelia added.

"Thanks for the lesson," Rod said sourly. "But how did you know about this, Magnus?"

The boy reddened. "I did not wish to trouble thee, Papa . . ."

"Oh, really?" Rod looked the question at Gwen; she shook her head. "Didn't want to worry Mama either, I gather. Which is fine, until we find out about it. From now on, we'll *always* be worried—that you've discovered a new way to use your power, and are trying dangerous experiments without letting us know."

Magnus looked up, startled. "I had not meant . . ."

"I know. So don't. Worry me, son—that's what I'm here for." For a second, he wondered if that was truer than he knew.

Magnus sighed. "Well enough, then. I have found thoughts in things people have used, Papa."

Rod nodded. "Let Mama be near next time you experiment with it, okay? So much for the 'calling up' part. I take it the 'throwing out' is talking about projective telepathy?"

"By that," Gwen explained to the children, "he doth mean a witch or warlock who can send their thoughts out to folk who have not witch power."

"Oh!" Cordelia nodded. "Such she was, Papa. What she saw in her mind, she could make others see, also."

Rod nodded. "So we weren't seeing real ghosts—just reflections of the memories 'recorded' in the rocks of that hall . . . uh, Gwen?"

"Aye, my lord?"

"Remember those ghosts we met, way back when, in Castle Loguire?"

"Aye, my lord. Mayhap they were, at first, raised in just such a manner."

"Why the 'at first'?"

"Why, for that they endured after the witch who raised them—long after, by accounts."

"Oh, yeah." Rod nodded. "That's right—that castle was supposed to have been haunted for a century or two, wasn't it?" He glared at the sudden gleam in Magnus's eye. "Don't go trying any surprise visits. Those ghosts weren't harmless."

"Save for thy father." Gwen couldn't resist it.

Rod gave her a glower. "That was diplomacy, not necromancy. And, come to think of it, this witch of Alfar's wasn't too bad at persuasion, herself."

"Aye," Gwen agreed. "Her words, when we had unmasked her, were meant more for Count Drulane and his folk, than they were for us."

"Trying to boil up all the old fears of witches, to boost their Reign of Terror," Rod growled. "Never mind what the peasants might do to the witches in the rest of the kingdom."

"Nay, *do* mind it!" Gregory cried. "For if they take fright, and are hurted enough to become bitter and hateful, might they not flee to Alfar, and swell his strength?"

Rod thought about it, then slowly nodded. "I hate to admit it, son, but you're right." He turned a somber gaze on Gwen, then dropped his gaze to look at his children, one at a time.

"What thoughts dost thou engender, husband?" Gwen asked softly.

Rod lifted his gaze to her again. "This mission has definitely turned dangerous, darling. Time for you and the children to go home."

The night was silent for a moment. Then: "'Tis not fair!" Cordelia cried.

"Only now doth it gain interest!" Gregory protested.

"Nonetheless . . ." Rod began.

"'Tis the tactics of magic!" Geoffrey cried. "Assuredly, Papa, thou'lt not deny me the chance to witness such!"

"You're apt to get hurt!" Rod snapped. "And preventing that, is my main job in life!"

"Then wither wouldst thou be, without us?" Magnus demanded, catching at his sleeve.

"Lonely," Rod snapped, "but effective. A lot *more* effective than if I'm worrying about you while I'm in the middle of a fight!"

"Yet thou hast no need to fear for us!" Cordelia cried.

"Send an *army* 'gainst us, ere thou dost fear!" Geoffrey howled.

"Yeah." Rod's jaw tightened. "You'd just love to have an army to box with, wouldn't you? Unfortunately, it just might have a stronger arm than you, and..."

"Husband." Gwen's low voice bored through his building anger. "Thou didst say, even now, that thou didst protect them."

Rod's head snapped up, indignation flaring. "Are you implying...?"

But Gwen was already talking to the children, rapidly. "Thy father has said there is danger in this; and if thou dost believe thyselves strong, only think—how wouldst thou fare if thou didst confront a grown warlock, at the height of his powers, an thou wert alone? If thou hadst been split away from thy brothers and sister—how then?"

Geoffrey started to answer.

Gwen pressed a hand over his mouth. "Nay, do think carefully ere thou dost speak! There is a thrill of pleasure in it, aye—but only till thou dost truly fear! Then all of thy joy in it doth die a-borning." Her gaze came up to meet Rod's. "'Tis even as thy father doth know, for he hath been in peril. Nay, if he saith 'tis dangerous, then assuredly the danger could strike deepest fear in thee, could kill thee."

The children stared up at her gravely, thinking they understood.

"Yet, husband, be mindful." Gwen looked straight into Rod's eyes. "The foes Alfar hath sent against us thus far, have scarce begun to tax our powers. Were Alfar to send all his force against us, 'twould be great danger, aye; but I misdoubt me an he would risk more than a moiety of his force, when he knoweth not the true depth or breadth of our power. Were he to send an army, in truth, we ought then to flee; yet if he sends only witches, the High Warlock and his family have little to fear."

"Only enough to make it fun, eh?" Rod managed a harsh smile.

"I could not deny it," Gwen admitted. "'Tis but exercise, for a brood such as ours."

"Yes..." Rod frowned. "He's testing us, isn't he?"

Geoffrey spun around, wide-eyed. "Papa! Wherefore did I not see that?"

"Experience," Rod assured him. "But that means the attacks will become stronger, until he thinks he knows our limits. *Then* he'll hit us with twice the force he thinks he needs, just to make sure."

Geoffrey had a faraway look in his eyes. "Therefore . . . it doth behoove us to use as little power as we must, to defeat them."

Rod nodded. "Which we haven't exactly been doing, so far."

"We may stay then?" Cordelia cried, jumping up and down.

Rod fixed them all with a glare.

They pulled themselves into line, hands clasped in front of them, heads bowed a little—but looking up at him.

"Do I have your *absolute* promise that you'll all go right home, without *any* argument, the next time I say to?"

"Oh, yes, Papa, yes!" they cried. "We will flee, we will fly!" Cordelia avowed.

"We wouldn't *want* to stay, if this sorcerer really were dangerous, Papa," Magnus assured him.

"But you don't believe he could be, eh?" Rod fixed his eldest with a glare.

"Well . . ."

"That's all right." Rod held up a palm. "I've got your promises. It's okay—you're still on board, at least until the next attack. And if it's too close to being dangerous, home you go!"

"Home," they averred.

"Still don't believe me, eh?" Rod looked up at Gwen. "How about you? Promise?"

"I shall heed thee as strongly as ever I have done, my lord," she said firmly.

"That's what I was afraid of," Rod sighed. "Well, I suppose I'll have to be content with that. C'mon kids, let's set up camp."

Gwen threw her head back with a happy sigh. "Ah, 'tis good to be aloft again."

"I'm glad for you." Rod gripped the broomstick tighter and swallowed heavily. His idea of flying was inside a nice, warm spaceship, with a lounge chair and an autobar. "This shooting around on a broomstick is strictly for the birds. On second thought, strike that—even the birds wouldn't touch it."

"Oh, certes, they would, Papa." Cordelia shot up alongside, matching velocities. A robin sat on the tip of her broomstick, chirping cheerily.

Rod gave the bird a jaundiced glance. "Odd friends you're making, up here."

Gregory shot past them, flipping over onto his back to look back and wave bye-bye.

"Show-off," Rod growled, but his heart sang at the sight of a smile on the face of his sober little son. It was good to see him be a child again.

"Regard thy way," Gwen called after him. Gregory nodded cheerfully and flipped over onto his tummy again.

Magnus swung up alongside. "I thank thee, Papa! We are free again!"

"Delighted." Rod tried to mean it. "Might as well, since Alfar knows who we really are, anyway."

"Yonder." Magnus pointed ahead. Rod looked up, and saw a line of hills, blued by distance. Magnus informed him, " 'Tis the Titans' Rampart."

"The Romanov boundary." Rod felt his stomach suddenly grow hollow. "Somehow, I find myself less than eager to cross it."

"But 'twill be exciting, Papa!" Geoffrey cried, flying up on his port side.

"That's a kind of excitement I think I can live without. Besides, I'm hungry. Darling, what do you say we find a town large enough to have an inn, this side of the boundary?"

"I misdoubt me an they'd welcome folk so poorly dressed as we, my lord."

"Yeah, but they'd let us sit in the innyard, if we buy our food with real silver."

"Hot sausage!" Geoffrey cried.

"Stew!" Magnus caroled.

"Toasted cheese!" Cordelia exulted.

"Hungry children," Gwen sighed. "Well, husband, an thou dost wish it."

"Great. Land us in a nice little copse, about half a mile out, will you? Tinkers they might accept in the innyard, but not if they use it for a landing strip." He stared ahead hungrily. "Terra firma!"

5

As they came into the town, Cordelia gave a happy little sigh. "'Tis *so* nice that the nasty old sorcerer knows we come toward him!"

"Oh, indeed yes," Rod muttered. "This way, he can have a wonderful reception all ready for us! Why do *you* like it, dear? Because you can fly?"

"Oh, aye!"

"I dislike disguise, Papa," Geoffrey explained.

Rod gave his son a measuring stare. "Yes, I suppose you would—even when you see it's necessary."

"As 'tis, I know," the little boy sighed. "Yet doth it trouble me, Papa."

"I understand." Rod frowned. "What bothers *me*, is trying to figure out how Alfar saw through our disguises."

The family walked on in brooding silence—for a few seconds. Then Gwen said, "'Tis widely known that the High Warlock doth have a wife, and four bairns—and that one is a lass, and the other three lads."

Rod scowled. "What are you suggesting—that they had their illusionist attack every family who came North?" His gaze wandered. "Of course, I suppose there aren't that many families *coming* North . . . and the kids' ages are pretty much a matter of public record . . ."

"It doth seem unlikely," Gwen admitted.

"And therefore must be seriously considered. But we would have heard about it, wouldn't we? Monsters, attacking families . . ."

"Not if the witch and her monsters won out," Geoffrey pointed out.

"But no sooner would they have attacked, than the witch would have seen the families had no magical powers!" Cordelia protested. "Surely she would then have called off her monsters."

Geoffrey's eyes turned to steel. "She would not—if she wished to be certain no word reached the King."

"That does seem to be their strategy," Rod agreed.

"But—to kill *bairns?*" Cordelia gasped.

"They are not nice people," Rod grated.

The children were silent for a few minutes, digesting an unpleasant realization. Finally, Gregory pointed out, "We do not *know* that, Papa."

"No, but I wouldn't put it past them. Still, it does seem a little extravagant."

"Mayhap they did post sentries," Geoffrey suggested.

Rod nodded. "Yes, well, that's the most likely way— but what kind of sentries? I mean, we haven't seen any soldiers standing around in Alfar's livery. So his sentries must be disguised, if he has them. And I suppose they'd have to know what we looked like. . . ."

"Eh, no!" Magnus cried, grabbing Rod's wrist. "They need only be . . ."

"Telepaths!" Rod knocked his forehead with the heel of his hand. "Of course! Just station mind readers on each of the main roads—and maybe even out in the pastures, if you're the suspicious type—and they'd be almost impossible to spot! They could be anybody—the farmer who passes in his cart, the varlet in the kitchens, the merchant and his draymen . . ."

The children looked around them, suddenly alert.

". . . and they'd be almost impossible to spot," Rod finished, "since all they have to do is sit there, with their minds wide open for every stray thought!"

"We *could* have masked our minds," Geoffrey mused.

"Yes, but we didn't." Rod shook his head. "Besides, it's not as easy as it sounds. You're all beginning to get pretty good at it..." He caught Gwen's glance. "... every time you're doing something you don't want Mama and me to know about."

The children exchanged quick, guilty glances.

"Of course, Mama and I are getting even better at probing *behind* the masks," Rod went on, "so I suppose it's very good training for all of us. In fact... that might not be a bad idea." He flashed a grin at each of them. "Start poking around inside minds here and there, kids."

Instantly, all four faces turned blank, their eyes losing focus.

"No, no! Not *now!* I mean, if they *have* been listening to us, they'll have heard us, and just wiped their minds and started thinking disguise thoughts! You've got to catch them when they're *not* ready, take them by surprise. Listen and probe for them whenever you just happen to think of it, at odd moments."

"But will they not always be masked to us, Papa?" Cordelia protested.

"Not when they're trying to listen to your thoughts," Rod explained. "They can't do both at the same time—mask *and* listen. You've tried it yourselves—*you* know."

This time, the glance the kids exchanged was startled—and worried. Just how much *did* Daddy know, that they didn't know he knew?

"Try to catch them unaware," Rod urged.

The children sighed philosophically.

"I know, I know," Rod growled, "this unpredictable Daddy! First he tells you *to* do it, then he tells you not to! So balance it—sometimes you do it, and sometimes you don't." He looked up. "Gee, that's a nice looking horse, up there. I think I'll steal it."

The children gasped with shock, and looked—and gave their father a look of disgust. "Thou canst not steal him, Papa," Gregory said sternly. "He is already thine."

"Makes it more convenient that way, doesn't it?" Under his breath, Rod muttered, "Nice of you to come ahead to meet us, Old Iron. How about I ride you, on the next leg of the trip?"

"Motion sickness, Rod?"

But it was Gwen and Cordelia who rode, at least as far as the inn, and the innkeeper was very obliging—once Rod caught his attention.

It wasn't easy. Rod left the family at the door and stepped inside, bracing himself for an unpleasant scene. He saw a tall, wiry man with a stained apron tied around his waist, setting a double handful of mugs on a table and collecting coppers from the diners. As he turned away from the table, his gaze fell on Rod. "Be off with you," he ordered, but he didn't even stop turning. "We've no alms to give." By the time he finished the sentence, he was facing the kitchen again, and had started walking.

"I've got money!" Rod called.

The man kept on walking.

Rod dodged around him and leaped into his path, shoving his purse under the innkeeper's nose and yanking it open. The man stopped, frowning. Slowly, his eyes focused on the purse.

Rod shook a few coins out onto his palm. "See? Silver. The real thing."

The innkeeper scowled at the coins as though they were vermin. Then his expression lightened to musing, and he pinched up one of the coins, held it in front of his nose to stare at it as though it were some new variety of bug, then methodically set it between his teeth and bit.

Rod couldn't resist. "Hors d'oeuvres?"

"'Tis silver." The innkeeper seemed puzzled.

"Genuine," Rod agreed.

The man focused on Rod. "What of it?"

Rod just stared at him for a second. "We'd like something to eat."

"We?" The innkeeper turned his head from side to side, inspecting the walls and corners.

"My wife and children," Rod explained. "I didn't think you'd want us inside."

The innkeeper thought that one over for a while, then nodded, frowning. Rod wondered how the man ever managed to make a profit. Finally, the innkeeper spoke. "Wise." He kept nodding. "Wise." Then he focused on Rod again. "And what food dost thou wish?"

"Oh, we're not choosy. A big bowl of stew, a plateful of sausage, a couple of loaves of bread, a pitcher of milk, and a pitcher of ale should do us. Oh, and of course, six empty bowls. And six spoons."

The innkeeper nodded judiciously. "Stew, sausage, bread, milk, and ale." He turned away, still nodding. "Stew, sausage, bread, milk, and ale." He headed for the kitchens, repeating the formula again and again.

Rod watched him go, shaking his head. Then he turned away to find Gwen and the kids.

He found them sitting under an old, wide oak tree with a huge spread of leaves. "Will they have us, husband?" Gwen didn't really sound as though she cared.

"Oh, yeah." Rod folded a leg under him and sat down beside her, leaning back against the trunk. "He was very obliging, once he tasted our silver and found out it wasn't pewter."

"What troubles thee, then?"

"Frankly, my dear, he didn't really give a d—" Rod glanced at the eager faces around him, and finished, ". . . darn."

"Assuredly, Tudor doth lack in gallantry," said a large man, walking into the inn with a companion.

"Aye; it doth pain me to say it, but our noble Earl hath ever been clutch-fisted," answered his companion. "This sorcerer Alfar, now—all one doth hear of him, doth confirm his generosity."

They passed on into the inn. Rod sat frozen, staring into space.

Magnus put it into words for him. "Do they speak against their own *lord?*"

"They do," Gwen whispered, eyes huge.

"And in *public!*" Rod was flabbergasted. "I mean, peasants have spoken against their rulers before—but never out in the open, where a spy might overhear them. For all they know, we could be. . ." He ran out of words.

"Yet the lord would have to be *greatly* wicked, for his own folk to complain of him!" Cordelia cried. "Could they break faith with him so easily?"

"Not ordinarily," Rod said grimly. "But we didn't come up here because things were normal."

A maid came ambling up to them, bearing a tray of food.

Her face was smudged, and her apron was greasy—from the scullery, Rod guessed. He braced himself for the contempt he'd grown used to from the peasants, and reminded himself that everybody had to have somebody they could look down on. Maybe that was what they *really* needed tinkers for.

But the maid only held the tray down where they could reach it, shaking her head and marvelling, "Tinkers! Why doth the master spare good food for tinkers?"

Rod took a plate warily, and sniffed at it. A delighted grin spread over his face. "Hey! It *is* good!"

"May I?" Magnus sat still, with his hands in his lap. So did the other children, but their eyes fairly devoured the tray.

"Why . . . certes." The scullery maid seemed surprised by their politeness.

Magnus seized a bowl. "May I?" Cordelia cried, and the younger two chorused, "May I?" after her.

"Certes," the wench said, blinking, and three little hands snatched at bowls.

Rod handed the plate to Gwen and lifted down a huge bowl of stew, then the pitchers. "Take your cups, children." Gwen scooped up the remaining two flagons, and the spoons.

The kitchen wench straightened, letting one edge of the tray fall. A furrow wrinkled between her eyebrows. "Strange tinkers ye be."

She was trying to think, Rod realized—and she'd have been trying very hard, if some mental lethargy hadn't prevented her. "Still wondering why your master is serving us more than kitchen scraps?"

Enlightenment crept over her face. "Aye. That is what I be thinking."

"Best of reasons," Rod assured her. "We paid in silver."

She lifted her head slowly, mouth opening into a round. "Oh. Aye, I see." And she turned away, still nodding, as she began to amble back to the kitchen.

"Why doth she not ask how mere tinkers came by silver money, Papa?" Magnus watched her go.

"I expect she'll think that one up just as she gets to the kitchen. . . ."

"Why is she so slow, Papa?" Cordelia seemed concerned.

Rod shook his head. "Not just her, honey. That's what the innkeeper was like, too." He gazed after the scullery maid, frowning.

Two men in brocaded surcoats with grayed temples strolled past them toward the inn door. "Nay, but our Earl doth seek to rule all our trade," the one protested. "Mark my words, ere long he will tell to us which goods we may not sell, for that he doth grant patents on them to those merchants who toady to him."

"Aye, and will belike tax the half of our profit," the other agreed, but he spoke without heat, almost without caring.

They passed on into the inn, leaving Rod rigid in their wake. "*That* is the most blatant lie I've heard since I came here! Earl Tudor is so *laissez-faire*-minded, you'd almost think he just doesn't care!"

"Folk will believe any rumor," Gwen offered.

"Yeah, but businessmen check them out—and those two were merchants. If they stray too far from the facts, they go bankrupt."

A string of donkeys plodded into the innyard, heads hanging low, weary from their heavy packs. Their drovers bawled the last few orders at them, as the inn's hostlers strolled past the Gallowglass family toward the donkeys, chatting. "They say the sorcerer Alfar is a fair-minded man."

"Aye, and generous withal. Those who come under his sway, I hear, need never be anxious for food or drink."

The first shook his head, sadly. "Our Earl Tudor doth care little for the poor folk."

"Are they *crazy?*" Rod hissed. "Tudor is practically a welfare state!"

"'Tis e'en as thou dost say," the second mused. "Yet at the least, our Earl doth not tax his peasants into rags and naught for fare but bread and water, as Duke Romanov doth."

"Oh, come *on,* now!" Rod fumed. "Nobody ever claimed Romanov was a walking charity—but at least he realizes the peasants can't produce if they're starving."

But Gregory had a faraway look in his eyes. "Papa—I mislike the feel of their minds."

Gwen stopped ladling stew and gazed off into space. She nodded, slowly. "There is summat there..." Then her eyes widened. "Husband—it doth press on me, within mine head!"

Instantly, the children all gazed off into space.

"Hey!" Rod barked in alarm. He clapped his hands and snapped, "Wake up! If there is something messing with people's minds here, it could be dangerous!"

They all started, blinking, then focused on their father. "'Tis as Mama doth say, Papa," Magnus reported. "Something doth press upon the minds of all the people here—and at ours, too. Only, with us, it cannot enter."

"Then it knows all it really needs to know about us, doesn't it?" Rod growled. He frowned, and shrugged. "On the other hand, it already did. Here, I've got to have a feel of this."

It wasn't as easy for him as it was for Gwen and the kids. They'd grown up with extrasensory power; they could read minds as easily as they listened for birdsongs. But Rod's dormant powers had just been unlocked three years ago. He had to close his eyes, concentrating on the image of a blank, gray wall, letting his thoughts die down, and cease. Then, when other people's thoughts had begun to come into his mind, he could open his eyes again, and see while he mind read.

But he didn't have to look about him this time. He could feel it, before he even heard another person's thoughts. When he did, he realized that the thoughts resonated perfectly with the pressure-current. It was a flowing wave, rocking, soothing, lulling; but modulated on that lethargic mental massage was a feeling of vague unease and suspicion—and riding within that modulation, as a sort of harmonic, was the central conviction that the sorcerer Alfar could make all things right.

Rod opened his eyes, to find his whole family staring at him—and for the first time on this trip, fear shadowed the children's faces.

Rage hit, hot and strong. Rod's whole nervous system flamed with it, and his hands twitched, aching for the throat of whatever it was that had threatened his children.

"Nay, husband." Gwen reached out and caught his hand. "We need thy wisdom now, not thy mayhem."

He resented her touch; it pushed his anger higher. But

he heeded her words, and concentrated on the feel of that
beloved hand, whose caresses had brought him so much of
comfort and delight. He let it anchor him, remembering
how his rage had made him do foolhardy things, how his
wrath had played into the hands of the enemy. He took slow,
deep breaths, trying to remember that he was really more
dangerous when he was calm, trying to regain the harmony
of his emotions. He concentrated on his shoulders, relaxing
them deliberately, then his back, then his upper arms, then
his forearms, then his hands. Anger wouldn't help anybody
now; anger would only destroy—everything but the enemy.
He shivered as he felt the rage loosen, and drain away; then
he swallowed, and closed his eyes, nodding. "I'm . . . all
right, now. Thanks, darling. Just . . . be careful about grabbing me when I'm like that, okay?"

"I will, my lord." She released him, but held his gaze
with her own.

"Okay." He took a deep breath, and looked up at the
children. "You know what hypnosis is."

"Aye, Papa." They stared at him, round-eyed.

"Well, that's what we're facing." Rod's lips drew back
into a thin, tight line. "Somebody's sending out a mental
broadcast that's putting everybody's conscious minds asleep.
This whole town is in the early stages of mass hypnosis."

The children stared, appalled.

Rod nodded. "Someone, or something, up there, is a
heck of a lot more powerful a projective telepath, than we've
ever dreamed of."

"But it hath not the feel of a person's mind, my lord!"
Gwen protested. "Oh, aye, the thoughts themselves do—
but that lulling, that pressure that doth soothe into mind-
lessness—'tis only power, without a mind to engender it!"

Rod had a brief, lurid memory of the genetically altered
chimpanzee he'd had to fight some years ago. Actually, it
was its power he'd had to fight; the poor beast had no mind
of its own. The futurians, who were continually trying to
conquer Gramarye, had just used it as a converter, trans-
forming minute currents of electricity into psionic power-
blasts that could stun a whole army. When they'd finally
found the chimp, it had been one of the ugliest, most obscene
things he'd ever seen—and one of the most pitiable. Rod

shuddered, and looked into his wife's eyes. "I don't know what it is—but I don't like the climate. Come on—eat up, and let's go."

They turned back to their food, with relief. But after a bit, Cordelia looked up. "Not hungry, Papa."

"I know the feeling," Rod growled, "but you will be. Choke down at least one bowlful, will you?" He turned to Gwen. "Let's take the bread and sausage along."

She nodded, and began to wrap the food in his handkerchief.

Rod turned back to his children—and frowned. There was something wrong, some flaw in their disguise...

Then he found it. "Don't forget to bicker a little, children. It's not normal, to go through a whole lunch without being naughty."

They passed the last house at the edge of the village. Rod muttered, "Not yet, kids. Another hundred yards; then we're safe."

For a moment, Geoffrey looked as though he were going to protest. Then he squared his shoulders like his siblings, gritted his teeth, and plowed on for another three hundred feet. Then Rod stopped. "Okay. *Now!*"

With one voice, the whole family expelled a huge sigh of relief. Cordelia began to tremble. "Papa—'tis horrid!"

Gwen reached to catch her up, but Rod beat her to it. He swept the little girl into his arms, stopping her shuddering with a bear hug. "I know, I know, baby. But be brave—there'll be worse than this, before we're done with Alfar." *Or he's done with us;* the thought fleeted through his mind, but he helped it fleet on out; a father whose children could read minds couldn't afford defeatist thinking. *Talk about thought control....* Rod cast an appealing glance over Cordelia's shoulder, at Gwen. "Don't you think it's time for you folks to go home now?"

Gwen's chin firmed and lifted. Below her, three smaller chins repeated the movement. "Nay, my lord," she said firmly. "'Tis eerie, and doth make one's flesh to creep—yet for us, there is, as yet, no greater danger than we saw last night, and thou mayest yet have need of our magics."

"I can't deny that last part," Rod sighed, "and I suppose

you're right—that village may have been nasty, but it wasn't any more dangerous than it was last night. Okay—we go on as a family."

The boys broke into broad smiles, and Cordelia sat up in Rod's arms and clapped her hands together. Rod set her down, set his fists on his hips, and surveyed his children with a stern eye. "You do realize what's going on back there, don't you?"

They all nodded, and Magnus said, "Aye, Papa." Geoffrey explained, "Alfar doth prepare the town for conquest."

Rod nodded, his gaze on his second son. "How will he take them?"

The boy shrugged. "In peace. He will march in, and they will acclaim him as their friend and master, and bow to him—and all of this without a ever a drop of blood shed."

There was a definite note of admiration in his voice. Rod shook his head. "Good analysis—but be careful, son. Don't start thinking that ability implies goodness."

"Oh, nay, Papa! Ne'er could I think so! He is a worthy enemy—but that's just to say, he would not be worthy an he were not able; but he would not be an enemy were he not evil."

Rod took a deep breath and stilled, with his mouth open, before he said, "We-e-e-ll . . . there *are* enemies who might not be really *evil*—they'd just be trying to get the same thing you're trying to get."

But Geoffrey shook his head firmly. "Nay, Papa. Such be rivals, not enemies."

Rod stilled with his mouth open again. Then he shrugged. "Okay—as long as you make the distinction." He took a deep breath, looking around at his family. "So. I think we've got a better idea, now, about how Alfar works. First he takes over most of the population with long-range hypnosis. Then he sends his minions in to intimidate anybody who didn't hypnotize easily."

"There be such, Papa?" Cordelia asked in surprise.

Rod nodded. "Oh, yes, dear. That particular kind of magic isn't exactly foolproof; there'll always be a few people who aren't terribly open to letting somebody else take over their minds—I hope."

"And there be those who will not bow to him from fear, either," Geoffrey said stoutly.

"Oh, yes. And if any of those happen to be knights, or lords, and march against him with their men-at-arms—by the time they get to Alfar, he'll have most of the soldiers convinced they don't *want* to win."

"Aye. 'Tis the way of it." Geoffrey looked up at his father with a glow of pride.

"Thanks, son." Rod smiled, amused. "Just adding things up." Then his smile faded. "But *what* the *heck* kind of projective telepath does he *have,* that can reach out over a hundred miles to hypnotize a whole *village?*"

They set up camp, with trenches for beds and pine boughs for mattresses. The kids rolled up in their blankets, and were instantly asleep—at least, as far as Rod could see.

He didn't trust them. "What child is this who, laid to rest, sleeps?" he asked Gwen.

She gazed off into space for a moment, listening with her mind. He decided to try it, himself, so he closed his eyes and blanked his mind, envying the ease with which she did it. After a few seconds, he began to hear the children's low, excited, mental conversation. He rolled his eyes up in exasperation and started to get up—but Gwen caught his arm. "Nay, my lord. Let them speak with one another, I prithee; 'twill lull them to sleep."

"Well . . ." Rod glanced back at her.

"Yet what will lull us?" she murmured.

He stared down at her, drinking in her beauty. Her femininity hit him with physical force, and he dropped back down beside her, one arm spread out in return invitation. "I'm sure I'll think of something, dear—but it takes some creativity, when the kids are watching."

She turned her head to the side, watching him out of the corners of her eyes. "Their lids are closed."

"But not their minds." Rod pressed a finger over her lips. "Hush up, temptress, or I'll put you back in your teapot."

"And what wilt thou do with me, once thou hast me there?" she purred, nestling up against him.

The contact sent a current coursing through him. His

breath hissed in. "I said a teapot, not a pumpkin shell!"
He reached out to caress her gently, and it was her turn
to gasp. He breathed into her ear, "Just wait till they fall
asleep. . . ."

"Beshrew me! But they have only now waked from several hours' rest!" Gwen gazed up at him forlornly.

"Hmm!" Rod frowned. "Hadn't thought of that . . ."

"Aye di me!" Gwen sighed, snuggling a little closer.
"E'en so, the comfort of thy presence will aid me greatly,
my lord."

"Fine—now that you've made sure *I* won't sleep!"

"Yet must not a husbandman be ever vigilant?" she murmured.

"Yeah—waiting for my chance!" He rested his cheek
against her head. "Now I know why they call you a witch. . . ."

"Papa-a-a-a!"

Rod waked instantly; there'd been tears in that little voice.
He opened his eyes and saw Gregory leaning over him
clutching his arm, shaking him. "Papa, Papa!" Tears were
running down the little boy's cheeks. Rod reached up an
arm to snake around him and pull him down, cradling him
against his side. The little body stayed stiff, resisting comfort. Rod crooned, "What's the matter, little fella? Bad
dream?"

Gregory gulped, and nodded.

"What was it about?"

"Nasty man," Gregory sniffled.

"Nasty?" For some reason, Rod was suddenly on his
guard. "What was he doing?"

"He did creep upon us." Gregory looked up at his father,
eyes wide. "Creeping up, to hurl things at us."

Rod stared into his eyes for a second, then began to pat
his back gently. "Don't worry about it. Even if the nasty
man did sneak up on us, your brothers and sister would
gang up on him before he could do much damage." He
smiled, and saw a tentative, quivering lift at the corners of
Gregory's mouth. He tousled the boy's hair and turned to
look at his wife. He saw a large pair of eyes staring back
at him. "Kind of thought you'd wake up, if one of the kids
had a problem."

"I did hear him," Gwen said softly. "I did see his dream. And, my lord..."

Rod couldn't help feeling that being on his guard was just the thing for the occasion. "What's wrong?"

"Gregory's mind would not conjure up so mild a phantasm, nor one so threatening."

The tension was building inside Rod. Anger began to boil up under it. Rod tried to hold it down, reminding himself that he and Gwen could probably handle any attempt to hurt them. But the mere thought that anyone would dare to attack his children, to plant nightmares in their sleeping minds...!

Magnus, Cordelia, and Geoffrey suddenly sat bolt-upright. "Papa," Cordelia gasped. "what dost thou?"

"Is it that bad already? I'm trying to *hold* my temper."

"Thou dost amazingly." Magnus blinked the sleep out of his eyes and leaned closer, on hands and knees, to peer at his father. "In truth, thou dost amazingly. I would never guess thy rage, to look at thee. Papa, what..."

The night seemed to thicken a few feet away from the children. Something hazy appeared, coalesced, hardened, and shot to earth, slamming into the ground a few feet from Magnus's hand. His head snapped around; he stared at a six-inch rock. Cordelia's gaze was rivetted to it, too, in horror; but Geoffrey leaped to his feet. "Ambush!"

The night thickened again, just over Magnus's head. Something hazy appeared...

...and began to coalesce...

"Heads up!" Rod dove for his son. His shoulder knocked Magnus sprawling, and a foot-thick rock crashed down, grazing Rod's hip. He bellowed with pain—and anger at the monster who dared attack his children. His full rage cut loose.

"Ware!" Magnus cried. The children were already looking up, as their father had bade them, so they saw the rocks materializing—two, three, all plummeting to earth as they became real.

"Dodge ball!" Magnus shouted. Instantly, he and his brothers and sister were bounding and bobbing back and forth, Cordelia weaving an aerial dance that would've given a computer tracker a blown fuse, the boys appearing and disappearing here, there, yonder, like signal lights in a storm. Through their flickering pavane, Magnus called in suppressed rage, "Art thou hurted, Papa?"

"Nothing that a little murder won't cure," Rod yelled back. "Children—seek! Discover and destroy!"

The children seemed to focus more sharply, and stayed visible for longer intervals.

Gwen was on her feet, still, her eyes warily probing the night above them.

Then Geoffrey hopped to his left, just as a small boulder materialized right where his chest had been.

Rod stood rigid with horror. If the boy hadn't happened to jump aside, just at that instant . . . "Somebody's trying to teleport rocks into the kids' bodies!"

"'Twould be instant death." Gwen's face was pale, but taut with promised mayhem.

Rod stood tree-still, his eyes wide open; but the night blurred around him into a formless void as his mind opened, seeking. . . .

Cordelia seized her broomstick and shot up into the sky. For a moment, all three boys disappeared. Then Magnus reappeared, far across the meadow, dimly seen in the moonlight. He disappeared again just as Geoffrey reappeared ten feet away, twenty feet in the air. Air shot outward with a pistol-crack, inward with firecracker-pop. The meadow resounded with reports, like miniature machine gun fire. Geoffrey disappeared with a dull boom, and a treetop nearby swayed with a bullwhip-crack as Gregory appeared in the topmost limbs.

And stones kept falling, all over the meadow.

"Husband!" Gwen's voice was taut. "This enemy will mark us, too, ere long."

That jolted Rod. "I suppose so—if he doesn't just pick on little kids. Better split up."

Gwen seized her broomstick and disappeared into the dark sky.

That left Rod feeling like a sitting duck. He supposed he would be able to float up into the sky himself, if he just thought about it—but he'd never done it, and didn't want to have to pay attention to trying to keep himself up while he was trying to find and annihilate an enemy. Capture, he reminded himself—capture, if you can.

But he hoped he'd find he couldn't.

Magnus appeared ten feet away, shaking his head. "He doth cloak his thoughts well, Papa. I cannot . . ." Suddenly, his eyes lost focus. Geoffrey's laugh carolled over the meadow, clear and filled with glee. Magnus disappeared with a pistol-crack. Rod leaped for Fess's back and shot across the meadow, a living missile with a double warhead.

He was just in time to see Geoffrey and Magnus shoot up out of the trees, carrying a young man stretched like a tug-of-war rope between them. He struggled and cursed, kicking and whiplashing about with his legs and torso, but the boys stretched his arms tight, laughing with delight, and pulling with far more strength than their little bodies could account for.

The young man shut his mouth, and glared at Magnus.

Foreboding struck, and Rod sprang from Fess's back in a flying tackle.

He smacked into the young man's legs so hard they bruised his shoulder. Above him, the warlock yowled in pain.

Then it was daytime, suddenly full noon. The glare stung Rod's eyes, and he squinted against it. He could make out fern leaves closely packed above, and a huge lizardlike monstrosity staring at them from five feet away. Then its mouth lolled open in a needle-fanged grin, and it waddled toward them with amazing speed. Panic clawed its way up Rod's throat, and he almost let go to snatch out his knife— but the enemy warlock panicked first.

It was night again, total night. No, that was moonlight, wasn't it? And it showed Rod water, endless waves heaving below him. One reached up to slap at his heels, and its impact travelled on up to hit his stomach with chilling dread. He could just picture himself falling, sinking beneath those undulating fluid hills, rising to thrash about in panic, clawing for land, for wood, for something that floated. . . . Instinctively, he tightened his hug on the ankles.

Then sunlight seared his eyes, the sunlight of dawn, and bitter cold stabbed his lungs. Beyond the legs he clung to, the world spread out below him like a map, an immensity of green. Jagged rocks stabbed up, only a few yards below his heels. It had to be a mountain peak, somewhere on the mainland.

Darkness again, blackness—but not quite total, for moonlight filtered through a high, grated window, showing him blocks of granite that dripped with moisture, and niter webbing the high corners of the cramped chamber. Huge rusty staples held iron chains to the walls. A skeleton lounged in the fetters at the end of a pair of those chains. Another held a thick-bodied man with a bushy black beard. His brocade doublet was torn and crusted with dried blood, and a grimy bandage wrapped his head. He stared at them in total amazement. Then relief flooded his face, and his mouth opened. . . .

Limbo. Nothingness. Total void.

There wasn't any light, but there wasn't any darkness, either—just a gray, formless nothingness. Rod felt an instant conviction that he wasn't seeing with his eyes—especially when colors began to twist through the void in writhing streaks, and a hiss of white noise murmured in the distance. They floated, adrift, and the body in Rod's arms suddenly began to writhe and heave again. A nasal voice cursed, "Thou vile recreants! I will rend thee, I will tear thee! Monstrous, perverse beasts, who . . ."

Geoffrey cried out, "Abandon!"

Suddenly Rod was hugging nothing; the legs were gone. He stared blankly at the space where they'd been. Then panic surged up within him, and he flailed about, trying to grasp something solid, anything, the old primate fear of falling skewering his innards.

Then a small hand caught his, and Geoffrey's voice cried, "Gregory! Art there, lad? Hold thou, and *pull!*"

Gentle breeze kissed Rod's cheek, and the scents of pine and meadow grass filled his head with a sweetness he didn't remember them ever having, before. Moonlight showed him the meadow where they'd camped, and Gwen darting forward, to throw her arms about him—and the two boys who clung to him. "Oh, my lord! My bairns! Oh, thou naughty lads, to throw thyselves into such danger! Praise Heaven thou'rt home!"

Cordelia was hugging Rod's neck hard enough to gag

him, head pressed against his and sobbing, "Papa! I feared we had lost thee!"

Rod wrapped his arms around her, grateful to have something solid to hold on to. He looked up to see Geoffrey peeking at him over Gwen's shoulder. Rod nodded. "I don't know how you did it, son—but you did."

6

"'Twas not so hard as that."

The blankets were around their shoulders now, and a small campfire danced in the center of the family circle. Cordelia turned a spit over the fire from time to time, roasting a slow rabbit for breakfast.

"'Not so hard?'" Rod frowned at Geoffrey. "How could it have been anything *but* hard? That young villain had to be one of the best teleporters in the land! I mean, aside from you boys, the only warlock we've got who can teleport anything but himself, is old Galen—and nobody ever sees him!"

"Save old Agatha," Gwen murmured.

"Nobody ever sees *her* either," Rod retorted.

"Save old Galen," Cordelia reminded him.

"He's going to need it," Rod agreed. He turned back to the boys. "Toby's the best of our young warlocks, and he's just beginning to learn how to teleport other objects. He's almost thirty, too. So Alfar's sidekick has to be better than Toby."

"Nay, not so excellent as that." Magnus shook his head. "And he was a very poor marksman."

"For which, praise Heaven." Rod shuddered. "But he was *too* good at teleporting himself—even over his weight allowance! I didn't begin to recognize most of the places he took us to!"

"Any child could do the same," Magnus answered, annoyed.

"I keep telling you, son—don't judge others by yourself. Why didn't he just disappear, though?"

"He could not," Geoffrey grinned. "We could tell where he would flee to, and fled there but a fraction of a second behind him."

"How could you tell where he was going?"

"They held his hands," Gwen reminded. "Thoughts travel more readily, by touch."

Magnus nodded. "We could feel, through his skin, where he meant to go next."

Rod stared at him for a moment, then sat back, shaking his head. "Beyond my comprehension. Thoughts can't travel any FESSter just by touching—can they?"

"No," Fess's voice murmured through the earphone implanted in the bone behind Rod's right ear. "But there would be less signal-loss than with a radiated waveform."

Cordelia sighed, striving for patience with her dullard father. "'Tis not that one doth hear faster, Papa—only that one doth hear more. With touch, even tinges of thought speak clearly."

"I bow to the guest expert." Rod managed to keep the fond amusement out of his tone, giving the words a sour twist.

Fess plowed on. "The neurons in the warlock's hand did, in all probability, induce the signal directly into the neurons in the boys' hands."

"He couldn't hide his thought-traces from you." Rod turned back to Geoffrey. "So you always had just enough clues to follow him. But how did you manage to bring *me* along?"

Gregory shook his head, eyes round. "That, Papa, we cannot say."

"We thought thou couldst," Magnus added.

Rod scowled. "No . . . can't say that I did. Except that I was bound and determined that I wasn't going to let go of him. . . ."

The children stared at one another, then at their mother.

"What's the matter?" Rod demanded. "What am I—a monster?"

"Nay, Papa," Cordelia said softly, "thou'rt only a warlock—yet a most puissant one."

"You mean it was just my determination that took me wherever he went?"

Magnus nodded. "Thy magic followed all else that was needful."

Rod was still, gazing at the fire for a few minutes while he tried to absorb that. It was unnerving to think that he was beginning to be able to work magic the way his wife and children did—just by thinking of it. Now he was going to have to watch his step, to make sure he didn't do it accidentally. He could just hear a casual passerby asking, "How do you think the weather's going to be today, Mr. Warlock?" "Well, to tell you the truth, I think it's going to rain. . . ." and, *sploosh!* They'd be drenched. . . .

He shook off the mood, and looked up to find the children's gazes glued to him. They looked worried; he wondered what they'd been up to. "So. Finally, he took us into a dungeon."

"'Twas the sorcerer Alfar's dungeon," Geoffrey explained, and Cordelia gasped.

Rod nodded. "Convenient. If he could just have figured out some way to get rid of us, we'd be right there to hand for the jailers. But how did he figure he was going to be able to keep you there? How could he prevent you from teleporting out?"

"I do not think he had thought that far," Magnus said slowly.

Rod was still nodding. "Makes sense. I wouldn't be too good at the details, if I was trying to run from the enemy, but he was coming right along."

"He was not attempting that," Geoffrey said, with conviction. "He meant only to take us to a place in which we would be unwilling to stay."

Rod smiled slowly. "Clever kid. Chose a nice one, didn't he?"

"Aye." Magnus shivered. "I was well relieved, to be quit of that place."

"But how're you so sure?" Rod asked Geoffrey.

"Because we tried to hale him out, and he would not come."

Rod stared. Then he took a deep breath and said, delicately, "Little chancey, wasn't it?"

"Nay. We sought to bring him to Mama."

Gwen's eyes gleamed. Rod glanced at her, and turned back to the boys with a shudder. "That's what put us into Limbo?"

"Where?" Magnus frowned. "Oh! Thou dost speak of the Void!"

Rod didn't like the familiarity with which he spoke of it. "Been there before, have you?"

Magnus caught the look, and realized its significance. "Nay, not so often..... 'Tis only that..."

"Spells go awry sometimes, Papa," Geoffrey explained. "Assuredly thou must needs realize that."

"That," Rod said tightly, "is why you're supposed to wait till Mama can supervise."

"She did, the first time."

"*First*...time?"

"Peace, husband." Gwen touched his arm. "'Tis naught so dangerous as that."

"Aye," Magnus said quickly. "When thou dost arrive in that place that is not a place, thou hast but to think of where thou dost wish to be, and lo! Thou art there indeed!"

"I'll try to remember that," Rod said grimly. He noticed that Cordelia was managing to hold her tongue, but she looked chartreuse with envy. He caught her hand, and she squeezed back. "So," he said to Geoffrey, "how did we wind up in Limbo this time?"

"Why, because we wished to bear him to Mama, and he did not wish to go."

"I don't blame him, when she's in that mood. So you were trying to go, and he was trying to stay, so..."

"We went nowhere." Geoffrey nodded. "I saw, then, that we could not win, so I sought safety."

"What was so tough about it?" Rod frowned. "I thought you only needed to think yourselves home!"

"We did need some aid," Geoffrey admitted, and he reached out to clap his three-year-old brother on the shoulder. "This one had followed us with his mind, where e'er we had gone. I had but to call out to him, and he helped pull us, and showed us the road to home."

"Yes..." Rod's gaze fastened on his youngest. "He's had some experience doing that."

Gregory looked totally blank.

"Not that he'd remember it," Rod explained. "He was a little young, at the time—eleven months old.

"But! Here you are, safe at home—praise Heaven!" He gathered them all into his arms, and squeezed. They gave mock yells of dismay, and Rod relaxed, looking down into their faces. "And now—you can go home."

They let loose a squall that must've waked villagers for miles around.

"Nay, Papa, not so soon!"

"It was just beginning to be fun!"

"We're not ready, Papa!"

"Boys get to do all the fun stuff," Cordelia pouted.

Geoffrey looked straight into Rod's eyes. "There is no danger, Papa."

"No danger!" Rod exploded. "You have a maverick warlock raining cannonballs on you, and you tell me there's no danger? You have a monster magus trying to conjure rock chunks into your bodies, and you tell me it's *safe?* You have a felon enchanter, straight from the glass house, throwing stones at you, and you tell me it's *tame?"*

"But we are whole," Magnus spread his hands. "Naught save a bruise or two."

"Chance! Sheer, freakish good fortune! You're just lucky that sorcerer was a lousy shot!"

"Yet we outnumber him, Papa!"

"He outweighs you! And that's just the *human* danger! What's going to happen the next time you get into a tug-of-war with one of those sorcerer interns? You might be stranded out in that void with no way to get home!"

"Surely not, Papa!" Geoffrey protested. "'Tis as I've said—thou hast but to *think* of..."

"Yeah, if you've got somebody tuned in to act as your safety line!"

"But Gregory..."

"Gregory might be *with* you!" Rod bawled.

"Yet that doth not afright me, Papa," the three-year-old cried. "That gray place doth please me! 'Tis comforting, and . . ."

"Makes you feel right at home, does it?" Rod felt a bitter stab of guilt. "You should; your mind spent enough time searching there, when you were a baby, trying to find out where Mama and I had gone."

"An thou sayest it. Therefore do I know my way. There is truly no dange–"

"Now I say NO!" Rod roared, slamming his fist into the turf. Pain shot up his forearm, but his rage shoved it aside. "What the *hell* do you think you're doing, talking back to your father!" He snatched Magnus's collar, and yanked the boy's face up to his. "Think you're getting big, do you? Let me tell you, you will *never* be old enough to argue with me!" He threw Magnus back, and whirled to catch at Geoffrey. The six-year-old ducked aside, automatically bringing his arm up to block, managing to knock Rod's arm aside.

Rod froze, eyes bulging, staring down at the boy, rigid as a board, white with rage, nostrils pinching in.

Geoffrey flinched away. "Papa—I did not mean . . ."

"I *know* what you meant!" Rod strode forward. "I know damned well what you . . ."

But he bumped into something, and Gwen's eyes were looking directly into his. Her voice bored through his fury, droning, demanding, "Come out! I know thee, Rod Gallowglass, born Rodney d'Armand. I know thee for my lover and husband, and know that thou art there, beneath this beastliness that overcomes thee. Come out, Rod Gallowglass! Let not this shell of anger overwhelm and overmaster thee. Ever hast thou been a caring husband, and a gentle father to my children. Thou art of Gramarye, not Tir Chlis! Thou art my treasure, and my children thy gems! Husband, turn! Come out to me, Rod Gallowglass!"

Rod stared at her, fury mounting higher, but held by the truth of her words. An evil spell . . . He shuddered, and his rage fell into slivers, and ebbed. He sagged, his knees giving way for a moment, and stumbled—and Magnus was there beside him, shoulder under his father's arm, staring up at Rod in fright and concern.

Concern for his father's safety—even after Rod had been so cruel! This son could not only forgive—he could even run to help! Remorse charged his anguish, and made him harsh. He recovered his balance and stood, stiffening. "Thank you." But he clasped the boy's shoulder firmly.

Magnus winced, but stood steadfast.

Rod held the boy's shoulders with both hands, but his gaze held Gwen's. "That was foolish, you know. Very risky. Likely to get you slugged."

Answering anger flared in her eyes—flared, and was smothered. "'Twas worth the risk, my lord."

He gave her a brief, tight nod. "Yes. Thank you. Very much." He shook his head. "Don't do it again. It won't work, again. When it hits me, just ... go. Anywhere, as fast as you can. Just go."

"That, also, would be foolish," she cried, almost in despair. "If we do flee, thou wilt pursue—and then thou wilt not hear, no matter what appeal I plead."

He stared at her, immobile.

Finally, he closed his eyes, clenching his fists so tightly that they hurt. He took three slow, deep, even breaths, then looked up at her and said, "But you must. Not when I'm angry—no, you're right, that would be dangerous." He forced himself to say it: "For both of us." It left an astringent taste behind. "But now. Now. It's getting too wild up here. Alfar and his henchmen aren't playing games. They're too dangerous. I'm too dangerous. And if I don't hurt the children, he will."

She stared at him for a long moment. The children were very silent.

Then, slowly, Gwen said, "An thou dost wish it, my lord, we will go. Yet I prithee, think again—for we are safer if we are with thee, as thou'lt be. For then can we ward one another's backs. Yet if we are apart from thee— if we dwell back in Runnymede—then may thine enemies seek to strike at thee by hurting us—and thou wilt not be by us, to defend."

It was an excuse. It was a rationalization. It was specious and hollow, and Rod knew it.

But he was scared. He was very scared of what might

happen, inside him, if he started arguing with her. He was afraid for her, afraid for the children. . . .

But he was also afraid for them if Alfar ever realized that none of his henchmen could handle the Gallowglasses alone. When he did, he'd probably do the sensible thing—gang up on them, all his sorcerers together. And the children were powerful espers already, but they were still children.

But he was more afraid of what might happen to them, if he lost his temper again.

Abruptly, he bowed his head. "All right. Stay."

The children cheered.

Their raucous clamor bounced off Rod's ears. He stood in the midst of the rain of their sound, swearing under his breath that he would not let his temper turn against them again.

He was still swearing the next day, inside his head, and searching frantically for a way to ensure their safety. Other than sending them home—he wasn't going to argue with them about that, again. Arguments turned into rages.

"Wilt thou not ride now, my lord?" Gwen sat up on Fess's saddle, with Cordelia in front of her.

Rod shook his head, mute, and plowed on.

The children glanced at their mother, then back at him, and followed him silently.

Around the curve ahead of them, a husky peasant and his equally husky wife came into view, with five children trudging wearily beside them—wearily, even though it was early in the morning. The husband pushed a handcart piled high with sacks and household belongings.

"More refugees," Rod grated. "How many is that, Delia?"

"Fourteen, Papa."

Rod nodded. "Fourteen in how long?"

"An hour and a half, Papa," Gregory answered, glancing at the sun.

Rod shook his head. "That's real evil happening up there, children. People don't leave their homes for mild likes and dislikes—not even for hates. They flee because of fear."

"We do not fear, Papa," Magnus said stoutly.

"I know," Rod returned. "That's what worries me."

They plodded on toward the peasant family. Then Geoffrey took a chance and said, "The sorcerer's guards grow careless, Papa."

"Why?" Rod frowned. "You mean because they let these people pass?" He shook his head. "That's not where they're coming from. Here, I'll show you." He stepped over to the side of the road as the big peasant and his family came up. The man looked up at him, surprised, and scowled. Then weariness overcame him, and he relaxed, humbling himself to talk to someone who was below his station. "Hail, tinker! Dost thou travel north, then?"

"Aye," Rod answered. "Poor folk must seek their living where they can. Why, what moves in the North?"

The peasant shook his head. "We know only what Rumor speaks. We ourselves have not seen it."

Rod frowned. "So fearsome? What doth Rumor say?"

"That an evil sorcerer hath risen," the peasant answered. "He hath overcome the Sire de Maladroit, the Baron de Gratecieux, and even the Count Lagorme."

Rod stared, incredulous. "Why? Who doth speak so?"

Geoffrey looked unbelieving, too, at the idea that Alfar's men could have let someone slip out to bear word.

The big peasant shrugged wearily. "Rumor flies, tinker— and well thou shouldst know it, for 'tis thy tradesmen that do carry such tidings, more often than not."

"Is it that, then?" Rod's eyebrows lifted. "Only that a cousin told a neighbor, who told a gossip, who told an uncle, who told..."

"Aye, belike." The big peasant shrugged. "I know only what my god-sib Hugh son of Marl told unto me—and that the whiles he packed a barrow like to this, and set packs to the backs of his wife and sons. 'Whither comes this word?' quoth I; and spake he, 'From Piers Thatcher...'"

Rod interrupted. "Lives he on the Count's estates?"

The peasant shook his head. "Nay, nor on Gratecieux's, nor on Maladroit's. Yet he hath a cousin whose god-sib's nephew hath a brother-in-law whose cousin hath a niece who doth live hard by the good Count's manor—and thus the word doth run."

"Is't so?" Rod glanced back at Geoffrey, then back to the peasant, bobbing his head and tugging a forelock. "I thank thee, goodman. We shall wend our way a little farther north—but we shall ponder well thy words."

"Do," the big peasant advised, "and turn back toward the South."

"These things are not certain," Gwen protested.

"Nay," the peasant's wife agreed. "Yet we have heard this word again and, aye, again, for all these months of spring. First Rumor spoke of the Sire—but then of the Baron, and now of the Count. If Rumor doth begin to speak of the Duke, belike we'll find we *can* not flee." She shook her head. "Nay, an thou lovest thy little ones, chance not the truth of Rumor."

"Mayhap thou hast the right of it," Gwen said, with a pensive frown. "I thank thee—and farewell."

"God be with thee, goodman." Rod tugged at his forelock again.

"God be," the man returned, and took up the handles of his cart again.

As the peasant and his family slogged away toward the South, Geoffrey spun toward his father and fairly exploded in a hissing whisper. "So easily, Papa! Is all the work of so many guards and sentries brought low so easily, by naught but *gossip?*"

"Indeed it is," Rod answered sourly. "Remember that when you command. The fence isn't made, that can stop a rumor."

Geoffrey threw up his hands in exasperation. "Then why mount a watch at all?"

"Proof." Rod grimaced. "If none of the lords have proof, they won't go to the expense of sending an army northward. After all, what did the King himself do, when he heard the unconfirmed word? Sent us!"

"All this, to hold back proof?"

Rod nodded. "Without that, anybody who wants to believe the news is false, can."

"Until the sorcerer and his minions overrun them," the boy said darkly.

"Yes," Rod agreed, with a bleak smile. "That is the idea, isn't it?"

"Papa," said Cordelia, "I begin to fear."

"Good." Rod nodded. "Good."

• • •

Half an hour later, they saw a small coach in the distance, hurtling toward them. As it came closer, they saw that the horses were foaming and weary. But the woman who sat on the coachman's box flogged them on, with fearful glances over her shoulder at the troop of men-at-arms who galloped after her on small, tough Northern ponies, and the armored knight who thundered at their head on a huge, dark warhorse that would have made two of the ponies.

"What churlishness is this," Gwen cried, "that armed men pursue a woman shorn of defense?"

"Don't blame 'em too hard," Rod snapped. "I don't think they're terribly much aware of what they're doing."

"Thou must needs aid her, my lord!"

"Yes," Rod agreed. "It isn't too hard to tell who the bad guys are, is it? Especially since we've seen their livery before. Ambush stations, kids."

"Magnus and Gregory, guard the left," Gwen instructed. "Cordelia and Geoffrey, do thou ward the right. Flit toward them, as far as thou canst." She turned to Rod. "How wouldst thou have them fell their foes, husband?"

"One by one. Unhorse them." Rod felt a warm glow at her support.

Delia caught up her broomstick with a shout of glee.

"How shall we fell them, Mama?" Geoffrey grinned. "Throw rocks at them?"

Gwen nodded. "Aye—but take thou also thy belts of rope, and discover how thou mayst make use of them."

They all quickly untied the lengths of hemp that were lashed about their waists. "Mama," said Magnus, "I think that I could make the nails to disappear from the horses' shoes."

Rod nodded slow approval. "I pity the poor horses—but they shouldn't be damaged. They will stop, though."

"Naught of these will avail against the knight," Gregory pointed out.

Rod gave him a wolfish grin. "He's mine."

"Begone from sight now, quickly!" Gwen clapped her hands.

The children dodged off the roadside into the underbrush, and disappeared.

Gwen hopped down from Fess's back, and caught her broomstick from its sling alongside the saddle. "Wilt thou need thine horse, my lord?"

"'Fraid so, dear. Can you manage without him?"

"Why, certes." She dimpled, and dropped him a quick curtsy. "Godspeed, husband." Then she turned away to dive into the underbrush after her children.

Rod sighed, jamming a foot into the stirrup. "Quite a woman I've got there, Fess."

"Sometimes I wonder if you truly appreciate her, Rod."

"Oh, I think I do." Rod swung up into the saddle and pulled on the reins. "We'd better imitate them. Off the road, Steel Stallion."

Fess trotted off the shoulder and down into the underbrush. "What did you have in mind for the knight, Rod?"

"About 120 volts. Got a spare battery?"

Fess's answer was lost in the racket, as the coach thundered by them.

Rod looked up at the mounted squad. "A hundred yards and closing. Got some cable?"

"Forward port compartment, Rod." A small door sprang open under Fess's withers.

Rod reached in and pulled out a length of wire. He drew out his dagger and stripped the insulation off in a few quick strokes. "Where do I plug it in?"

The horsehead turned back to look at him. "Simply place it in my mouth, Rod. I will route current to it. But are you certain this is ethical?"

"Is the sword he's carrying?" Rod shrugged. "A weapon is a weapon, Fess. And this one won't do him any permanent damage—I hope. Okay, *now!*"

They darted up out of the roadside as the squad pounded up. Rod swerved in alongside the knight. The helmet visor turned toward him, but the knight raised neither sword nor shield, no doubt flabbergasted at seeing a tinker riding up alongside him on a horse that would've done credit to a lord. Besides, what need was there to defend against a piece of rope?

Rod jabbed the end of the wire at him, and a fat blue spark snapped across the gap; then the wire was in contact with the armor, and the knight threw up his arms, stiffened.

Rod lashed out a kick, and the knight crashed off his horse into the dust of the road.

Someone gave a shout of horror, behind him. Rod whirled Fess around, then darted off to the side of the road before the sergeant could get his thoughts together enough to start a try for retribution.

Along the side of the road, three soldiers lay sprawled, one every hundred feet or so. Another four lined the verge on the far side. Some of the horses were grazing, very contentedly, next to their fallen masters. A few of the others, obviously more intelligent, were galloping away into the distance.

As Rod watched, a small figure exploded into existence right in front of one of the remaining riders. Startled, the horseman flinched back, and his mount reared, whinnying. Geoffrey lashed out a kick to the man's shoulder, and the soldier overbalanced, tipped, and fell. The child slapped the horse's rump, and the beast turned to gallop away with a whinny.

On the other side of the road, a length of rope shot flying through the air like a winged serpent, and wrapped itself around another soldier's neck. He grabbed at it with both hands, then suddenly jolted backward, and slammed down onto the road, still struggling with the coil. With a gun-crack, Magnus appeared beside him, stick in hand. He swung downward, and the soldier went limp. The rope uncoiled and flew off to look for a new victim. Pocket thunder made a boomlet, and Magnus disappeared.

Rod winced. "Bloodthirsty brood I've got, here."

"They are only doing as you told them, Rod—and taught them."

"Maybe I'd better revise the curriculum."

"Do not be overly hasty," the robot murmured. "That soldier still breathes."

"I hope it's widespread. Well, back to work." Rod turned the horse back onto the road—and saw all the soldiers lying in the dust, unconscious. Already, Gwen knelt by the nearest, gazing intently at his face. Cordelia arrowed in to land beside her, and the boys began to appear, like serial thunder.

"They work fast, too," Rod muttered. He trotted up beside the family grouping, and leaned down to touch Magnus on the shoulder. The boy's head snapped up in surprise. He saw his father, and relaxed, with a sigh of relief.

"You did wonderfully." Rod beamed with pride. "All of you. But keep an eye on the soldiers, son. A few of them might come to while you're still trying to overhaul their minds."

Magnus nodded, glowing with his father's praise. "I will ward them well, Papa."

"Stout fellow. I should be back before they wake up— but, just in case." He straightened up, turning Fess southward.

"Wither goest thou, Papa?"

"To tell that lady she can stop panicking." Rod kicked his heels against Fess's sides. "Follow that coach."

The robot-horse sprang into a gallop. "Drumming your heels against my sides really serves no purpose, Rod."

"Sure it does—keeping up appearances. You wouldn't want people to know you weren't a real horse, would you?"

"Surely you cannot be concerned about that with your own family. They all know my true nature."

"Yeah, but I've got to stay in the habit. If I start trying to remember who knows about you and who doesn't, I'll start making little mistakes, and . . ."

"I understand," the robot sighed. "The coach approaches, Rod."

"Might be more accurate to say we approach the coach."

"I was under the impression that you had become a Gramaryan, not a grammarian."

Rod winced. "All right, already! I'll go for the content, and stop worrying about the form."

"Then you would make a very poor critic. . . ."

"Oh, shut up and head off the coach."

Fess swerved in front of the coach horses, and the animals reared, screaming with fright. The woman hit the brake with frantic strength, then lashed out with the whip at Rod.

"Hey!" He ducked, but too late; the lash cracked against the side of his head. The roadway tilted and circled, blurring; distantly, he heard the whip crack, again and again. Then the world levelled, and he began to see clearly. The familiar rage surged up in him. Appalled, he tried to remember her fear. The woman stood on the box, brandishing the whip for one more try.

Rod held up a palm. "Whoa! Hold it! I'm on *your* side!" He pointed to his chest. "No uniform. See?"

The woman hesitated, but anger and fear still held her eyes wide.

Rod was working hard to stifle a huge flood of anger of his own; his head ached abominably. "You wouldn't hit a poor, wandering tinker, would you?"

"Aye, if he threatened me or mine." But sanity began to return to the woman's eyes. "And why would a poor tinker stop a noble Lady, if not to harm her?"

"To tell you, you can stop running!" Rod cried. "We knocked out your enemies!"

The woman stood frozen, but hope flared in her eyes.

Rod pointed back along the road. "Take a look, if you doubt me!"

She darted a quick glance back up the road, then glanced again. She turned back to him, joy beginning to flower in her face. Then her knees gave way, and she collapsed onto the box. "Praise Heaven! But how didst thou . . ."

"I had a little help," Rod explained.

She was instantly on her guard again. "From whom?"

"My wife," Rod explained, "and my children."

She stared. Then weariness filled her face. "I see them; they pick the corpses of the soldiers. Do not lie to me, fellow. How could a tinker and his bairns and wife, fare against an armored knight and a dozen soldiers?" She hefted the whip again.

"Now, hold on!" Rod felt his anger mounting again, too. He took a deep breath, and tried to remember that the poor woman had been chased for most of the night—probably. "My wife and kids aren't robbing bodies—they're trying to break the enchantments that bind living men. Unconscious, but living—I hope. You see, we're not quite what we seem to be."

"Indeed," she hissed between her teeth, and forced herself to her feet again, swinging the whip up. "So I had thought!"

"Not *that* way! This tinker outfit is just a disguise!" Rod straightened in the saddle, squaring his shoulders. "I am Rodney Gallowglass, Lord High Warlock of Gramarye—and that woman back there is the Lady Gwendylon."

She stared. Then her lips parted, and she whispered, "Give me a sign."

"A *sign?*" Exasperated, Rod bit down on his irritation and forced himself to imagine just how paranoid he'd be feeling in her place. He took another deep breath, expelled it. "Oh, all right!" Rod closed his eyes and let his mind go blank, concentrating. His usual haze of needs and responsibilities seemed to ebb and clear, till he could hear his children's voices, as though they were right next to him. He singled out the one who looked least threatening and thought, *Gregory! Come here!*

Air popped outward, and Gregory floated next to his shoulder. "Ayé, Papa?"

The woman stared.

Then her knees gave way again, and she sat down, nodding weakly. "Aye. Thou art the High Warlock."

"Papa?" Gregory cocked his head to the side, frowning up at his father. "Why didst thou call?"

"For what you just did, son."

The child stared. "What did I?"

"You proved I'm what I said I was." He turned back to the woman. "And whom have I the pleasure of addressing?"

Now it was her turn to pull herself together and remember her dignity. "I am Elyena, Duchess of Romanov."

7

Rod steered the tottering horses off the road and into the meadow near Gwen, holding up the Duchess with his left arm. As he pulled them to a halt, she raised her head, looking about, then crowded closer to him. "The soldiers..."

Rod turned, and saw all the soldiers gathered in a knot under a low tree. Most of them held their heads in their hands. Some had lifted their gazes and were looking around, blinking, their faces drawn and uncertain. The knight lay by them with his helmet off. Gwen knelt over him.

"Don't worry," Rod said, trying to sound reassuring. "They feel as though they've just awakened from a bad dream. They're on your side again." He jumped down from the box. "Just stay there."

She did, huddling into herself—and not looking at all reassured.

Rod sighed, and thought sharply, *Cordelia!*

The little girl leaped up halfway across the meadow and looked around. She located her father and jumped on her broomstick, zooming straight over to him. "Aye, Papa?"

Rod noticed the Duchess staring. Well, at least she was distracted. "Cordelia, this lady needs..."

But Cordelia was staring past him, toward the windows

of the coach, and a delighted grin curved on her lips. "Children!"

Rod turned, suprised.

Two little faces filled one of the windows, looking about with frank curiousity.

Cordelia skipped past Rod, hands behind her back. The Duchess's children watched her warily. Cordelia stopped right below them and cocked her head to the side. "I am hight Cordelia."

They didn't answer; they just stared.

Rod touched her shoulder. "They've been having some bad scares lately, honey."

The elder boy looked up in indignation. "Was *not* scared!"

"Yeah, sure, you were calm as a mill pond. Just go easy, honey."

"Oh, Papa!" she said, exasperated. "Can they not see I wish them no harm?" Before he could answer, she whirled away to the Duchess. "May I play with them?"

The Duchess stared down at her. Then, slowly, she said, "Why . . . an they wish it . . . certes."

That they would wish it, Rod did not doubt; he knew his daughter. Already, the two boys were watching her with marked interest.

"Oh, good!" Cordelia spun back to the children. "I have brothers, too. Thou mayst play with them also, an thou dost wish it."

The two boys still looked wary, but Cordelia's friendliness was infectious. The younger opened the coach door, and stepped out. "I," he said, "am Gaston."

Rod turned away, quite certain the Duchess's attention would be fully occupied for a while, and went over to his wife.

As he came up, she sat back on her heels, gazing down at the knight and shaking her head. Instantly, Rod was alert. "What's the matter? Is the hypnosis too strong?"

Gwen shook her head again. "I have broke the spell, my lord. Yet I can bring him no closer to life than this."

Rod turned, staring down at the knight. He saw a lined face and bald head, with a fringe of gray hair. His skin was gray, and covered with a sheen of sweat. Guilt swept through

Rod. He knelt beside the knight. "But it was only 120 volts! Only fifteen amperes! And I only hit him with it for a few seconds!"

Gwen shook her head. "It may have as easily been the fall, my lord. His heart had stopped, and I labored to make it begin to beat again."

"Heart attack?" Rod took a closer look at the knight. "He's middle-aged—and he's let himself sag out of shape." He shook his head, looking up at Gwen. "There was no way I could tell that. He had his helmet on, and the visor was down."

"In truth, thou couldst not," she agreed, "and anything thou hadst done to stop him, might have hurt him this badly." She lifted her eyes, gazing into his. "Yet, my lord, I misdoubt me an 'twas any action of thine that did strike him down. He had ridden too many miles in harness."

Rod nodded slowly. "Whoever sent him out to lead a troop in full armor, at his age, must've seen him only as a thing, not a person. Who . . . ? No, cancel that. Of course— who else? Alfar."

"We will tend him, milady."

Gwen looked up, and saw the sergeant kneeling across from her.

"Sir Verin is old, but dear to us," the soldier explained. "How he came to this pass, we know not. We will tend him." He lifted his head, showing haunted eyes. "Lady— what have our bodies done, the whiles our souls slept?"

"Naught that is any fault of thine." She touched his hand, smiling gently. "Trouble not thine heart."

Geoffrey darted up beside her. "Mama! There are children! May we go play?"

Gwen looked up, startled. "Why . . ."

"We've got company," Rod explained.

A short while later, the parents sat around a hasty campfire while the children played nearby. The Duchess sat, shivering in spite of the sun's midday warmth. Gwen had fetched a blanket from Fess's pack and wrapped it around her, but the poor lady still shivered with reaction. She gazed at the children, who were winding up a raucous game of tag. "Ah, bless them! Poor mites." Tears gathered at the corners of her eyes. "They know not the meaning of what hath happed."

"Thou hast not told them, then?" Gwen said softly.

The Duchess shook her head. "They know what they have seen, and no more." She looked up at Rod, a hard stare. "And I will not tell them until I *know*."

Rod stared back, and nodded slowly. "Why not? Your husband could still be alive. It's even possible that he's well."

The Duchess nodded slowly, maintaining the glare. But she couldn't hold it long, and her head dropped.

Nearby, the children collapsed in a panting tangle.

"Nay, but tell!" Cordelia cajoled. "Didst thou truly see the evil sorcerer?"

"Nay," said the youngest; and "We saw naught," said the eldest. "Naught save the inside of our keep. Mother penned us there, and would not even let us go so far as the window."

"Yet thou didst come in a coach," Magnus reminded. "Didst thou see naught then?"

The boys shook their heads, and the youngest said, "We knew only that Mother bade us follow her down to the courtyard, and placed us in the coach. Through the gate house, we heard the clash of arms afar off; yet she drew the curtains closely, and bade us open them not."

The oldest added, "We could hear the rumble of the wheels echoing about us, and knew that we passed through the gatehouse. Then the portcullis did crash down behind us, and the noises of war began to grow nearer."

Geoffrey's eyes glinted.

"Then they began to grow fainter, till they were lost behind us," the eldest went on, "and we heard naught but the grating of the coach's wheels."

The youngest nodded. "When at last we did part the curtains, there was naught to see but summer fields and groves."

The Duchess pressed her face into her hands, and her shoulders shook with more than shivering. Gwen tucked the blanket more tightly around her, murmuring soothing inanities. She glanced at Rod and nodded toward the children.

Rod took the cue. "Uh, kids—could you maybe change the subject?"

"Eh?" Cordelia looked up and took in the situation at a glance. "Oh!" She was instantly contrite. "We are sorry, Papa." She turned to the other children, catching the hands of the Duchess's sons. "Come, let us play at tracking."

The fatuous look they gave her boded well for her teen-aged future, and ill for Rod's coming peace of mind. But they darted away, calling to one another, and Magnus hid his face against a large tree, and began to count.

The Duchess lifted her head, turning it from side to side in wonder. "They so quickly forget such ill!"

"Well, yes—but you haven't really told them the bad parts," Rod said judiciously. "For all they know, their father's winning the battle. And can you really say he didn't?"

"Nay," she said, as though it were forced from her. "Yet I did not flee till I looked down from the battlements, and saw that the melee had begun to go against him—even as we had feared." Then she buried her face in her hands, and her shoulders heaved with sobbing. Gwen clucked over her, comforting, and Rod had the good taste to keep quiet until the Duchess had regained some measure of control over herself. She lifted her head, gazing out over the meadow with unseeing eyes. "When first the reeves began to bring us tales of villages suborned, we dismissed them with laughter. Who could come to rule a village, whiles its knight stood by to shield it? Yet the first tale was followed by a second, and a second by a third, then a fourth, then a fifth—and ever was it the same: that a sorcerer had made the people bow to him. Then it was a witch who forced the homage, with the sorcerer's power supporting her; then a warlock."

"How'd they do it?" Rod asked. "Did the reeves know?"

The Duchess shook her head. "They had heard only rumors of dire threats, and of barns bursting into flame, and kine that sickened and fell. Yet for the greater part, there had been only surliness and complaining from the peasants, complaining that swelled louder and louder. Then the witch or warlock stepped amongst them, and they turned with joyful will to bow to him or her, and the sorcerer whose power lay 'neath. My lord did bid one of his knights to ride about his own estates, and visit the villages therein. The knight returned, and spoke of peasant mobs that howled in fury, brandishing scythes and mattocks, and hurling stones. When he charged, they broke and ran; yet when he turned away, eftsoons they gathered all against him once again." Her mouth hardened. "Thus were they bid, I doubt not."

"Sudden, rabid loyalty." Rod glanced at Gwen. "Would you say they didn't really seem to be themselves? The peasants, I mean."

"Nay, assurdly not!" The Duchess shuddered. "They were as unlike what they had been, as Maytime is from winter. Such reports angered milord, but not greatly. They angered his vassal, the Baron de Gratecieux, far more; for, look you, the greater part of Milord Duke's revenues was yielded to him by his counts, who gained theirs from their barons. Yet the barons gain theirs from their knights."

Rod nodded. "So a knight's village resisting payments is a little more serious to the baron than to his duke."

The Duchess nodded too. "He did implore Milord Duke for arms and men, which my lord did give him gladly. Then rode the Baron 'gainst the sorcerer."

She fell silent. Rod waited.

When she didn't go on, Rod asked, "What happened?"

The Duchess shuddered. "Eh, such reports as we had were horrible, in truth! The Baron's force did meet with a host of magics—fell creatures that did pounce from the air, fireballs and rocks that appeared among them, hurtling; arrows that sped without bows or archers, and war-axes and maces that struck without a hand to bear them. Then peasant mobs did charge upon them, howling and striking with their sickles. Yet far worst of all was a creeping fear, a sense of horror that overcame the Baron's soldiers, till they broke and ran, screaming hoarsely in their terror."

Rod met Gwen's eyes, and her words sounded in his ears alone: *I count a witch-moss crafter, and the warlock who doth hurl stones 'mongst us; and there be witches who do make the weapons fly. Yet what's this creeping horror?*

Rod could only shake his head. He looked down at the Duchess again. "What happened to the Baron?"

The Duchess shuddered. "He came not home; yet in later battles, he has been seen—leading such soldiers as lived, against the sorcerer's foes."

Rod caught Gwen's eye again; she nodded. Well, they'd met that compulsive hypnosis already. "How many of the soldiers survived?"

"There were, mayhap, half a dozen that lived to flee, of the threescore that marched to battle."

Rod whistled softly. "Six out of sixty? This sorcerer's efficient, isn't he? How many of the defeated ones were following Baron de Gratecieux in the next battle?"

The Duchess shrugged. "From the report we had—mayhap twoscore."

"Forty out of sixty, captured and brainwashed?" Rod shuddered. "But some got away—the six you mentioned."

"Aye. But a warlock pursued them. One only bore word to us; we know not what happened to the other five."

"It's a fair guess, though." Rod frowned. "So right from the beginning, Alfar's made a point of trying to keep word from leaking out." Somehow, that didn't smack of the medieval mind. "You say you learned this afterwards?"

The Duchess nodded. "It took that lone soldier a week and a day to win home to us."

"A lot can happen in a week."

"So it did. The sorcerer and his coven marched against the Castle Gratecieux; most of the household acclaimed Alfar their suzerain. The Baroness and some loyal few objected, and fought to close the gates. They could not prevail, though, and those who did acclaim the sorcerer their lord, did ope the gate, lower the drawbridge, and raise the portcullis."

Rod shrugged. "Well, if they could make whole villages switch allegiance, why not a castleful?"

"What did the sorcerer to the Baroness?" Gwen asked, eyes wide.

The Duchess squeezed her eyes shut. "She doth rest in the dungeon, with her children—though the eldest was wounded in the brawling."

Gwen's face hardened.

"How did you learn this?" Rod tried to sound gentle.

"Servants in Gratecieux's castle have cousins in my kitchens."

"Servants' network." Rod nodded. "So Alfar just took

over the castle. Of course, he went on to take over the rest of the manor."

"Such villages as did not already bow to him, aye. They fell to his sway one by one. At last, the other barons did take alarm, and did band together to declare war upon him."

"Bad tactics." Rod shook his head. "The hell with the declaration; they should've just gone in, and mopped him up."

The Duchess stared, scandalized.

"Just an idea," Rod said quickly.

The Duchess shook her head. "'Twould have availed them naught. They fought a sorcerer."

Rod lifted his head slowly, eyes widening, nostrils flaring. He turned to Gwen. "So he's got people thinking they can't win, before they even march. They're half defeated before they begin fighting."

"Mayhap," the Duchess said, in a dull voice, "yet with great ease did he defeat the barons. A score of sorcerer's soldiers did grapple with the barons' outriders, on the left flank. The scouts cried for a rescue, and soldiers ran to aid them. The sorcerer's men withdrew; yet no sooner had they vanished into the forest, than another band attacked the vanguard of the right flank. Again soldiers ran to bring aid, and again the sorcerer's men withdrew; and, with greater confidence, the barons' men marched ahead."

Even hearing the story, Rod felt a chill. "Too much confidence."

The Duchess nodded, and bit her lip. "When they came within sight of Castle Gratecieux, a wave of soldiers broke upon them from the forest. At t'other side of the road, rocks began to appear, with thunder-crashes, and also from that side came a swarm of thrown stones—yet no one was there to throw them. The soldiers recoiled upon themselves, then stood to fight; yet they fell in droves. Three of the five barons fought to the last with their men, and were lost. The other two rallied mayhap a score, and retreated. The sorcerer's army pressed them hard, but well did they defend themselves. Naetheless, a half of the men fell, and one of the barons with them. The other half won through to the High Road, whereupon they could turn and flee, faster than the sorcerer's men could follow. A warlock followed them, and rocks appeared all about them; yet he grew careless and, of a sudden, an archer whirled and let fly. The arrow pierced the warlock, and he tumbled from the sky, screaming. Then away rode the baron and his poor remnant—and thus was the word brought to us. And I assure thee, mine husband did honor that archer."

"So should we all," Rod said. "It always helps, having a demonstration that your enemy can be beaten. Didn't your husband take these rumors of danger seriously before then?"

"Nay, not truly. He could not begin to believe that a band of peasants could be any true danger to armored knights and soldiers, even though they were witches. Yet when the Baron Marole stood before him and told him the account of his last battle, my lord did rise in wrath. He summoned up his knights and men, and did send his fleetest courier south, to bear word of all that had happed to Their Royal Majesties."

Rod frowned. "He sent a messenger? How long ago?"

The Duchess shrugged. "Five days agone."

Rod shook his head. "He should have been in Runnymede before we left."

She stared at him for a long moment, her eyes widening, haunted. "He did not come."

"No," Rod answered, "he didn't."

The Duchess dropped her gaze. "Alas, poor wight! Need we guess at what hath happed?"

"No, I think it's pretty obvious." Rod gazed north along the road. "In fact, he might even have dressed himself as a peasant, in hopes he'd be overlooked. In any case, he's probably the reason Alfar sent his new army out to cut down refugees."

"Refugees?" The Duchess looked up, frowning. "What are these?"

"Poor folk, who flee the ravages of war," Gwen explained.

Rod nodded. "Usually because their homes have been destroyed. In this case, though, the only ones who've been heading south are the ones who realized what was coming, and got out while they could."

"You've seen such folk, then?"

Rod nodded. "A few. I'd say we've been running into one every mile or so."

The Duchess shook her head slowly. "I marvel that they 'scaped the sorcerer's soldiers!"

"They started early enough, I guess—but I'm sure the soldiers caught up with plenty of other bands. And, of course, we did manage to, ah, interfere, when a squad of men-at-arms was trying to stop a family we bumped into."

The Duchess studied his face. "What had this family seen?"

"Not a darn thing—but they'd heard rumors."

"And were wise enough to heed them." The Duchess's mouth hardened. "Yet will Their Royal Majesties send an army north, after naught but rumor?"

Rod shook his head. "Not a chance."

She frowned. "Yet how is it *thou* dost..." Then she broke off, eyes widening in surprise, then hope. "Yet thou *dost* come, thou!"

Rod answered with a sardonic smile. "Quick-witted, I see. And yes, the King sent us—to find out the truth of the rumors."

"And thou dost lead thy wife and bairns into so vile a brew of foulness?" the Duchess cried. She turned on Gwen. "Oh lady, nay! If thou dost thy children love, spare them this horror!"

Gwen looked up at Rod, startled.

Like a gentleman, Rod declined the unexpected advantage. He only said, "Well...you'll understand that my wife and children are a bit better equipped to deal with evil witches than most might be—so they're not really in so great a danger."

It earned him a look of warmth from Gwen, but the Duchess cried, "Danger enow! Lord Warlock, do not let them go! Thou dost not comprehend the might of this fell sorcerer!"

"We've had a taste of it."

"Then let that taste make thee lose thine appetite! A fulness of his work will sicken thy soul! 'Tis one thing to see a mere squadron of his victims, such as these poor folk..." She waved toward the soldiers. "Yet when thou dost see them come against thee by the hundreds, thine heart

shall shrink in horror! 'Tis not that his magic is so fell—
'tis the purely evil malice of his soul!"

Rod's eyes gleamed. "You've seen him yourself, then?"

She dropped her eyes. "Aye, though only from a distance. 'Twas enow." She shuddered. "I could feel his hatred
washing o'er me, as though I stood 'neath a cloudburst of
dirtied water. Methought that I should ne'er again feel clean!"

"But how could the Duke let you come so near the battle!"

"He fought against it, I assure thee—yet the battle did
come nigh to me. For when he had dispatched the courier
southwards, and his knights had come up with all their men,
he donned his armor and rode forth to meet the sorcerer."

Rod nodded. "Sounds right. I never would've accused
Duke Romanov of hesitating—or of the slightest bit of
uncertainty."

"Error, though?" The Duchess looked up, with a sardonic
smile. "I know mine husband, Lord Warlock. Dearly though
I love him, I cannot help but be aware of his rashness. Yet
in this matter, I believe, even full caution would have impelled him to battle—for 'twas fight or flee, look you, and,
as Duke, he could not flee—for he was sworn to the protection of his people. 'Twas his duty, then, to fight—and
if he must needs fight, 'twas best to fight just then, when
the sorcerer and his forces were newly come from battle,
and would therefore be weakened with battle losses."

"But strengthened with the men he'd captured." Rod
frowned. "Or didn't you realize..." He gazed at her, and
let the words gel in his mouth.

"What?" She frowned.

Rod cleared his throat, and shifted from one foot to the
other. "Well, uh...where he recruited his men from. His
army, I mean."

"Ah." She smiled bitterly. "From those he had defeated,
dost thou mean? Aye, that word was brought to us with the
news of Baron Gratecieux's lost battle. The soldier who
came back, did tell us of old friends he'd seen who, he
knew, had fought in the train of one of Gratecieux's vassal
knights."

"Well, at least it's not a surprise now," Rod sighed. "I
suppose it would take Alfar a little while to process his new
recruits..."

"To bind them under his spell?" The Duchess shook her head. "I know not. I know only that my lord did march out toward the castle that had been Gratecieux's—and I went up to the highest turret, to see them go."

Rod lifted his head a little. "Could you see all the way to Gratecieux's castle?"

"Aye; his towers are taller even than those of Their Royal Majesties. We can see only the battlements—yet we can see that much. Not that I had need to."

Rod frowned. "You mean they didn't even get that far?"

The Duchess nodded. "The sorcerer had marched out to meet him. Even when my lord set out, the sorcerer's forces already stood, drawn up and waiting, by a ravine midway betwixt the two castles. 'Tis as though he knew aforetime of my lord's coming."

"He did," Rod growled. "All witches and warlocks here are mind readers."

The Duchess looked up, surprised. Then her mouth tightened in exasperation. "Aye, certes. And I knew it. I had but to think—and I did not."

"It matters not," Gwen said quickly.

"Truth. What aid could I provide?" The Duchess spread her hands helplessly. "I could but watch. Yet though the sorcerer had magics, my lord the Duke had guile."

"Oh, really? You mean he managed to escape the ambush?"

"Aye, and drew them onto ground of his choosing. For they waited on the road, look you, with a wooded slope to the left, and a bank strewn with boulders on the right."

Rod nodded. "Good ambush country. What'd your husband do about the roadblock?"

"He saw it afar off, and marched his force off the road ere the slopes had begun to enfold it. Out into the open plain they went, and away toward Castle Gratecieux."

"Oh, nice." Rod grinned. "Go knock on the door while the army's out waiting for you." His opinion of Duke Romanov went up a notch. No matter; it had plenty of room.

"The sorcerer did not appreciate his wisdom," the Duchess assured Rod. "He marched his men posthaste out into the plain, to once again block my lord's path, and more men than had bestrode the road, burst from the trees and rock."

"Of course. Your husband knows an ambush point when he sees one—and it *is* nice to be proven right now and then, isn't it?"

The Duchess exchanged a wifely glance with Gwen.

Rod hurried. "I gather they did manage to cut him off."

"They did indeed; yet my lord's troops were drawn up in battle array, and fresh, whiles the sorcerer's straggled hard from a chase. Then they met, with a fearful clash of arms and a howling of men, that I could hear clearly over the leagues. And, at first, my lord's forces bore back the sorcerer's. Little could I see from my tower; but the coil of men did move away, and therefore did I know that the sorcerer retreated, and my lord did follow."

"Delightful! But I take it that didn't last?"

"Nay." She spread her hands. "I cannot tell why, or what did hap to change the tide of battle. I only know that the coil began to grow again, and swelled far too quickly. Thus I knew that my husband's forces did flee—in truth, that I did witness a rout. I stayed to see no more, but flew down to gather up my boys, and bundle them into the coach. I bade them keep the curtains close, and lie upon the floor; then turned I to old Peter, the groom, and I did cry, 'The coachman hath gone to fight by my lord's side! Up, old Peter, and aid us in our flight!' Yet he did not stir; he only glowered up at me, and spat at my feet. 'Not I,' he growled. 'Ne'er again shall I serve a lordling!'"

Rod didn't speak, but flint struck steel in his gaze.

Gwen saw, and nodded. "'Twas even so. The sorcerer's spells had reached out to entrap his mind."

"What did you do?" Rod asked the Duchess.

"I fled," the Duchess said simply. "I did not stay to seek another coachman, lest old Peter's surliness turn to malice. I had no wish to have spellbound creatures seek to drag me down. Nay, I sprang up on the box myself, and seized the whip. I attempted to crack it over the horses' heads, but it only whistled past them; yet that was enow, and they trotted forward. Through the gates and over the drawbridge I drove, with my heart in my throat, for fear the team would seize the bits, and run wild away; yet they trotted obediently, and I found that I had moved in barely ample time. For even as my coach's wheels roared onto the drawbridge, the portcullis shot down behind me with a crash, and the bridge beneath me began to tremble. As soon as I was clear, I did look back, and, surely, did see the bridge begin to rise."

"Yet thou wast free!" Gwen breathed.

The Duchess shook her head. "Nay, not yet. For as I raced away from the castle, I did see my lord's soldiers charging towards me with the sorcerer's men-at-arms hot on their heels. I knew I must pass near to their flight ere I could win free to the southward road; I prayed that our faithful men, seeing me, would turn to fight, and gain us that last vital moment in which to escape. Yet were my hopes dashed, for as they came nigh me, fire kindled in their eyes, and a dozen of them ran to catch my horses' reins, howling for my blood and my children's heads—they, who but minutes before had fought in our defense!" She buried her face in her hands, sobbing.

Gwen wrapped an arm around her, and murmured, "They did not know. I have broke this spell from two bands of men now, and thus can tell thee how it is: Their minds are put to sleep, and the thoughts that float above that slumber are not theirs. The men themselves, who swore thee faith and served thee well, do keep the faith they swore! If they are waked, and learn what their bodies did while their minds slept, they will be heart-struck, even as these." She nodded toward the soldiers gathered under the tree.

"Heart-struck, as am I!" the Duchess sobbed. "For when they are waked from their enchantment, what shall I say to them? 'That scar upon thy cheek is my own doing, but I did not truly mean to do it?' For, look thee, as they threw themselves at the horses' bits, I struck out with the whip, and scored them wheresoe'er I might—on their hands, their arms, their chests or, aye, even their faces! And they fell back, then they fell back . . ." Her voice dissolved into weeping again.

"You had no choice." Rod's voice was harsh.

"No choice, in truth!" Gwen cried. "Wouldst thou have let them drag thine horses to a halt, wrench ope thy carriage, and drag out thy bairns, to take to Alfar?"

The Duchess shuddered. "'Tis even as thou dost say." She caught her breath, swallowed, and nodded. "'Tis even so. I could not let them triumph."

"But Alfar did?"

"Oh, aye, of that am I certain—and my lord doth lie in the sleep of death! Or, if I am blessed, only battered and bloody, but alive in a dungeon! Ah, how shall I look into his eyes again, if ever he is freed, if ever we do meet again? For which, pray Heaven! Yet what shall I say? For I was not there to hold his castle against his return!"

"He was probably in chains before he came anywhere near home." Rod carefully didn't mention the alternative. "If I know Duke Romanov, he probably didn't even start the return trip."

Gwen nodded. "All the land doth know that thy husband would sooner die than flee, milady. Belike they dragged him down fighting, and bore him away to prison."

"Aye." She took a deep breath, and squared her shoulders. "Aye, that is most likely. He would not have even known his men had fled. And they would seek to capture him, no matter the cost—would they not? For surely, an imprisoned Duke is a mighty weapon! Yet I did flee."

"And thus he would have bade thee do!"

Rod nodded. "Yes, he would have. If he'd thought you might have stayed to fight against an enemy like *that,* he'd have been in a panic—and a less effective fighter for it; his fear for you would have shackled his sword arm." He shook his head. "No, knowing that you'd do everything you could to get the children to safety, if he lost the battle, was all that gave him a clear enough mind to fight the battle."

The Duchess sat still, head bowed.

"'Tis even as milord doth say," Gwen murmured, "and thou dost know it to be true. Thou art thyself the daughter of noblemen."

Slowly, then, the Duchess nodded. "Aye, 'tis true. I have done naught but my duty."

"And your lord will praise you for it," Rod assured her. "Bewail his loss—but don't bewail your own conduct. You know you did exactly as you should have."

The Duchess sighed, straightening and poising her head. "Indeed, 'tis true—yet I did need to hear one speak it anew. I thank thee, Lady Gallowglass—and thou, Lord Warlock." But her eyes were on Gwen's when her sudden smile showed.

Rod heaved a sigh of relief. "I take it you've been driving without a rest."

"Aye, the poor horses! Though I slowed to a walk as often as I dared—yet are the poor beasts near to foundering."

"They lasted." Rod turned to glance at the horses grazing. A couple had already dozed off. "It's a wonder, though—they must've been going for a whole day and night."

The Duchess nodded. "Less a few hours. We began our flight late in the afternoon."

Gwen caught Rod's eye, with a covert smile. He didn't hear her thoughts, but he didn't have to; they no doubt would've been something along the lines of: *Subtle as a nuclear blast.*

"Papa! PapaPapaPapaPapaPapa!"

Rod looked up, glad of the reprieve.

The children came pelting across the meadow—or at least, the Duchess's two did. Rod's brood behaved more like spears.

"Papa!" Javelin Geoffrey struck into him, and clung. Rod staggered back a step, caught his breath, and said, "Yes. What's so important that it can't wait a second?"

"Illaren's papa!" Geoffrey crowed. "We saw him!"

Illaren, the elder of the Duchess's children, nodded eagerly.

His mother sat galvanized.

"You *what?*" Rod caught his son under the shoulders and held him at arm's length. "Now, be very careful what you say, son. Remember, you could hurt people's feelings very badly, if you're making a mistake. . . . Now. You don't mean to tell me you just saw Duke Romanov *here,* do you?"

"Oh, no, Papa!" Geoffrey cried in disgust; and Magnus exploded. "'Twas last night, Papa—when we chased the warlock!"

"The nasty one, who threw rocks," Gregory chimed in. "Art thou mindful, Papa, of when he took thee to the dungeon?"

"Yes, I remember." Suddenly, vividly, in his mind's eye, Rod saw the prisoner shackled to the wall again. "You mean . . . the man in chains . . . ?"

"Aye! Wouldst thou not say, Papa, that he was . . ." He

turned to Illaren, nose wrinkling. "How didst thou picture thy father?"

"A great bear of a man," Illaren supplied.

"Aye!" Geoffrey whirled back to Rod. "With hair of so dark a brown 'twas near to black. And richly clad, with gilded armor!"

Rod nodded, faster and faster. "Yes . . . yes! Yes on the armor, too—what there was left of it, anyway."

"But that is Father!" cried the younger boy.

"Art thou certain!" The Duchess came to her feet, staggering.

Geoffrey stilled, staring at her, eyes huge. "In truth, we are."

"Dost thou truly mean . . ."

"They're right." Rod turned a grave face to her. "I didn't recognize him, at the time—but I should have. It *was* your husband, my lady Duchess. I'm sure of it."

She stood rigid, staring at him.

Then her eyes rolled up, and she collapsed.

Gwen stepped forward, and caught her in an expert grip. "Be not affrighted," she assured the two boys. "Thy mother doth but swoon—and 'tis from joy, not grief."

"But Illaren's papa is sorely hurted, Papa!" Magnus reminded Rod.

"Yes." Rod fixed his eldest with an unwavering stare. "He was hurt—and imprisoned. Remember that."

Magnus stared up at him, face unreadable.

"A Duke." Rod's tone was cold, measured. "With all his knights, with all his men-at-arms, with all his might, he was sorely wounded, captured, and imprisoned." He turned his head slowly, surveying his children. "Against a power that could do *that,* what could four children do? And what would happen to them?"

"But we are *witches!*" Cordelia cried.

"Warlocks!" Geoffrey's chin thrust forward.

"So," Rod said, "are they."

"They have come against us," Geoffrey cried, "and we have triumphed!"

"Yes—when there were six of us, and one of them. What's going to happen if we meet all of them together?" He stared into Geoffrey's eyes. "As the Duke did."

"We will *not* go back!" Cordelia stamped her foot.

Rod stiffened, his face paling. "You . . . will . . . do . . . as . . . I . . . tell you!"

Magnus's face darkened, and his mouth opened, but Gwen's hand slid around to cover it. "Children." Her voice was quiet, but all four stilled at the sound. Gwen looked directly into Rod's eyes. "I gave thy father my promise."

"*What* promise?" Cordelia cried.

"That if he did insist, we would go home." She raised a hand to still the instant tumult. "Now he doth insist."

Rod nodded slowly, and let his gaze warm as he looked at her.

"But, *Mama* . . ."

"Hush," she commanded, "for there is this, too—these horrors that the Duchess hath spoke of to me. Nay, children, 'tis even as thy father hath said—there is danger in the North, horrible and rampant. 'Tis no place for children."

Cordelia whirled on her. "But *you,* Mama . . ."

"Must come with thee, to see thee safely home," Gwen said, and her tone was iron. "Or dost thou truly say that I have but to bid thee 'Go,' and thou'lt return to Runnymede straightaway? That thou wouldst truly not seek to follow thy father, and myself, unseen?"

Cordelia clenched her fists and stamped her foot, glaring up at her mother with incipient mutiny, but she didn't answer.

Gwen nodded slowly. " 'Tis even as I thought." She lifted her gaze to Rod. "And there is this, too—I do not believe the Duchess and her sons are safe yet."

Rod nodded. "Very true."

Gwen nodded too, and turned back to the children. "We must needs guard them."

"But the soldiers . . ."

"Did lately chase them," Gwen reminded. "Who is to say the sorcerer's power may not reach down from the North to ensnare them again, and turn them 'gainst the Duchess and her boys?"

Illaren exchanged a quick, frightened look with his brother.

"But, Mama . . ." Geoffrey cried.

"Thou wilt do as thou art bid," Gwen commanded, "and thou wilt do it presently. Thou, whose care is ever the ordering of battles—wilt thou truly deny that the course of wisdom is to guard this family, and take them to King Tuan, to bear witness?"

Geoffrey glowered back up at her, then said reluctantly, "Nay. Thou hast the right of it, Mama."

"Doesn't she always," Rod muttered; but nobody seemed to hear him.

She turned to him. "We shall go, husband—even as thou dost wish."

"But Papa won't be safe!" Cordelia whirled to throw her arms around his midriff.

Rod hugged her to him, but shook his head. "I've faced danger without you before, children. There was even a time when I didn't have your mother along to protect me."

Magnus shook his head, eyes wide with alarm. "Never such danger as this, Papa. A vile, evil sorcerer, with a whole army of witches behind him!"

"I've gone into the middle of an army before—and I only had a dagger against all their swords, and worse. Much worse."

"Yet these are witches!"

"Yes—and I've got more than a mental dagger, to use against them." Rod held his son's eyes with a grave stare. "I think I can match their sorcerer, spell for spell and power for power—and pull a few tricks he hasn't even dreamed of, since he was a child." He hauled Magnus in against him, too. "No, don't worry about me this time. Some day, I'll probably meet that enemy who's just a little too much stronger than I am—but Alfar isn't it. For all his powers and all his nastiness, he doesn't really worry me that much."

"Nor should he."

Rod looked up to see his youngest son sitting cross-legged, apart from the huddle. "I think thou hast the right of it, Papa. I think this sorcerer's arm is thickened more with fear, than with strength."

"An that is so," said Geoffrey, "thou must needs match him and, aye, e'en o'ermatch him, Papa."

"Well." Rod inclined his head gravely. "Thank you, my sons. Hearing you say it, makes me feel a lot better." And, illogically, it did—and not just because his children had, when last came to last, become his cheering section. He had a strange respect for his two younger sons. He wondered if that was a good thing.

Apparently, Cordelia and Magnus felt the same way. They pried themselves away from Rod, and the eldest nodded. "If Gregory doth not foresee thy doom, Papa, it hath yet to run."

"Yes." Rod nodded. "Alfar's not my Nemesis." He turned back to Gregory. "What is?"

The child gazed off into space for a minute, his eyes losing focus. Then he looked at his father again, and answered, with total certainty, "Dreams."

8

The Duchess slapped the horses with the reins, and the coach creaked into motion as they plodded forward. They quickened to a trot, and the coach rolled away. Gwen turned back from her seat beside the Duchess, and waved. Four smaller hands sprouted up from the coach roof, and waved frantically too.

Rod returned the wave until they were out of sight, feeling the hollowness grow within him. Slowly, he turned back toward the North, and watched the soldiers moving away, bearing their wounded knight on a horse-litter. They had decided to go back into the sorcerer's army, disguised as loyal automatons. Gwen had told them how to hide their true thoughts with a surface of simulated hypnosis—thinking the standardized thoughts that all Alfar's army shared. She had also made clear their danger; Alfar would not look kindly on traitors. They understood her fully, every single man jack of them; but their guilt feelings ruled them, and they welcomed the danger as expiation. Rod watched them go, hoping he wouldn't meet any of them again until the whole rebellion had been squelched.

Somehow, he was certain that it would be. It was assinine to place faith in the pronouncements of a three-year-old—but his little Gregory was uncanny, and very perceptive.

Acting on the basis of his predictions would be idiocy—but he could let himself feel heartened by them. After all, Gregory wasn't your average preschooler.

On the other hand, just because he had a ten-year-old's vocabulary, didn't mean he had a general's grasp of the situation. Rod took his opinions the way he took a palm reading—emotionally satisfying, but not much use for helping decide what to do next. He turned to Fess, stuck a foot in the stirrup, and mounted. "Come on, Alloy Animal! Northward ho!"

Fess moved away after the departing squadron. "Where are we bound, Rod?"

"To Alfar, of course. But for the immediate future, find a large farmstead, would you?"

"A farmstead? What do you seek there, Rod?"

"The final touch in our disguise." But Rod wasn't really paying attention. His whole being was focused on the devastating, terrifying sensation of being alone, for the first time in twelve years. Oh, he'd been on his own before during that time—but never for very long, only a day or two, and he'd been too busy to think about it. But he had the time now—and he was appalled to realize how much he'd come to depend on his family's presence. He felt shorn; he felt as though he'd been cut off from his trunk and roots, like a lopped branch. There seemed to be a knot in his chest, and a numbing fear of the world about him. For the first time in twelve years, he faced that world alone, without Gwen's massive support, or the gaiety of his children—not to mention the very considerable aid of their powers.

The prospect was thoroughly daunting.

He tried to shake off the mood, throwing his shoulders back and lifting his chin. "This is ridiculous, Fess. I'm the lone wolf; I'm the man who penetrated the Prudential Network and overthrew its Foreman! I'm the knife in the dark, the vicious secret agent who brings down empires!"

"If you say so, Rod."

"I *do* say so, damn it! I'm *me*, Rod Gallowglass—not just a father and a husband! . . . No, damn it, I'm Rodney d'Armand! That 'Gallowglass' is just an alias I took when I came here, to help me look like a native! And Rodney d'Armand managed without Gwen and the kids for twenty-nine years!"

"True," Fess agreed. "Of course, you lived in your father's house for nineteen of them."

"All right, so I was only on my own for ten years! But that's almost as long as I've been married, isn't it?"

"Of course."

"Yes." Rod frowned. "On the other hand, it's *only* as long—isn't it?"

"That, too, is true."

"Yeah." Rod scowled. "Habit-forming little creatures, aren't they?"

"There, perhaps, you have touched the nub of it," the robot agreed. "Most people live their lives by habit patterns, Rod."

"Yeah—but they're *just* habits." Rod squared his shoulders again. "And you can always change your habits."

"Do you truly want to, Rod?"

"So when I get home, I'll change them back! But for the time being, I can't have them with me—so I'd better get used to it again. I can manage without them—and I will."

"Of course you will, Rod."

Rod caught the undertone in Fess's voice and glared at the back of his metal skull. "What's the 'but' I hear in there, Fess?"

"Merely that you will not be happy about it. . . ."

"Rod, no! This is intolerable!"

"Oh, shut up and reverse your gears."

The robot heaved a martyred blast of white noise and stepped back a pace or two. Rod lifted the shafts of the cart and buckled them into the harness he'd strapped onto Fess in place of a saddle.

"This is a severe debasement of a thoroughbred, Rod."

"Oh, come off it!" Rod climbed up to the single-board seat and picked up the reins. "You used to pilot a spaceship, Fess. That's the same basic concept as pulling a cart."

"No—it is analogous to *driving* a cart. And your statement is otherwise as accurate as claiming that a diamond embodies the same concept as a piece of cut plastic."

"Hairsplitting," Rod said airily, and slapped Fess's back with the reins.

The robot plodded forward, sighing, "My factory did not manufacture me to be a cart horse."

"Oh, stuff it! When my ancestors met you, you were piloting a miner's burro-boat in the asteroid belt around Sol! *I've* heard the family legends!"

"I know; I taught them to you myself," Fess sighed, again. "This is merely poetic justice. Northward, Rod?"

"Northward," Rod confirmed, "on the King's High Way. Hyah!" He slapped the synthetic horsehide with the reins again. It chimed faintly, and Fess broke into a trot. They swerved out of the dirt track onto the High Road in a two-wheeled cart, leaving behind a ragged yeoman gazing happily at the gold in his palm, and shaking his head at the foolishness of tinkers, who no sooner came by a bit of money, than they had to find something to spend it on.

As they trotted northward, Fess observed, "About your discussion with your wife, Rod..."

"Grand woman." Rod shook his head in admiration. "She always sees the realities of a situation."

"How are we defining 'reality' in this context, Rod?"

"We don't; it defines us. But you mean she was just letting me have my own way, don't you?"

"Not simply that," Fess mused. "Not in regard to anything of real importance."

"Meaning she usually talks me into doing things her way." Rod sat up straighter, frowning. "Wait a minute! You don't mean that's what she's done this time, too, do you?"

"No. I merely thought that you achieved her cooperation with remarkable ease."

"When you start using so many polysyllables, I know you're trying to tell me something unpleasant. You mean it was too easy?"

"I did have something of the sort in mind, yes."

"Well, don't worry about it." Rod propped his elbows on his knees. "It was short, but it wasn't really easy. Not when you consider all the preliminary skirmishes."

"Perhaps . . . Still, it does not seem her way . . ."

"No . . . If she thinks I'm going to lose my temper, she

stands firm anyway—unless she sees good reason to change her mind. And I think having given me a promise is a pretty good reason. But at the bottom of it all, Fess, I don't think I'm the one who convinced her."

"You mean the Duchess?"

Rod nodded. "Mother-to-mother communication always carries greater credibility, for a wife and mother."

"Come, Rod! Certainly you don't believe yourself incapable of convincing your wife of your viewpoint!"

"Meaning I think she won't listen to me?" Rod nodded. "She won't. Unless, of course, I happen to be right. . . ."

It wasn't hard to tell when they reached the border; there was a patrol there to remind him of it.

"Hold!" the sergeant snapped, as two privates brought their pikes down with a crash to bar the road.

Rod pulled in on the reins, doing his best to think like a crochety old farmer—indignant and resentful. "Aye, aye, calm thysen! I've held, I've held!"

"Well for thee that thou hast," the sergeant growled. He nodded to the two rankers. "Search." They nodded, and went to the back of the cart, to begin probing through the cabbages and bran sacks.

"'Ere! 'Ere! What dost thou?" Rod cried, appalled. "Leave my cabbages be!"

"'Tis orders, gaffer." The sergeant stepped up beside him, arms akimbo. "Our master, Duke Alfar, demands that we search any man who doth seek to come within the borders of Romanov."

Rod stared, appalled—and the emotion was real. So Alfar had promoted himself! "Duke Alfar? What nonsense is this? 'Tis Ivan who is Duke here!"

"Treason!" another private hissed, his pike leaping out level. Rod's fighting instincts impelled him to jump for the young man's throat—but he belayed them sternly, and did what a poor peasant would do: shrank back a little, but manfully held his ground. He stared into the boy's eyes, and saw a look that was intense, but abstracted—as though the kid wasn't quite all here, but wherever he was, he cared about it an awful lot.

Hypnoed into fanaticism.

The sergeant was grinning, and he had the same sort of shallow look behind the eyeballs. "Where hast thou been, gaffer? Buried in thy fields, with thine head stuck in a clod? Ivan is beaten and gaoled, and Alfar is now Duke of Romanov!"

"Nay, it cannot be!" But Rod eyed the soldiers' uniforms warily.

The sergeant saw the glance, and chuckled in his throat. "Aye. 'Tis Alfar's livery." He scowled past Rod. "Hast thou not done yet? 'Tis a cart, not a caravan!"

Rod turned to look, and stared in horror.

"Aye, we've done." The troopers straightened up. "Naught here, Auncient."

"Nay, not so," Rod snapped. "I've still a few turnips left. Hadst thou not purses large enow for all on't?"

"None o' yer lip," the sergeant growled. "If thou hast lost a few cabbages, what matter? Thou hast yet much to sell at the market in Korasteshev."

"Why dost thou come North?" demanded one of the men-at-arms—the one with the quick pike.

Rod turned to him, suddenly aware of danger. He gazed at the trooper, his eyes glazing, as the world he saw became a little less than real, and his mind opened to receive impressions. What was really going on behind the soldier's face?

He felt a pressure, almost as though someone were pressing a finger against his brain. Mentally, he stilled, becoming totally passive. He sensed the differences in the minds around him; it was like smelling, as though each mind gave off its own aroma.

But four of them were all thinking the same thought: *Stop those who flee, to make Alfar stronger and greater.* However, someone coming into the Duchy was very boring. He was no threat—just more potential, just one more mind that would help magnify Alfar's glory.

But the fifth mind was alive and alert, and teeming with suspicion. A dozen questions jammed up at its outlet, demanding to be asked. Underneath them lay the suspicion that the stranger might be a spy or, worse, an assassin. And at the bottom of the mind writhed a turmoil of unvoiced thoughts, all rising from a brew of emotions: ambition, suspicion, shame, anger, hatred. Rod carefully suppressed a shudder, and bent all his efforts toward thinking like a peasant farmer. He was a rough, unlettered country man, who labored twelve hours a day on his lord's fields, and four hours a day on his own—the four to raise a cash crop that could all be fitted into one small cart. Of course, he tried hard to get the most money he could, for all that work—the small, additional amount that would make the difference between poverty, and an adequate living for himself and his family during the winter. What did these arrogant bastards mean by trying to keep him from Duke Romanov's fat market in Korasteshev! And where did they get the idea to act so high and mighty? Just because they were wearing leather armor and carrying pikes! Especially when anyone could see that, under the green and brown uniforms, they were dirt peasants, like himself—probably less. Probably mere serfs, and the sons of serfs.

The soldier shifted impatiently. "Tell, peasant! Why dost thou seek to come into—"

"Why, t' sell m' bran 'n' cabbages 'n' turnips," Rod answered. "Dosta think I'd wast m' horse for a day's pleasure?"

The sentry ignored the question. "You're Earl Tudor's man," he growled. "Why not sell in Caernarvon? Why come North all the way to Korasteshev?"

"'Tis not 'all the way,'" Rod snorted. "I live scarce three leagues yon." He nodded toward the road behind him. "Korasteshev is closer for me." He glared at the trooper—but he let his mind dwell hungrily on the thought of the prices he could get in Korasteshev. Everyone knew Duke Romanov's barons were fighting among themselves—and the more fool the Duke, for letting them! And every peasant knew that, when armies fought, crops got trampled. Nay, surely the folk in Korasteshev would be paying far more for cabbages than those in Earl Tudor's peaceful Caernarvon!

The soldier's face relaxed. *So, the cranky old codger's greedy! Well and good—greed, we know how to deal with. . . .*

Rod just barely managed to restrain a surge of indignation. Old?!? Codger, okay—but, *old?* He diverted the impulse into suspicious fuming: Who was this bare-cheeked brat, to be asking *him* questions? Why, he was scarcely done suckling his mother's milk!

He was gratified to see the young man redden a little—but the boy's suspicion wasn't quite finished yet. He ran a trained eye over Fess. "How comes a poor dirt farmer to have so fine a horse?"

Panic! Anxiety! The one thing that men might really blame him for. Rod had been caught. And hard on the heels of that emotion, came a surge of shame. He glanced at Fess. *Eh, my wife was beautiful, ten years agone! Small wonder that Sir Ewing took notice of her....*

He turned back to the young man. "Sir Ewing gave him to me, saying he was too old to bear an armored knight still."

The suspicion was still there in the young soldier's mind; it just changed direction. The young man was trying to find a flaw in the story. "Why would a knight give even a cast-off charger to a poor peasant?"

The shame again. Rod let it mount, burning. "Why, for ...favors...we did him, me and mine." *Mostly 'mine.'* There was a brief, lurid image of a strapping, tow-headed man in bed with a voluptuous young woman, with chestnut hair—not that you could see much else of her...and the vision was gone. But the shame remained, and rage mounted under it. "For favors." Rod's face had turned to wood. "Not that 'tis any affair of thine."

"'Affair,' is it?" The young man let a mocking grin spread. "Aye, thine 'affair' now, is only the selling of thy cabbages, I warrant." He turned to the sergeant. "Why do we linger, wasting time on this peasant, Auncient?"

"Why, for that he hath not set his horse to going," the sergeant growled. "Be off with thee, fellow! Get thy cart out from our station! Get thee hence to the market!"

"Aye—and I thank thy worships," Rod said sourly. He turned away and slapped the reins on Fess's back—but very gently, to avoid the metallic ring. Fess started up again, plodding away.

Rod kept a tight rein on his thoughts. It was such a huge, aching temptation to indulge himself in speculation! But he was certainly still in range of the young telepath, and would be for several miles at least—even if the kid's powers were weak. And if they were strong...No, Rod kept a steady mental stream of embarrassment and anger seething. That the young bastard should have subjected him to such personal questions! What a filthy mind he must have! And where did such a low-born serf's son get any right to be questioning *him,* old Owen, about his comings and goings?

Underneath that surface spate, in bursts of pure thought not encoded into words, boiled the host of questions. Interesting, that the ranker had asked the questions, and the sergeant hadn't even seemed to notice that his authority was being usurped. Interesting, that the sorcerer's sentries would pose as underlings; they had, at least, some craftiness in their disguises. That the young warlock was one of those who had volunteered to work for Alfar, completely willingly, Rod had no doubt; the youngster clearly had the inferiority complex and paranoia of the persecuted witchling grown to manhood—and the ambition that stemmed from it. Inwardly, Rod shuddered—if he'd been Alfar, he'd never have been able to sleep easily, knowing that his underlings would very cheerfully have sliced him to bits and taken his place.

On the other hand, the fact that they hadn't indicated that Alfar was either an extremely powerful old esper, or was surrounded by a few henchmen who were genuinely loyal. Or both.

But the chance that telepaths were constantly running surveillance over the duchy, was just too high. Rod couldn't afford to take chances. His concentration might falter at just the moment that one of the sentry-minds happened to be listening to the area he was in. He had to take more thorough mental precautions.

Accordingly, he let the tension from the confrontation at the border, begin to ebb away, and began to relax—as "old" Owen, of course. *What does it matter, what the fuzz-cheeked brat said? I'm in Romanov—and I can sell my crop for that much greater price! But my, it's been a long day!* He'd been up before dawn, Owen had—as he always was, of course; but travelling was more wearying than threshing. His eyelids were sagging. How nice it would be, to nap for a bit—just a little bit! Maybe the half of an hour, or so. In fact, he was beginning to nod. It wasn't safe, driving when he was so sleepy. Nay, surely he'd better nap.

So he steered the cart off to the side of the road, reined

the horse to a stop, lashed the reins to the top bar of the
cart, clambered over the seat into the back, and found himself a small nest among his baskets. The boards weren't too
much harder than his pallet at home—and at least he could
lean back.

He let his head loll, eyes closing, letting the drowsiness
claim him, letting his thoughts darken and grow still. . . .

"Rod."

Rod jolted upright, blinking, hauling his mind out of the
fringes of the web of sleep. "Huh? Wha? Wha's'a mattuh?"

"Did you intend to doze, Rod?"

"Who, me? Ridiculous!" Rod snorted. "Just putting on
a very good act. Well . . . okay, maybe I got carried away. . . ."

"As you wish, Rod." Fess was peacefully nibbling at the
roadside grass. Rod made a mental note to dump the robot's
wastebasket. For the time being, of course, Fess's act was
as necessary as Rod's.

Of course, he did have to keep it an act. He lay back
against a bran sack, closed his eyes, and let drowsiness
claim him again, let the surface of his mind flicker with the
images of Owen's imaginary day.

Underneath, he tried to remember what had happened
inside his head when he had first come to Gramarye, how
it had felt.

He remembered the shock when he had found out that
someone was reading his mind. He had been eyeing one of
the teenaged witches with admiration, speculating about her
measurements, when she had gasped, and turned to glare
at him. He remembered how embarrassed he'd been, and
the clamoring panic inside as he realized someone could
read his mind. Worse, that any of the Gramarye "witches"
could—and that there were dozens of them, at least!

But by the time he'd met Gwen, only a week or so later,
she hadn't been able to read his thoughts. For nine years,
that had been the one mar on an otherwise blissful marriage.
There had been spats, of course, and there had been the
constant, underlying tension that always stems from two
people trying to make one life together; but the loving re-
assurance she'd had every reason to look forward to, the
warmth of being able to meld her mind with her husband's,
just hadn't been there. That had put a continuing, unspoken

strain on the marriage, with Gwen hiding feelings of having been cheated—not by Rod, but by life—and Rod trying less successfully to bury his feelings of inferiority.

Then, when the family had been kidnapped to the land of Tir Chlis in an alternative universe, Rod had encountered his analog, the alternate High Warlock, Lord Kern—who was very much like Lord Gallowglass, enough so to be Rod's double. But there had been some major differences under the skin—such as Kern's roaring temper. And huge magical powers—one of which was the ability to blend his mind with Rod's, to lend him Kern's powers. That had wakened Rod's own slumbering esper powers—and afflicted him with a hair-trigger temper. Fortunately, it had also roused a mind reading ability he'd never suspected he'd had. And, suddenly, Gwen had been able to read his mind; he'd no longer been telepathically invisible.

So, if he had been open to mind reading when he came to Gramarye, but had been telepathically invisible when he'd met Gwen, his mind had probably closed itself off in that first panic of embarrassment, finding out that somebody could read his thoughts when he most definitely hadn't wanted her to.

Of course, when the girl got done looking indignant, she *had* looked rather pleased. . . .

He tried to remember how he had felt at that moment, and caught it—exposed, vulnerable. Being so open was intolerable; he couldn't allow other people to know so much about him, that they might be able to use to hurt him. He couldn't let them have the advantage of knowing what he was going to do, before he did it.

He could feel himself pulling back, withdrawing, pulling inward, politely but firmly closing himself off, locking out the rest of the world. He would smile, he would still interact with them—but they could not, would not, know his inner self. . . .

He came out of the reverie with an inward shudder. With an attitude like that, it was amazing his marriage had lasted the first nine years. On second thought, knowing Gwen, it was understandable; he hoped he'd made it up to her, since then.

By turning into a howling demon whenever a few things

went wrong all at the same time?

Be fair, he told himself, frowning. If she'd rather have him emotionally open, she had to accept everything that implied. Could he help it if, underneath the mask, he wasn't really a very nice guy?

Now he was being unfair to himself. Wasn't he? Surely there had to be a way to be open, without going berserk every so often.

There had to be, and he'd get busy searching for it—as soon as the current crisis was out of the way.

He stilled, suddenly remembering that his technique might not have worked. He might not have managed to regain his telepathic invisibility; he might still be exposed to passing telepaths.

So he sat very still, letting his mind open up, eyes still closed in mock slumber. He let his thoughts slumber, too, let them idle into dreams, while his mind opened up to all and any impressions.

He didn't hear a thought.

He would've believed there wasn't a thinking being for a hundred miles—and it wasn't just human thoughts that were missing, either. When he concentrated on mind reading this way, he always heard a continuing background murmur of animal minds—simple, vivid emotions: hunger, rage, desire. Even earthworms radiated sharp, intense little spikes of satisfaction as they chewed their way cheerfully through the dirt.

But not now. Either the worms had plowed into sandy soil, or his mind was closed off from both directions. He couldn't hear anything—not the background murmur, not the defiance of a skylark, nothing. He felt as though a vital part of him had been chopped off, that he was less than he had been. After three years as a telepath, this was a sudden, devastating impoverishment.

But it was necessary. Without it, he'd very quickly be detected and, shortly thereafter, be dead.

He felt a little better, after that realization. No, he decided, mental deafness was definitely preferable to permanent sleep. Besides, the 'deafness' was only temporary.

He hoped.

He shrugged off the thought, and cranked his eyelids open

just enough to see through the lashes. The road was clear, as far as he could see. Of course, someone might be coming up behind him, so he kept up the act: He sat up slowly, blinking around him as though he couldn't remember where he was. Then he lifted his head, as though remembering, smiled, yawned, and stretched. He leaned forward, elbows on knees, and blinked at the scenery around him while he waited for his body to come awake. Finally, Owen reached down to untie the reins, sat up, and clucked to his horse, giving his back a light (very light) slap. The horse lifted his head, looked back to see his master awake, then turned front again and leaned into the horsecollar. The wagon creaked, groaned, and clattered back onto the High Road again.

As the wooden wheels rolled away on the paving stones, Rod worked at fighting down a rising fear—that, when this struggle with renegade espers was over, he might not be able to come out of his shell again, might be permanently maimed mentally, and never again able to be fully with his family. "It's done, Fess. I've closed my mind off. The rest of the world is telepathically invisible to me."

"And you to it?" Fess sounded surprised. "Wasn't that a bit drastic, Rod?"

"Yes—but in a land of hostile telepaths, I think it was necessary."

The robot was silent for a few hoofbeats, then nodded slowly. "It is a wise course, Rod. Indeed, I would have counselled it, if you had asked me."

Rod caught the implied reproach. "I couldn't, though— not while an enemy telepath might have been able to read my mind." He was silent for a few seconds, then added, "It's scary, Fess."

"I can understand that it would be, Rod, after three years as a telepath. But I should think Alfar would be even more frightening."

"What, him?" Rod shrugged. "Not really. I mean, if worst comes to worst and I don't come back, Tuan will start marching."

"A rather gruesome interpretation. What *do* you fear, Rod?"

"Being stuck here, inside myself." Rod shuddered. "And not being able to unlock my mind again."

9

The sun was low, ahead and to the left, bathing the road, and the dusty leaves that bordered it, in an orange glow that made the whole world seem somewhat better than it really was—and Rod began to relax as he gazed at it. It was a magical road, somehow, twisting away through gilded leaves to some unguessable, wonderful faery world ahead.

Around the turn, a man cried out in alarm, and a chorus of bellowing shouts answered him. Quarterstaves cracked wood on wood, and clanked on iron.

Rod stared, snapping out of his reverie. Then he barked "Charge!" and Fess sprang into a gallop. The cart rattled and bumped behind him, melons and cabbages bouncing out into the roadway. Rod swerved into the turn with one wheel off the ground—and saw a gray-haired man whirling a quarterstaff high, low, from side to side, blocking the furious blows of three thick-bodied, shag-haired thugs with five-day beards. Two of them had iron caps—which was just as well, since they weren't very good with their staves. Even as Rod watched, the gray-head managed to crack his staff down on one of their skulls. The man howled and flinched back, pressing a hand to his head; then, reassured that he wasn't injured, he roared and leaped back into the fight, flailing a huge, windmilling arc of a blow that would

137

have pulverized anything in its way. But the older man's staff snapped out at an angle, blocking the blow—and the thug's stick shot down the smooth wood, straight toward the victim's knuckles. The traveller's staff pushed farther, though, coming around in a half circle, and the thug's stick plowed into the ground. By that time, the other end of the older man's staff was swinging up to block a short, vicious blow from the thug on the other side.

Anger flared in Rod, the smoldering resentment of injustice. "Anybody that good has *earned* help!" Rod snapped. "We can't let him be killed just because he's outnumbered! *Never!*"

Fess's hooves whipped into a blur that no real horse could have managed. Rod swung his whip back, fighting against his own anger to withhold the blow until the right moment.

A handful of soldiers broke through the screen of brush at the roadside, riding into view from a woodland track.

Rod hauled on Fess's reins—not that the horse needed it; but it helped Rod to force down his anger, contain the frustration at not striking out. "Hold it, Fess! Company's coming. Maybe we'd better leave this goodman to natural processes."

The sergeant saw the fracas, swung his arm in an overhand circle that ended pointing toward the thugs, and shouted as he kicked his mount into a gallop. His troopers bellowed an answer, and their horses leaped into a charge.

The thugs were making too much noise to hear, until the soldiers were only thirty feet away. Then one of them looked up and shouted. The other two turned, stared for one moment of panic, then whirled and plunged into the underbrush with howls of dismay.

The sergeant reined in just in front of the older man.

"I thank thee, Auncient." The traveler bowed, leaning on his staff. "They'd have stripped me bare and left me for wolf-meat!"

"Nay, certes! We could not allow such work, could we, then?" The sergeant grinned to his men for a chorus of agreement, and turned back to the traveler. "Such goods as wayfarers own, are ours to claim." He leaned down, shoving an open palm under the traveler's nose. "Thy purse, gaffer!"

The older man stared at him, appalled. Then he heaved

a sigh, and untied his purse from his belt. He set it in the sergeant's hand. "Take it, then—and surely, I owe thee what I can give, for thy good offices."

"Dost thou indeed?" The sergeant straightened, opening the purse with a sly grin. But it faded quickly to a scowl of indignation, as he looked into the little bag. He glared down at the traveler. "Here, now! What manner of jest is this?"

"Why, naught!" the traveler said, surprised. "What few coins I have, are there!"

"Few indeed." The sergeant upended the purse, and five copper coins clinked into his palm. He growled and tossed them into the dust. "Come, then! None take to the road without a few shillings at least, to provide for themselves."

The older man shook his head. "I had no more—and my daughter's near to term with her first. I must be there; she'll have need of me."

"She will, indeed," the sergeant growled, "and thou'lt be wanting." He nodded to his men. "Strip him, and slash his clothes. We'll find shillings, though they be within his flesh."

The traveler stepped back, horrified, as the soldiers crowded in, chuckling. Then his face firmed with resignation, and his staff lifted.

"Seize him!" the sergeant barked.

"So much for natural processes." Rod's anger surged up, freed. "*Now,* Fess!"

The great black horse sprang forward.

One of the soldiers chopped down at the traveler with his pike; but his victim's quarterstaff cracked against the pike-shaft, and it swerved, crashing into the shield of the trooper next to him. "Here now!" the man barked, and swung his own axe.

"Nay, nay!" the sergeant cried in disgust. "Is one lone . . ."

A bellow of rage drowned him out, and his eyes bulged as Rod's whip wrapped itself around his throat. Rod yanked back as Fess crashed into a trooper, and the sergeant shot out of his saddle. The trooper screamed as his horse went flying. Fess slammed into another horse, reaching for its rider with steel teeth, as Rod turned to catch up a club he'd hidden among the grain sacks, and whirled it straight-armed

down at the steel cap of a third trooper with a bellow of
fury. The blow rang like the parish bell on a holy day, and
the soldier slumped to the ground, his helmet flying off.
Fess tossed his head as he let go of the second trooper's
arm, and the man spun flying to slam into a tree. Rod turned,
just as the fourth trooper hit the ground. The traveler's staff
rose, and fell with a dull thud. Rod winced, his rage ending
as suddenly as it had begun, transmuting into leaden chagrin.
He looked about him at the three fallen men. He fought
against it. He'd been right, damn it! And none of them were
really hurt. Nothing permanent, anyway . . .

Then he turned, and saw the older man looking up, panting, eyes white-rimmed, staff leaping up to guard again.

Rod dropped the reins and held his hands up shoulder-
high, palms open. "Not me, gaffer! I'm just here to help!"

The staff hung poised as the battle tension ebbed from
the traveler's muscles. Finally, he lowered his guard, and
smiled. "I give thee thanks, then—though I'm no one's
'gaffer.'"

"Not yet, maybe—but you will be, soon." Rod forced
a weak smile. "I couldn't help overhearing."

"Nay, I think thou didst attempt such hearing—and I
thank thee for it." The traveler grounded the butt of his
staff, and held out his hand.

"I am called Simon, and my village is Versclos."

"I am, uhhh . . ." Rod leaned down to shake Simon's
hand, groping frantically to remember the name he'd used
for his "old farmer" act. "Call me Owen. Of Armand."

"Owen of Armand?" Simon lifted an eyebrow. "I've not
heard of that village."

"It's far from here—to the south." *Galactic south, anyway.*

"I thank thee for thy good offices, Owen of Armand."
Simon's handclasp was warm and firm. "Indeed, had it not
been for thee . . ." He broke off suddenly, staring.

Rod frowned.

Simon lifted his head with a jolt and gave it a quick
shake. "Nay, pardon! My mind wanders. Had it not been
for thee, these liveried bandits would have stripped me
bare—and sin' that there were no shillings for them to
find . . ."

Rod's mouth thinned and hardened. "They probably would have stripped you down to your skin, then used their knives to look for pockets."

"I do not doubt it." Simon turned toward the soldiers. "Yet 'tis not their doing. They labor under a wicked enchantment. Come, we must attend to them." And he turned away, to kneel down by one of the troopers, leaving Rod with a puzzled frown. That had been rather abrupt—and, polite though he was, Simon had very obviously been trying to change the subject. What had he suddenly seen in Rod, that had so offended him? "Odd victim we have, here," he muttered.

"Odd indeed," Fess agreed. "To judge by his vocabulary and bearing, one would think him too well-qualified to be a road wanderer."

Rod lifted his head slowly. "Interesting point . . . Well, let's give him a hand." He lashed the reins around the top bar of the cart and swung down to the ground.

Simon was kneeling by the sergeant, hand on the man's shoulder, but still holding to his staff with the other. He stared into the man's face, frowning, head cocked to the side, as though he were listening. Rod started to ask, then saw the abstracted glaze in Simon's eyes, and managed to shut his mouth in time to keep the words in. He'd seen that same look in Gwen's face too many times to mistake it—especially since he'd seen it in all his children's faces, too, now and then—especially Gregory's. Exactly what was going on, Rod didn't know—but it was certainly something psionic.

The sergeant's eyes opened. He blinked, scowling against pain, then sat up, massaging his throat. "What hast thou . . ." Then his eyes widened in horror. "Nay, I! what have *I* done to *thee?*"

Rod relaxed, reassured. The sergeant had his conscience back.

The man's eyes lost focus as he took a quick tour back through memory. "I have . . . nay, I have oppressed . . . I have murdered! Eh, poor folk!" He squeezed his eyes shut, face clenched in pain. "I have seen these hands cut down fleeing peasants, then steal what few coins they had! I have heard mine own voice curse at villagers, and hale forth their sons to serve in the sorcerer's army! I have . . ."

"Done naught." Simon spoke sternly, but without anger, his voice pitched and hardened to pierce the sergeant's remorse. "Be of good cheer, Auncient—for thou didst labor under enchantment. Whilst thy mind slumbered, ensorceled, thy body moved at the bidding of another. His commands were laid in thee, and thy body remembered, and governed its actions by his orders. Whatsoe'er thou dost recall thine hands doing, or thy voice crying, 'twas not thine own doing, but Alfar's."

The sergeant looked up, hope rising in his gaze.

Rod held his face carefully impassive. Interesting, very interesting, that Simon knew the nature of the spell. Even more interesting, that he could break it.

Which meant, of course, that he was a telepath. And which meant that the startled look he had given Rod, was because he saw a man before him, but didn't sense a mind to go with it. Rod could understand his amazement; he'd felt the same way a few times, himself. . . .

It also raised the interesting question of how Simon had escaped Alfar's dragnet. Or did the sorcerer routinely leave witches and warlocks free to roam about the countryside, even though they hadn't signed up with him? Somehow, Rod doubted it.

The sergeant gave Simon a glance up from the depths of despair. "What nonsense dost thou speak? When could so vile a spell have been laid upon me?"

"Why, I cannot tell," the traveler answered, "for I was not there. Yet, think—'twas in all likelihood hard after a battle, when thou hadst been taken prisoner."

The sergeant's eyes widened, and he turned away, but he was not seeing the roadside, nor the trees. "Aye, the battle . . . Our gallant Duke led us against the sorcerer's vile army, and they fought poorly, advancing on us with pikes lowered, but with their gazes fixed. 'Twas daunting, for their pikes never varied, nor the even tread of their feet; but our Duke cried, 'Why, they are puppets! And they can do only what their master wills, when he pulls their string. Onward, brave hearts—for he cannot govern a thousand separate fights!' And he lowered his lance, charging straight toward the foe. We took heart with a shout and followed, and 'twas even as he said, for we had but to sidestep the pikes. Though the men behind them sought to follow, we could move faster, and step through to stab and cut. Thus the sorcerer's army began to give ground—not through retreat, but through being forced back bodily.

"But something vile and huge struck at us from the sky with a scream and, of a sudden, the air was filled with flying rocks. Sheets of fire enveloped our army, and we cried out in fear. Daunted, we gave ground, and the sorcerer's troops strode after, to follow.

"Then, of a sudden, the man in front of me turned, with a strange look in his eye—eerie and fey. 'Turn, man!' I cried, and stabbed past him with my pike, knocking aside a blow that would have slain him. 'Turn, and fight for thy Duke!' 'Nay,' quoth he, 'for what hath the duke done ever, save to take from us as much, and return as little, as he might? I shall fight for the sorcerer now!' And he raised his pike to strike at me. Yet whatever spell held him, it had slowed him. I stared in horror at what I had heard him say, then saw his pike sweeping down at me. I struck it aside; but all about me, the Duke's soldiers in the front of the army were turning to strike at their comrades behind. In an instant, I was hard put to defend myself—yet 'twas from men of mine own livery! Distant behind them, I saw the Duke on his tall horse, surrounded by pikes; yet those at his back, that jabbed at his armor, were held by his own men! He turned, roaring in rage, and his sword chopped in a half circle, reaping pike-heads like corn; yet a dozen sprang up for every one that fell.

"Then, of a sudden, there was a fellow who floated in midair, above the Duke, who dropped a noose about our lord and cast loops of rope to follow it, binding his arms to his sides. He roared in anger, but the warlock shot away from him, jerking him from his horse. He crashed down below the hedge of pikes, and I cried out in despair, striking out with my own pike, blocking the blades about me; yet a heaviness crept over me. I struggled against it and, praise Heaven, felt anger rise to counter; yet even so, the heaviness grew greater and greater. I scarce seemed to feel the pike in my hands. Then all darkened about me, as though I had fallen asleep." Slowly, he lifted his head, looking up at

Simon. "I recall no more of the battle."

Simon nodded. "Belike thou, in thy turn, didst turn upon thy comrades behind. Yet be of good cheer; for they, belike, fell also under the spell. What else dost thou recall?"

"Why..." The soldier turned away again, his eyes glazing. "Only brief snatches. I am mindful of marching in the midst of a troop, a thousand strong or more. The sorcerer's livery bounded its rim, with those of us who wore the Duke's colors within; and in our center rode our great Duke himself, his helmet gone, a bloody rag tied about his head—and his arms bound behind him!" He squeezed his eyes shut, bowing his head. "Alas, my noble lord!"

"Buck up!" Rod reached out to clasp the man's shoulder. "At least he's still alive."

"Aye, verily! For he did glare about him, cursing!" The sergeant's eyes glittered. "Ah, gallant Duke! Him the spell could not entrap!"

"He's a strong-willed man," Rod agreed. "What else do you remember?"

"Why... coming home." The sergeant's mouth tightened. "Eh, but what manner of homecoming was this? For I saw an armed band haling milord Duke away to his own dungeons. Then, with wild cheering, all soldiers turned, to welcome the sorcerer Alfar as he rode through the gates in a gilded coach—and I, I was one of them!"

"What did he look like?" Rod demanded.

The sergeant shook his head. "I cannot truly say. 'Twas naught but a brief glimpse 'twixt the curtains of a rolling coach, as he went by. A slight man, with a flowing beard and a velvet hat. No more could I tell thee."

Simon nodded. "And after that?"

"After? Why—the guardroom. And those of us who wore the Duke's livery had no weapons. Yet we played at dice, and quaffed wine, the whiles they who wore the sorcerer's livery took us, one by one, away, and brought us back wearing Alfar's colors." His face worked; he spat.

"What happened when you were taken away?" Rod asked gently.

The sergeant shrugged. "I went willingly; wherefore not? The sorcerer was all-wise and good; assuredly his folk could not harm me!" His mouth tightened, as though he'd tasted

bitterness. "They took me, one soldier on either side, their
pikes in their hands, though there was no need for such."

"And wither did these two take thee?"

"To the chamber of the Captain of the Watch; yet 'twas
not he who waited there within. And I would not have known
the place, for 'twas darkened, and filled with sweet aromas.
A candle burned on a table, and they sat me in a chair beside
it, the whiles the door closed behind. 'Twas all dark then,
and I could see that one sat across from me; yet I could not
tell his face nor colors, for they were lost in shadow. 'Sleep,'
he bade me, 'sleep well. Thou hast fought hard; thou hast
fought bravely. Thou hast earned thy reward of slumber.'

Thus he spake; and truly, mine eyes did close, and darkness folded about me, and 'twas warm and comforting."

He looked up, blinking. "The rest, thou hast heard. I have
but now waked from that slumber. What I remember, I recall
as though 'twere a dream."

"What was the dream?" Rod frowned, intent. "What
happened after they hyp–, uh, put your mind to sleep?"

The sergeant shrugged. "Naught. We lazed about the
guardroom for a day, mayhap two, and all the talk was of
the excellence of the sorcerer, and how well-suited to the
duchy would be his rule.

"Then, of a sudden, the captain cried, 'To horse!' and
we ran for our weapons. 'The peasant folk flee,' cried he.
'They have taken to the roads; southwards they wander, to
bear treacherous words to Earl Tudor and King Loguire.
Out upon them, barracks scum! Out upon them, and haul
t'.em back or slay them were they stand!' And out we rushed,
to horse and to road, and away to the South we thundered,
galloping, seeking poor folk to slaughter." He squeezed his
eyes shut, pressing his hand over his eyes. "Alas, poor souls!
What guilt was theirs? Only that they sought to shield their
wives and bairns from war and evil! What fault was theirs,
that earned so harsh a reward?" He lifted his gaze to the
traveler, and his eyes were wide and haunted. "For we found
them, a single family; and we found a dozen such, one by
one; and one by one, we slew them. Our swords whirled,
cleaving through blood and bone, flinging wide a spray of
crimson. Then, when all the corpses lay pooling all their
scarlet gore together in a single pond, we did dismount, slit

their purses, and search their bodies, to carry away what few coins they had hoarded, to bear back to Alfar the sorcerer." He buried his face in his hands. "Ay me! How shall I live, with such pictures seared upon my brain?" He turned to Rod. "But we have plunder—aye, booty rich indeed! For every peasant family had a coin or two—and we have thirty shillings! A pound, and half again! Wealth indeed, to hale home to Alfar!" He threw back his head, and howled, "A curse upon the man, and all his minions! A curse upon one who could do such evil to his fellow man! And curses, too, upon the witches who do serve him—on all witches, for surely such evil lies in all their hearts!"

"Nay, not so!" Simon spoke sternly. "'Tis only this handful of miserable recreants who do evil to their fellow men! Belike they are unable to gain fellowship of other men and women, and blame their loneliness not on themselves, but on the other folk, who do not befriend them. I doubt me not an they do tell themselves the goodfolk envy them their magic, and therefore spurn all witches. Thus do they reason out some license for themselves to steal, and lord it over other folk."

Rod was impressed. He hadn't expected such insight, in an average yeoman.

Neither had the sergeant. He stared up at Simon, wide-eyed. "How well thou dost know them!"

"As well I should." Simon's mouth tightened at the corners. "For I am myself a warlock. But!" He held up a palm, to stop the sergeant's startled oath. "But like the greater number of my fellows, I have learned the ways of hiding all my powers, and deal with other folk as well as any man. I have had a wife who was not a witch. Together, we reared children who, though they had some Power, learned well to hide it, and have grown up in the liking of their fellows. We do not seek for power; we do not seek for wealth. We have already what we most care for—the good regard of others."

The sergeant's mouth went crooked. "An thou hast so deep a regard for we humble common folk, why canst thou not ward us from these evil ones?"

"Why, so they did," Simon answered, "those warlocks and witches who had real power. I knew one crone who was a healer—many had she mended in both mind and body; and I have known warlocks, gentle men who did speak with those whose minds were laboring in confusion, or disarranged, and led them out into the light of sanity again. But I myself?" He shrugged. "My powers were never so great. I have known warlocks who can disappear, and appear again some miles distant, and I have heard of some who can make their thoughts be heard in others' minds—aye, even those who are not witches. But I?" He shook his head, with a sad smile. "I am none of these. I have power, aye; yet it is weak and feeble—enough to prevent my being a man, like other men, yet not enough to make me a warlock like to other warlocks. Neither fish nor flesh, I know not where to nest. Oh, I can hear what others think if they are near to me—but that is all. I did not know I could do more..." his smile hardened, "...until Alfar did bind with his spell, boys from mine own village—and they did drop their hoes, and turn to march away toward his castle, for his army, I doubt not. I ran after one, and caught him by the arm. 'Whither dost thou go?' I cried; but he turned sneering to me, and raised his fist, to strike me away. Yet..." and Simon's lips curved in a small smile, "...I have some skill in arms. I fended off his blow, and struck ere he could draw his fist again, and I did stretch the poor lad senseless upon the road. And whiles he lay thus, unwillingly in slumber, I knelt beside him, frantic in my need, crying out to him, 'Wake! Dost'a not see thou art ensorceled?' For this was my neighbor's son, look you, who had been my children's playfellow. I could not stand aside to let the sorcerer take him while breath yet passed within my lungs. With every grain of my poor, puny witch power, I did seek to reach and wake his slumbering mind, where it lay 'neath Alfar's spell."

The sergeant stared at him, round-eyed. "And did he waken?"

Simon nodded, closing his eyes. "He did. Praise Heaven, for he did. And when his body likewise woke, he sat up bewildered, for he'd no notion how he'd come to be there, lying in the midroad, half a league from home. I took him back to his father; yet I bethought me that what I could do for one, I might so hap to do for others. Thus, when any boy from our village did gain that far-off gaze and wander toward the High Road in a trance, I followed, struck him down, and woke his mind; and when the spell began to wrap itself around my neighbors' minds also, I waited till night fell, and they slumbered, then passed from house to house, standing against the wall and seeking to wake them from their enchantments. At length I fell ill from exhaustion—but my village held, alone free from the weird.

"And so, at last—two days agone—a warlock came himself, a meager, pimply-faced lad, but with soldiers at his back. Then I could do naught; the boys all marched away; yet, at the least, their parents saw they were compelled."

"Yet did the warlock not seek thee out?"

Simon shrugged. "He did attempt it; for with a whole village yet free-minded, he knew there must needs be a witch or warlock who had prevented it. Yet as I've told thee, my power's weak; I can only hear thoughts. And that I was adept at hiding what little force I had. I was careful not to think of witch powers, or spell breaking; I thought only of suspicion, and how much I did resent Alfar's dominion." He shook his head slowly. "He could not find me; for every mind in all that hamlet thought as I did."

"And this was but two days agone?" the sergeant cried.

"Two days," Simon confirmed.

"Then 'tis months that thou hast held thy neighbors' minds 'gainst Alfar's spell!"

"It is. Yet in all comely truth, 'tis not till now that Alfar's had soldiers to spare for such an errand."

"Aye." The sergeant's face hardened again. "Yet with the Duke captured, he could spare the men, and the time— for all present threats were laid."

"I doubt it not. Yet I assure thee, I did tremble with relief when that warlock passed from our village.

"Then I bethought me that I'd cheated Death quite long enow. Nay, I reasoned that I'd done my part, and had escaped thus far more by luck than skill—and, in comely truth, my daughter doth draw near to her confinement. Accordingly, I sought the better part of valor, and turned my steps southward, hoping I might break from his evil-seized, ensorceled realm into the free air of Earl Tudor's county."

He turned to Rod. "And I have come near—so near! 'Tis but a half day's journey now, is't not?"

Rod nodded. "Guards at the border, though. You'd have trouble getting across."

Simon smiled, amused. "Not I."

"Aye." The soldier gave him an appraising glance. "Thou hast something of the look of the wild stag about thee. I doubt not an thou couldst find thy freedom through the forest trails, where no sentry's eye doth watch."

"Just so. Yet I think I must not go."

"Nay!" The sergeant leaned forward. "Go thou must! Make good thine escape whilst thou may!"

"And if I do? Wilt thou?"

The sergeant lowered his gaze. "I must go back—for I've blood on mine hands, and must atone."

"Stuff and nonsense!" Simon snorted. "These deaths were Alfar's doing, and none of thine. Do thou make thine escape, to join King Tuan's army, and march back to take thy vengeance 'gainst the sorcerer."

The sergeant shook his head. "Nay. 'Twould take too long. And . . . if we journey north again, my men and I, and take our places amidst the sorcerer's force—then there will be peasant lives spared, when next they send out to sweep the roads. And when King Tuan comes, there will be swords to fight for him, within the sorcerer's ranks."

"'Tis worthy," Simon mused.

"And stupid!" Rod snorted. "The first warlock who runs a security check on the army, listening for traitorous thoughts, will find you out. All you'll accomplish is an early execution."

The sergeant glared at him, then turned back to Simon. "Canst thou not teach us the way of hiding our thoughts?"

"I can tell thee the way of it," Simon said slowly, "yet 'tis not quickly learned. It will require constant practice— and never mayest thou relent. Such vigilance is well-nigh impossible, for one who hath but newly learned. Thou mayest quite easily be found out."

"Then give them choice," the sergeant said. "Wake them from their spellbound sleep, and say to them what thou hast said to me. I doubt me not an all of them will choose as I do—to ride back North."

Simon smiled, and shrugged. "Can I do less? I, who am practiced at such dissimulation? Nay. I shall be a half day's ride behind thee."

"That," Rod said, "is just a form of suicide. The only thing that's uncertain about it, is the date."

Simon looked up, in mild surprise. "Yet thou dost journey northward."

"Well, yes," Rod admitted, "But I have duty involved. It's required of me—never mind why."

"As it is of me—no matter why." Simon gave him the sardonic smile and rose to his feet, standing a little taller, a little straighter. "Craven was I, to ever flee. My work remains. I must turn back, and set my face against the North, that I may go to aid more souls who labor in enchanted sleep, the whiles their bodies wake."

"Nay, thou must not!" The sergeant stepped forward, alarmed. "In truth, thou hast done all any man should ask of thee!"

"'Tis good of thee, to speak so." Simon smiled with gentle warmth. "Yet I'm beholden to them—for look you, these are my people, and have been all my life. They have aided me in all the daily trials that a poor man undergoes, and tended me and mine in illness, and consoled us in bereavement—as I have done for them. Such bonds are not severed only for reason that I'm the only one able to give aid now. Nay, i' truth I played the craven, when that I did flee."

"Thou didst not," the sergeant asserted. "What will it profit them, for thou to turn back? Thy spell-breaking will but draw the warlock to thee again—and when he hath taken thee, thy folk will rest spellbound once more."

Simon fairly beamed, but shook his head. "I may escape his notice, as I've done already. Nay, I'll not again play coward."

The sergeant sighed. "Thou wast not craven to be afeared; for certes, thou hast much to fear. Therefore, an thou wilt wake my men from this foul spell, we all shall company thee."

"And make the danger greater!" Rod stepped forward, frowning. "How much chance do you think you boys would have against a squad of twenty, Auncient?"

The sergeant hesitated, frowning.

Rod pressed the point. "One civilian, going North with five armed men? Alfar's witch-sentries would smell a rat, even if they didn't have noses."

Simon's face lit with a delighted smile. "Yet think, goodman! They could say I was their prisoner!"

Rod gave the sergeant a jaundiced eye. "Do you have any orders about taking prisoners?"

"Nay," the sergeant admitted. "We were commanded to but slay and rob."

"You'd stand out like a haystack in a cornfield." Rod shook his head. "Pleasant fellow, isn't he, this Alfar? Efficient, though. Nasty, but efficient."

"Nay; he's most plainly evil," the sergeant growled.

"Yeah, but you don't fight evil by standing out in front of a full army and declaring war on them. At least, not when you're only a handful."

Simon gave the sergeant a sad nod. "'Tis even so, Auncient. Thou and thy men were best to fare on southward."

The sergeant's jaw tightened; he shook his head. "I will not choose to go—nor, I think, will even one of my men."

"Well, if you're bound and determined," Rod sighed, "let's make your lives as expensive as possible. Even just a handful of men can do an amazing amount of damage."

"Indeed?" The sergeant turned to him eagerly. "How dost thou mean?"

"You could be guerillas," Rod explained. "The word means 'little war,' and that's just what you do—make little wars within a big war. Most of the time, you see, you'd be riding along like good little Alfarites—but whenever there's a chance, you can turn into raiders."

The sergeant clamped his lips, turning away in exasperation. "What use are bandits, 'gainst an army?"

"A lot, if you choose the right targets. For example, if you break into the armoury and steal all the crossbow bolts, or even break all the arrows . . ."

The sergeant lifted his head, eyes lighting. "Aye—that would hamper an army's fighting, would it not?"

"Some," Rod agreed, "though there are still spears, pikes, and swords. At this level of technology, commandoes have a tougher time hurting the main army. Actually, I was thinking of you getting into the kitchens and pouring a few bucketfuls of salt on the food."

Slowly, the sergeant grinned.

"It'll work even better if you can link up with the other groups who've had their spells broken," Rod added.

The sergeant stared. "There be others?"

"There will be." Simon's eye glittered.

Rod glanced at him, and tried to suppress a smile. He turned back to the sergeant. "Yes, uh, a Southern witch, yesterday—she broke the spell on another squad, like yours, and they opted to go back North, too."

"Allies!" the sergeant cried, then frowned in doubt. "But how shall we know them? We cannot ask every soldier in the sorcerer's army, 'Art thou of the band whose spell is broke?'"

"Scarcely," Rod agreed. "But any bands Simon frees from now on, he can give secret names—ones you can say aloud for everyone to hear, but that only the ones whose spells are broken will recognize. For example, from now on, you'll be, um . . . Balthazar." He turned to Simon. "And you can name the auncients of the next two groups you free, 'Melchior' and 'Casper.'"

"What use is this?" the sergeant demanded.

"Well, if another soldier comes up to you, and says he has a message from Auncient Melchior, you can exchange information, because you'll know he's a part of the freedom movement. But you shouldn't get together, mind you. The bigger your force, the easier you'll be to find."

"Then what use this sending of messages?"

"So you can all agree to hit the same target at the same time. For example, you might want to make a big enough raid to actually take over a castle, or something. And, of course, when King Tuan's army marches North, you can all meet just behind the sorcerer's army, and hit them from the back while he hits 'em from the front."

"Doth he come, then?" The sergeant fairly pounced on the idea.

"Oh, he'll come," Rod said, with more certainty than he felt. "A message went South, yesterday."

Simon and the sergeant both stared at him.

With a sinking heart, Rod realized he'd made a bad slip.

"I couldn't help overhearing," he added, lamely.

"Certes, thou couldst not," Simon murmured. "Yet I bethink me thou'rt not the humble yeoman farmer that thou dost seem."

"Aye," the sergeant agreed. "Thou'rt a man of arms, by thy knowledge. What rank hast thou? What is thy station?"

"Proxima Centauri Terminal," Rod answered. "And as to my rank, just take my word for it—I've got enough to know what I'm talking about. And as to the name, call me, uh—'Kern.'"

Instantly, he knew it was a bad choice. *If people call you Kern,* said his id, from its morass of superstitious fear, *you'll lose track of who you are. You'll start thinking you are Kern, and you'll be absorbed into him.*

Ridiculous, his ego responded. *Kern's will can't reach across universes. The name's just a word, not a threat to your identity.*

His superego surveyed the two, came to its own conclusions, and declared it a draw.

Rod swallowed, firmed his jaw, and stuck to his story. "Kern," he said again. "That's all you need to know. Just take it and go with it as far as you can, Auncient."

"Indeed I will. Yet why ought I not to know who it is who doth command me?"

"Not command," Rod pointed out. "I'm just giving you advice. It was your idea to go back North, not mine. If you want a command, I'll tell you to go South."

"Nay," the sergeant said quickly. "Yet I thank thee for thy good, um, 'advice.'"

"My pleasure, I'm sure. And, of course, if the worst should happen, and they should capture you . . ."

"I will not betray thee," the sergeant said firmly. "Let them bring hot irons; let them bring their thumbscrews. I shall breathe no word."

"You won't have to. All they'll have to do is read your mind. You may be able to keep from saying it aloud, but you can't keep from thinking about it."

The sergeant looked doubtful.

Rod nodded. "So the whole idea is to not know anything more than is absolutely necessary. But—just in case we should be able to get something moving, mind you . . ."

"Aye!"

"If someone should come to you, and say that Kern says to attack a given place at a given time, you'll know what to do."

The soldier lifted his head, with a slow grin. "Aye. I shall indeed now. And I swear to thee, I will execute what thou dost command."

"Good man." Rod slapped him on the shoulder. "Now—let's get to waking up your men." He turned to Simon. "If you would, Master Simon? The sooner we can split up and hit the road, the better."

Simon nodded, with a smile, and turned away to the fallen troopers.

"Well done," Fess's voice murmured behind Rod's ear. "You excel as a catalyst, Rod."

"Oh, I'm great at knocking over the first domino," Rod muttered back. "Only trouble is, this time I have to set them up, too."

10

The osprey circled above them, its wings dipping as it balanced in the updraft. Rod scowled up at it, wondering if its eyes were green, like Gwen's. "Simon, how far are we from the coast?"

"Mayhap a day's ride." Simon followed Rod's gaze. "Ah, I see. 'Tis a fish-hawk, is't not?"

"Far as I know. But if the ocean's only twenty miles off, it's probably genuine." Rod turned to his companion. "Thought you were a dirt farmer. How would you know what a fish-hawk looks like?"

Simon shrugged. "As I've said, the ocean's not so far."

Which was true enough, Rod reflected. He didn't really have anything to be suspicious about—but in enemy territory, he couldn't help it. He wasn't that far from suspecting the nearest boulder might be a witch in disguise.

"Then, too," Simon said, amused, "I've never claimed to be a farmer."

Rod looked up, surprised. "True enough," he said slowly. "I did just assume. After all, what other occupations would there be, in a small village?"

"'Tis hard by the King's High Way," Simon explained. "I keep an inn."

Rod lifted his head, mouth opening before the words

came. "Oh." He nodded slowly. "I see. And quality folk stop in frequently, eh?"

"Mayhap twice in a month. There was ever a constant coming and going with the castle of Milord Duke. I did hearken to their speech, and did mimic it as best I could, the better to please them."

He'd hearkened to a lot more than their speech, Rod reflected. The aristocrats would no doubt have been aghast, if they'd known a mind reader served them. And, of course, Simon couldn't have had too many illusions left, about the lords.

So why was he still loyal?

Probably because the alternative was so much worse. "I don't suppose they taught you how to read?"

"Nay; my father sent me to the vicar, for lessons. He kept an inn before me, and knew 'twould be useful for an innkeeper to read and write, and cast up sums."

So. Unwittingly, Rod had stumbled into one of the local community leaders. "An enlightened man."

"Indeed he was. And what art thou?"

Every alarm bell in Rod's head broke into clamor. Admittedly, he'd made a pretty big slip; but did Simon have to be so quick on the uptake? "Why . . . I'm a farmer. Do I look so much like a knight, as to confuse you? Or a Duke, perhaps?" Then his face cleared with a sudden, delighted smile, and he turned to jab a finger at Simon. "*I* know! You thought I was a goldsmith!"

Simon managed to choke the laugh down into a chuckle, and shook his head. "Nay, goodman. I speak not of thine occupation, but of what thou *art*—that thou art there, but thou'rt not."

Rod stared, totally taken aback. "What do you mean, I'm not here?"

"In thy thoughts." Simon laid a finger against his forehead. "I have told thee I can hear men's thoughts—yet I cannot hear thine."

"Oh." Rod turned back to the road, gazing ahead, musing—while, inside, he virtually collapsed into a shuddering heap of relief. "Yes . . . I've been told that before. . . ." *Glad it's working . . .*

Simon smiled, but with his brows knit. "'Tis more than simply not hearing thy thoughts. When my mind doth 'listen' for thee, there is not even a sense of thy presence. How comes this?"

Rod shrugged. "I can guess, but that's all."

"And what is thy guess?"

"That I'm more worried about mind readers than your average peasant."

Simon shook his head. "That would not explain it. I have known some filled with morbid fear their thoughts would be heard—and I think they had reason, though I sought to avoid them. Still, I could have heard their thoughts, an I had wished to. Certes, I could sense that they were there. Yet with thee, I can do neither. I think, companion, that thou must needs have some trace of witch power of thine own, that thy will doth wrap into a shield."

"You trying to tell me I'm a witch?" Rod did a fairly good imitation of bristling.

Simon only smiled sadly. "Even less than I am. Nay, I'd not fear that. Thou canst not hear thoughts, canst thou?"

"No," Rod said truthfully—at least, for the time being.

Simon smiled. "Then thou'rt not a witch. Now tell me—why dost thou come North? Thou must needs know that thou dost drive toward danger."

"I sure must, after you and the auncient finished with me." Rod hunched his shoulders, pulling into himself. "As to the danger, I'll chance it. I can get better prices for my produce in Korasteshev, than I can in all of Tudor's county! And my family's always hungry."

"They will hunger more, an thou dost not return." Simon's voice dropped, full of sincerity. "I bid thee, friend, turn back."

"What's the matter? Don't like my company?"

Simon's earnestness collapsed into a smile. "Nay—thou art a pleasant enough companion. . . ."

Personally, Rod thought he was being rather churlish.

But Simon was very tolerant. "Yet for thine own sake, I bid thee turn toward the South again. The sorcerer's warlocks will not take kindly to one whose mind they cannot sense."

"Oh, the warlocks won't pay any attention to a mere peasant coming to market." At least, Rod hoped they wouldn't.

"The prices in Romanov cannot be so much better than they are in Tudor." Simon held Rod's eyes with a steady gaze. It seemed to burn through his retinas and into his brain. "What more is there to thine answer?"

Reluctantly, Rod admitted, "There is more—but that's all you're going to get."

Simon held his gaze for a minute.

Then he sighed, and turned away. "Well, it is thy fate, and thou must needs answer for it thyself. Yet be mindful, friend, that thy wife and bairns do depend upon thee."

Rod was mindful of it, all right. For a sick instant, he had a vision of Gwen and the children waiting weeks, without word of him. Then he thrust the thought sternly aside, and tried to envision the look on his boys' faces if he abandoned his mission and came back to be safe. "You have obligations to the people of your village, Master Simon. So have I."

"What—to the folk of thy town?"

"Well, to my people, anyway." Rod had the whole of Gramarye in mind, not to mention the Decentralized Democratic Tribunal. "And once you've accepted an obligation of that sort, you can't put it aside just because it becomes dangerous."

"Aye, that's so," Simon said, frowning. "'Tis this that I've but now come to see."

Rod turned to him, frowning too. "But you've already done your part, taken your risks. No one would call you a coward for going South now!"

"I would," Simon said simply.

Rod looked directly into his eyes for a moment, then turned away with a sigh. "What can I say to that, goodman?"

"Naught, save 'gee-up' to thine horse."

"Why?" Rod asked sourly. "This cart may be pulled by a horse, but it's being driven by a pair of mules."

Sundown caught them still on the road, with grainfields at either hand. "Nay," Simon assured Rod, "there is no town near."

"I was afraid of that," Rod sighed. "Well, the earth has been my bed before this." And he drove off the road, pulling Fess to a stop in the weeds between the track and the field. He was cutting vegetables into a small pot before Simon could even volunteer.

The innkeeper eyed him quizzically, then asked, "Dost ever have a pot with thee?"

"I was a tinker once. Habits stick."

Simon smiled, shaking his head, and leaned back on an elbow. "I think such travels are not wholly new to thee."

"We're even," Rod snorted. "I get the feeling spell-breaking isn't all that new to *you.*"

Simon was still for a moment, but his eyes brightened. "Almost could I believe thou didst read minds."

"If I did, I'd need to have yours translated. So when did you start spell-breaking?"

Simon sat up, hooking his forearms around his shins, resting his chin on his knees. "The men of the village came oft to mine inn for drinking of beer, which they took as part-price for the produce they brought. Anon would come one whose heart was heavy, with thoughts in turmoil, to drink and be silent—mayhap in hopes that beer would quiet his unrest."

Rod nodded. "Strange how we keep trying that solution. Especially since it never works."

"Nay; but speaking thy thoughts to a willing ear, can help to calm them; and the troubled ones would talk, for I would hearken, and give what sympathy I could. Yet one there came who seemed like unto a wall in winter—like to spring apart at the first freeze. He could not talk, but huddled over his flagon. Yet the jumble of his thoughts rode upon such pain that they fairly screamed. I could not have shut my mind to them, even had I wished to—and brooding over all was the shadow of a noose."

Rod looked up sharply. "The kid was suicidal?"

"Aye. And he was no child, but in his thirties. 'Tis these passages from one state to another that do wreak their havocs within us, and his children all had grown."

Rod couldn't understand the problem; but he had Gwen for a wife. "What could you do about it?"

"Fill another flagon, and one for myself, and go to sit

by him. Then, 'neath the pretext of conversing—and 'twas very much a pretense, for I alone did speak—I felt through the snarl of his thoughts, found the sources of his pain and shame, then asked aloud the questions that did make him speak them. And 'twas not easy for him thus to speak— yet I encouraged, and he did summon up sufficient resolution. I meant only to have him thus give me pretext to discuss his secret fears, to tell him they were not so fearsome—yet I found that, once he had spoken them aloud, and heard his own voice saying them, these secrets then lost half their power. Then could I ask a question whose answer would show him the goodness within him that could counter his hidden monsters, and, when we were done, he'd calmed tolerably well."

"You saved his life," Rod accused.

Simon smiled, flattered. "Mayhap I did. I began, then, to give such aid to all such troubled souls that I encountered. Nay, I even sought them out, when they did not come into my inn."

"Could be dangerous, there," Rod pointed out. "Just so much of that hauling people back from the edge, before the neighbors decided you had to be a witch to do it. Especially since you were poaching on the parish priest's territory."

Simon shook his head. "Who knew of it? Not even those I aided—for I gave no advice nor exhortation. And look, you, 'twas a village. We all knew one another, so there was naught of surprise should I encounter any one of them, and chat a while. Yet withal, the folk began to say that troubled souls could find a haven in mine inn."

Definitely poaching on the priest's territory," Rod muttered. "And that was an awful lot of grief to be taking on yourself."

Simon shrugged, irritated. "They were my people, Master Owen. *Are,* I should say. And there were never more than three in a year."

Rod didn't look convinced.

Simon dropped his gaze to the campfire. "Thus, when Tom Shepherd lapsed into sullenness, his brothers brought him to my taproom. In truth, they half-carried him; he could no longer even walk of his own." He shook his head. "'Twas an old friend of mine—or should I say, an old neighbor."

"What was the matter with him?"

Simon turned his head from side to side. "His face was slack; he could not move of his own, and did but sit, not speaking. I drew a stool up next to his, and gazed into his face, the whiles I asked questions, which he did not answer; yet all the while, my mind was open, hearkening at its hardest, for any thought that might slip through his mind."

"Sounds catatonic." Rod frowned. "I shouldn't think there would've been any thoughts."

"There was one—but only one. And that one did fill him, consuming all his mind and heart with a single graveyard knell."

"Suicidal, again?"

Simon shook his head. "Nay. 'Twas not a *wish* to die, look thou, nor even a willingness, but a sureness, a certainty, that he *would* die, was indeed that moment dying, but slowly."

Rod sat very still.

"I labored mightily 'gainst that compulsion. Yet I could but ask questions that would recall to mind the things that would make him wish to live—wife, and bairns, and careful neighbors; yet naught availed." He shook his head. "One would have thought he had not heard; for still throughout him rang the brazen knell of death." Simon sighed, turning his head slowly from side to side. "In the end, I could but bid his brothers take him to the priest, but the good friar fared no better than I." He shrugged. "I could not cast into his mind thoughts to counter that fell compulsion. The power was not in me."

Rod nodded, understanding. Simon was only a telepath, not a projective.

Simon picked up a stick, and poked at the fire. "He died, in the end. He ate not, nor drank, and withered up like a November leaf. And I, heartsick, began to wonder how such a doom came to burden him. For he'd ever been a cheerful fellow, and I could see that one had laid a spell upon him. Aye, I pondered how one could be so evil as to do so fell a deed.

"So I commenced long walks throughout the county till at length I found that same wholehearted, whole consumption of a mind—yet 'twas not one mind, but a score; for I came into a village, and found that half the folk who lived there were bewitched. Oh, aye, they walked and spoke like any normal folk—but all their minds were filled with but one single thought."

"Death?" Rod felt the eeriness creeping over the back of his skull.

"Nay." Simon shook his head. "'Twas praise of Alfar."

"Oh-h-h." Rod lifted his head slowly. "The sorcerer's enchantment team had been at work."

"They had—and, knowing that, I went back to mine own village and, in chatting with my fellow villagers, asked a question here, and another there, and slowly built up a picture of that which had occurred to Tom Shepherd. He'd met a warlock in the fields, who had bade him kneel to Alfar. Tom spat upon the ground, and told that warlock that his Alfar was naught but a villein, who truly owed allegiance to Duke Romanov, even as Tom Shepherd did. The warlock then bade him swear loyalty to Alfar, or die; but Tom laughed in his face, and bade him do his worst."

"So he did?"

"Aye, he did indeed! Then, knowing this, I went back to the village where half had been of one thought only, and that thought Alfar's. I found only ten of a hundred still free in their thoughts, and those ten walking through a living nightmare of fear; for I spoke with some, and heard within their thoughts that several of them had defied the warlocks, and died as Tom Shepherd had. Even as I stood there, one broke beneath his weight of fear, and swore inside himself that he'd be Alfar's man henceforth, and be done with terror." Simon shuddered. "I assure thee, I left that village as quickly as I might."

He turned to look directly into Rod's eyes, and his gaze seemed to bore into Rod's brain. "I cannot allow such obscenities of horror to exist, the whiles I sit by and do naught." He shook his head slowly. "Craven was I, ever to think I could walk away and leave this evil be."

"No," Rod said. "No, you can't, can you? Not and still be who you are."

Simon frowned. "Strangely put—yet, I doubt me not, quite true."

The campsite was quiet for a few minutes, as both men sat watching the flames, each immersed in his own thoughts.

Then Rod lifted his head, to find Simon's gaze on him. "Now," said the innkeeper, "'tis thy turn. Is't not?"

"For what?"

"For honesty. Why dost thou go North?"

Rod held his gaze for a few moments, then, slowly, he said, "Same reason as yours, really—or one pretty much like it. I've seen some of Alfar's work, and it's sickened me. I can't call myself a man if I let that happen without fighting it. At the very least, I've got to help keep it from spreading—or die trying."

"As indeed thou mayest," Simon breathed. "Yet that is not the whole of thine answer, is it?"

"No—but that's all you're going to get."

They gazed at one another for several heartbeats, the blade of Rod's glare clashing off the velvet wall of Simon's acceptance. Finally, the innkeeper nodded. "'Tis thine affair, of course." He sounded as though he meant it.

He turned back to the fire. "Thou art mine ally for this time. I need know no more than that the sorcerer's thine enemy."

"Well, that—and that the stew's ready." Rod leaned over to sniff the vapors. "Not bad, for field rations. Want some?"

When Simon rolled up in his cloak to sleep, Rod went over to curry Fess. The job wasn't really stage dressing at all—Fess's horsehair may have owed more to plastic than to genetics, but it still collected brambles and burrs on occasion.

"So." Rod ran the currycomb along Fess's withers. "Alfar started out with nothing but feelings of inferiority, and a grudge against the world."

"An ordinary paranoid personality," Fess noted.

"Yeah, except that he was an esper. And somewhere along the line, he all of a sudden became a lot more powerful than your average warlock." He looked up at Fess. "Maybe just because he managed to talk some other witches into joining him?"

"Perhaps." The robot sounded very skeptical. "I cannot help but think there is more to the matter than that."

"Probably right, too . . . So. Alfar had a sudden boost in power, and/or got together a gang. Then he started leaning on the local citizenry, like any good gangster."

"The process seems to begin with intimidation," Fess noted.

Rod stopped currying for a minute. "Maybe . . . Even the soldiers were scared, when they were marching against him. . . ." He shrugged. "Hard to say. In any event, he's finally able to mass-hypnotize whole villages—though from the soldier's account, it needs to be redone in depth, on an individual basis."

"The soldiers' mass hypnosis was done during the heat of battle, Rod, and very quickly. The peasant villages seem to have been done more leisurely, by Simon's statement— over a period of days, perhaps even weeks."

"True—so it would be more thorough. Though, apparently, some are harder to hypnotize than others." He looked up at Fess again. "And espers appears to be immune."

"So it would seem, to judge by Simon."

"Yes . . ." Briefly, Rod wondered about that. Then he shrugged it off. "Anyhow. When Alfar'd built enough of a power base, one of the local knights got worried, and tried to knock him down before he grew too big. But he was already too big."

"Indeed," Fess agreed. "He was already powerful enough to overcome a knight with his village force."

Rod nodded. "And by the time he was big enough to worry the local baron, he'd absorbed the forces of several knights. So the baron fell, and the chain reaction began— the baron, then the count, then finally the duke himself— and it doesn't end there, does it?"

"Certainly not, Rod. After all, he now has the resources of a duchy to draw on."

"Yes. We all know what he's going to do now, don't we?"

"But surely Gwendylon and the children have already borne word to Tuan and Catharine, Rod—and the Duchess's personal account must certainly have been very persuasive. I doubt not that Tuan is already gathering his forces."

"Gathering them, yes. But it's going to be at least a week or two before he can march North."

"Surely Alfar cannot consolidate his newly won forces

with sufficient speed to enable him to carry the attack to Tuan!"

"Oh, I don't think he would, anyway." Rod looked up into Fess's imitation eyes. "All the Duke's horses and all the Duke's men aren't quite enough to take on the King's army."

"True," the robot conceded. "Therefore, he will attack Earl Tudor."

"You really think he'd dare strike that close to Tuan?"

"Perhaps not. Perhaps he will seek to conquer Hapsburg first."

"It's just great, having outgoing neighbors . . . and if he manages to swallow Hapsburg, he'll have to digest him before he can take on Tudor."

"I doubt that he would try. He might be able to defeat the Earl quickly, but he must surely need a week or two to complete the indoctrination of the captured soldiers."

"And while he's digesting, he's right next to Tuan. No, you're right. He'd try to march through Tudor, and attack Tuan right away. Which means *our* job is to keep him from being able to attack another baron, before Tuan attacks him."

"What methods do you propose, Rod?"

Rod shrugged. "The usual—hit and run, practical jokes, whispering campaigns—nothing sensible. Keep him off-balance. Which shouldn't be too hard; he's going to be feeling pretty insecure, right about now."

"He will indeed. And, being paranoid, he will seek to eliminate whatever enemies he does see, before he turns his attention to attack."

"Maybe. But a paranoid also might decide to attack before the next baron can attack him, and start his own secret police to take care of internal enemies." Rod clenched a fist in frustration. "Damn! If only you could predict what a single human being would do!"

"Be glad you cannot," Fess reminded, "or VETO and its totalitarians could easily triumph."

"True," Rod growled. "Truer than I like. And speaking of our proletarian pals, do you see any evidence of their meddling in this?"

"Alfar's techniques do resemble theirs," Fess admitted.

"Resemble? Wish fulfillment, more likely! He's got the kind of power they dream of—long-distance, mass-production brainwashing! What wouldn't any good little dictator give for that?"

"His soul, perhaps?"

"Are you kidding? Totalitarianism works the other way around—everybody *else* gives their souls to the dictator!"

"Unpleasant, but probably accurate. Nonetheless, there is no evidence of futurian activity."

"Neither totalitarians nor anarchists, huh?"

"Certainly not, Rod."

"Not even the sudden, huge jump in Alfar's powers?"

"That ability does bother me," Fess admitted. "A projective telepath, who seems to be able to take on a whole parish at one time . . . Still, there's no reason to believe the totalitarians would be behind it."

"Oh, yes there is," Rod countered. "From everything Simon's told me, and it just backed up what Gwen said—the trance these people seem to walk around in, is thoroughly impersonal."

"Almost depersonalized, you might say? I had, had something of the same thought too, Rod. I recognize the state."

"Yes—mechanical, isn't it?"

"True. But that is not conclusive evidence of futurian meddling."

"No—but it does make you wonder." Rod gave the synthetic horsehair a last swipe with the brush. "There! As new and shiny as though you'd just come from the factory. Do you mind a long tether, just for appearances?"

"I would mind not having it. It is certainly necessary, Rod."

"Must keep them up, mustn't we?" Rod reached into the cart, pulled out a length of rope, tied one end to Fess's halter and the other to a convenient tree branch. "Besides, you can break it easily, if you want."

"I will not hesitate to do so," Fess assured him. "Sleep while you can, Rod. You will need the rest."

"You're such an optimist." Rod pulled his cloak out of the cart and went back to the campfire. "I'm not exactly in a great mood for emptying my mind of the cares of the day."

"Try," the robot urged.

"If I try to sleep, I'll stay awake." Rod lay down and rolled up in his cloak. "How about trying to stay awake?"

"Not if you *truly* want to sleep. I could play soft music, Rod."

"Thanks, but I think the nightbirds are doing a pretty good job of that."

"As you wish. Good night, Rod."

"I hope so," Rod returned. "Same to you, Fess." He rolled over toward the fire . . .

. . . and found himself staring into Simon's wide-open, calm, and thoughtful eyes.

"Uh . . . hi, there." Rod forced a sickly grin. "Say, I'll bet you're wondering what I was doing, rambling on like that—aren't you?"

"Not greatly," Simon answered, "though I do find thy conversation to be of great interest."

"Oh, I'm sure." Rod's stomach sank. "Does it, uh, bother you, to, uh, hear me talk to my horse."

"Not at all." Simon looked faintly surprised. "And 'tis certainly not so desperate as talking to thyself."

"That's a point . . ."

"'Tis also scarcely amazing." Simon favored him with a rather bleak smile. "Be mindful, I'm an innkeeper, and many carters have stopped at my inn. Every one I've known, has spoken to his horse."

"Oh." Rod hoped his surprise didn't shown in his face. "You mean I'm not exactly unusual?"

"Only in this: thou'rt the first I've heard who, when he spoke to his horse, made sense."

Rod supposed it was a compliment.

11

They were up at first light, and on the road by dawn. With the main issues out of the way, the two of them chatted together easily—Simon the innkeeper, and Owen the farmer. And if, as morning wore on, Owen's tales of his children bore a startling resemblance to the experiences of Rod Gallowglass, it can scarcely be surprising. On the other hand, all the stories had nothing to do with juvenile witch powers; Rod stayed sufficiently on his guard not to make that particular slip.

It wasn't easy. Rod found they had a lot in common—wives, and children. He also found Simon to be surprisingly refreshing. Instead of their usual dire predictions about the horrors of adolescence that lay in store for the unwary father, Simon restricted his anecdotes to childhood disasters—though, when pressed, he admitted that all his children were grown, and the tale of his daughter's impending first birth was quite true. Rod immediately began insisting, all over again, that Simon turn back to the South and his daughter, the more so because Simon had mentioned earlier that his wife had died quite a few years ago; but the innkeeper merely informed Rod that his daughter really lived north of his home village—wherefore, he had been doubly cowardly to flee. There wasn't much Rod could say to that, so he relaxed and enjoyed Simon's company. So, by the time they came to the first village, Rod was feeling in fine form—which was fortunate, because they were greeted by a mob.

The peasants stormed out of the village, howling and throwing stones and waving pitchforks—but not at Simon and Rod. Their target was a small man, who sprinted madly, managing to stay a dozen yards ahead of them.

"Slay the warlock!" they cried. "Stone him!" "Stab him! Drain his blood!" "Burn him! Burn him Burn Him BURN HIM!"

Simon and Rod stared at each other, startled. Then Simon snapped, "He could not be of Alfar's brood, or soldiers would even now be cutting down these peasants! Quickly, Owen!"

"You heard him!" Rod cracked the whip over Fess's head, keeping up the act. "Charge!"

Fess leaped into a gallop. Cartwheels roared behind him.

Rod pulled up hard as they passed the fleeing warlock, and Simon shouted, "Up behind, man! For thy lifeblood's sake!"

The running man looked up, startled, then jumped into the cart, as Simon rose to his feet and cried out, in a voice that seared through the crowd's shouting:

"I, too, am a magic worker! *Two* warlocks face thee now! Dost thou still wish wood to kindle?"

The crowd froze, the words of violence dying on their tongues.

Simon stood relaxed, but his face was granite. Slowly, he surveyed the crowd, picking out individual faces here and there. But he didn't say a word.

Finally, a fat little man stepped forward, shaking a club at Simon. "Step aside, fellow! Withdraw thy cart and horse! Our quarrel's with this foul warlock, not with thee!"

"Nay," Simon answered. "To the contrary; every warlock's business is every other's, for there are few of us indeed."

"*Every* warlock?" the fat man bleated in indignation. "Is Alfar's business also thine?"

His words set off an ugly murmur that increased in ugliness as it built.

"Alfar's business ours?" Simon's eyes widened. "Why would it not be?"

The noise cut off as the crowd stared at him, frozen.

Then the people began to mutter to one another, worried, a little fearful. One scrawny warlock by himself was one thing—but two together, with Alfar's backing...

Simon's voice cut through their hubbub. "'Twould be better an thou didst now go back unto thine homes."

"What dost thou speak of!" the fat little man cried. "Turn to our homes? Nay! For we have one who must be punished! What dost thou think thyself to..."

His voice ran down under Simon's stony glare. Behind him, the crowd stared, then began to whisper among themselves again. Rod heard snatches of "Evil Eye!" "Evil Eye!" He did the best he could to reinforce the idea, staring at the fat little leader with his eyes narrowed a little, teeth showing in a wolfish grin.

"Thou wilt go," Simon said, his voice like an icepick.

Rod could scarcely believe the transformation. He could've sworn Simon was at least two inches taller and four inches broader. His eyes glowed; his face was alive and vibrant. He fairly exuded power.

Cowed, the crowd drew in upon itself, muttering darkly. Simon's voice rose above. "We have shown thee plainly wherein doth lie the true power in this land—but it need not be turned against thee. Go, now—go to thine homes." Then he smiled, and his aura seemed to mellow—he seemed gentler, somehow, and reassuring. "Go," he urged, "go quickly."

The crowd was shaken by the transformation. Their emotions had been yanked back and forth; they didn't know whether to resent Simon, or be grateful to him. For a moment, they stood, uncertain. Then one man turned away, slowly. Another saw him, and turned to follow. A third saw them, and turned, then a fourth. Then the whole crowd was moving back toward the village.

The fat little man glanced at them, appalled, then back toward Simon. "Retribution shall follow," he cried, but fear hollowed his voice. "Retribution, and flames for all witches!"

Rod's eyes narrowed to slits, and he gathered himself; but Simon laid a restraining hand on his shoulder, and said mildly, "Go whilst thou may—or retribution there shall be indeed, and I shall not lift one finger to stay it."

The little man glanced at Rod in sudden terror, then whirled about, and hurried to follow the villagers back toward the houses.

Rod, Simon, and the stranger only watched him, frozen in tableau till he'd disappeared among the buildings. Then, the moment he was out of sight, Simon heaved a long sigh, going limp.

"I should say," Rod agreed. "You do that kind of thing often?"

"Nay." Simon collapsed onto the board seat. "Never in my life."

"Then you've got one hell of a talent for it." Privately, Rod had a strong suspicion that Simon was at least a little bit of a projective, but didn't realize it.

Even with his nerves a-jangle from facing down a mob for the first time, Simon remembered the fugitive. He turned, looking back into the cart. "Art thou well, countryman?"

"Aye," the stranger wheezed, "thanks to thee, goodmen. And thou hadst not come, there had been naught but a bloody lump left of me. E'en now I tremble, to think of them! From the depths of my soul I thank thee. I shall pray down upon thee one blessing, for every star that stands in the sky! I shall . . ."

"You shall live." Rod couldn't repress the grin. "And we're glad of it. But if you're a warlock, why didn't you just disappear?" Then a sudden thought hit him, and he turned to Simon. *"Is* he a warlock?"

"Aye." Simon nodded, his eyes on the stranger. "There is the feeling I've had, twice aforetime, when I've met another warlock and heard his thoughts—that feeling of being in a mind enlarged, in a greater space of soul."

Rod knew the feeling; he'd met it himself. With a variant form and intensity, it was one of the great benefits of being married to another esper—and one of the curses of being an esper himself, when he was near another telepath whom he didn't like. He'd decided some time ago that it was mental feedback—but controlled feedback. It must've been, or it would've torn both minds apart. The born witch, he thought, must develop a perceptual screen in infancy, a sort of blocking mechanism that would reduce the recycled mental energy to comfortable levels.

"He is a warlock," Simon said again. "Why, therefore, didst thou not disappear, goodman?"

"Why, for that I could not." The stranger smiled apologetically, spreading his hands and cocking his head to the side. "What can I say to thee? I am a very poor warlock, who can but hear others' thoughts, and that only when they're hard by me. E'en then, I cannot hear them well."

"I, too," Simon said, with a sad smile. "I can but hear one that's within the same house as I."

"And I, only when they are within a few yards," the stranger said, nodding. "But so little as that is enough, I wot, so that, now and again, summat of others' thoughts do come into mine head, unknowing—the thought comes that so-and-so is a-love with such-and-such, or that this one wishes the other dead. And, again and now, I let slip an unguarded word or two, and the one I'm speaking to doth stare at me, in horror, and doth cry, 'How couldst thou know of that? None have heard it of me; to none have I spoken of it!'"

"So they figured out what you were." Rod nodded.

"Aye; and it cost me what few friends I had, from my earliest years; yet it made me no enemies; for I am, as I've said, a most powerless warlock, and all, thankfully, knew that I meant no one harm."

Rod could believe it. The stranger was short, slump-shouldered and concave-chested, flabby, with a little potbelly. His hair was dun-colored. He had large, pale eyes, a snub nose, and a perpetual hangdog look about him. He couldn't have been much over thirty, but already his cheeks were beginning to sag. In a year or five, he'd have jowls. A *schlemiel*, Rod decided, a poor soul who would never intentionally hurt anybody, but would always be clumsy, both physically and socially. "Nobody really wanted you around, huh? But they didn't mind you, either."

"Aye," the stranger said, with a rueful smile.

"I know the way of it," Simon sighed. "There was such a lad in my village."

"There always is," Rod said. "It's a necessary social

function. Everybody needs somebody whose name they can't quite remember."

"Well said." Simon smiled. "And thou dost touch my conscience. How art thou called, goodman?"

"Flaran," the stranger answered, with the same smile.

"Flaran," Simon repeated, thoughtfully. "Tell me, Flaran—when Alfar the sorcerer began to rise to power, did thy fellows expect thee to hail him?"

Flaran's smile gained warmth. "They did that. Thou hast endured it thyself, hast thou not?" And, when Simon nodded, he chuckled. "So I thought; thou hast spoke too much of what I have seen myself. Aye, all my neighbors did think that, solely because I've a touch of the Power, I should cry that Alfar was the greatest hope this duchy hath ever seen. Yet I did not. In truth, I said I did not trust the man."

Simon nodded. "Yet they thought thou didst give them the lie."

"They did," Flaran agreed. "Straightaway, then, mine old friends—or neighbors, at least—began to mistrust me; in truth, as Alfar's fame and power have grown, they have doubted me more and more."

"Still, thou'rt of them." Simon frowned. "When last came to last, thou wert of their clan and kind. I would think they would not hound and stone thee."

"Nor did I—and still I misdoubt me an they would have. But folk began to pass through our village, pushing hand-carts and bearing packs upon their backs; and, though we did not have great store of food or ale, 'Stay,' we urged them. 'Nay,' they answered, 'for the sorcerer's armies do march, and we do flee them. We dare not bide, for they'll swallow up this village also.' Then they turned, and marched on toward the South."

Rod and Simon exchanged a quick glance. Simon nodded in corroboration. Rod understood; Simon had been one of the ones who had come marching through the village, and had not stayed. "And this small ball of a man with the great mouth?" Simon turned back to Flaran. "Was he of thy village, or of the strangers?"

"Of the strangers," Flaran answered, "and he did come into our village crying doom upon all who had any powers.

None could be trusted, quoth he, for all witch folk must needs hate all common men, and must needs fight them; therefore, any witch or warlock must needs be an agent of Alfar's."

Simon's eyes burned. "Indeed? Would I could have done more than send him back to thy village."

"Nay, friend. Thou wouldst but have made my neighbors certain in their hatred. Even as 'twas, he did turn my fellows against me—though, in all truth, the news from the North had made them so wary, they needed little turning. I came into the inn for a pint, but when I stood near to the landlord, I heard his thoughts, his rage and mistrust, his secret fear that the fat little stranger might be right, that mayhap all witch folk *should* be stoned. Nay, I dropped my flagon and fled."

"And, of course, they all ran after you." Rod reflected that the pack instinct must have taken over.

Flaran shuddered. "'Tis even as thou dost say. 'Twas not even an hour agone. I dodged and hid, then dodged and ran. At last they found me out, and I could hide no longer. Nay, I fled off down the road—but I was wearied, and must needs fight to stay running. Heaven be praised that thou didst come up the High Road then, or I had been a paste of a person!"

Simon reached out to clap Flaran on the shoulder. "Courage, friend—this bloodlust shall fade, as it hath aforetime. Ever and anon have they come out hunting witches—and ever and anon hath it passed. This shall, also."

Flaran braved a small smile, but he didn't look convinced.

Rod wasn't, either—the whole thing had too much of the deliberate about it. It was preplanned, well-organized whipping-up of sentiment, and there was only one group organized enough to do the whipping-up—but why would Alfar be trying to work up antiesper sentiment?

The answer hit him like a sap, in instant balance to the question: Alfar would whip up the witch hunt to eliminate his competition. After all, the only force in the duchy that could stand against him, were the witches who hadn't signed up with him. Left alone long enough, they just might band together in self-defense—as Simon and Flaran were doing, even now. If they organized a large enough band of fugitive witches and warlocks, they would constitute a power that might actually unseat him. And what better way to eliminate the independents, than the time-tried old witch hunt?

When you looked at it that way, it made excellent sense— especially since the unaligned espers would tend to be opposed to him; they'd be the most sensitive to his kind of hypnotic tyranny. "Say, uh—did either one of you ever feel one of Alfar's men trying to take over your mind?"

Both men looked up, startled. Then Simon nodded, gravely. "Aye. It was . . ." he shuddered, ". . . most obscene, friend Owen."

"I could barely feel it," Flaran added, "yet it turned my stomach and made my gorge to rise. And it raised such a wave of fear in me, that I thought it like to shake me to pieces. To feel fingers of thought, stroking at thy mind . . ." He broke off, looking queasy.

"Try not to think of it," Rod said, cursing his impulsiveness. "Sorry I brought it up." And these two, he reflected, were the gentle kind. What would happen when Alfar's men tried to take on a warlock who had a bit more arrogance? Or even just one who liked to fight? He would have flown into a rage, and gone hunting for Alfar.

And Rod couldn't blame him. The thought of someone meddling with *his* mind started the sullen flow of anger. He recognized it, and tried to relax, let it drain away—but the image of Gwen and the children rose up in his mind, with the instant thought of some overbearing young warlock trying to touch *their* minds—and the rage exploded with a suddenness that left him defenseless against it, shaking his body with its intensity, wild and searing, searching for a target, any target, striving to master Rod, to make him its instrument. He held himself still, fighting to contain it, to keep it inside himself, to keep it from hurting anyone else.

But both warlocks were staring at him. "My friend," Simon said, wide-eyed, "art thou well?"

Such a mild question, and so well-intentioned! But it broke the fragile membrane of Rod's control.

He hurled himself away from the cart, off the road and

into the field beside. *Don't hurt them. Let it blow, but don't hurt them*. He needed some way to channel the anger, some way to let it spend itself harmlessly, and running was as good as anything else.

A boulder loomed up ahead of him, a rock outcrop four feet high, with smaller boulders around the base. Rod seized one about a foot across, hefting it up above his head with a grunt of agony. He stood for a moment, poised, glaring at the boulder, then hurled his rock with all his might, shouting, "Blast you!"

The rock hit the boulder with a crack like a gunshot. Stone chips flew, and the smaller rock split and clattered to the base of the boulder.

"Burn in your own magic!" Rod screamed at it. "Fall down a rathole, and forget how to teleport! Jump into the sky, and don't come back down!" He raged on and on, a five-minute stream of incoherent curses.

Finally, the anger ebbed. Rod sank to one knee, still glaring at the boulder. Then, slowly, he bowed his head, gasping for breath, and waited for the trembling to stop.

When his heartbeat had slowed, he stood up, swaying a little. Then he forced himself to turn back toward the cart, fifty yards away—and saw Flaran staring at him.

But Simon stood near him, leaning on his staff, waiting, watching him with gentle sympathy.

That was what stung—the sympathy. Rod winced at the sight; it magnified his chagrin tenfold. He turned away, muttering, "Sorry about that. I, uh . . . I don't do that too often." *I hope*.

"Thou didst only as I did feel," Simon assured him.

"Well . . . thanks." That didn't really help. "I just get outraged at the thought of someone trampling on other people, without even thinking about them!"

Simon nodded. "And when the object of thy wrath is not nigh thee, 'tis harder to forebear. Indeed, thou didst well to seek a thing of stone unfeeling, to wreak thy vengeance on."

"But the force of it's wasted—is that what you're thinking? Why spend all that energy, without hurting the thing I'm angry at?"

Simon scowled. "I had not thought that—but aye, now that thou dost say it. 'Tis better husbandry, to contain thine anger till thou canst use its force to right the wrong that angers thee."

"Easy enough to say," Rod said, with a sardonic smile. "But how do you contain your anger? I know it sounds simple—but you should try it, sometime! You would..." He broke off, staring at Simon. Slowly, he said, "You have tried it, haven't you?" Then, nodding, "Yes. I think you have. That last line had the ring of experience behind it."

"'Tis even so," Simon admitted.

"*You* had a temper? *You* flew into rages? *You?* Mr. Nice Guy himself? Mr. Calmness? Mr. Phlegmatic? *You?*"

"Indeed," Simon admitted, and, for the first time, his smile was tinged with irony. "'Tis not so easy, friend Owen, to hide thy knowledge of others' thoughts. 'Tis most tempting, in moments of anger, to use those thoughts against them—to say, '*Me* a coward? When thou didst face the battle with panic clamoring through thy veins, and would have fled, had thy captain not stood behind thee with his sword?' For indeed, he *had* marched forward, and none who saw him would have thought him less than brave. Yet I knew, I—and was fool enough to speak it aloud. Then, to another, 'How canst thou call me a lecher, Father, when thou hast thyself lusted after Tom Plowman's wife?"

Rod whistled. "You *don't* take on the clergy!"

"Aye, but in my youthful pride, I thought that I had power o'er all—for I had but newly learned that I could hear other's thoughts and, in my delight and careless strength, did hearken to the thoughts of all about me. No person in that town was free from my thought-hearing. When one did sneer at me, I used my hoarded knowledge of his darkest secrets and proclaimed his shame for all to hear! He did swell up with rage, but durst not strike where all might see, and know the truth of what I'd said. Nay, he could only turn away with snarls—and I would gloat, rejoicing in my newfound power."

Rod frowned. "How long did you get away with that?"

"Thrice." Simon grimaced, shaking his head. "Three times only. For when the anger passed, the folk I'd wronged began to ponder. They knew they'd never spoken of their secret fears or lusts to any person living. By chance, they spoke to one another. . . ."

"By chance, my rabbit's foot! You'd insulted each one publicly; they knew who to compare notes with!"

"Like enough," Simon sighed. "And once they all knew that I'd spoken things none of them had ever said aloud, 'twas but a small step to see that I must needs be a warlock, and one who would not hesitate to use what knowledge I gained, from others thoughts to their harm. They spread that word throughout the town, of course . . ."

"'Of course' is right," Rod murmured, "especially with the village priest in there. Who'd doubt his word? After all, even if he did covet his neighbor's wife, at least he didn't *do* anything about it."

"Which is more than could be said for most of his flock," Simon said, with a tart grimace. "Aye, he too did speak of my 'fell power'—and the rumor ran through all the town, to harry all my neighbors out against me." His face twisted with bitterness. "'I' truth, 'twas no more than my desert; yet I felt betrayed when they came against me as a mob, screaming, 'Thought thief!' 'Slanderer!' and 'Sorcerer!' —betrayed, for that most of them had gossiped 'gainst me, one time or another—yet I'd forgiven them."

"Yes—but you had a weapon they couldn't use."

"Aye—not 'wouldn't,' but 'couldn't.'" Simon's grimace turned sardonic. "And for that reason, they did raise the hue and cry, and harried me from their town." He shuddered, closing his eyes. "Ah, praise Heaven that I have no powers other than thought-hearing! For in mine anger, I would have turned and hurled great stones at them, fireballs, sharp knives; I would have raised these folk up high, and slammed them to the earth!" He shuddered again, and his eyes sprang open, staring.

Rod could see the anger rising in him again, and spoke quickly, calmly. "Easy, easy. It was a long time ago."

"And the wrong's been righted. Aye." Simon managed to dredge up his smile again. "I did learn the error of my ways; I did repent, and did full pennance. For when I fled my native village, I wandered, blind with rage, immersed in bitterness, neither knowing nor caring whither my steps progressed. Forty leagues, fifty leagues, an hundred—till at last, worn out with hatred, I sank down in a cave and slept. And in my slumber, a soothing balm did waft to me, to calm my troubled spirit. When I waked, I felt refreshed, made new again. Wondering, I quested with my mind, to seek out the agency that had wrought this miracle. I found a well of holy thought which, in my slumber, I had drawn upon, unwitting. 'Twas a company of holy brothers and, by great good fortune, the cave I'd tumbled into was scarce an hundred yards from their community." Simon gazed off into the distance. "My soul did seek their solace, and did lead my steps unto them."

"Possible," Rod agreed. "But I thought there was only one monastery in this land—the Abbey of St. Vidicon, down South."

"Nay; there's another, here in Romanov, though 'tis not overlarge."

Rod nodded, musing. He knew that the main monastery was a conclave of espers, who knew about the outside universe and modern technology, and who were continually experimenting with their psi powers, trying to find new ways to use them. Could this northern monastery be the same type of thing? Maybe not, if they hadn't noticed Simon's troubled spirit so close by.

On the other hand, maybe they had... "So just being near the monks, healed your soul."

Simon nodded. "Indeed, their peace pervaded me. I made a broom, and swept the cave; I made a bed of branch and bracken. As the days passed, I made a cozy house there, and let the friars' peace still my rage, and fill my soul." He smiled, gazing off into the past. "Their serenity abides within me still, so deeply did it reach." He turned to Rod. "After some weeks, I did begin to ponder at their peace and calmness. What was its source? How did they come by it? I hearkened more carefully to their thoughts. And of them all, I found most wondrous were those that dwelt on herbs and their effects. So I commenced to spend much time within the minds of the monks who labored in the stillroom, distilling liquors and elixers. I drank up every fact, each notion.

As the leaves turned toward winter, I built a door to my

cave; I tanned furs and made a coat, then sat down by my
fire and hearkened all the more closely; for the monks were
pent up for the winter. The snows lay deep; they could not
venture forth. Then even friends could grate each upon the
other's nerves. The brotherhood was ripe for rifting. Quar-
rels did erupt, and I hung upon their every shout, eager to
see if they might still be holy. Yet I was amazed; for, even
when their tempers flared, the monks remembered their
devotions. They forgave each other, turned away!" Simon
sighed, shaking his head. "How wondrous did it seem!"

"Damn straight!" Rod croaked. "How'd they do it?"

"By their devotion to their God," Simon said, with a
beatific smile, "and by being ever mindful that He, and His
Way, were more important than themselves, or their pride—
or, aye, even their honor."

"Their honor?" Rod stiffened, staring. "Hey, now! You
can't mean they thought that God wanted them to be hu-
miliatied!"

Simon shook his head. "Nay, quite the contrary! They
trusted their God to prevent such!"

Rod felt a certain foreboding creeping over him. He
turned his head to the side, watching Simon out of the
corners of his eyes. "How was He supposed to do that?"

"By giving them to know, within themselves, which deeds
were right to do, and which were wrong. Then, even though
a man forebore to do some deed that other men did expect
of him, he might yet know himself to be worthy, even though
his fellows did jeer. Thus might he turn aside in pride,
without a trace of shame—for look thou, when all's said
and done, humiliation is within thee, not something visited
upon thee by thy fellows."

Rod frowned. "Are you trying to tell me a man can save
face, even though everybody else is pointing the finger of
scorn at him?"

Simon shook his head. "There was never need to. For if
any man stepped aside from a quarrel, and another ridiculed
him for it, the first had but to say, 'My God doth not wish
it,' and the other would comprehend, and only respect him
for his forebearance. Indeed, 'twas not even needful for the
first man to say aught aloud; 'twas only needful that he say

unto himself, in his heart, 'My God hath commanded me to love my neighbor,' and he would not think less of himself for retreating." He looked directly into Rod's eyes. "For this 'honor' that thou dost hold dear, this 'face' thou speakest of, is most truly but thine own opinion of thyself. We commonly suppose that 'tis what others think of us, but 'tis not so. 'Tis simply that most of us have so little regard for ourselves, that we believe others' opinions of us to be more important than our own. Therefore have we the need to save our countenances—our 'faces,' which term means only what others see of us. Yet we know that only by what they *say* they think of us—so our 'faces,' when all is truly said, are others' opinions of us. We feel we must demand others' respect, or we cannot respect ourselves." He shook his head, smiling. "But 'tis false, dost thou see."

"Surprisingly, I think I do." Rod frowned. "If any man really has a high opinion of himself, he won't care what others think of him—as long as *he* knows he's good."

In the cart, Flaran shifted impatiently. He had been following the conversation from a distance and seemed displeased by its direction.

Simon nodded, eyes glowing. "'Tis true, 'tis true! Yet few are capable of that. Few are so sure of themselves, that their own opinion can matter more to them than all the rest of their fellows' regard—and those few who are, be also frequently insufferable in their arrogance."

"Which means," Rod pointed out, "that they really don't have much faith in themselves—or they wouldn't have to make such a show of their supposed superiority."

"'Tis true, by all accounts. Nay, most of us, to have any sure sense of worth, must needs rely on some authority that's above us all, that doth assure us we are right. It will suffice, whether it be law, philosophy—or God. Then, should tempers flare, and thou dost draw back thine hand to smite me, and I, in wrath, set mine hand upon my dagger—one of us must needs retreat, or there will be mayhem sure."

"Yes," Rod agreed, "but what happens if neither of us is willing to? We'd lose face, we'd lose honor."

Simon nodded. "But if I can say, 'I will not strike, because my Lord hath commanded me to love mine enemy'—

why, then can I sheathe my dagger, step back, withdraw, and think myself no less a man for the doing of it." His smile gained warmth. "Thus may my God be 'the salvation of my countenance.'"

Rod nodded slowly. "I can see how that would work—but you'd have to be a real believer."

"Indeed." Simon sighed, and shook his head. "'Tis the work of a saint, friend Owen—and I am certainly none such."

Well, Rod had his own opinion about that.

"Yet there was sufficient of the monks' peace that did invest me so that, when the seasons turned to spring, and a villager came to beseech me for a cure for his cow, which was a-calving, but had taken ill—why, in my lone-ness, I delighted in his company, even for so short a while. I did distill the herbs that he did need, and sent him on his way. Some weeks later, another came—then another, and another. I welcomed their company, and strove to gain their liking—yet I minded me what I had learned of the good brothers—that the folk themselves were of greater import than their actions, or careless words. Thus did I learn to contain mine anger, and never reveal in wrath aught that I might have learned from their thoughts. Eh, but there were times it was not easy; for though their lips spoke courteously, their minds could hold insults grievous about the weird wood-hermit whose aid they sought. He smiled, amused at the memory of himself, the staunch innkeeper, as a wild-eyed anchorite. "Yet I was mindful that they were my fellow men, and of infinite worth thereby. Sorely tried I was, from time to time, to utter words that would have blasted pride—the hidden truths about themselves that would have made them shrink within. Yet I forebore, and was ever mindful that they were for cherishing. I served them all, from the poor peasant to the village priest, who first felt me to be a challenge yet finally came to respect me."

Rod smiled, amused. "Yes. I suppose if you can deal with those who wear their authority like mantles, you can deal with anything."

"Aye." Simon frowned, leaning forward. "And even as I have done, so mayest thou do also."

Rod stared at him a minute, then turned away. He started back toward the roadway, to avoid having to meet Simon's gaze. "What—withhold my anger, even against such a sink of corruption as Alfar?" He shook his head. "I can't understand how you can do that, with someone who's caused so much misery to so many people!"

At the mention of Alfar's name, Flaran climbed out of the cart, and came to join them where they stood.

"Loose anger at the deeds," Simon murmured, "but withhold it from the man."

Rod ground his teeth. "I hear your words, but I can't comprehend their meaning. How can you separate the man from his actions?"

"By being mindful that any human creature is a precious thing, and can turn aside from his own evil, if he can but recognize it."

"Can, sure." Rod's shoulders shook with a heave of inner laughter. "But, will? What are the odds on that, Master Simon?"

"Any person may be misled."

Rod shook his head. "You're assuming that Alfar's basically good—just an ordinary man, who's given in to the temptation for revenge, discovered he can actually gain power, and been corrupted by it."

"Certes." Simon peered up at him, frowning. "Is it not ever thus, with those who wreak wrong?"

"Maybe—but you're forgetting the possibility of evil. Actual, spiritual evil." Rod looked up, and noted Flaran's presence. He weighed what he was about to say, and decided that he didn't mind Flaran's hearing it. "Sure, all human souls have the potential for goodness—but in some, that potential is already buried before they're two years old. And it's buried so deeply that it's almost impossible to uncover it. They grow up believing that nobody's really capable of giving. They themselves can't love, or give love—and they assume everybody who talks about it is just putting on an act." He took a deep breath, and went on. "Though it's not really necessary to talk about that. All you really need is the word 'corruption.' Alfar succumbed to the temptation to do something he knows is wrong, because he loved the idea of being powerful. And now that he's tasted power, he'll do anything rather than give it up. No matter who he has to hurt, how many he has to kill, how much suffering he causes. Anything's better than going back to being what he really is—just an ordinary, humdrum human being, who probably isn't even very well-liked."

Flaran's eyes were huge; he stood frozen.

"Yet be mindful, he's human," Simon coaxed. "Hath that no meaning for thee, friend Owen?"

Rod shook his head. "Don't let the fact that he's human, make you believe that he thinks *you* are. He can't—he's treating people as though they were bolts for a crossbow— something to use, then forget about. He tramples through other minds without the slightest thought. Doesn't he realize these are real, feeling people, too?" He shook his head. "He can't, or he wouldn't be doing it. He's got to be totally without a conscience, totally calloused—really, actually, evil."

"Yet he is a person withal," Flaran piped up, timidly. "Even Alfar is not a devil, Master Owen."

"Not in body, maybe," Rod grunted. "I can believe he doesn't have horns, or a barbed tail. His soul, though . . ."

"Yet he doth have a soul," Flaran pleaded. "Look you, he may be an evil man—but he's a man nonetheless."

Rod drew a deep, shaky breath, then let it out slowly. "Friend Flaran . . . I beg you, leave off! I've seen Alfar's works, and those of his minions. Let us not speak of his humanity."

Flaran was silent, but he stared at Rod, huge-eyed.

Rod steeled himself against the look and picked up the reins. He slapped them on Fess's back, and the robot-horse started forward.

When the silence had grown very uncomfortable, Rod asked, "That fat little loudmouth, who was leading that mob—how did he figure out that Flaran was a warlock?"

"Why . . . he heard my neighbors speak of it. I would guess. . . ."

"Doesn't seem likely," Rod said, frowning. "He was a stranger, after all. How would he find out about the local skeletons, so quickly?"

"I think," Simon said, "that Alfar doth have adherents, minor witches and warlocks who can do little but read minds, salted here and there about the duchy—and their prime duty is to espy those of Power."

"Oh?" Rod held himself still, kept his tone casual. "How'd you hear about that?"

"I did not; but now and again, I've felt the touch of a mind that quested, but did not seek anything, or anyone, of which it was certain. And, anon, I've caught snatches of thought clearly between warlocks, warning that such-and-such had some trace of Power."

"How did they not espy thee?" Flaran asked, surprised.

Simon smiled. "I am, as we've said, rather weak at warlockery. And, too, I've learned to hide what poor weak powers I have, thinking like one who hath none at all, keeping the surface of my thoughts ever calm, and quite ordinary. 'Tis the key to not letting slip the odd comment that doth reveal thee—to think like an ordinary man; then you'll speak and act like one."

Flaran nodded, gaze locked onto Simon's face. "I will hearken to that. I will heed thee."

"Do so; 'twill save thee much grief. Nay, begin to think like John Common even now, for we never know when Alfar's spies may be listening."

Flaran started, darting a quick glance over each shoulder, then huddled in on himself.

"And, friend Owen, there's naught to fear for thee," Simon reassured Rod, "no spy would even know thou'rt there!"

Flaran looked up, astounded. "Why! How is that?"

"Oh, I'm, er, uh—invisible. To a mind reader." Rod said it as nonchalantly as he could, and tried to throttle down a burst of anger. How dare Simon let slip information about him! *Serves you right,* he told himself, in an attempt at soothing. And it was true; he should've known better than to confide in a stranger. But Simon was so damn like-able. . . .

"Ah, if only I could so hide me!" Flaran cried. "Nay, then, tell! How dost thou do it?"

"Nice question," Rod grated. "I really couldn't tell you.

But I think it has something to do with my basic dislike of all human beings."

Flaran stared at him, shocked.

"When you really get down to it," Rod admitted, "I guess I just don't really like people very well."

That rather put a damper on the conversation for a while. They rode on northward, each immersed in his own thoughts.

For his part, Rod couldn't help feeling that both of his companions were trying to become immersed in *his* thoughts, too. Not that they didn't both seem to be good people— but Rod was beginning to be very suspicious. The talk about mental spies had made him nervous, and he found himself remembering that Simon and Flaran *were* both strangers, after all.

A wave of loneliness hit him, and he glanced up at the skies. In spite of the longing, he was relieved to see the air clear, with a singular dearth of winged wildlife. At least his family was safe from getting mixed up in the mess.

Odd, though. He wasn't used to having Gwen listen to him.

12

He did notice the squirrel peering at him from the branches, and the doves stopping their preening to watch him from the roof of the inn, as they pulled the cart into an innyard. Rod climbed down and stood, surprised how much his joints ached from the four-hour ride. He tied the reins to a hitching post, and turned back to see Flaran climbing down from the cart also, and Simon stretching his legs carefully.

"Don't worry," Rod assured him, "they still work."

Simon looked up, and smiled. "The question is, do I wish they wouldn't?"

"Just at a guess, I'd say you're still having fun." Rod turned into the inn. "Shall we see what the kitchens hold?"

The question was as much good business as hunger; Rod was able to trade a bushel of produce for three lunches. Flaran insisted on paying Rod the penny he'd been planning to spend on beer, and Simon matched him. Rod protested, but wound up accepting.

Dinner came with a liberal supply of gossip. "Ye come off the road?" the landlord asked, as he set their plates in front of them. "Then say—is't true, what they say of Alfar?"

"Uh—depends on what you've heard," Rod said, feeling wary. "Myself, I've heard a lot about the man."

"Why, that he has dropped from sight!" A peasant leaned

over from another table. "That none have seen him since he took Castle Romanov."

"Oh, really?" Rod perked up noticeably. "Now, that's one I hadn't heard!"

"'Tis most strange, if 'tis true," the peasant said. "Here's a man who hath appeared from nowhere, conquered most of the duchy—and vanished!"

"Ah, but there's reason, Doln," an older peasant grinned. "Some say he was stole away by a demon!"

"Eh, Harl—there's some as says he *is* a demon," chirped a grandfather.

"Well, that would certainly explain why he appeared out of nowhere," Rod said, judiciously.

The third peasant caught the note of skepticism, and looked up with a frown. "Dost'a not believe in demons?"

"Dunno," Rod said, "I've never seen one."

"Such talk of demons is nonsense, Kench," Doln scoffed. "Why would demons take him away, when he's doing good demons' work?"

"Some say he's roaming the land, clad as a peasant," Harl grunted.

"Wherefore should he not?" Kench grinned. "He is a peasant, is he not?"

"Aye, but he's also a warlock," Harl reminded, "and they say he seeks through the land for folk who would aid him well in his governing."

Doln looked up, with a gleam in his eye. "That, I could credit more easily."

"Thou wilt credit aught," Kench scoffed.

"Belike he doth prowl unseen," Harl mused. "Would he not seek out traitors?"

Flaran and Simon stiffened, and Rod could feel little cold prickles running up his spine.

The peasants didn't like the idea, either. They glanced quickly over their shoulders, twisting their fingers into charms against evil. "How fell it is," Harl gasped, "to think that one could spy on thee, and thou wouldst never know it!"

Rod thought of mentioning that spies usually tried very hard to make sure nobody noticed them, but decided not to.

"Take heed of those rumors, and thou dost wish it," the

landlord chuckled. "For myself, I note only that the land is well-run."

The others turned to look at him, lifting their heads slowly.

"That's so," Doln nodded. "Dost'a say, then, that Alfar's still in his castle?"

"Belike," the landlord shrugged. "'Tis that, or his captains govern well in their own rights."

"That, I doubt." Rod shook his head. "I never yet heard of a committee doing any really effective governing. There has to be one man who always has the final say."

"Well, then." The landlord turned to Rod with a grin. "I must needs think Alfar's in his castle." And he turned away to the kitchen, chuckling and shaking his head. "Rumor! Only fools listen to it!"

"In which case, most people are fools," Rod said softly to Simon and Flaran. "So, if there's a rumor going around that you don't want people to believe, the thing to do is to set up a counter-rumor."

"Which thou dost think Alfar hath done?" Simon had his small smile on again.

"No doubt of it. Just look at the results—anybody who might 'been thinking of a counter-coup while Alfar was gone, would be thoroughly scared off. On the other hand, he *might* really be roaming the countryside in disguise."

"Would that not make witch folk loyal to him?" Flaran grinned. "For would he not be most likely to choose his own kind, to aid him in his governing?"

With his usual unerring social grace, he had spoken a bit too loudly. Harl looked up, and called out, "All witch folk would be loyal to Alfar. Wherefore ought they not to be?"

Flaran and Simon were instantly on their guard.

Rod tried to pull the sting out of it. He turned to Harl, deliberately casual. "For that matter, wouldn't every peasant be loyal to him? The rumor's that he's looking for talented *people* for his, uh, reign."

"Why . . . 'tis so." Harl frowned, suddenly doubtful.

Doln looked up, eyes alight. "Aye! He could not find witches enough to do *all* the tasks that are needed in governing, could he?"

"No." Rod repressed a smile. "He certainly couldn't."

Doln grinned, and turned to discuss the possibility with Harl and Kench. Rod reflected, with some surprise, that even a Gramarye peasant could have ambition. Which, of course, was perfectly natural; he should have foreseen it. He'd have to discuss the issue with Tuan when he went back to Runnymede; if it wasn't planned for, it could become dangerous.

He turned back to Flaran. "We can't be the only ones who've figured this out. Now, watch—the common people will all of a sudden start being *really* loyal, to Alfar— because they're going to think they have a chance to rise in the world."

"Indeed they may." Flaran grinned. "Would not the low-born have opportunity under the rule of an upstart?"

Rod frowned; the comment was a little too Marxist for his liking. "Yeah, if they happen to be the lucky ones out of thousands, the ones he wanted."

"Yet I should think that he has these by him already," said Simon. "He hath chosen his people ere he began this madcap climb. I would not look for him to place any great trust in those new to his banner."

Flaran frowned; he had definitely not wanted to hear that.

"But the hope of it could make a lot of people like him," Rod pointed out. "Just the idea that a lowborn peasant's son has come to rule a duchy, will pull an amazing amount of support to him."

"Can rumor truly do so much?" Flaran breathed.

"That, and more," Rod said grimly. "Which is the best reason of all for thinking Alfar's still in his castle."

Flaran stared. Then he closed his eyes, shook his head, and opened them again.

"I, too, am puzzled." Simon frowned. "How can a rumor mean..." His voice trailed off as his face cleared with understanding.

Rod nodded. "All he has to do is stay inside the castle and make sure the rumor gets started. Once it's running, it's going to keep building peasant loyalty on the one hand, and make everybody a little more wary about thinking disloyal thoughts, or doing any plotting, on the other—for fear Alfar himself might be listening in."

Flaran shuddered, and glanced quickly about the room—

and, suddenly, Rod had a sinking feeling in his stomach. Alfar could indeed be in that very taproom, could be one of the peasants, could be the landlord, lying in wait for one of Tuan's agents to come by—such as Rod himself. He could be about to spring the trap on Rod, any second. . . .

Then chagrin hit, and hard on its heels, anger. This was just what Alfar wanted Tuan's agents to be thinking. It was called "demoralization," and it had almost worked. Rod's respect for the sorcerer went up, as his animosity increased. He was amazed that a medieval peasant could be so devious.

On the other hand, maybe he had some help. . . .

Simon leaned over to Rod and murmured, "Do not look, or disguise it if thou must—but yon wench hath kept her eye on us, since we came through the door."

"That is a little odd," Rod admitted. "None of us is exactly what you'd call a model of masculine pulchritude."

"True enough," Simon answered, with a sardonic smile. "Yet 'tis not with her eyes alone that she's kept watch over us."

"Oh, really?" All of a sudden Rod's danger sensors were tuned to maximum—not that they'd done much good so far. He pulled out a coin, flipped it—and made sure it "accidentally" flipped her way. As he turned to pick it up, he managed a quick glance at her, and decided it wasn't much of a surprise that he hadn't noticed her sooner. She was average size, no heavier than she ought to be, with a pretty enough face and dark blond hair.

Rod picked up the coin and turned back to Simon. "Not exactly your stereotyped witch, is she?"

Simon frowned. "A very ordinary witch, I would say."

"That's a contradiction in terms. She's also not very experienced at hiding her interest."

"Oh, she doth well enough," Simon demurred. "Yet I've more experience at this sort of hiding than most, Master Owen—and, when one of us doth say that which doth amaze her, her shield doth slip."

Rod frowned. "Then why didn't she head for the door as soon as we started talking about her?"

"Because thy mind is hid, let alone thy thoughts—and for myself, I'm thinking one thought and saying another."

He grinned at Rod's surprise. "Be not amazed—what women can do, we men may learn to do also. As for Flaran, I speak so softly that he cannot hear."

Rod glanced quickly at the klutz; he was looking rather nettled. Rod turned back to Simon. "Then there's no real danger, is there?"

"Oh, there is alarm in her." Simon glanced at the serving-wench, then back at Rod. "We had best be on our way, Master Owen, and quickly, ere she calls another who doth serve Alfar."

Rod turned toward the girl, considering risks and coming to a quick decision. "No, I don't think that's really neces-sary." He beckoned to the wench. Fear leaped in her eyes, but she had no reason for it, and did need to keep her cover while she studied them—so she came. Slowly, as though she were being dragged, but she came. "What may I offer, goodmen? Ale? Or more meat?"

"Neither, just now." Rod plastered on a friendly smile. "Tell me—does it bother you that I'm not here, when I really am?"

She stared at him in shocked surprise, and Simon mut-tered, "Well done; she is quite disarmed. Certes, Alfar's her master. She holds watch for witches."

Rod's dagger was out before Simon finished the first sentence, its point touching the wench's midriff. She stared at the naked steel, horrified.

"Sit." Rod kept the smile, but it had turned vicious.

"Sir," she gasped, gaze locked on the blade, "I dare not."

"Dare not disobey me? No, you don't. Now sit."

Trembling, she lowered herself to the empty stool. Rod took her hand, gave her a glowing smile. "Simon, dig around and see what you can find." He let the smile turn fatuous, clasped both hands around hers, and leaned forward, croon-ing, "Now, pretty lass, sit still and try to pay no heed to the fingers you'll feel in your mind—and if their touch disgusts you, be mindful that you would have spoken words with your mind, that would have sent soldiers to slay us." He lifted her hand to his lips, kissed it, then beamed at her again. "I know—you feel like nothing so much as leaping up and screaming. But if you do, my knife is close at hand— and do not think that you can snatch it with your mind faster

than I can stab—for, in this case, the hand is quicker than
the mind." He saw her glance at the knife, and warned, "I
assure you, I've dealt with witches before." Which, he
reckoned, was his understatement for the year.

Her gaze darted back to his face, terrified. "But . . . why
dost thou kiss mine hand, when thou'rt mine enemy?"

"So that anyone watching . . . there, young Doln is staring
at me—no, don't look!—and his gaze is anything but
friendly. In fact, I think he favors my heart for the main
course. No, don't hope—I assure you, I'm a better fighter
than he, far better." He saw the flicker of fear in her eyes,
and decided to press it. "Sit very still, now. You wouldn't
want me to hurt him, would you?"

"Oh, do not!" she cried. Then, realizing she'd given away
more than military secrets, she blushed and dropped her
eyes.

"Aye, well done," Simon purred. "Gaze at the tabletop,
there's a good lass, and naught else; think of naught but its
grain, and its color . . . Now!"

The girl stiffened with a gasp, head flung back, eyes
shut; then she slumped in her chair.

"Stand away from her!" Doln was on his feet, knife out.

Rod stood slowly, his grin turning wolfish, knifepoint
circling. "Why, it shall be as you say—I shall stand away
from her. Shall I stand toward you, then?"

Harl scowled and stood up behind Doln, but the youth's
eyes showed doubt. He stood his ground, though—swal-
lowing hard, but he stood.

"Gently, now, gently," Simon soothed. "She sleeps, lad—
she but sleeps."

Doln glanced at him, then at the unconscious girl, and
the white showed all around his eyes.

"Softly, lad." Rod followed Simon's lead. "We're not
hurting her." He darted a quick glance at Simon. "Nay,
unless I mistake, my friend seeks to aid her."

"What manner of aid is this, that steals away her sense?"
Doln cried.

"What manner indeed!" Flaran huddled back in his chair,
eyes wide with terror.

Kench's glare would have killed a viper, and Harl gathered himself and stepped up behind Doln.

The girl sighed, and her head rolled back.

"Ask her," Rod said softly. "She'll be awake in a minute."

Doln's gaze darted to her. Her eyelids fluttered, then opened. She looked around her, uncomprehending, then suddenly realized where she was, and her eyes widened; she gasped.

"Marianne!" Doln dropped to one knee, clasping her hand. "What have these fellows done to thee!"

Her gaze darted down to him; she shrank away. Then she recognized him, and relaxed a little. She looked around, and her gaze centered on Rod. Slowly, it turned to Simon, then back to Doln, and her lips quivered with a smile. "Nay, be not afeared for me, good Doln. I am well—aye, more well than I have been for some weeks." She turned back to Simon, frowning, then back to Doln. "These goodmen have aided me."

Doln looked from one to another wildly, "What manner of aid is this, that makes thee to swoon?"

"That, thou dost not need know," Simon advised. "Stand away, now, I beg thee, for we must have further converse with thy Marianne."

"I am not his," she said, with a touch of asperity, then instantly balanced it with a dazzling smile at Doln. "I did not know thou hadst concern of me."

Doln swallowed heavily, and stood, but his eyes were still on her. "I . . . I do care for thy welfare, Marianne."

"I know it, now—and I thank thee." Her color had come back completely, now. She clasped his hand, and looked up at him through long lashes. "Most deeply do I thank thee. Yet I prithee, do as this goodman doth bid thee, and stand away, good Doln, for truly must I speak with them."

Reluctantly, Doln backed away from the table—and bumped into Harl, who muttered a curse, and turned away to his stool. Doln did, too, gaze flicking from Simon to Marianne, then to Rod, then back to Marianne again. Then Kench muttered something, and Doln turned to him, frowning, then fell to muttering with Harl and the gaffer, casting frequent glares at Rod and Simon.

He didn't notice Flaran. But then, who ever did?

Marianne turned back to Simon with a happy smile,

patting her hair into place. "I must needs thank thee for more things than one. Nay, ask what thou wilt. I will most gladly answer."

Rod rubbed a hand over his face to cover a smile, then turned to Simon. "Mind telling me what went on there?"

"Only what thou hast seen aforetime," Simon answered. "She labored under a spell. I have broken it."

"A *spell?*" Rod stared at Marianne, appalled. "A *witch!!?!*"

"Even so." The girl bowed her head in shame. "I see now that I must have been."

Simon reached out and caught her hand. "There's no shame in it, lass. 'Tis no fault of thine, that thou wert enchanted."

"But it is!" She looked up at him, wide-eyed. "For I hid my witch power from the goodfolk, full of guilt and embarrassment—till I began to believe that I was better than they, for I could read minds and make things move by mere thought, whilst they could not. Nay, it did come to seem to me that we witch folk were the true nobility, the new nobility, who could and should rule the world—aye, and better than the lords do!"

"This, thou dost count fault of thine own?" Simon asked, with a smile.

"Is't not?" She blushed, and looked down. "Alas, that ever I thought so! Yet I did—and no other witch did seem to feel as I did, no honest one; for I listened for their thoughts, and heard them afar. Nay, none thought to lead the witches to their rightful place—not even within the Royal Coven. Thus, when Alfar began to reach out for vassals, declaring he would lead the witch folk on to glory and to rule, I declared him my leader on the instant, and pledged him my fealty. All that he asked, I swore I would do."

"And the service that he asked of thee?"

"Only this." She gestured around at the inn in disgust. "Here is my glory and rule! To work as I had done, and watch, then speak to them of any witchfolk I found who, in either deed or thought, did struggle 'gainst Alfar. So I did—and most joyously." She plunged her face into her hands, "Eh, what a bitch I have been, what a vile, dastardly traitor! For three witches have I delivered unto them—poor, weak souls, who only sought to flee to safety!" She lifted tragic eyes to gaze at Simon. "Yet truthfully did it seem to me that any witch who did not acclaim Alfar, must needs be a traitor to her own kind. Therefore did I summon aid from Alfar's coven, and soldiers came, under the command of a warlock, to take those witches away, and..." She buried her face in her hands again. "Aiee! What did they to those poor folk!"

Her shoulders shook with weeping. Simon reached out to touch her, clasping her shoulder. "Nay, be not so grieved! For thou didst these things not of thine own free will and choice!"

Her gaze leaped up to his, tears still coursing down her cheeks. "Yet how could it be otherwise?"

"When first thou didst begin to think thyself greater than thy neighbors, the sorcerer's folk had already begun their vile work on thee." Simon's smile hardened. "These first thoughts, that witches ought to govern by right of birth, were not truly thine. But they were oh, most gently and skillfully worked in, among thoughts of thine own, that thou mightst think them so."

'Truly?" she gasped, wide-eyed.

Simon nodded. "Be sure. I have myself slipped through thy thoughts, witch—I must ask they pardon—and I know."

"Oh, the pardon is instantly given!" she cried. "How can I thank thee, for breaking this spell?" Then her face lit up, and she clapped her hands. "I know! I shall wander northward, and myself seek to break spells that bind goodfolk!"

Rod darted a quick glance at Simon, and saw the foreboding in his face. He turned back to Marianne. "Uh—I don't think that would be the best idea."

Her face fell. "Would it not? What, then..."

"Well, basically the same thing—just do it right here." Rod managed to smile. "What Alfar was having you do, but for our side. Keep working as a servingwench, and spy out witch folk who're going south. But when you find them, *don't* report them to Alfar's henchmen."

"But that is so small an aid!" she cried, disappointed.

"Those whom thou dost save will not think it so," Simon assured her.

"But they would be just as much saved if I were not here at all."

"Not so." Rod shook his head. "If you left this post, Alfar's men would find it out quickly enough, and they'd send some other witch here to do the job. The only way you can protect the fugitives, is to stay here and cover for them."

"Assuredly there must be work of greater import I can do!"

An imp pricked Rod with temptation. He grinned, and succumbed. "There is, now that you mention it. You can find another witch or two, who plan to stay."

"Others?" She stared, amazed. "How will that aid?"

"Because each of them can find two other witches," Rod explained, "and each of those, two more, and so on and on—and we can build up a network of witches opposed to Alfar, all throughout the duchy of Romanov."

She frowned, shaking her head. "What aid will that be?"

"King Tuan will march North, sooner or later. When he does, we'll send word through the net, for the witches to gather where the battle's going to be, to help."

"Help in a battle?" Her eyes were round. "How?"

"Well send word about that, too. Just be ready to do it."

Slowly, she nodded. "I do not fully comprehend—yet I do trust in thee. I shall do as thou dost bid."

"Good lass! And don't worry, you'll understand plenty. It won't be very complicated—just to gather at a certain place, and attack whatever part of the sorcerer's army you're assigned."

"An thou sayest it." She still seemed doubtful. "But how shall I know what to do, or when?"

"Someone will tell you. From now on, your name is, uh, 'Esmeralda,' to anyone else in the anti-Alfar network. So, if someone comes in and says he has word for Esmeralda, from Kern..." Again, Rod wished he hadn't chosen that name. "...you'll know it's a message from me."

"But wherefore ought I not to be called Marianne?"

"So nobody can betray you. This way, if they tell Alfar or his men they've a traitor named 'Esmeralda,' they won't know who it really is."

"And 'Kern' is thy false name?"

I sure hope so. "It's as good a name as any. The whole idea is that we don't know each other's real names, remember. Will you do it—be Esmeralda, and watch for witches to *not* report?"

Slowly, she nodded. "Aye—if thou dost truly believe this is the greatest aid I can offer."

"Good lass!" Rod clasped her hand, relieved—she was too young, and really too sweet, to wind up in Alfar's torture chambers. Better to leave her where it was safe. "Now, uh—would you please go reassure your friend Doln, there? I can't help this feeling that he's just dying to shove a knife between my ribs."

"Certes." She flushed prettily, and stood. "I thank thee, goodman." She turned away, becoming shy and demure as she neared her swain.

"I think she hath forgot thee quite," Simon said, with his small smile.

"Yes. And that's the way it should be, isn't it?" Rod was watching Doln, whose gaze was riveted to Marianne's face. He caught her hand, and Rod turned back to Simon and Flaran with a sigh. "Young love! Isn't it wonderful?"

"In truth." Simon watched the young couple over Rod's shoulder. "Yet I cannot help but think, friend Owen, that there's some truth to her words—not that her thoughts of overweening greatness were her own, nay, but that, shall we say, Alfar's seeds fell on fertile ground?"

"Oh, well, sure! People can't be hypnotized if they *really* don't want to be—and this particular kind of long-range telepathic hypnosis couldn't have worked so well if she didn't already have a bit of that resentful attitude—it's called 'feelings of inferiority.'"

"Inferiority?" Flaran stared. "Yet how can that be? Witch power makes us greater than other folk!"

Rod didn't miss the 'us.' "Yeah, but they don't *feel* that way. All they know is that they stand out, that they're different, and that if people find out just *how* different, nobody'll like them." He shrugged. "If nobody likes you,

you must be inferior. I know it doesn't really make sense, but that's how our minds work. And, since nobody can stand to think so little of themselves pretty soon, the warlock starts telling himself that he's not really inferior—it's just that everybody's picking on him, because they're jealous. And, of course, people do pick on witches—they've been doing it, here, for hundreds of years."

"Aye!" Flaran seized the thought. "'Tis not merely a matter of our telling ourselves others bully us—'tis true!"

"Oh, yeah, it's easy to feel persecuted, when you really are. But that must mean you're *worse* than inferior." He made a backwards arc with his forefinger. "If people're picking on you, and they're nice people, ones you ordinarily like, and all of a sudden, they're picking on you—then you must be worse than second-rate; you must be evil! But who can stand thinking they're outright evil?"

"Evil folk," Flaran answered quickly.

"And there you have it." Rod spread his hands. "Instead of saying, 'I'm second-rate,' they're saying, 'I'm evil'— they'd rather be first-rate evil than second-rate good."

Flaran stared, lost.

"Or!" Rod held up a forefinger. "Or you decide that you're not evil, and you're not second-rate, either—they're just picking on you because they're jealous. So their picking on you proves that you're better than they are. They're just afraid of the competition. They're out to get you because you're a threat to them."

Flaran's head lifted slowly, and Rod could see his eyes clearing with understanding.

Rod shrugged. "All the witch folk probably have that attitude to some degree—it's called paranoia. But they keep it under control; they know that even if there're wisps of truth attached to the notion, there's more truth in thinking of their neighbors as being basically good folk—which they are. And if the witch has even a grain of humility, she's as much aware of her faults as she is of her powers—so they manage to keep their feelings of persecution under control. It's a sort of a balance between paranoia and reality. But it does make them ready, even eager, victims, for Alfar's style of brainwashing—uh, persuasion."

Flaran turned away, staring at the table. The color had

drained out of his face, and his hands trembled.

Rod watched him, shaking his head with a sad smile. *The poor kid*, he thought, *the poor innocent*. In some ways, Flaran probably would have preferred to just go along from day to day for the rest of his life, feeling inferior and picked-on. And it must've been very demeaning, to find out that his feelings were, if not normal, at least standard for his condition—it was bad enough being born an esper, but it was worse finding out you weren't even exceptional.

He turned away, to catch Simon's eye. The old man had a sympathetic look, and Rod smiled back, nodding. They both knew—it was rough, learning the facts of life.

Back on the road, Rod and Simon tried to strike up a cheerful family topic conversation again; but the mood had changed, and it was an uphill fight all the way. When they each realized that the other guy was trying just as hard, they gave it up.

Of course, the ambiance wasn't helped much by Flaran riding along on Rod's other side sunk in gloom, glowering at the road.

So they rode along in silence, the unease and tension growing, until Rod'd had about as much as he could take. "Look Flaran, I know it's hard to accept the idea that Alfar's turning the whole population into puppets—but that is what he's doing. So we have to just admit it, and try to go beyond it, to figure out what we can do about it. See? Feeling lousy won't do anybody any good."

Flaran looked up at Rod, and his attention came back, as though from a great distance. Slowly, his eyes focused. "Nay. Nay, 'tis not that which hath me so bemused, friend Owen."

Rod just looked at him for a moment.

Then he said, "Oh." And, "Really?"

He straightened in his seat and tilted his head back, looking down at Flaran a little. "What *is* bothering you?"

"These thoughts which the servingwench hath uttered."

"What—about witches being naturally superior?" Rod shook his head. "That's nonsense."

"Nay, 'tis good sense—or, if not good, at least sense."

Flaran gazed past Rod's shoulder at the sky. "Truly, witches should rule."

"Oh, come off it! Next thing I know, you'll be telling me how Alfar's really a good guy, and is really freeing the peasants, not conquering them!"

Flaran's eyes widened. "Why—that is true." He began to nod, faster and faster. "In truth, 'tis all true. He doth free the peasants from the rule of the lords."

Rod turned away, his mouth working, and swallowed heavily. He looked up at Simon. "Check him, will you? Give him the once-over. He sounds as though the spell's beginning to creep over him."

"Oh, nay!" Flaran said in scorn, but Simon frowned, gazing off into space for a moment. Then he shook his head. "I do not read even so much as he doth utter, Master Owen— only thoughts of how goodly seem the fields about us, and the face of the wench who served us." His eyes focused on Rod's again. "Still, those are not the thoughts of a spell-bound mind."

"Spellbound? Nay, certes!" Flaran cried. "Only because I speak truth, Master Owen?"

"Truth?" Rod snorted. "Somebody must have warped your mind, if you think that's truth!"

"Nay, then—lay it out and look at it!" Flaran spread his hands. "It doth seem the common people must needs have masters . . ."

"I could dispute that," Rod growled.

"But not gainsay it! From all that I have seen, 'tis true!" Flaran craned his neck to look over Rod's shoulder at Simon. "Wouldst thou not say so, Master Simon?"

"Someone must govern," Simon admitted reluctantly.

"And if one must govern—why, then, one must be master!" Flaran slapped his knee. "And is it not far better for the peasant folk to have masters who were born, as they were, peasants? Who know the pain of poverty, and the grinding toil of the common folk? Is that not far better for them than the rule of those who are born to silver plates and ruby rings, in castles, who have never known a hard day's work, nor a moment's want? Nay, these lords even look down from their high towers, and speak of we poor folk as though we were chattels! Things to be owned! Cattle! Not men and women!"

Rod stared, horrified. "Where'd you hear that line of rubbish?"

Flaran reddened. "Can there be truth in rubbish?"

"I don't know who you've been talking to," Rod said, "but it sure wasn't a lord. Most of 'em don't say things like that—and where would you have had a chance to hear 'em talking, anyway?"

"Mine ears do be large, Master Owen. I may be foolish in my speaking, but I am wise in my listening. I have spoken with folk who serve the lords, and thus have I learned how they speak of us. And, too, I have hearkened to my neighbors, to their groans and cries of grief under the lords' rule—and I cannot help but think that they do not serve the best of masters." Flaran shook his head. "Nay, the words of that servingwench do make most excellent sense—for who could better know the people's wants, than those who can hear their thoughts? And who can better guard them in their labors, than one who knows what it is to labor so?"

"Excuses," Rod growled. He turned away, and saw, in the distance, a party of peasants coming out of a side road, clad in rough homespun and bowed under the weight of huge packs. "There!" He stabbed a finger at them. "That's the kind of sense you've been making! Poor people, wandering the roads, lost and alone, because their homes have been destroyed in battle! Folk bereft, whose villages still stand, but who have packed what they can carry and have fled, because they fear the rule of an upstart they don't trust!"

"Yet peasants' homes do ever burn in wars," Flaran cried, "ever and aye, when the lords do seek to resolve some private quarrel with their armies! This time, at the least, the war may bring them some benefit, for he who wins will have been born among them!"

"Excuses," Rod said again, "rationalizations!" He turned to look squarely at Flaran. "Let me tell you what that is— a rationalization. It's giving something the appearance of rationality, of reason, when it doesn't have the reality of it. It's finding a way to justify what you want to do, anyway. It's finding an excuse for something you've already done—a way to make it seem to be good, when it really isn't. That's all you're doing here—trying to find a way to make the wrong things you want to do, seem right. All your arguments really boil down to, 'I want power, so I'm going to take it.' And the real reasons are envy and revenge!"

He noticed, out of the corner of his eye, that the peasants had stopped, staring up at them, on both sides of the cart. All the better—let witnesses hear it!

"Yet how canst thou speak so?" Flaran frowned, cocking his head to the side. "Thou hast thyself an enormous power!"

Rod froze. How had he let his cover slip? "What... power... is... that?"

"Why, the talent of not being seen by the mind! Our friend Simon hath said it—to a thought-hearer, thou dost not seem to be here at all!"

"Nay, then!" the younger man cried, "even I have noticed it, weak though my powers are!"

Rod shrugged; that was explanation enough, for the moment.

"How great a talent that is!" Flaran cried. "What great advantage must it needs give thee, if one doth seek thee with evil intent! If thou wert of Alfar's band, he would surely create thee Duke of Spies!" He smiled, leaning forward, eyes glittering. "Would that not be most excellent, Master Owen? Wouldst thou not be delighted to be a duke?"

"I'd say it would be horrible," Rod grated. "Do you realize what that would mean? I'd be helping to enforce one of the harshest tyrannies humanity has ever known! Stop and think!" He held up a forefinger. "Even under the tightest dictatorships Old Terra ever knew, people have still been able to have one thing that was theirs, alone to themselves— their minds. At least their thoughts were free. But Alfar's trying to change that; he's trying to set up a tyranny so complete that nobody can even call his thoughts his own!"

"How small a thing that is!" Flaran waved away the objection. "Thoughts are naught, Master Owen—they are gossamer, mere spiders' webs! What are free thoughts against a filled belly, and an ease of grinding toil? What is freedom of thought, against freedom from want? What worth hath the secrecy of the mind, when weighed against the knowledge that the King doth hold every least peasant to be his own equal? But think!" He gazed off into space, eyes glittering. "Think how sweet this land could be, an witches ruled it! What an earthly paradise we could make here for ourselves, an folk of good heart could labor freely with their minds, to build it!"

Rod stared, astounded by the younger man's enthusiasm.

Then he leaned back, letting his mouth twist to show his skepticism. "All right—tell me."

"Why! What could they not do, an witches could use their power openly? Never would there be drought or flood, for witches could move the storms about so as to water all the land! Never would murrain slay cattle or other stock, for witches could be open in their curing! Nor, for that matter, would folk need to die from illness, when witch-physicians could be by to aid them! Never would the peasants go hungry, to give their substance unto their lord, that he might deck himself with finery, or gamble through the night! Never would the people grumble in their misery, unheard, for a warlock would hear their thoughts, and find a means of ending that which troubled them!"

"Yeah, unless those peasants were grumbling because the king-warlock was doing something they didn't like! Then he'd just shut them up, by hypnotism!"

"Oh, such would be so few!" Flaran gave him a look of disgust. "Why trouble thyself for a mere handful of malcontents? Ever will some few be discontented with their lot!"

"Right—and Alfar's one of them! But it wouldn't be just a few malcontents, if the witch folk ruled—it'd be the vast majority, the normals, who'd be feeling like half-humans, because they didn't have any witch power! And they'd resent the governing ones who did—but they'd know the witches would wipe out anybody who dared utter it! So they'd keep quiet, but live in terror, and their whole lives would be one long torture! Just ordinary people, like these men around us!" He gestured at the peasants, who were pressing close all about them, eyes burning. "Better move along, boys. I'm having trouble keeping my temper; and when warlocks fight, bystanders may get hit with stray magic."

"Ah, art thou a warlock, then?" Flaran cried.

Rod ground his teeth in frustration, furious with himself for the slip he'd made; but he made a brave try at covering. "According to you, I am. Didn't you just say my invisible mind was a great talent?"

"In truth I did—and if thou art a warlock, then art thou also a traitor!" Flaran leaped to his feet, face dark with anger, suddenly seeming bigger—almost a genuine threat.

Rod wasn't exactly feeling pacific, himself. "Watch your tongue! I'm a King's man, and loyal to the bone!"

"Then art thou a traitor to witchhood!" Flaran stormed. "Naught but a tool for hire, and the King's pay is best! Nay, thus art thou but a tool of the lordlings, a toy in their games—but it is we who are their pawns and moved about the land for their mere amusement! And thou dost abet them! Thou, who, by blood, ought to join with Alfar and oppose them! Nay, thou'rt worse than a traitor—thou'rt a shameless slave!"

"Watch your tongue!" Rod sprang to his feet, and the cart rocked dangerously. But Flaran kept his footing easily, and, for some reason, that ignited Rod's anger into a blow-torch. "Beware who you're calling a slave! You've fallen so far under Alfar's spell that you've become nothing but his puppet!"

"Nay—his votary!" Flaran's eyes burned with sudden zeal. "Fool thou art, not to see his greatness! For Alfar will triumph, and all witch folk with him—Alfar will reign, and those self-sold witches who do oppose him, will die in torments of fire! Alfar is the future, and all who obstruct him will be ground into dust! Kneel, fool!" he roared, leaping up onto the cart-seat, finger spearing down at Rod. "Kneel to Alfar, and swear him thy loyalty, or a traitor's death shalt thou die!"

The thin tissue of Rod's self-control tore, and rage erupted. "Who the hell do you think you are, to tell me what to swear! You idiot, you dog's-meat gull! He's ground your ego into powder, and there's nothing left of the real you! You don't exist anymore!"

"Nay—*I* exist, but *thou* shalt not!" Flaran yanked a quarterstaff from the peasant next to him and smashed a two-handed blow down at Rod.

Rod ducked inside the swing, coming up next to Flaran with his dagger in his hand, but a dozen hands seized him and yanked him back, the sky reeled above him, framed by peasant faces with burning eyes. He saw a club swinging down at him—and, where the peasants' smocks had come open at the necks, chain mail and a glimpse of green-and-brown livery.

Then pain exploded through Rod's forehead, and night came early.

13

A blowtorch, set on "low," was burning its way through Rod's brain. But it was a very poor blowtorch; it seemed to go over the same path again and again, in a regular, pulsing rhythm. He forced his eyes open, hoping to catch the bastard who was holding the torch.

Blackness.

Blackness everywhere, except for a trapezoid of flickering orange. He frowned, peering more closely at it, squinting against the raging in his head, and figured out that it was the reflection of a flame on a rock wall. There were stripes up and down—the shadows of bars, no doubt. There were a couple of other stripes, too, zigging and zagging—the trails of water droplets. Then Rod became aware of fragile orange webs, higher up—gossamer niter, lit by the firelight.

He added it all up, and enlightenment bloomed—he was in a dungeon again. The firelight was a guard's torch, out in the hall, and the trapezoid was the shadow of the little barred grille in the door.

He heaved a sigh and lay back. This kept happening to him, time and again. There'd been the gaol in Pardope, the Dictator's "guest chamber" in Caerleath, the dungeon under

the House of Clovis, and the cell in the Duke's castle in Tir
Chlis, where Father Al had taught him how to use his ESP
talents . . . and the list went on. He frowned, trying to remember back to the first one, but it was too much for his
poor, scrambled brain.

He put the list away, and very slowly, very carefully,
rolled up onto one elbow. The blowtorch shot out a fiery
geyser that seemed to consume his whole head, right down
his backbone, but only for a few moments; then it subsided,
and fell into perspective as a mere headache. A real beaut,
Rod had to admit—those soldiers hadn't exactly been deft,
but they'd made up for it with enthusiasm. He pressed a
hand to his throbbing forehead, remembering the chain mail
under the peasant tunics. It was a very neat little trap he'd
walked into—but he couldn't imagine a less appetizing bait
than Flaran.

Not that it hadn't worked, though.

He lifted his head slowly, looking around him. Compared
to the other dungeons he'd been in, this one was definitely
second-rate. But, at least he had a couple of roommates,
manacled to the wall across from him—though one of them
had lost quite a bit of weight over the years; he was a pure
skeleton. Well, not "pure"—he did have some mold patches
here and there. The other one had some patches, too, but
they were purple, shading toward maroon. It was Simon,
and his chin was sunk on his chest.

Rod squeezed his eyes shut, trying to block out the headache, trying to think. Why should Simon be here? He wasn't
a spy. Rod considered the question thoroughly, till the brain-
storm struck: He could ask. So he cleared his throat, and
tried. "Uh . . . Simon . . ."

The other man looked up, surprised. Then his face relaxed into a sad smile. "Ah, thou dost wake, then!"

"Yeah—kind of." Rod set both palms against the floor
and did a very slow push-up. The headache clamored in
indignation, and he fell back against the wall with a gasp—
but victorious; he was sitting up. The headache punished
him unmercifully, then decided to accept the situation and
lapsed into the background. Rod drew in a long, shuddering
breath. "What . . . what happened? You shouldn't be here—
just me. What'd Flaran have against you?"

"He knew me for what I was," Simon sighed. "When the soldiers had felled thee, young Flaran turned on me, raging. "Who was this 'Owen?' Thou, vile traitor, will speak! Wherefore did this false, unminded man march northward into our domain?"

"Our?" Rod frowned.

Simon shrugged. "By good chance, I did not know the answers he sought. I said as much, and he whirled toward the soldiers, pointing back at me, screaming, 'Torture him! Hale him down now, and break his fingers, joint by joint!' 'Nay,' I cried, 'I have naught to hide,' and I abandoned all pretence of cloaking my mind, casting aside all shields and attempts at hiding."

"What good could that do? As mind readers go, he was barely literate."

"Oh, nay! He was a veritable scholar!" Simon's mouth tightened. "Thou, my friend, wert not alone in thy deceptions. I felt naught, but I saw his face grow calm. Then his eyes lit with excitement—but they soon filled with disappointment, and he did turn away to the soldiers in disgust. 'There's naught here—naught but an old man, with some talent for spell-breaking. He could have gone free but, more's the fool, he hath come back North to seek to undo our work.' Then the auncient said, 'He's a traitor, then,' and the look that he gave me was venomed—yet there was that strange emptiness behind it."

Rod nodded. "Spellbound."

"Indeed. Then the auncient said further, 'Shall we flay him?' and cold nails seemed to skewer my belly. But Flaran gave me a measuring glance, and shook his head. 'Nay. He may yet prove useful. Only bind him and bring him.' Then he did fix his gaze upon me, and his eyes did seem to swell, glowing, to burn into my brain. 'An thou dost seek to break spells on these soldiers,' he swore. 'I will slay thee.'"

"So." Rod lifted his eyebrows. "Our young klutz wasn't quite the fool he seemed to be, was he?"

"Nay. In truth, he did command. He bade the soldiers march home, and all did turn to take up the journey. Some hundreds of yards further, we came to tethered horses. The soldiers untied them and mounted—and there were pack mules for myself and for thee, and a great chestnut charger with a saddle adorned with silver for Flaran."

Rod watched Simon for a moment, then said, "Not exactly an accident we ran into them, was it?"

Simon smiled, with irony. "In truth, 'twas quite well-planned."

"Even to the point of rigging up a peasant mob to be chasing Flaran, at just the right time to run into us on the road." Rod's mouth tightened. "He knew that was a sure way to make us take him in. And he stayed with us just long enough to make sure we were what he thought we were, before he turned us over to his bully boys."

"He did give us the opportunity to turn our coats to Alfar's livery," Simon pointed out.

"Yes. Generous of him, wasn't it?" Rod scowled. "But how did he catch onto us?"

Simon sighed, and shook his head. "I can only think that some spy of his must have sighted us, and followed unbeknownst."

"Yeah—that makes sense." With a sudden stab of guilt, Rod realized that Alfar had probably had spies watching him from the moment he crossed the border. After all, he'd certainly had Rod in sight before then. Rod just hadn't counted on the sorcerer's being so thorough.

Nothing to do about it now. Rod shook himself—and instantly regretted it; the headache stabbed again. But he thrust it all behind him, and asked, "How far did they ride?"

"All the rest of the day, and far into the night," Simon answered.

"But it was only mid-morning." Rod frowned. "That must have been . . . let me see . . ." He pressed a hand against his aching head, and the clank of the wrist-chain seemed to drive right through from ear to ear. But he absorbed the pain and let it disperse through his skull, trying to think. "Sixteen hours. And I was out cold all that time?"

Simon nodded. "Whenever thou didst show sign of wakening, Flaran bade his soldiers strike thee again."

"No *wonder* my head's exploding! How many times did they hit me?"

"More than half a dozen."

Rod shuddered. "I'm just lucky I don't have a fracture. On the other hand . . ." He frowned, and lifted a hand to probe his skull, then thought better of it. "I guess I'll have to hope. Why didn't he want me awake?"

"He did not say; yet I would conjecture that he did not wish to chance discovery of the range of thy powers."

Rod felt an icicle-stab. "Powers? What're you talking about? I just happen to be invisible to any listening witches, that's all."

"Mayhap; yet in this, I must needs admit that, in Flaran's place, I would have done as he did. For whether thou dost shield thy mind by chance, or by intention, truly matters not—such shielding bespeaks great witch power. Nay, thou'rt a true warlock, Master Owen, whether thou dost know it or not—and a most puissant one, to be able to hide thy mind so thoroughly." Simon leaned back against the wall. "And there is ever, of course, the chance that thou dost know it indeed, and dost hide thy thoughts by deliberation. And if that were the case, and if I were thine enemy, I would not wish to gamble on the extent of thy powers. I, too, would not chance thy waking."

Rod just gazed at Simon.

Then he looked away, with a sigh. "Well, I can't fault your logic—or his wisdom. But why did he bring you along?"

Simon shrugged. "Who can say? Yet I doubt not he'll seek to force thee to answer certain questions, whether thou dost know them or not—and if thine own pain is not enough to make thee speak, mayhap he'll think that mine will."

Rod shivered. "That boy's a real charmer, isn't he?"

"In truth. He did turn to me, jabbing with a finger. 'Do not seek to hide thy thoughts,' he cried, 'nor to disguise them, or I shall bid them slay thee out of hand.' I assured him I would not, the more so since I saw no point in such disguising. For what could he learn from my mind, that's of any import?"

"And that he didn't learn from traveling with the two of us." Rod was glad that the light was too dim for Simon to see his face burning. "Or that he couldn't find out by, let us say, more 'orthodox' means? For example, if he's keeping tab on your thoughts, he knows I'm awake now."

"Aye. I doubt me not an we'll see him presently."

"No doubt at all; I'm sure he's still in charge of our case.

...So he was giving the orders, huh? To the soldiers, I mean."

"Aye. There was no doubt of that."

Rod nodded. "Then he's probably the one who arranged the ambush."

Simon gazed at him for a moment, then nodded slowly. "That would be likely."

"So he's not exactly the simple half-telepath he claimed to be."

Simon's lips curved with the ghost of his smile. "Nay, Master Owen. He is certainly not that."

"He didn't happen to let out any hints about his real self, did he?"

Simon shook his head. "The surface of his thoughts stayed ever as it had been. For aught that I could hear from him, his name was ever Flaran; yet his thoughts were all extolling Alfar, and how greatly advantaged the land was, since he'd taken power."

Rod frowned. "Nothing about the job at hand?"

"Aye; he did think how greatly thy capture would please Alfar."

"I should think it would." Rod closed his eyes, leaning his head back against the wall, hoping the cold stone might cool the burning. "No matter what else we might say about our boy Flaran, we've got to admit he was effective."

A key grated in the lock. Rod looked up at a slab of dungeon warder with a face that might have been carved out of granite. He didn't say a word, just held the door open and stepped aside to admit a lord, gorgeously clad in brocade doublet and trunk-hose, burgundy tights and shoes, fine lace ruff, and cloth-of-gold mantle, with a golden coronet on his head. His chin was high in arrogance; he wore a look of stern command. Rod had to look twice before he recognized Flaran. "Clothes do make the man," he murmured.

Flaran smiled, his lips curving with contempt. "Clothes, aye—and a knowledge of power."

The last word echoed in Rod's head. He held his gaze on Flaran. "So the rumor was true—Alfar was wandering around the country, disguised as a peasant."

Flaran inclined his head in acknowledgement.

"Well, O Potentate Alfar." Rod leaned back against the

wall. "I have to admit you did a great job of disguising yourself as a peasant. Could it be you had experience to draw on?"

Alfar's eyes sparked with anger, and Simon seemed to shrink in on himself in horror. The sorcerer snapped. "Indeed, I was numbered 'mongst the downtrodden till a year agone."

"But that's all behind you now, of course."

His voice was a little too innocent. Alfar's gaze hardened. "Be not mistaken. Think not that I'm a peasant still—for thou dost lie within my power now, and thou wilt find it absolute."

Rod shrugged. "So you're a powerful peasant. Or did you honestly think you could be something more?"

"Greatly more," Alfar grated, "as thou wilt discover."

"Oh?" Rod tilted his head to the side. "What, may I ask?"

"A duke—Duke Alfar, of the Northern coast! And thou, slave, shalt address me as such!"

"Oh." Rod kept his lips pursed from the word. "I'm a slave now, am I?"

"Why?" Alfar's eyes kindled. "What else wouldst thou call thyself?"

Rod watched him for a second, then smiled. "I'm a peasant, too. Aren't I?"

"Assuredly," Alfar said drily. "Yet whatsoever thou art, thou art also a most excellent thought-hearer, an thou hast been able to probe 'neath my thoughts to discover who I truly am."

"Oh, that didn't take mind reading. None at all. I mean, just look at it logically: Who, in all the great North Country, would be the most likely one to go wandering around disguised as a *schlemazel* peasant, supporting Alfar's policies with great verve and enthusiasm, and would have authority to command his soldiers?"

"One of my lieutenants, mayhap," Alfar said, through thinned lips.

Rod shook his head. "You never said one word about having to refer a decision to someone higher up—at least, not from Simon's reports about what happened while I was out cold. But you did mention 'our' domain, which meant that you were either one of the lieutenants, viewing himself as a partner—and from what I'd heard of Alfar, I didn't think he was the type to share power..."

"Thou didst think aright," Flaran growled.

"See? And that left the 'or' to the 'either'—and the 'or' was that the 'our' you'd used was the royal 'our.' And that meant that Flaran was really Alfar." Rod spread his hands. "See? Just common sense."

"Scarcely 'common.'" Alfar frowned. "In truth, 'tis a most strange mode of thought."

"People keep telling me that, here," Rod sighed. He'd found that chains of reasoning were alien to the medieval mind. "But that was the royal 'our,' wasn't it? And you are planning to try for the throne, aren't you?"

Alfar's answer was an acid smile. "Thou hast come to the truth of it at last—though I greatly doubt thou didst find it in such a manner."

"Don't worry, I did." Rod smiled sourly. "Even right now, with you right next to me, I can't read your mind. Not a whisper."

"Be done with thy deception!" Alfar blazed. "Only a warlock of great power could cloak his thoughts so completely that he seems not even to exist!"

Rod shrugged. "Have it your way. But would that mighty warlock be able to read minds when his own was closed off?"

Alfar stared.

Then he lifted his head slowly, nodding. "Well, then." And, "Thou wilt, at least, not deny that thou art Tuan's spy."

"*King* Tuan, to you! But I agree, that much is pretty obvious."

"Most excellent! Thou canst now tell to Tuan every smallest detail of my dungeon—if ever thou dost set eyes upon him again."

For all his bravado, a shiver of apprehension shook Rod. He ignored it. "Tuan already knows all he needs."

"Indeed?" Alfar's eyes glittered. "And what is that?"

"That you've taken over the duchy, by casting a spell over all the people—and that you'll attack him, if he doesn't obliterate you first."

"Will he, now! Fascinating! And how much else doth he know?"

Rod shrugged. "None of your concern—but do let it worry you."

Alfar stood rigid, the color draining from his face.

Then he whirled, knife whipping out to prick Simon's throat. "Again I will demand of thee—what information hath Tuan?"

His gaze locked with Rod's. Simon paled, but his eyes held only calm and understanding, without the slightest trace of fear.

Rod sighed, and capitulated. "He knows your whole career, from the first peasant you intimidated, up to your battle with Duke Bourbon."

"Ah," Alfar breathed. "But he knoweth not the outcome. Doth he?"

"No," Rod admitted, "but it was a pretty clear guess."

"'Twas the Duchess, was it not? She did escape my hunters. Indeed, my spies in Tudor's county, and in Runnymede, attacked her, but were repulsed by puissant magics." His gaze hardened. "Magics wielded by a woman and four children."

Inwardly, Rod went limp with relief, hearing his family's safety confirmed. But outwardly, he only permitted himself a small smile.

"Yet thou wouldst know of that, wouldst thou not?" Alfar breathed. "Thou didst dispatch them on that errand, didst thou not?"

Rod looked at the drop of blood rising from the point of the dagger, considered his options, and decided honesty wouldn't hurt. "It was my idea, yes."

Alfar's breath hissed out in triumph. "Then 'twas thy wife and bairns who did accompany the Duchess and her brats, whilst yet they did live!"

Alarm shrilled through Rod. Did the bastard mean his family was dead? And the anger heaved up, rising.

Oblivious, Alfar was still speaking. "And thou art he who's called Rod Gallowglass, art thou not?"

"Yes. I'm the High Warlock." Rod's eyes narrowed, reddening.

Simon stared, poleaxed.

Alfar's lips were parted, his eyes glittering. "How didst thou do it? Tell me the manner of it! How didst thou cease to be, to the mind, the whiles thou wert apparent to the eye?"

"You should know," Rod grated. "Weren't you eavesdropping?"

"Every minute, I assure thee. I held thy trace the whiles thou didst buy a cart and didst drive out to the road. Then, of a sudden, there were no thoughts but a peasant's."

"Quite a range you've got there."

"More than thirty leagues. How didst thou cloak thy thoughts?"

"I didn't—not then." Rod throttled the rage down to a slow burn, keeping his mind in control, floating on top of the emotion. "I just started thinking like a peasant."

Alfar stared.

Then he frowned. "Then thou dost counterfeit most excellently."

"I had some acting lessons." And they were coming in handy, helping him keep the rage under control. "I didn't pull the real disappearing act until I was across the border." Privately, he found it interesting that Alfar could have been so thoroughly deceived. Either he wasn't very good at reading thoughts in depth, or Rod was even better at believing himself to be somebody fictitious than he had thought.

"Ah, 'twas then? Tell me the manner of it." But his knife hand was trembling.

Nonetheless, Simon was staring at Rod, not Alfar, and with awe, not fear.

And he'd been friendly to Rod, and he was an innocent bystander . . .

Rod shrugged. "I withdrew, that's all. Pulled back into my shell. Decided nobody was worth my trouble."

Alfar stared at him.

Then he frowned. "Canst say no more than that?"

Rod shrugged. "Details. Techniques. Remembering times in my past when I wanted to get away from people, and letting the feeling grow. None of it could teach you how to do it. The first time, it just happens."

Alfar watched him, eyes narrowed.

Then he straightened, sliding the knife back into its sheath, and Simon almost collapsed with a sigh of relief.

Rod felt a little relief, too, but the anger countered it.

"'Tis even as I've thought," Alfar said, with grim satisfaction. "From aught I've heard of thee, thy chivalry exceeds thy sense."

"Would you care to explain that?" Rod's voice was velvet.

"Why, 'tis plainly seen! Would a sensible captain risk his own pain, or mayhap even life, on a perilous mission? Nay! He would send a spy, and let the underling be racked and torn! But thou, who dost pride thyself on thine honor..." he made the word an obscenity, "... wouldst rather waste thine hours spying out the enemy thyself!"

Now Rod understood the man—and he didn't bother hiding his contempt. "Just sit back in Runnymede and read through intelligence reports, huh?"

"That would be wise." Alfar stood, arms akimbo, smirking down at him. "Or dost thou truly believe thou couldst accomplish more in thine own person?"

Rod studied the sorcerer—cocky stance, chip on the shoulder, the whole arrogant air (and didn't overlook the menace, or the sadistic glitter at the back of the eye) and wondered why he didn't feel more fear. He did know, though, that he'd better not let Alfar know that.

So he stuck his chin out just that little bit farther, and made his tone defiant. "I only know this: by the time I realized that it was really dangerous, it was too much a hazard to let anyone else go in my place."

"How gallant." Alfar's scorn was withering.

"It seems I was right." Rod held his gaze on Alfar's eyes. "If you could catch onto me, you could catch onto anybody I might send. How'd you see through my disguise?"

A slow smile spread over Alfar's face. He lifted his head, chest swelling, and stepped toward Rod, almost strutting. "I did sense danger when my spies sent word that the High Warlock did journey northward. Yet sin' that thou didst come with thy wife and bairns, it might well have been naught but a pleasure jaunt. Naetheless, he did note that thou hadst but lately spoken with Tuan and Catharine."

Rod shrugged. "I do that all the time." But his interest was piqued. "So your man couldn't eavesdrop on my conversation with Their Majesties, huh?"

Alfar flushed, glowering.

"Well." Rod leaned back against the wall. "Nice to know my wife's noise-shield works so well."

"Is that how thou dost manage it!" Alfar's eyes gleamed. "In truth, their thoughts are well-nigh impossible to single out from all that buzzing hum of thoughts that doth surround them." He nodded, with a calculating look. "Thy wife hath talent."

Rod quailed at the threat his tone implied—especially since Gwen hadn't held a shield around the royal couple. "Just be glad I sent her back."

"Mayhap I had ought to be. Mayhap 'tis fitting that what my lieutenants could not accomplish, mine actions could."

"'Lieutenants?'" Rod stared in disbelief, then let a slow smile grow. "You mean that lousy marksman was one of your *best?*"

Alfar's gaze darkened. "'Twas purposely done. I bade him discourage thee, not slay thee or thine."

"Wise." Rod nodded. "If you had, I'd've broken off the spy mission right there, and shot back to Runnymede to tell Tuan to call out the army. But you did a great job of warning us you were there."

"Aye—and did secure a gauge of the range and strength of thy powers, and thy wife's and bairns'. Wherefore did I send mine other lieutenants to afright thee a second, then a third time, that I might learn thy pattern of attack, and its weaknesses. Nay, if thy wife and bairns had come north farther, I would have known well how to deal with them."

The chill had settled around Rod's backbone, and wasn't leaving. "I did have some notion that it was getting a little too thick. So when the Duchess and her boys came along, I took advantage of the excuse to send my family back South, to safety."

Alfar nodded. "And went on northward thyself. Then thou didst stop by a farmstead, where thou didst buy a horsecart and peasant garb—and my man lost trace of thee, the whiles thou didst don thy smock and buskins."

Very interesting! Rod hadn't gone invisible until he'd crossed the border. "Let me guess: that's when you decided you'd better get involved on the personal level."

Alfar nodded. "Even as thou hadst, I did don peasant garb, and took the southward road, afoot and unguarded." He smiled, amused, as though to say, *Why would Alfar need guards?*

Rod resolved to take the first possible opportunity to demonstrate exactly why. Aloud, he said, "Why didn't you ride to the border first? You could have intercepted me there."

"Oh, I was certain I would discover thee as I went! Thou hadst, after all, no need to use aught but the High Road—and good reason not to, for thou wouldst then have been most strikingly noticed, in byways where only villagers do journey. Yet long ere I encountered thee, I did come upon a troop of guardsmen, and something about them caught my notice. I did look deeply into their auncient's eyes and thoughts and, 'neath the surface, discovered that he was no longer spellbound! That, even though they wore my colors!" His smile was not pleasant. "I found occasion to journey with them, begging their protection and, as we walked, wove my spell about each one in turn. When only the auncient remained disenchanted, I bade his troopers seize him; so they did. Then did I pose him questions, the whiles I hearkened to the answers that rose within his mind, unspoken."

Rod decided he'd better find a new interrogation technique; this one was obviously so easy to invent that it boded fair to becoming common.

"From his mind," Alfar went on, "I gained the image of the man who'd broke his spell...." He nodded toward Simon. "And I saw, to my surprise, that he was accompanied, by a most ill-favored, surly peasant."

Rod straightened in indignation. "Hey, now!"

Alfar smiled, satisfied that his barb had drawn blood. "But 'twas easily seen that the spell-breaker must needs be the High Warlock. Why, he had so great a look of dignity!"

Simon looked up, startled.

Alfar's eye glinted. "And his serving man had so churlish a look!"

But Rod wasn't about to bite on the same bait twice. He shrugged. "I won't argue. When it comes to churls, you should know what you're talking about."

Alfar flushed, and dropped a hand to his dagger.

Rod leaned back lazily. "What did you do with the soldiers?" He was tense, dreading the answer.

Alfar shrugged. "What ought I to do? I enchanted the auncient too, and sent them on northward to rejoin mine army."

Rod lifted his head, surprised. "You didn't punish them? No racks, no thumbscrews? No crash diets?"

Alfar looked equally surprised. "Dost thou punish an arrow that has fallen to earth, if thine enemy hath picked it up, and set it to his bowstring? Nay; thou dost catch it when he doth loose it at thee, and restore it to thy quiver. Oh, I sent them on northward. I did not wish to chance their beholding thee again—or, more's to the point, thy spell-breaker. But at the next guardpost, I showed my badge of authority..." He fingered the medallion on his breast. "... and bade the soldiers disguise themselves as peasants, to wait in ambush where a country way joined the High Road. Then I summoned a lesser warlock to abide with them, in readiness to transmit orders to march, when he should receive a thought-code—Alfar's greatness, and why all witches ought to join with him." He smiled, vindictively.

Rod knew better than to withhold ego-oil when the one with the inferiority complex held the knife. "So that's why the sudden diatribe, eh?"

"Certes." Alfar's eyes danced. "There's method in aught I do. Then did I march southward, my thoughts ranging ahead of myself, till I heard Simon's. I found a village warlock, then, and bade him lead his people out to chase me...."

"The little fat guy. But of course, you made sure all their rocks would miss, and they wouldn't catch you."

"Why, certes." Alfar grinned, enjoying the account of his own cleverness. "And as I had foreknown, thou couldst not forebear to save a poor weakling, beset by human wolves."

"Yes." Rod's mouth twisted with the sour taste of his own gullibility. "We fell right into it, didn't we? Just picked you up, and carried you right along."

"Thou wast, in truth, most gracious," Alfar said, with a

saccharine smile. "'Twas but a day's work to discover that 'twas Simon broke the spells, yet that he could do little more—and that thou must needs be the High Warlock."

"My natural greatness just shone through those peasant rags, huh?"

"Oh, indubitably. Yet 'twas more truthfully thy face."

"Naturally noble, eh?"

"Nay, only familiar. Mine agents had borne me pictures in their minds, more faithful than any painter could render. Oh, thou hast disguised thyself somewhat, with peasant's smock and grime; yet I know something of deception myself, and can look past surface features to those that underlie them. Yet I knew thee even ere I'd set eyes upon thy face; for thou wast there to mine eyes, but not to my mind, and only a most puissant warlock could shield himself so thoroughly."

Rod shrugged. "I seem to have had that knack before I started doing any of what you call magic. . . . But, go on."

"Pay heed!" Alfar held up a forefinger. "Even then, I offered thee thine opportunity to join with me and mine! And only when thou didst refuse, and that with such force that I knew thou couldst not be persuaded, did I seize thee." His gaze intensified, locked on Rod's eyes. "E'en now, an thou dost wish to join with me, I will rejoice, and welcome thee!"

"Providing, of course, that I can prove I mean it."

"Of course. What use art thou, if I cannot rely on thee to the uttermost?" His eyes glittered, and his mouth quivered with suppressed glee. "Indeed, I've even now the means to insure thy loyalty."

Dread shot through Rod and, hard after it, anger. He throttled it down and growled, "What means?"

"Thou hast no need to know. Thou dost not, after all, wish to ally thy fortunes with mine."

The rage surged up, and Rod let it rise. "I'll grind your head under my heel, if I can ever find a forked stick big enough to hold your neck down!"

Alfar went white, and sprang at Rod, his knife slipping out. Fear shot through Rod, like a spark to gunpowder and the anger exploded, shooting through his every vein and nerve, smashing out of him in reaction.

Alfar slammed back against the far wall and slid to the floor, dazed.

Rod's chains jangled as they broke apart, and fell.

He thrust himself away from the wall, rising to his feet, borrowed rage-power filling every cell of his body. The headache throbbed through him, darkening all he saw except for an oval of light that contained Alfar, crumpled in a heap. Rod waded toward the fallen man, feeling anger envelop him, pervading him, as though Lord Kern's spirit reached across the void between the universes, to take possession of him. His finger rose with the weight of all his manslayings, pointing out to explode the sorcerer.

Then Alfar's eyes cleared; he saw Rod's face, and his eyes filled with terror. Rod reached out to touch him—but thunder rocked the cell, and the sorcerer was gone.

Rod stood staring at the empty space where the sorcerer had been, finger still pointing, forgotten. "Teleported," he choked out. "Got away."

He straightened slowly, thrusting outward with his mind, exploding his mental shield, opening himself to all and every sense impression about him, concentrating on the human thoughts. Nowhere was there a trace of Alfar.

Rod nodded, perversely satisfied; Alfar hadn't just teleported out of the cell—he'd whipped himself clean out of the castle, and so far away that he couldn't be "heard."

14

Rod sagged back, sitting against the cell wall as the biggest reason for his anger abated. His emotions began to subside, but still within him there was an impulse toward violence, a lust for battle that kept the anger and built it, filling his whole body with quaking rage.

That scared Rod. He tried to force the mindless rage down; and as he did, Simon's voice bored through to him: "Owen! Owen! Lord Gallowglass! Nay, I'll call thee as I knew thee!" A hand clasped his wrist; fingers dug in. "Master Owen! Or Rod Gallowglass, whichever thou art! Hast thou lost thyself, then?"

"Yes," Rod grated, staring at the wall, unseeing. "Yes. Damn near."

Simon groaned. "Is there naught of the High Warlock left in thee?"

"Which one?" Rod growled. "Which High Warlock?"

Simon answered in a voice filled with wonder. "Rod Gallowglass, High Warlock of Gramarye! What other High Warlock is there?"

"Lord Kern," Rod muttered, "High Warlock of the land of Tir Chlis." He rose to his feet, and stood stock-still, stood against the humming in his mind, the thrumming in his veins. Then he forced the words out. "What is he like— this High Warlock?"

"Which one?" Simon cried.

"Yes." Rod nodded. "That's the question. But tell me of this Rod Gallowglass."

"But thou art he!"

"Tell me of him!" Rod commanded.

Simon stared, at a loss. But no matter what he thought of the oddness of Rod's question, or the irrationality of what he did, Simon swallowed it, absorbed it, and gave what was needed.

"Rod Gallowglass is the Lord High Warlock."

"That doesn't help any," Rod growled. "Tell me something different about him."

Simon stared for a moment, then began again. "He is somewhat taller than most, though not overmuch..."

"No, no! Not what he *looks* like! That doesn't help at *all*! What's he like *inside*?"

Simon just stared at him, confounded.

"Quickly!" Rod snapped. "Tell me! *Now*! I need an anchor, something to hold to!"

"Hast thou lost thyself so truly, then?"

"*Yes!*"

Finally, the actuality of the emergency struck home to Simon. He leaned forward and said, earnestly, "I have not known thee overlong, Rod Gallowglass, and that only in thy guise as old Owen. Yet from what I've seen of thee, thou art... well, aye, thou art surly. And taciturn. Yet art thou good-hearted withal. Aye, thou hast ever the good of thy fellows at heart, at nearly every moment." He frowned. "I've heard it said of thee, that thou hast a wry humor, and dost commonly speak with wit. Yet I've not seen much of that in old Owen, save some bites of sarcasm—which are as often turned against himself, as against any other."

"Good." Rod nodded. "Very good." He could feel the anger lessening, feel himself calming. But underneath it, there was still fury, goading him to action, any action. Lord Kern. "Tell me..." Rod muttered, and swallowed. "Tell me something about myself, that doesn't apply to Kern— for most of what you've said might be true of him, too. I don't know; I scarcely met the man. It might, though. Tell me something about me, that's definitely mine alone, that couldn't be his!"

"Why..." Simon floundered, "there is thy garb. Would he go about as a peasant?"

"Possible. Try again."

"There is thy horse..."

"Yes!" Rod pounced on it. "Tell me about him!"

"'Tis a great black beast," Simon said slowly, "and most excellent in his lines. Indeed, 'twas the one great flaw in thy guise; for any could see that he was truly a knight's destrier, not a common cart horse." He frowned, gazing off into space. "And now I mind me, thou dost call him 'Fess.'"

"Fess." Rod smiled. "Yes. I could never forget Fess, no matter what. And Lord Kern couldn't possibly have one like him. He's been with me as long as I've been alive— no, longer. He's served my family for generations, did you know that?"

"Assuredly, I did not." Simon watched him, wide-eyed.

"He's not what he seems, you know."

"Aye, certes, he's not!"

"No, not just that way." Rod frowned. "He's, uh, magical. But not your kind of magic—mine. He's not really a horse of any kind. He could be anything."

"A pooka," Simon murmured, unable to tear his gaze away.

"No, not *that* way! He's cold iron, underneath that horsehair—well, an alloy really. Plus, he's got a mind that's really a thing apart." Rod remembered how easily he could take the basketball-sized sphere that held Fess's computer-brain out of the horse-body and plug it into his starship, to astrogate and pilot. "I mean, his brain's *really* a thing apart. But he's always calm—well, almost always. And supremely logical. And *always* has good advice for me." The core of anger was shrinking; it had almost disappeared, and Rod could feel the last tendrils of rage withdrawing into it. If Lord Kern really had reached across the void between the universes in response to Rod's anger, he had lost his grip. And if it was really just his own bloodlust driving him toward violence, it was under control again now. Rod's mouth quirked into a sardonic smile. "Thank you, Milord. I appreciate your assistance, and will call upon it frequently, when there is need. But for now, I am myself again, and must trace this foul sorcerer in the ways which I deem best, in this world in which horses may be of metal, with machines for brains."

Simon cocked his head, trying to hear, but not quite catching Rod's words.

Rod felt Kern's presence—or the bulk of his own anger, whichever it was—ebb. Whether "Kern" was real, or just a projection of his subconscious, it was now as thoroughly gone as it could be. He heaved a sigh, and turned to Simon. "Thank you. You pulled me out of it."

"Gladly," Simon said, "though I misdoubt me an I comprehend."

"It's really very simple. You see, there's another High Warlock, in another kingdom, far, far away—*extremely* far away; there isn't even a way to measure it. It's in another universe, if you can believe that."

"Believe it, aye. Understanding it's another matter."

"Just try and drink it in," Rod advised. "We won't have an examination in this course. Now, this other High Warlock is my analog. That means that he corresponds to me in every detail; what he does in his universe, what I do in mine. I visited his country for a while, and had occasion to borrow his powers; he channelled them through me, of course. But now it seems that was habit-forming; he keeps trying to reach across to this universe, and take up residence in my body."

Simon paled. "Surely he cannot!"

Rod shrugged. "Maybe not. Maybe it's just my own lust for violence, the temptation to commit mayhem, and I'm labelling it 'Lord Kern' to try to separate the actions I believe to be wrong, from my conscience." He glowered off into space. "That doesn't really work, of course, The responsibility's mine, no matter what illusion I create as an excuse. Even if I *say* Lord Kern did it, it'll really be me who committed the deed. It'll still be me, even if I try to disguise it." He turned to Simon with a bleak smile. "But I seem to be able to lie to myself very convincingly. I'm thoroughly capable of persuading myself that I'm somebody else, when I want to."

"So." Simon frowned. "I have convinced thee that thou art thyself again?"

Rod nodded. "More importantly, you've shown me that

I can restore myself to my real personality, instead of the make-believe one, welding my thoughts and my actions back into a whole again. It's a matter of remembering who I am. Fess was the key; Fess was the final thing that did it. Because, you see..." He quirked a smile. "...Fess couldn't exist in Lord Kern's universe."

Simon frowned. "I do not understand why not; yet will I accept thine assurance." Then his eyes sparked, and widened. "Yet mayhap I do comprehend. Thine horse doth stand for thee, doth he not? For if he could not be, in this Lord Kern's land, then neither couldst thou!"

"Not without being imported, no." Then Rod stiffened, turning aside from Simon, feeling as though an electric current were passing through him. "Yes... he does stand for me in a lot of ways, doesn't he?" The computer mind in the horsehair body was rather symbolic of technological Rod in Gramarye's medieval culture....

But of himself...?

"I think 'tis so," Simon was saying. "And even as thine horse is the key to returning thee to control of thine actions, so thine anger is the key to summoning this 'Lord Kern' which, thou dost say, thou hast created, to take responsibility for thine own fell deeds, that thou mayest give thyself the lie that 'tis no fault of thine own."

Rod stood still for a moment, then nodded slowly. "Yes. And it is a lie." He dropped down, to sit on his heels. Simon sat by him. "Ever since I came back from Lord Kern's universe, I've been flying into rages—and it's scary, very scary."

"So." Simon's eyes glinted. "Thou hast been afraid to draw on thine own powers, for fear of summoning him."

Rod stared at him for a while. Then, slowly, he nodded. "Yes, that would make sense, wouldn't it? Association. Using magic for the first time, resulted in Lord Kern's being a house guest within my skull; so using them again, should bring him back. A certain illogical sort of reason to it, isn't there?"

"It doth sound so, when thou dost say it."

"Yes—but stating it also makes me able to see that it doesn't make sense." Rod grinned. "I *have* to draw on my powers, though. There have been times when they came in almighty handy. Just now, for example—Alfar had his dagger at my throat, so I had nothing to lose." He shuddered. "And 'Lord Kern' almost took over completely, this time."

"Aye." Simon smiled. "Thou didst fear, didst thou not? To use thy powers, for fear of summoning 'Lord Kern.'"

Rod nodded, chagrined. "Even if he's just an illusion I made up. Yeah. I'd still be afraid of it."

"Yet thou dost wish to use these powers." Simon raised a forefinger. "Whether they be Lord Kern's, or but thine own magics, that thine anger doth conjure up, thou dost fear to use them, lest thou shouldst yield to temptation, and let thine hands do what thou dost abhor."

Rod nodded slowly. "Nicely said. Separating the thought from the action. Yes. I *have* always been a bit schizoid."

"Then contain the power thou dost conjure up," Simon urged. "Thus thou mayst reunite thy thoughts with thine action, by containing thine active part within the pen thy thoughts do make. Contain 'Lord Kern,' even as thou dost contain thine anger. Assuredly thou hast not forgot our conversation, touching on that point? 'Twas directly after thou . . ."

"After I beat up on that poor, unsuspecting, defenseless rock. Yes." Rod nodded, lips tight with chagrin. "Yeah, I remember it. But I still don't understand how you keep the lid on your anger."

"Nay, I do not!" Simon frowned, shaking a finger at Rod. "If the anger rises, do not attempt to bury it, nor to pretend that it's not there. Let it be in thine awareness, and do not seek to throttle it—but contain it."

Rod frowned. "And how do you manage that?"

"By distancing thyself from the person who doth anger thee," Simon answered. "'Tis not easily done, I know— for when the folk of the village had come to like me, and their priest had become my friend, I did come from out mine hermitage, to live among them. I built myself mine inn—with their aid. And, in good time, I found myself a wife." His head lifted, gazing off into the past again. "She bore me bonny bairns, and together we labored to rear them."

"That's right—you do have a daughter."

"Two—and a son. Who, by Heaven's grace, went for a soldier in the last war, and remained in the South, to serve Lord Borgia. Beshrew me, but I love him! Yet whilst he grew, he tried me sorely!"

"I wouldn't say I know *all* about that," Rod growled, "but I'm sure learning. How did you deal with it?"

"By holding in my mind, and never letting go, the notion that 'twas not me his anger aimed at, but at that which I stood for."

"Authority," Rod guessed. "Limits on his actions."

"Aye—and the tree from which he needed to separate himself, the shoot, or he'd not be a being in his own right. Yet 'twas more than that—'twas that he was not angry at me, but at what I'd done or said."

"That doesn't make much sense." Rod frowned. "What you're trying to say is, it was anger, not hatred."

Simon gazed off into space. "Mayhap that is the sense of it. Yet whether it be anger or hatred, anger at thee or at what thou hast done, be mindful that, if worst comes to worst, thou hast but to recall that this person, this event, is but a part of thy life, not the whole of it—a part with which thou mayest have to deal but, when the dealing's done, canst lock out from thy life."

"What if you *can't?*" Rod exploded. "What if you're tied to them? What if you have to deal with them continually, every day? What if you *love* them?"

Simon sat, grave and attentive. He nodded. "Aye. 'Tis far more easy to hold thy temper with one whom thou dost see for but an hour or two each day, for thou canst go to thine home, shut the door behind thee, and forget them." His face eased into a gentle smile. "Be mindful that these you love are people too, and deserving of as much respect and care as those with whom thou dost deal for but an hour or two each day. If thou dost not treat thy family well, pretend they're friends."

The thought gave Rod an icy chill. "But they're not! They're inextricable parts of my life—parts of myself!"

"Nay!" Simon's eyes blazed, and his face was the countenance of a stern patriarch. "Never must thou believe them so! For look you, no one else can be a part of thee; they are themselves withal, and are *apart* from thee!"

Rod just stared, astounded by the intensity of Simon's emotion.

Simon shook his head slowly. "Never think that, simply because thou dost love a person, or she doth love thee, that she is no longer her self, a separate thing, apart."

"But . . . but . . . but that's the *goal* of marriage!" Rod sputtered. "For two to become one!"

"'Tis a foul lie!" Simon retorted. "'Tis but an excuse for one to enslave another, then make her cease to be! Thy wife is, withal, one person, contained within her own skin, and is, and ought to be, one whole, of which all the parts are fused together, a being, separate, independent—one who loves thee, yet who is apart." Suddenly, he smiled, and his warmth was back. "For look you, an she were not a separate person, thou wouldst have none to love thee."

"But . . . but, the word marriage! Isn't that what it means— two people, being welded together into a single unit?"

Simon shook his head impatiently. "That may be what the word doth mean. Yet be not deceived; two cannot become one. 'Tis not possible. I confess it hath a pretty sound— but doth its beauty suffice to make it right?"

Rod stared at Simon, astounded by the older man's words.

"What of thee?" Simon demanded. "Would it be right for one to attempt to make thee someone other than thou art?"

"No! I'm me, damn it! If anybody tried to make me somebody else, he'd eliminate me!"

"Then 'tis wrong for thee to attempt to make another become part of thee!" Simon stabbed at him with a forefinger.

Rod frowned, thinking it over.

"An two folk do wed," Simon said softly, "they should take pleasure in one another's company—not essay to become one another." He smiled again, gently. "For how canst thou become a part of someone else, save by erasing either themselves, or thee?"

Rod lifted his head, then slowly nodded. "I see your point. And as it is with my family, so it is with Lord Kern, isn't it? He keeps trying to become Lord Gallowglass—and if he did, Rod Gallowglass would cease to exist."

"Ah, then!" Simon's eyes lit. "Dost thou, then, mislike this notion of thyself and Lord Kern merging together, fusing, growing, into something larger and greater?"

"I'd kill the man who tried to wipe me out that way!" Rod leaped to his feet in anger. "That's not making me bigger and better—that's stealing my soul!"

Simon only smiled into Rod's wrath, letting its force pass him by, untouched. "Yet if the thought so repels thee with this Lord Kern—who, thou hast told me, is thine other self—how can it be right if the 'other half' is thy wife?"

Rod stared, poleaxed, his anger evaporated.

"Is it thy wife, or thy bairns—or the fear of ceasing to be?"

Rod dropped down to sit crosslegged again, leaning forward intently. "Then why do I only get angry when they oppose me? Why don't I get angry when they agree with me?"

"For that, when they oppose thee, there is danger of *thy* self being digested; but when they agree with thee, 'tis they who may be merged into thee."

Rod mulled that over. "So it's a threat. I get angry when there's a threat."

"Certes," Simon said, surprised. "What else is anger's purpose?"

"Yes—self-preservation," Rod said slowly. "It's the impulse to fight—to get rid of a threat." His mouth quirked into a sudden smile, and his shoulders shook with a silent, internal laugh. "My lord! Me threatened, by my three-year-old son?"

"Art thou not?" Simon said softly.

Rob sobered. "It's ridiculous. He couldn't possibly hurt me."

"Oh, he can," Simon breathed, "in thy heart, in thy soul—most shrewdly."

Rod studied his face. Then he said, "But he's so little, so vulnerable!" Then he scowled. "But, damn it, it *is* hard to remember that when he's coming up with one of those insights that make me feel stupid!"

Simon nodded, commiserating. "Thou must, therefore, be ever mindful, and tell thyself again: 'He doth not lessen me.' For that is what we truly fear, is it not? That our selves will be diminished, and, if 'tis diminished too much, 'twill cease to exist. Is that not what we resist, what anger guards against?"

"But it's so assinine," Rod breathed, "to think that such a small one could hurt big me!"

"Aye—and therefore must thou bring it to mind anew, whenever thou dost feel the slightest ghost of anger." Simon sat back, smiling. "And as 'tis with thy bairns, so 'tis with Lord Kern."

Rod just sat, spellbound, then, slowly, he nodded. "So that's the key to holding my temper? Just remembering that I'm myself?"

"And that Lord Kern is not Rod Gallowglass. Just so." Simon closed his eyes and nodded. "Yet 'tis not so easily done, Lord Warlock. To be mindful of thyself, thou must needs accept thyself—and to do that, one must be content with his self. Thou must needs come to believe that Rod Gallowglass is a good thing to be."

"Well, I think I can do that," Rod said slowly, "Especially since I've always felt Rod Gallowglass is an even better thing to be, when he's with his wife Gwen."

"Thy wife?" Simon frowned. "That hath a ring of great wrongness to it. Nay, Lord Warlock—an thou dost rely on another person for thy sense of worth, thou dost not truly believe that thou hast any. Thou shouldst enjoy her company because she is herself, and is pleasing to thee, is agreeable company—not because she is a part of thee, nor because the two of thee together make thy self a worthwhile thing to be."

Rod frowned. "I suppose that makes sense, in its way. If I depend on Gwen for my own sense of worth, then, whenever she finds me less than perfect, or finds anything at all wrong with me, I'll believe I'm not worth anything."

Simon nodded, his eyes glittering, encouraging.

"And that would feel to me, as though she were trying to destroy me, make me less than I am—which'll make me angry, because I'll feel that I need to fight back, for my own survival."

Simon still nodded. "'Tis even as it happed to me—'til I realized why, with my wife and myself, each quarrel was worse than the last—for, of course, she felt even as I did—that she must needs attack me, to survive." He shook his head, like a cautioning schoolteacher. " 'Tis wrong of thee, to make her the custodian of thy value. That is thine own burden, and thou must needs accept it."

Rod nodded. "Learn to like being inside my own skin, eh?"

"Aye." Simon smiled, amused. "And do not seek to so burden thine horse, either."

"Yeah—Fess." That jolted Rod back to the issue. "He was the symbol that pulled me back to my own identity. Does that mean I'm closer to my horse, than to my wife?"

"I think not." Simon throttled a chuckle. "For when all's said and done, a horse is a thing, not a person. It may have a temperament all its own, and some quirks and snags of mood, just as a person hath; and each horse may be as unique and separate as each human is from another—yet when all's said and done, it hath not an immortal soul, and cannot therefore challenge thee in any way that will truly make thee feel any less. It cannot lessen thy sense of self, any more than a shoe or a shovel can."

Rod nodded slowly. That made sense—more than Simon knew; for Fess wasn't a living horse, but a computer in a body full of servo-mechanisms. Sure, the computer projected a personality by its vocodered voice—but that personality was only an illusion, a carefully-crafted artifact, albeit an intangible one. Fess was, really, only a metal machine, and his identity was as much an illusion as his ability to think. "My horse is like a sword, in a way," he said thoughtfully.

Simon laughed softly. "In truth, he doth seem to be somewhat more than a shoe or a shovel."

"No, I was thinking of mystique. For a knight, his sword was the symbol of his courage, his prowess—and his honor. Each sword was a separate, unique, individual thing, to the medieval mind, and its owner invested it with a full-fledged persona. He even gave it a name. Sometimes, in the legends, it even had a will of its own. You couldn't think of a famous sword, without thinking of the knight who owned it. Excalibur evoked the image of King Arthur, Durandal evoked pictures of Roland, Gram brought to mind Siegried slaying Fafnir. The sword was the symbol of the knight who bore it."

"As thine horse is the symbol of thee?"

Rod frowned. "That doesn't quite feel right, somehow—but it's close. Metaphorically, I suppose Fess is my sword."

"Then use him." Simon's eyes glowed. "Draw thy blade, and go to slay the monster who enslaves us."

Rod sat still a moment, feeling within him for fear—and, yes, it was there; but so was the courage to answer it. But courage wouldn't do much good, really; in this case, it'd just let him go ahead into a situation that was too dangerous for him to survive. How about confidence, though? Could he summon Lord Kern, let himself fill with anger, and not be mastered by it? He thought of Fess, and all the qualities in himself that Fess represented, and felt calm certainty rising in response to the mental image. He nodded. "I'm up to it. But if I start to fall in, pull me out, will you?"

"Gladly," Simon answered, with a full, warm smile.

"Then hold on." Rod stood, grasped Simon's shoulder, and thought of Alfar, of his arrogance, his insolence, and the threat he represented to Rod and his children. Hot anger surged in answer, anger building toward rage. Rod felt Lord Kern's familiar wrath—but he was aware of it, now, as something that was a part of him, truly, not implanted from someone else—and, being of himself, it was as much under his control as his fingers, or his tongue. He opened his mind, concentrating on the world of thought. The world of sight dimmed, and his blood began to pound in his ears. Only the thoughts were real—the darting, scheming thoughts of the warlocks and witches; the dulled, mechanical plodding thoughts of the soldiers and servants—and the ceaseless background drone that had to be the projective telepath, who had hypnotized a whole duchy. What else could it be, that emitted such a constant paen of praise, such a continual pushing of thought against mind?

Whatever it was, Rod was suddenly certain that it was the key to all the pride and ambition that was Alfar's conquest. He scanned the castle till he found the direction in which it was strongest, then willed himself to it.

15

It was a small room, a round room, a room of gray stone blocks with three tall, skinny windows. But those windows were sealed with some clear substance, and the air of the chamber was unnaturally cool—climate-controlled. Every alarm bell in Rod's head screamed. He glanced at Simon. The older warlock tottered, dazed. Rod held him up, growling, "Steady. That's what happens when a warlock disappears."

"I had . . . ne'er had the opportunity aforetime," Simon gasped. He looked around him, whites showing all around his eyes. Finally, he turned back to Rod, awe-struck. "Eh, but thou'rt truly the Lord Warlock, thou."

"The same," Rod confirmed, "but nonetheless your pupil in fathering and husbandry."

"As I am to thee, in wizardry." Simon pointed a trembling finger at the metal box in the center of the room. It sat on a slender pedestal at chest height, and had a gray, irridescent cylinder atop one end. The other sprouted a cable that dropped down to the floor, ran over to the wall and up it, to a window, where it disappeared—probably to a transmitting antenna, Rod decided. "What," Simon asked, in a voice that shook, "is that spawn of alchemy?"

"Probably," Rod agreed. "It's a machine of some sort,

anyway." He could feel the insistent pounding of the message, extoling Alfar's virtues over and over again. It was much stronger than it had been when he was in the dungeon. It belabored him, convincing, persuading by sheer repetition. Alfar was master, Alfar was great, Alfar was rightful lord of all that was human.... "I think I know what it is, Simon—or, at least, what it does. If I'm right, the last time I saw one of these, it was alive."

"How?" Simon stared, horrified. "A living thing cannot be a machine."

"No more than a machine can be a living thing. But this one sure seems to be. If you didn't know better, wouldn't you swear that thing's thinking at us?"

"Wh ... *this?*" Simon pointed at the contraption, features writhing with revulsion. "Assuredly it doth not!"

"Assure me again—I could need it." Under his breath, Rod murmured, "Fess. Where are you?"

"Here, Rod, in the castle stables," Fess's voice answered from behind his ear.

"Close your eyes," Rod growled, "and don't worry about what's happening." He closed his eyes, envisioning Fess, and the stable he was in. In excellent repair, probably, since it had been Duke Romanov's just a week ago—but slipping a bit now. The straw surely needed changing, for example, and the manure needed clearing. But he needed Fess, needed him badly, right *here*.... He made the thought an imperative, an unworded summons, sharp, demanding.

Thunder rocked the little room, and Fess was there, looking about him wildly, Rod saw as he opened his eyes again. The robot's voice came out slurred. "Whhhaddt ... wherrre ... I have ... have I ... telllepo..." Suddenly his head whipped up, then slammed down. All four legs spraddled out, stiff, knees locked. The neck was stiff, too, pointing the head at the floor; then it relaxed, and the head began to swing between the fetlocks.

"Seizure," Rod explained. "It always happens, when he can't avoid witnessing magic."

But Simon didn't answer. He was staring at the electronic gizmo, and his eyes had glazed. He took a stumbling step toward it. *Of course,* Rod thought. *This close to the gadget*

... He grabbed Simon by the shoulders, and gave him a shake. "Simon! Wake up!" He clapped his hands sharply, an inch in front of Simon's nose. Simon started, and his eyes came back into focus. "What . . . Lord Warlock! For the half of a minute, I thought . . . I could believe . . ."

"That the background noise is right, and Alfar's a good guy." Rod nodded, mouth a thin, straight line. "Not surprising. Now I'm sure what that weird device is—but let's confirm it." He turned back to Fess, felt under the pommel of the saddle for an enlarged vertebra, and pushed it. It clicked faintly. After a moment, Fess's head lifted slowly and turned to look at Rod, the great plastic eyes clearing. "I . . . had a . . . seizure, Rrrod."

"You did," Rod confirmed. "But let me show you something you can cope with." He took a step toward the pedestal, pointing. "There's a background thought-message, constantly repeating, Fess. Over and over, it praises Alfar to the skies—and it's much stronger here than anywhere else."

The robot's head tracked him. Then Fess stepped closer to the metal box. The great horsehead lifted, looking at the box from the top, then from the front, then the back. Finally Fess opined, "There is sufficient data for a meaningful conclusion, Rod."

"Oh, ducky! What's it add up to?"

"That the futurian totalitarians are supporting Alfar's conquests."

"Are they really," Rod said drily. "Care to confirm my guess as to what it does?"

"Certainly. It's a device that converts electricity into psionic power. I would conjecture that the large, rectangular base contains some sort of animal brain in a nutrient solution, with wires carrying power from an atomic pack into the medulla, and leads from the cerebrum carrying power at human thought frequencies into a modulator. The cylinder at the rear of the machine would seem to perform that function. This modulated message is fed out through the cable, which presumably goes up to an antenna on the roof of this tower."

"Thanks." Rod swallowed against a suddenly queasy stomach. "Nice to have my guess confirmed—I suppose.

Their technology has improved since we met the Kobold, hasn't it?"

"The state of the art advances constantly, Rod."

"Relentlessly, you might almost say." Rod turned to Simon. "It projects thoughts. Not a living thought, you understand—a recorded one, made as carefully as people make chairs, or ships, or castles, but just as thoroughly made. Then that thought is set down, as you'd write a message in ink, almost—and sent out from this machine, to the whole of the duchy, again and again, drumming itself into people's heads. Warlocks and witches can at least realize they're being bombarded—but the average peasant in the field has no idea it's happening. But warlock or witch, it doesn't seem to matter—it converts them all."

"Who placed it here?" Simon's voice trembled.

"People from the future." Rod's face was set, stony. "People who want the whole universe to be ruled by one single power." He glared around at the blank stone walls. "Where're its builders? Hiding somewhere, out of harm's way, while Alfar and his coven do their dirty work for them. But I must admit I'm disappointed—I was hoping to find a few of them here, keeping guard." He could feel indignation spurring his anger higher; he began to tremble.

"Peace, peace." Simon grasped his forearm. "Wherefor would they? Why guard what none know of, and none need tend?"

"Yeah—it's fully automatic, isn't it? And just because I expected them to be here, doesn't mean they should feel obligated to show up. But I was at least expecting a human witch or warlock to be doing the thinking! Maybe hooked up to a psionic amplifier—but nonetheless one of Alfar's henchmen, taking it in relays! But . . . this is it!" He spread his hands toward the machine. "This is all there is! Here's the spectacular sorcerer—here's the arch-magus! Here's your rebel warlock warlord, fantastically powerful—until its battery runs down!"

"'Twill suffice," Simon said, beside him.

"Damn straight it will!" Rod turned to rummage in Fess's saddlebag. "Where's that hammer I used to carry?"

"May I suggest that it would be more effective, and more immediate, to turn the machine off, Rod?"

Rod shrugged. "Why not? I'm not picky—I'll wreck it any way I can!" He turned to the machine, looking it up and down. "Where's the off switch?"

"I detect a pressure-pad next to the cylinder," Fess said. "Would you press it, please, Rod?"

"Sure." Rod pressed the cross-hatched square. The machine clicked, whirred for a second, then pushed one end of the cylinder toward Rod. He lifted it off, holding it warily at arm's length. "What is it?"

"From the circuitry, Rod, I would conjecture that the cylinder is the transducer. This disc, therefore, would be the recorded message."

"Oh, is it, now!" Rod whipped his arm back for a straight pitch, aimed at the wall.

"Might I also suggest," Fess said quickly, "that we may find a use for the disc itself?"

Rod scowled. "Always possible, I suppose—but not very satisfying." He dropped it into his belt-pouch. "So we've stopped it from mass-hypnotizing the population. Now, how do we wake them up?"

"Why not try telepathy?" the robot suggested. "The message is recorded thought, placed in contact with the transducer; presumably it will function just as well, from contact with living thought."

Rod turned to his friend with a glittering eye. "Oh, Master Simon . . ."

In spite of himself, the older man took a step backward. But, stoutly, he said, "Wherein may I aid, Lord Warlock?"

"By thinking at the machine." Rod tossed his head toward the gadget. "But you'll have to put your forehead against it."

Simon's eyes bulged; his face went slack in horror.

"Oh, it won't hurt your mind," Rod said quickly. "That much, I'm sure of. This end of the machine can only receive thoughts—it can't send out anything." He turned, bowing, and pressed his forehead against the transducer. "See? No danger."

"Indeed," Simon breathed, awestruck. "Wherefore dost thou not give it thine own thoughts?"

"Because I don't know how to break Alfar's spell." Rod stepped back, bowing Simon toward the machine. "Would you try it, please? Just press your forehead against that round plate, and pretend it's a soldier who's been spellbound."

Simon stood rigid for a few seconds. Then he took a deep breath, and stepped forward. Rod watched him place his forehead against the transducer, with admiration. The humble country innkeeper had as much real courage as a knight.

Simon closed his eyes. His face tensed as he began his spell-breaking thought sequence.

Rod stiffened as the 'message' hit him, full-strength. It had no words; it was only a feeling, as though someone very sympathetic was listening to him, listening deeply, to everything Rod could tell, down to his very core—then, kindly, gently, but very firmly, contradicting. Rod shook his head and cleared his throat. "Well! He's certainly getting across, isn't he?" He turned to Fess. "How'll we know whether it works or not?"

"By Alfar's reaction, Rod. He doubtless detected our disabling his message, but refrained from attacking us, wary of your power."

Rod's head lifted, "I . . . hadn't . . . thought of that."

"I consider it a distinct possibility," Fess mused. "Now, however, Alfar must realize that we are destroying the very base of his power—that he must attack us now, or lose all he has conquered."

Quintuple thunder roared in a long, ripping sequence, and Alfar was there with three witches and a warlock at his back, chopping down at Rod with a scimitar.

Rod leaped back with a whoop of delight. The sword's tip hissed past him, and he and Fess instantly jumped into place between Simon and the sorcerer's band. One of the witches stabbed a hand at them, all five fingers stiff and pointing, and a dozen whirling slivers of steel darted toward them.

Fess took a step to his left, blocking Rod and Simon both. The darts clanged against his horsehide, and he stepped back—just in time to step on the witch's foot. She screamed and careened away, hobbling as Alfar lashed at Rod with the scimitar again. But this time, Rod leaped high and kicked the sword out of his hand as Fess reared, lashing out at the other warlock and witch with his forehooves. Rod sliced a karate chop at Alfar, and the sorcerer leaped back, but not quite quickly enough—Rod's fingertips scored his collarbone, and Alfar howled in pain. The witch was staring at Fess, wild-eyed, backing away slowly, and Rod could feel a crazy assortment of emotions crashing through him—anger, fear, confusion, love. She was the emotional projective, hitting Fess with everything she had, totally confounded by his complete lack of response.

Which reminded Rod who he was, and that the emotions were illusions. He managed to ignore them as Alfar wound up for a whammy. But he didn't have time; a stone leaped out of the wall, and slammed straight at Rod. He sidestepped, but the block caught him on the shoulder. Pain shot through him, and his temper leaped up in response. He slumped back against the wall, striving frantically to reign in his temper, trying to channel it, knowing that rage would slow his reflexes; they'd get under his guard, and chop him down. Another block shot straight at him and he dropped to a crouch, ducking his head. The block cracked into the wall behind; Another whirled tumbling and slammed into Fess's hindquarters. Rod galvanized with alarm—if that boulder had hit Fess in the midriff, it might've staved in his armored side, and damaged his computer-brain!

That was just distraction enough. He saw the stone coming, and spun away—but not fast enough. Its corner cracked into his hip, and agony screamed through his side, turning his whole leg into flame. His knee folded, and he fell.

And Alfar was above him with his scimitar again, chopping down with a gloating grin.

Rod rolled at the last second. The huge blade smashed into the stone floor, and twisted out of Alfar's hands. One of the fallen stones shot up off the floor, straight at his face. Alfar screamed in shock, and stepped back—and tripped over something, crashing down onto his back.

Rod was up on one knee, trying frantically to force himself to his feet. He stared at the obstacle Alfar had stumbled over, and it stared back for a fraction of a second—Geoffrey! The boy grinned just before he leaped to his feet, his eighteen-inch sword whipping out to stab down at the fallen sorcerer, who just barely managed to twist out of the way in time. His hand flailed about the floor till it found the scimitar's hilt, and wrapped fast around it.

A block of stone smashed at Geoffrey. He dodged, but Rod roared with rage when he saw how closely the block had come. He sprang at the telekinetic—but Alfar jumped into his path, slashing with the scimitar again. Rod leaped back, letting the blow whistle past him, then lunged over it with a chop. Alfar just barely managed to twist aside.

The telekinetic was surrounded by blocks of stone smashing into each other. Her lips were drawn back in a feral snarl, and drops of sweat beaded her forehead. Geoffrey ducked in under the hedge of stone and stabbed upward. The telekinetic screamed and jumped back, stumbled over Gregory, and fell. Magnus's cudgel whacked her at the base of her skull and she went limp.

Cordelia crouched glaring at the other witch—but between them was a storybook witch, complete with cone hat, broomstick, hooked nose, warts, and insane cackle, hands clawing at the child. A ghost materialized beside her, moaning, and something huge, flabby, and moist, with yellow, bloodshot eyes, lifted itself up off the floor, extruding pseudopod tentacles toward the little girl. But Cordelia spat, "Aroint thee, witch! Dost thou think me a babe?" and threw her broomstick at the illusionist. It speared through the storybook witch and arrowed toward the illusionist, who screamed and threw up her hands to ward it off—and the ghost, witch, and monster disappeared. But the broomstick whirled and whipped about, belaboring the woman from every side faster than she could block, whacking her about the head and shoulders. She screamed, and darted toward the chamber door—and Gwen's full-sized broomstick swung down from the ceiling and cracked into her forehead. Her eyes rolled up, and she crumpled.

Rod twisted aside from Alfar's scimitar and reached out to brace himself against the wall, just as his burning leg tried to give out under him again. He shoved against the stone, shifting his weight onto his good leg, and drew his sword just in time to parry another cut. He riposted and thrust, faster than Alfar could recover. The sorcerer darted back, just an inch farther than Rod's thrust, and saw two of his lieutenants on the floor. He was just in time to see

Fess's hoof catch the emotional projective a glancing blow on the temple. She folded at the knees and hit the flagstones, out cold. He shrieked, and Rod leaped, catching the sorcerer's arm with his left hand to steady himself. Alfar whirled, saw Rod's sword chopping down, screamed again—and Rod caught the unspoken image of another place. He closed his eyes and willed himself *not* there, just as Alfar teleported toward it. Dimly, Rod heard a thunder-boom, and knew Alfar had managed to disappear from the tower room. His eyes sprang open—and he found himself still clinging to the sorcerer's arm, in the midst of formless grayness, lit by dim, sourceless light. There was nothing, anywhere— nothing but his enemy.

Alfar looked about him, and screamed, "We are lost!" Then he squeezed his eyes shut, and Rod caught the impulse toward someplace he didn't recognize. He countered grimly. Their bodies rocked, as though hit by a shock wave, but stayed put. "You're in the Void," Rod growled, "and you're not getting out!"

Alfar screamed, hoarse with terror and rage, and whirled to chop at him with the scimitar. But Rod yanked him close, caught his sword hand, and cracked it against his good knee. Pain shot through him, almost making him go limp—but Alfar was still screaming, in hoarse, panting caws, and the scimitar went whirling away through empty space. Rod slammed an uppercut into the sorcerer's face. He dodged, but the blow caught him alongside the jaw. His head rocked, but he slammed a knee into Rod's groin. Rod doubled over in agony, but clung to Alfar's arm and a shred of sense; his right hand slipped the dagger out of his boot, and he shot his last ounce of strength into a sudden stab into Alfar's belly. The blade jabbed up under the ribcage, and Alfar folded over it, arms flailing, eyes bulging in agony. Conscience smote; Rod yanked the dagger out and stabbed again, quickly, mercifully, into the heart. He saw Alfar's eyes glaze; then the body went limp in his hands. Rod held it a second, staring, unbelieving. Then chagrin hit, and he felt his soul quail at the reality of another manslaughter. "It was him or me," Rod grated; but no one heard except himself.

He let go, shoving, and the body drifted away from him,

turning slowly, trailing an arc of blood. It swung away, revolving, and faded into the mists, a thin red line tracing its departure.

Rod turned away, sickened. For a long, measureless instant, he drifted in space, numbed, absorbing his guilt, accepting the spiritual responsibility, knowing that it had been justified, had been necessary—and was nonetheless horrible.

Finally, the tide of guilt ebbed, and he opened his mind to other thoughts—Gwen, and the children! Had they all come through that melee alive? And what the hell had they been doing there, anyway? Never mind the fact that if they hadn't been, they'd be short one husband and father by now—nonetheless! What were they doing where it was so dangerous?

Helping him, obviously—and they'd have to help him again, or he'd never find how to get out of here. He wasn't scared of the Void; he'd been here before, between universes.

And, of course, he'd get home the same way now. He closed his eyes, and listened with his mind. There— Gregory's thought, unvoiced, a frightened longing for his father—the same beacon that had brought him home before. Rod sighed and relaxed, letting the boy's thought fill his mind. Then he willed himself back to his three-year-old son.

"Is that all of them?" Rod ground his teeth against a sudden stab of pain from his upper arm.

"Be brave, my lord," Gwen murmured. She finished binding the compress to his triceps. "Aye, every one of them has come—every witch and warlock of the Royal Coven. E'en old Agatha and Galen have come from their Dark Tower, to flit from hamlet to village, speaking with these poor peasants, who have waked to panic, and the loss of understanding."

"I don't blame 'em," Rod grunted. "If I all of a sudden came to my senses and realized that I'd been loyal to an upstart for the last few weeks while my duke was casually bumped off, I'd be a little disoriented, too. In fact, I'd be frightened as hell." He winced as Gwen bound his arm to his side. "Is that really necessary?"

"It must," she answered, in a tone that brooked no argument. "Yet 'tis but for a day or two, 'til the healing hath begun."

"And I didn't even notice I'd been sliced, there." Rod looked down at the bandage. "Well, it was only a flesh wound."

Gwen nodded. "Praise Heaven it came no closer to the bone!"

"Lord Warlock!"

Rod looked up.

They were in the Great Hall of Duke Romanov's castle. It was a vast stone room, thirty feet high, forty wide, and eighty long—and empty, for the moment, since all the boards and trestles had been piled against the walls at the end of the last meal, for the evening's entertainments. The High Table was still up, of course, on its dais, and Rod sat in one of the chairs, with Gwen beside him—though pointedly not in the Duke's and Duchess's places.

An auncient, still wearing Alfar's livery, came striding toward them from the screens passage, eyes alight with excitement.

"Did you lock up the traitors?" Rod demanded.

"Aye, milord." The auncient came to a halt directly in front of Rod. "'Twas that to be said for the sorcerer's having used our bodies for his army, the whiles he lulled our souls into slumber—that when we waked, we knew on the instant which soldiers had been loyal to the usurper of their own wills, e'en though they'd remained wakeful."

Rod nodded. "By some strange coincidence, the ones who had been giving the orders." There had been a few opportunistic knights who had been loyal to Alfar without benefit of hypnotism, too. Rod had had to lock them in a dungeon himself, medieval caste rules being what they were. One of them had resisted; but after the others saw what happened to him, they went quietly. It was just too embarrassing, being defeated by a bunch of children. . . . A couple of them, quicker to react, had escaped as soon as peasants started waking up all around them. That was all right; Rod had a few thousand mortified soldiers on his hand, who needed something to do to appease their consciences. A hunt was just fine.

But the common soldiers who had allied with Alfar, could be left to the tender mercies of their erstwhile comrades—once Rod had made it clear that he expected them to, at least, survive. "So you found the deepest, darkest, dungeon, and locked them in it?"

"Aye, milord." The auncient's eyes glowed. "We loosed its sole tenant." He turned toward the screens passage with a bow, and in limped the prisoner. His doublet and hose were torn, and crusted with dried blood; his face was smeared with dirt, and his hair matted. There was a great livid gash along the right-hand side of his face, scabbed over, that would leave a horrible scar; and he limped heavily, his limbs sodden with inactivity; but his back was straight, and his chin was high. Two knights were with him, blinking, dazed, as disoriented as any of the soldiers, but straight and proud. Simon followed after, looking perplexed.

Rod shoved himself to his feet, ignoring the searing protest from his wounded hip, and the auncient announced:

"Hail my lord, the Duke of Romanov!"

Rod stepped down from the dais to clasp his one-time enemy by the shoulders. "Praise Heaven you're alive!"

"And thee, for this fair rescue!" The Duke inclined his head. "Well met, Lord Warlock! I, and all my line, shall ever be indebted to thee and thine!"

"Well, maybe more the 'thine' than the 'thee.'" Rod glanced behind him at the children who sat, prim and proper, on the dais steps with their mother fairly glowing behind them. "When push came to shove, they had to haul my bacon out of the fire."

"Then I thank thee mightily, Lady Gallowglass, and thee, brave children!" The Duke inclined his head again.

Blushing, they leaped to their feet and bowed.

When the Duke straightened, there was anxiety in his face. "Lord Warlock—my wife and bairns. Did they . . . escape?"

"They did, and my wife and children made sure they reached Runnymede safely." Rod turned to Gwen. "Didn't you?"

"Certes, my lord. We would not have turned aside from what we'd promised thee we'd do."

"Yes—you never did promise to *stay* safe, did you? But Alfar mentioned something about a dire fate in store for you. . . ."

"Indeed!" Gwen opened her eyes wider. "Then it was never taken out from storage. I wonder thou wast so merciful in thy dealings with him."

"Well, I never did like lingering deaths." But Rod couldn't help feeling better about it all.

"He also implied that the Duchess and her boys didn't stay safe. . . ."

"False again," Gwen said quickly, just as the Duke's anguish was beginning to show anew. "We saw them to Runnymede, where they bide safely, in the care of Their Royal Majesties."

"Yes . . . what are monarchs for?" But Rod noted the flash of shame that flitted across Romanov's features—no doubt in memory of his rebellion.

"We played with them not three hours agone, Papa," Geoffrey added.

The Duke heaved a sigh, relaxing. Then the father and host in him both took over. "Three hours? And thy children have not dined in that time?" He spun to the auncient. "Good Auncient, seek out the cooks! Rouse them from their dazes, and bid them bring meat and wine—and honeycakes."

The children perked up most noticeably.

"Three hours agone." The Duke turned back to the children with a frown. "Was this in Runnymede?"

The children nodded.

The Duke turned back to Rod. "How could they come to aid thee, then?"

"Nice question." Rod turned to Gwen again. "It *was* rather dangerous here, dear. Just how close were you, while you were waiting for me to need you?"

"The lads were in Runnymede, my lord, even as thou hast but now heard," Gwen answered. "They could bide there, sin' that they may travel an hundred leagues in the bat of an eyelash."

Rod had notion that their range was farther than that, much farther, but he didn't deem it wise to say so—especially not where they could hear (or mind read).

"At the outset," Gwen continued, "Cordelia and I did bide with them, for we could attend to thy thoughts e'en from that distance, and fly to thine aid if thou didst come near to danger. It did greatly trouble me, therefore, when thy thoughts did so abruptly cease."

Cordelia nodded confirmation, her eyes huge. "She did weep, Papa."

"Oh, no, darling!" Rod caught Gwen's hands. "I didn't mean to..."

"Nay, certes." She smiled. "Yet thou wilt therefore comprehend my concern."

Rod nodded slowly. "I'd say so, yes."

"I therefore did leave the boys in care of Their Royal Majesties, and Brom O'Berin, and flew northward again. I took on the guise of an osprey...."

Rod rolled his eyes up. "I *knew,* when I saw that blasted fish-hawk that far inland, that I was in trouble!" Of course, he knew that Gwen couldn't really shrink down to the size of a bird any more than a butterfly could play midwife to a giraffe. It was just a projective illusion, making people think that they saw a bird instead of a woman. "If I hadn't shielded my thoughts, I probably would've seen through your spell!"

"An thou hadst not shielded thy thoughts, I would not have had to fly near enough to see thee," Gwen retorted. "And though thou hadst disguised thyself, I knew thee, Rod Gallowglass."

That, at least, was reassuring—in its way.

"Then," Gwen finished, "'twas but a matter of hearkening to the thoughts of that goodman who did ride beside thee." Gwen turned to Simon. "I thank thee, Master Simon."

The older man still looked confused, but he bowed anyway, smiling. "I was honored to be of service, milady—e'en though I knew it not."

"And when thou wert taken," Gwen went on, "I did summon Cordelia to me, to bide in waiting, in a deserted shepherd's croft. Then, when thou didst burst forth from thy shield, I could not help but hear thy thoughts for myself."

"Not that you were about to try to ignore them," Rod murmured.

"Nay, certes!" Gwen cried in indignation. "Then, when thou didst come unto the tower chamber, I knew the moment of battle was nigh, and did summon Cordelia from her croft to fly to the tower; and when the unearthly device did cease to compel, and did commence to disenchant, I knew the time of battle had come. Then did I summon thy sons, that the family might be together once again."

"Very homey," Rod grinned. "And, though I was mighty glad to see you all, I don't mind saying I'm even gladder to know the kids were safe, right down until the last moment."

"Certes, my lord! I would not endanger them."

Rod gave her the fish-eye. "What do you call that last little fracas we went through—homework?"

"Oh, nay! 'Twas far too great a delight!" Geoffrey cried.

"Homework's delight," Gregory lisped.

"Papa!" Cordelia cried indignantly; and Magnus's chin jutted out a quarter-inch further. "'Twas scarce more than chores."

"We'd fought each of them aforetime," Geoffrey reminded him, "and knew their powers—save Alfar, and we left him to thee."

"Nice to know you have confidence in me. But there could've been accidents...."

"So there may ever be, with bairns," Gwen sighed. "Here, at least, they were under mine eye. Bethink thee, husband, what might chance an I were to leave them in the kitchen, untended."

Rod shuddered. "You've made your point; please don't try the experiment." He turned to the Duke. "Ever begin to feel redundant?"

"Nay, Papa," Magnus cried. "We could only aid thee in the ending of this campaign."

"Truly," Gregory said, round-eyed, "we knew not enough to bring the sorcerer to bay."

But Rod had caught the sly glance between Magnus and Geoffrey. Under the circumstances, though, he deemed it wiser not to say anything about it.

"Now, mine husband." Gwen clasped his hands. "In this last battle, I did hear thy thoughts at all times. Thine anger was there, aye, but thou didst contain it. Hast thou, then, so much ta'en this goodman's advice to thine heart?" She nodded at Simon.

"I have," Rod confirmed. "It worked this time, at least."

"Dost thou mean thou wilt not become angry again, Papa?" Cordelia cried, and the other children looked up in delight.

"I can't promise that," Rod hedged, "but I think I'll have better luck controlling it. Why—what were you planning to do?"

Whatever they would have answered was forestalled by the cooks, stumbling in with dinner. They set down the platters on the table, and the children leaped in with joyful cries. Magnus got there first, wrenched off a drumstick, and thrust it at his father. "Here, Papa! 'Tis thy place of right!"

"Why, thank you," Rod said, amused. "Nice to know I have some rank around here."

"I shall have the other." Cordelia reached for the other drumstick.

"Nay; thou hast never favored the legs of the fowl!" Geoffrey's hand darted out, and grabbed the bone before hers.

"Loose that!" Cordelia cried. "'Twas my claim was first!"

"As 'twas my hand!"

"Yet I came to the bird before either of thee!" Magnus laid a hand on the bone of contention. "My remembrance of our father, doth not bar me from this choice!"

"Uh, children," Rod said mildly, "quiet down, please."

"'Tis mine!"

"Nay! 'Tis mine!"

"I am eldest! My claim is first!"

"Children!" Rod hiked his volume a bit. "Cut it out!"

Gwen laid a restraining hand on his arm. That did it; his temper leaped.

Cordelia turned on her brothers. "Now, beshrew me an thou art not the most arrogant, ungentlemanly boys the world hath ever..."

"Wherefore beshrew thee? Thou art a shrew already!"

And the discussion disintegrated into wild shouts of accusation and counter-accusation.

Rod stood rigid, trying to contain his soaring anger. Then Simon caught his eye. Rod stared at the older man's calm, level gaze, and felt a measure of strength that he hadn't known he had. He took a deep breath and reminded himself that their bickering might make them look childish (as it should), but not him—if he didn't start shouting with them. The thought checked his anger and held it. He was himself, Rod Gallowglass—and he wasn't any the less himself, nor any less important, nor any less in any way, just because his children didn't heed him.

But he did know how to get their attention. He reached out, grasped the last drumstick, and twisted it loose.

The children whirled, appalled. "Papa!" "Nay! Thou hast no need!" "Thou already hast one, Papa!"

"'Tis not justice," little Gregory piped, chin tucked in truculently over folded arms.

"But it does settle the argument," Rod pointed out. He turned to Gwen, presenting the drumstick with a flourish and a bow. "My dear, you saved the day. Your glory is as great as mine."

"But, Papa!" Cordelia jammed her fists on her hips, glowering up at him. "Thou'rt supposed to be a *nice* daddy now!"

"Why," Rod murmured, "wherever did you get an idea like that?"